Chilli Birds

From Suburbia to Island King

Chilli Birds

From Suburbia to Island King

John McGinn

Winchester, UK
Washington, USA

First published by Roundfire Books, 2013
Roundfire Books is an imprint of John Hunt Publishing Ltd., Laurel House, Station Approach,
Alresford, Hants, SO24 9JH, UK
office1@jhpbooks.net
www.johnhuntpublishing.com
www.roundfire-books.com

For distributor details and how to order please visit the 'Ordering' section on our website.

ISBN: 978 1 78099 611 0

A CIP catalogue record for this book is available from the British Library.

Design: Stuart Davies

Printed and bound by CPI Group (UK) Ltd, Croydon, CR0 4YY

Acknowledgements

A Truck-Load of Gratitude and Shed-Full of Thanks goes out to:

Ada and Boston Securities Ltd

Sheila Spice and Barbie Bikini, purveyors of patience, food and drink

James, Ken and Dave the intelligent proof-readers

Helen the catalyst

Chapter 1

The black kite circled Giles several times, flying closer with each lazy flap of its huge wingspan. Settling a few feet away from his face, it coughed out evil smelling breath. The ugly raptor raised its sharp beak skywards and emitted a shrill whistling call.

Giles could only move his head to follow the approaching creature. His body lay there, impotent and paralysed. Fearful eyes watched, as the bird's powerful talons clawed at the object fallen from his outstretched right hand.

The kite tore large chunks out of the spicy red-stained burger meat, leaving the two dried out crusts of bread. After feasting, it eyed Giles hungrily, before spitting out junk food remnants on his face and hopping closer.

The burning chilli seeds, made him turn sharply away from his fate. To the left, through his watering eyes, he could just make out a slim figure with beautiful nylon-clad legs, wearing red high-heeled shoes.

Beelzebub nestled against the silky, black pantyhose of his female nemesis; the witch who had enchanted him with her sexy spell. His tail curled around her shapely calf and the feline raised an open clawed paw, in the trapped victim's direction.

Giles screamed as he felt his neck being pierced ...

"Meow..."

"Shit," he said, waking up and shaking the hungry black cat off his shoulder.

The feline gave him its best, *'I've saved you from certain doom, so feed me now'* look, and Giles responded by patting him.

"I wish these awful flashbacks would go away, puss. I'll get you dinner in five minutes, Bez."

The cat appeared to nod gratefully and Giles looked at his old watch. The Roman numerals told him it was six o'clock, on a late June evening and time to check the brewery.

There had been eight consecutive days of bright sunshine, a

little unusual for this time of year. Giles Morton wore brown sandals, a 'Keo Beer of Cyprus' T-shirt and washed out, cut-off denim jeans. The shorts were in good condition, apart from a large white paint smear on the back pocket.

He smiled to himself, as he remembered the last time that he wore them. The chain of events, which followed that day, eventually exposed the truth about his sham-marriage. His life had changed so much, since a fateful accident with a paint tin, three years ago.

Giles had been trying to avoid renovating their old wooden greenhouse for ages. His previous partner, Sandra, badly wanted him to tidy it up, until finally on a sunny day, he had agreed to turn his hand to some DIY. She went off to work with the parting sentence, "Don't mess up your new trousers…"

He remembered watching her trot off down the drive, three years ago, in her navy blue business suit and listening to her heels clip clopping along the path. Many years before that, he had found such attire rather fetching on her, but as time marched on, the thought of even spending the day together, used to test his patience to the limit.

There's plenty of time to restart this three-year-old painting job another day, he thought. It seemed to have commenced in another life. The black nylon dream returned for a second and he shook his head to empty it out.

"Focus Giles," he said to himself. "She's gone, just a bad memory."

He stood up from the sofa and stretched. His neck clicked to remind him of an injury sustained in a fight for his very survival, all those years ago. What's another day, he thought? Sandra wasn't around anymore to tell him what to do; so he retired to the small building at the back of the house.

At one time, before being extended, it may have been the outside lavatory. He imagined that other people would have trodden the same path years ago, just like him, with a newspaper under their arm. No old-fashioned way for him, though, any straining would be of a different kind. His new hobby resided here and this is where he liked to spend his time.

"Hello my beauties," he said, as he turned the corroded brass handle on the old tongue and groove door. A large, black spider annoyed that this intrusion had damaged the newly woven web, scuttled across the floor and watched him from underneath an old fan heater.

The dusty shelves were filled end to end with glass demijohns and the floor held several buckets of unappealing looking mixtures. The warmth that had built up in the room hit him as he walked in and his nostrils were filled with the warm smell of his concoctions.

He stirred the nearest one, with the piece of one-by-one-inch timber that stuck out of each pail and some gungy yellowed objects rose to the surface. They span around twice before submerging like a prehistoric sea monster. A string of little bubbles came to the surface. He repeated this with the other three buckets. "Very nice, indeed," he said to his unusual friends.

Giles looked up at the rank of empty demijohns on the shelf waiting to be filled and a thought hit him. Maybe the worse the initial bucketful looked; the better the new wine will taste? He glanced back down at the stained liquid. Hmm…

It can take a year to ferment some home wines. Fresh grapes are hard to come by, but real English fruit and veg may be found as close as the local grocer. He'd tried growing a black Tempranillo vine in his younger days, in the wooden greenhouse. A total failure, as the tiny fruits were usually so sour that even if he left some out on the bird-table, the sparrows just pecked them onto the floor, leaving pink stains on the patio.

A neighbour had introduced him to an alternative, the 'English Grape'. Otherwise known as the gooseberry, it's the nearest thing that will easily grow in our fair isle that contains enough sweet sugar to make a palatable wine.

Giles thought back to some of the neighbour's recipes that he'd tasted and their enchanting properties. He wondered if he'd be able to brew anything as fiery or adventurous. He sat down on an old wooden chair and let Bez the cat hop onto his lap. The look on the hungry cat's face said, *'You know how this stuff turned your life upside down three years ago. Just get my dinner and forget it'.*

"I can't forget it, Bez," said Giles, speaking out aloud. "It's part of me. I'm hiding again but the memories are still so real..."

Chapter 2

Three years ago, on the way back from the post box, Giles saw a woman at work in her front garden. The house had been empty for a while and he hadn't really noticed the plants before. He deliberately slowed down, pretending to look for something in his pocket in order to admire her tanned legs. She seemed to be picking something from one of the many shrubs, in her leafy front garden.

The lady suddenly pulled her hand out of the leaves and sucked at her index finger.

She became aware of him watching and waved her finger at him. The red nail-varnish glinted in the sun. "Only a flesh wound, one of the joys of gooseberry picking!" and before he could answer, "You may have some, if you help."

Boyhood memories of his mother's cooking instantly sprang to mind, along with his dislike for sour fruit puddings, gooseberry crumble included.

The vision in front of him smiled broadly and expunged all negative thoughts from his mind.

Her naked feet and long brown legs led up to white shorts, with big pockets stitched to the front. He could tell they were large because her hands and wrists disappeared into them, as he faced him. Her top half was covered by a lumberjack patterned shirt, most probably a man's.

She gave him a cheeky smile and winked.

He loved chatting to pretty ladies. His wife usually accompanied him and her radar would soon detect any potential rival. As he surveyed the slim, tomboyish, hands in pocket female, he instantly decided that this was an opportunity not to be missed, even if he had to appear grateful for some sour fruit afterwards.

Giles struggled to open the rusty front gate. The latch worked but it seemed to have an invisible lock. He rattled it a bit and looked at her bemused.

"Let me," she shouted, walked over and with a sweep of her hand which hardly seemed to touch the gate, it creaked open.

He glanced angrily at the gate as he walked through. Real men open doors for women; not the other way around, he thought. When he looked back at her, she stood on the newly cut lawn in her bare feet with her hands back in her pockets. There were little pieces of wet green grass stuck to her toes, which looked somewhat cute.

She took a hand out of her pocket and pulled the near shoulder-length brown hair over her left ear.

"I'm Suzie," she said. "We moved in a month ago. I've seen you with your wife in the car. Does she work in a bank?"

"No, deputy manager of an infertility clinic," he replied.

Suzie smiled, "Knew it, sperm bank, then!"

Giles nearly fell over laughing and at this exact moment, he fell in love with Suzie.

She laughed uncontrollably too. Her cute nose screwed up and the laughter lines became very visible around her eyes. In the morning sunlight, the freckles on her cheeks and nose added a girly twist to her tanned face.

She looked a young fortyish, wore no facial makeup and from her dress sense, he guessed she may be a little unusual by his standards.

"I'm Giles, by the way," he finally managed to say.

Suzie stopped and looked him in the eye. "I'm so glad to hear your name. It suits you," and pointed at a couple of bushes.

"We need to pick every little jewel. Mind your hands, they bite!" she instructed.

"How hard can it be?" he asked, reaching into the bush and tugging on a large green gooseberry. The fruit initially resisted him, until the stalk decided to let go and his hand recoiled into a thorny branch, which also scratched him as he attempted to pull it out.

"Shit." He watched helpless as the now dropped berry fell

deeper into the well-defended heart of the evil plant.

They looked at each other and another fit of laughter ensued.

"This means war," he said angrily.

An hour later, they had four large bowls brimming with bright green fruit from the half dozen shrubs. His arms and hands were covered in scratches.

They compared wounds. "We look like we work on a hedgehog farm," said Suzie and they both burst into laughter again.

"How many pies will these make?" asked Giles.

"Not pies, it's for wine. I'll show you. Come with me."

Suzie took him down the side of the house to the kitchen door. Just outside the entrance, she started unbuttoning her check shirt. Embarrassed, Giles turned around pretending not to look.

"It's okay," she giggled, "I'm not naked."

His eyes opened wider as he turned, to see her in a short light blue T-shirt that said 'Witch' across the chest. The perky boobs with their little points, poked enticingly behind the fabric.

Suzie quickly turned around and as she stepped up into the house, her short T-shirt revealed a glimpse of a thong and a tattoo on her lower back of a witch riding a broom.

"Come into the kitchen, Giles," she shouted, as she skipped in.

Giles followed her trim behind and watched fascinated, as she bent over and took a bottle from the fridge.

"One of last year's potions," she explained, as she stood up and winked.

"Try a glass," his newly found neighbour said to him. "You'll be surprised."

Gingerly, he took a sip, half expecting a pair of sharp scissors to emerge from the glass to nip his tongue.

"That's truly amazing," he said, after following his initial sip with two large gulps. "Why is it not sour like I expected?"

His neighbour explained that some extra sugar added during the home process, could make the wine as sweet or as dry as you wished.

"It's not magic," she said, standing there resplendent in her 'Witch' T-shirt.

She clasped her hands behind her back. This tightened the fabric across her chest and he marvelled at her bra-less nipples, wondering how a woman of her age could have such a fine figure.

"Finish your glass," she ordered, which he did and the next thing he recalled is being woken up by his wife.

"Wake up, sleepyhead," she said. "Quite a performance from you last night, don't suppose you want to repeat it this morning?"

He felt a soft breast press into his face and a nipple trail gently across his cheek. It homed in on his lips and attempted to part them with its eager tip.

Giles opened his eyes and mumbled "Coffee first, dear," before focusing on his unusually friendly wife, sitting on the bed next to him. She had lifted up her nightie with her left hand and was rolling the right nipple between the other fingers. The wide grin on her face and the tongue that she provocatively flicked out, told him that something had happened yesterday, which may have culminated in sex. A very unusual thing nowadays...

Chapter 3

After a long warm shower during which he had racked his brains trying to remember anything about yesterday afternoon, he went downstairs to face his wife over the kitchen table. She had just poured out a bowl of Coco Pops and they crackled busily as she poured hot milk onto them.

"Would you like tea or coffee, my darling?" asked Sandra, as she held up a pot in each hand. He pointed at the tall silver container and was rewarded with a mugful of steaming black liquid. "Help yourself to milk, although by the look of the bags under your eyes, you'll probably have it black," she chuckled.

"So," he said, probing. "Enjoy last night?" also hoping to hear something to jog his vacant memories.

"Why, of course, my darling, I had to look in the bin when I got up, to search for oyster shells or other aphrodisiacs," she said, "I even looked in your desk drawers for packets of little blue pills...but nothing. Why did you pounce on me when I arrived home? And can I book it once a week?"

"Oh-erm...yes, we'll see. Fifty years old now, gotta watch the old ticker," he replied, biding for time.

"Anyway, I've been called in to work today. Some funding crisis so I'll see you later," she said.

Suddenly, he realised that she had already dressed. He watched her as she walked to the back door and left for work. She seemed to have a little spring in her step and her head held high.

Giles finished his coffee. Either I'm going senile or Suzie's wine is rather strong, he thought. He decided to first have a shave and then pay Suzie another visit.

He felt a little happier until he looked in the shaving mirror. Definitely big bags under his eyes and the hair on his temples seemed greyer than yesterday. Trick of the light, he thought and wondered what to wear.

In the wardrobe, a shirt at the back drew his attention. He didn't know he owned it. For some reason, after trying it on, it felt just right. He looked in the mirror and the dark shirt complemented his physique. The chest hairs showing through the unbuttoned neck, didn't seem so grey and funnily enough neither did his hair. He chose a pair of his favourite jeans that his wife hated, found a pair of unloved trainers and made for the door.

With one final look at his smart dark shirt in the hall mirror, he suddenly became aware that he remembered everything about the last afternoon.

He'd drunk a bottle of wine with Suzie, gooseberry maybe (he never asked). They'd talked for ages and she'd made some sandwiches. Her husband stayed away for weeks at a time. She studied the 'Arts' and played housewife, whatever that is. She reckoned that she could size men up, by just looking and gave him a new shirt that too small for her husband. This was his reward for fruit picking because she could tell he didn't really like gooseberries, (so that's where the shirt came from, he thought).

Well, Suzie's spot on about the size and it did sort of suit him. He reached up to his right cheek, upon which he remembered her giving a thank you kiss, which left a funny tingle.

His cheek tingled again and a vision of her flashed into his head. Brown legs, short red leather skirt, white sleeveless jumper and those nipples...

Gorgeous isn't she, he thought, and after locking the door, strode purposefully along their avenue towards Suzie's house with no idea what to say. He had previously decided to go there, to ask what had happened but now he'd remembered. A voice inside him just kept saying "Go see her."

Chapter 4

Giles walked down the drive past his favourite car, an old seventies Triumph Stag in carmine red. The car used to make him feel really proud to be its owner but recently, he'd neglected it. Hadn't washed it for months and as he walked past, the twin headlamps scowled at him; he got the strange idea that the car had become jealous. She knew that he'd found a new love interest and the fact bugged him. He turned back and patted the dusty green-eyed lady on the boot. "Don't fret, Stella, I'll give you a rub and polish tomorrow." The car's rear lights gave him a nasty look which said *'Promises, promises, I know that you're up to no good'*.

He had decided his first stop would be the newsagent on the corner, just a street away. Picking up a paper would be a good excuse to be out, if Sandra became inquisitive. As he walked along the pavement, he noticed a black cat sitting on a fence almost motionless, apart from its head. It swivelled around watching him.

Giles stared back, and after making sure that the adjacent gardens were empty, he let out a loud hiss. The cat's ears twitched as its expression changed. For a split second, Giles thought it smiled at him. He shook his head and started to stroll on. For some reason, Suzie popped back into his mind and she looked upset. He stopped, turned around and mouthed, "Sorry," to the cat. Suzie liked cats but how do I know that, he wondered?

He looked at the window display through the dirty glass at the newsagents. An out-of-date advert for the lottery had been there for weeks. The glass had a crack in the corner where someone had whacked it. The owner had stuck wide clear plastic tape over it, seemingly hoping that it would fix itself. It hadn't. Shops always seemed immaculate to him as a kid and he wondered why some premises didn't bother to clean their glass and the surrounding framework any more.

He loved the local newsagents as a youngster. There were toys in cardboard boxes, cap guns with ammo and Airfix models in plastic bags, hanging from wire hooks. All interspersed with black-and-white newspapers, Woman's Realm, packets of flower and veg seeds. Neatly arranged boys' comics, such as Hotspur, Victor and Lion, great manly sounding titles, fought for the attention of eager fingers. He wanted to be all the heroic characters and save the world but never made the grade.

He walked in, forever hopeful that the clock would turn back. Only to gaze at the boring industry standard, long multi-coloured aisle of magazines on one side, balanced by hundreds of greeting cards along the other wall. A few shelves of books dominated the centre of the shop and he wandered over, to see if anything took his fancy.

He scanned over science fiction, love and romance, thriller and settled on horror and supernatural.

The illustrations on the front covers always fascinated him. How did the artists design such macabre pictures? He read some of the summaries on the back covers. He shivered and put each one back on the shelf.

Thank heavens it's all unreal; werewolves, goblins and witches.

He shivered, moved to the next shelf and spotted a book on card tricks. Giles knew a couple to tease his friends with. He'd learned them a few years ago. Leafing through it, he noted a few interesting ones and decided it may be a useful buy. Be good to pick up a few new pranks, he thought, as he went over to the newspaper section, found the Daily Express and went to the cashier.

Giles knew the woman on the till from ages ago. They'd had a date once, which like all of his early ones, turned into a disaster. She'd been married twice and always seemed on the lookout for another conquest, despite her forty-nine years. Christina said to him, "So the old dog's trying to learn new tricks? Why don't you come around to mine tonight and show me some," before winking and adding, "Nice shirt." She reached out to feel the collar between her bejewelled fingers.

"You know I'm happily married, Chris," Giles fibbed and blushed slightly. They'd flirted on and off over the years but definitely not if Sandra had accompanied him into the shop. The wife knew Christina was an old flame of his but if they were alone in the shop, Chris would always slip in a comment. Never touched him like that before, though, he realised. What is it about this shirt? Giles mused.

"Nice day today," she said, changing the subject as another customer walked in. "Look at him," she whispered in his ear.

Giles looked over his shoulder as nonchalantly as he could in the direction of the door.

An old man had come into the shop. He wore a large wide-brimmed hat, a tweed suit and leant on a silver cane. As Giles caught his eye, he tapped his cane sharply on the floor as though to gain attention.

Christina shouted, "Can I help you, sir?" and started to walk over.

Giles decided to wait until she'd dealt with the customer as he wanted to ask Chris a question.

The man reminded him of a character from a film or the theatre. He could hear them talking but for some reason couldn't make out any words or phrases. They weren't particularly whispering, yet it could have been a foreign language for all he could pick up. Must be my age, he thought and pretended to look at a few cards. From the way that they occasionally turned towards him, Giles got the idea that they might have been talking about him.

The old gent eventually doffed his hat to Chris, tapped his stick smartly on the tiled floor, making Giles jump and left.

Chris came back over to the till with a funny look on her face.

"What did Tweedy want?" asked Giles. "He didn't buy

anything."

"Erm…no, I don't think he asked for anything," she stammered. "I-I think that he just wanted a chat. I feel a little light-headed. I'll just sit on the stool, if you don't mind, Giles."

"He had such strange eyes. Did you see them?" she asked.

"No," said Giles. "I was too far away. Were you talking about me? You kept looking."

"I don't think so…not really…I can't remember what we talked about. How strange. I feel okay now but I feel like I've lost a few minutes," Chris replied.

"Must be going around, although my latest lapse may have been alcohol induced," he said. "Sure you're okay now because I have a few things to do?" (Suzie wearing black stockings and a short nightie had just popped into his head).

"Go on Giles. A cup of tea will sort me out. I'll have to give up talking to strange men. That's a nice shirt you're wearing by the way."

"Cheerio, then," said Giles. He didn't have the heart to tell her that she'd already told him about the shirt. Must still be a bit groggy, he thought. He'd wanted to ask her if she knew anything about Suzie. Maybe she went in there for a paper or cards but he decided to do it another time. Be just his luck for the old gent to come back again and foil him, he laughed to himself. The last few days have been a little odd.

As he stepped out into the sun, a coloured light partly blinded him. After screwing up his eyes and blinking they adjusted to the sunny day he saw a creature fluttering by. A butterfly…no, a dragonfly, wings shimmering in the bright light of the summer's day. A beautiful sight, he thought and he'd soon see another in Suzie…

The insect dive-bombed him at that point and he flinched as it bounced off the top of his head before it disappeared into the blue sky.

"Trying to tell me something?" he said quietly as he watched it go. He'd read that global warming affected insects in a nature article. Maybe they were getting a bad attitude?

The rest of the walk to Suzie's turned out to be spectacularly uneventful. When he was at the gate, he yet again struggled to open it.

A cheery voice shouted, "I'll get it," and Suzie came down the drive like a little missile. Her feet ran so fast they hardly seemed to touch the ground and likewise her hand hardly seemed to touch the gate as it opened with a loud creak, allowing him in.

He'd noticed the front door stood partly open before he fiddled with the gate and it still seemed open by the same small amount. Although Suzie looked slim, he wondered how she managed to fit through the small gap.

Before he could think any further, Suzie leaned over and kissed him on the cheek. He felt the same tingle in his face and rush he'd felt before.

"I just knew you would come and see me again today," she said and licked her lips. Giles couldn't work out if she gave him an appreciative look or if she wanted to devour him. Weird, he thought.

Then she smiled that unbelievably gorgeous smile. "Would you like to try a different wine today after you've helped me in the garden?"

The thought of helping in the garden hadn't even occurred to Giles in his rush to see her.

"Erm…okay, sure as long as there aren't any carnivorous plants to tend again," referring to the gooseberry bushes with a nod in their direction.

"There's no gain without pain," she said. "Sometimes a little discomfort makes the prize taste even better," she winked at him.

He noticed again that she didn't seem to have any visible make up, yet her complexion seemed flawless. The long, dark lashes that winked at him did not have a trace of mascara. Giles always liked made up eyes and thought that women without any sort of eye decor looked like they'd just woken up or were ill. He'd loved the 1980s with the heavy eye-tones and couldn't work out why this bare-eyelashed lady simply looked so attractive.

Her clothes seemed to have been made for her and the cut of her top and shorts complimented her svelte figure. She talked but he didn't listen, just looked at her, his mind devoid of thought apart from her prettiness.

"Wake up, Giles!" she snapped and laughed. "You must be easy to hypnotise..."

Giles almost jumped. "Sorry, Suzie, I felt miles away."

"Not so sure about that. Were you busy taking me somewhere miles away?" she teased.

"Oh...no...no," he lied. "So we're picking some late strawberries today then?"

"Very good, Giles, how did you know because I didn't tell you?" she asked quizzically...

"Oh...erm...seemed to pop into my head after I looked at you. You have lovely eyelashes," he stammered. What am I saying, he thought?

"Why thank you, Giles," she said, giving them a flutter in his direction, "and that's very clever of you to read my mind about the strawberries. I'll have to be careful in future."

Only a half-smile this time, he noted.

"Let's get on then. I have a box for both of us," she giggled.

Giles looked over to where she pointed and saw two empty strawberry punnets like the ones they give you on the 'pick your own' farms. He hadn't noticed them earlier. It was almost like they'd appeared behind his back, on the worktop. He grabbed both and followed her out through the back door, into the garden. As he did so, he looked at the neatly folded cream and red boxes with their little handles. He couldn't see a maker's name, only a black circle with a star inside it, on the underneath.

"These are cute little boxes. Where did they come from?" he said, making conversation.

"I guess you could say I made them," Suzie replied without looking. "I can make lots of things," she added with another half-smile, turning towards him. "You'll find out soon enough."

He trailed after her to the corner of the garden, marvelling at the swing of her hips. She bent down and said "Look at these little beauties."

Giles' gaze affixed itself to her firm rounded buttocks as she reached and fiddled in the greenery. "Wonderful," he replied.

She turned around and seemed to have a very red tongue. At first Giles thought she'd hurt herself, before realising that she'd bitten into a strawberry and the other half sat in the fingers of her right hand. She reached out to him with her left hand and said "Bite me."

"Pardon?" he said, before he realised she had another berry in her other hand. "Oh, okay then."

He started to raise his hand to take the fruit off her but she ignored him and it continued its relentless path towards his mouth and made light contact with his lower lip. "Go on then, you know you want to," she giggled.

Giles sank his teeth into the fruit not knowing what to expect. English strawberries varied wildly in their taste and sugar content. His mother grew some years ago that you could strip paint with. Each berry needed half a teaspoonful of sugar to make it even slightly palatable. His father would encourage him to eat them 'raw' by saying, "They'll put hairs on your chest, son." Only then did Giles decide he'd rather be smooth-chested.

But as soon as his incisors slid into this berry, he sensed a treat…

"Wow!" he said, a split second later, as the sweet syrupy favour seduced his taste buds with wild fruity fragrance. He felt dizzy for a few seconds, as a sugar-high pulsed through his veins. He realised that he'd closed his eyelids and opened them to see Suzie looking intently at him, her big brown eyes almost swallowing him up.

She asked, "Are they sweet enough for you, darling?

"Eat your heart out magic mushrooms," he answered. "You've got magic strawberries. Incredible, and you make wine from these?" he queried.

"Of course but you don't need too many or the wine will be overpowering. You have to know how to create with nature's produce. Not many people know how to bring out the true intensity and hidden properties. I'm one of the few, so to speak," she replied.

"I bet people would be after you, if they knew," he laughed.

"You're reading my mind again, Giles," Suzie answered with that funny half-smile. "Pick some with me now and later I'll have to get you try my strong strawberry wine."

That's twice she's mentioned mind reading, he noted, as he pulled berry after berry from underneath the low lying pinnate leaves. The garden creepy crawlies and hungry birds had completely ignored this harvest for some reason. His mothers were always half chewed to bits by some creature or other.

It didn't take long to fill the boxes with the delicious shiny scarlet trophies. Delicious definitely was the word but he felt a little worried to eat as he picked, which he always did at the PYO farms. The little dizziness that accompanied the first bite made him a bit wary. Can you have too much sugar in a strawberry, Giles mused? Anyway, there was the promise of a drop of wine or hopefully a glassful later to look forward too.

He started wondering if he could smuggle a few berries home and tried to remember if he had a tissue in his pocket when... "Well done, Giles," shouted her cheery voice. "Come into the kitchen with me and wash your hands. I'll take charge of the strawberries." The boxes were removed out of range of pilfering so he walked over to the sink to clean up.

When he turned around, he could see that a bottle and two goblet-shaped glasses had arrived quietly on the table. A white plate with a couple of slices of bread sat to the side.

Giles stood there watching from the sink as Suzie poured two glassfuls. She picked them up and approached him as he wiped his hands on a soft towel.

"Put that down," she ordered laughing. "There's work to do."

He laughed with her and took a glass from her left hand. She took a sip from her glass and motioned him to do the same. "Go on then, you know you want to."

He held it up and looked at the bright red transparent liquid through the side of the glass goblet. Giles could see the reflection of his eye on the shiny surface and also Suzie, her outline and features shrunken and distorted by the optical properties of the glass and liquid. She looked so old. How strange, he thought and took a deep inhalation of the heady aroma emanating from the glass.

As she'd approached him with the glass, he could smell the berry. Tasting, however, became an entirely different experience. The fermentation had allowed an amazing combination of fruity, sweet and alcoholic vapours to merge with others that he couldn't dream of identifying. The final result seemed indescribable. His vocabulary didn't have the words, in the same way that his nose and tongue swam out of their depth.

Giles took a mouthful, held it on the tip of his tongue at first to appreciate the sweetness and then swallowed holding his eyes closed.

The liquid tasted divine, lovely wine with a fragrant kiss. Suzie took a mouthful of hers and swallowed deeply. She said, "Ah," and licked her lips before looking at him. This encouraged him to swiftly sup two more tasty mouthfuls.

"And you've really made this yourself?" Giles questioned, then adding, "From strawberries that you've grown outside? This is wonderful nectar."

"I cannot tell a lie. Let's just say I had a hand in producing the ingredients and making the drink to my own secret recipe," she answered and then Suzie gave her usual big smile. "Let me top you up. I'm sure you've things that you want to say to me. You do want to stay a little longer, don't you Giles?"

He nodded because he didn't want to open his mouth and lose the amazing taste.

"You should try some of this bread that I've baked. It's new and I just know you'll like it."

Giles sat down on one of the pine chairs at the table. He looked at the clock on the wall, also in pine. Only eleven in the morning, there would be plenty of time, before he was missed. He hadn't noticed the clock before. It almost seemed like it appeared there to encourage him to stay. The pine chair with its padded seat felt very comfortable and he wondered why he'd not noticed that before, either.

He followed Suzie's lead, picked up a slice of bread and broke off a piece. She put the morsel in her mouth and took a sip of wine and closed her eyes. He did likewise…

Suzie said something softly but he couldn't make it out. Sounded foreign, Latin maybe? Possibly praying? He didn't want to open his eyes and look because he felt it might be rude.

Giles swallowed his sweet, bready mouthful or at least he tried. It wouldn't go down or his tongue seemed stuck or worse… He tried to open his eyes but neither would respond. Then he felt a floating sensation. He could see clouds, lovely fluffy white ones in an azure blue summer sky.

Should I panic? he thought. Or maybe I've fallen asleep? He looked down and astonishingly saw that the ground below burned brightly. Massive yellow and red flames with spikey tongues were striking up towards him, from deep in the heart of a hellish furnace.

Then he swallowed and his eyes opened. He gasped for air and then realised that he didn't have to.

His eyes refocused on Suzie.

"Poor Giles, you went quiet for a second then, did you nearly choke?" she asked. "Take another sip of wine. You were telling me about your wife."

Giles did as instructed, feeling none the worse for his vision or dream.

"Sorry, Suzie. I must have drifted off. Just thinking about something a little odd, erm… I was telling you about Sandra, yes?" he said, hoping for a lead.

"Yes, told me that you couldn't remember how you met her or what you really see in her. You were saying how different, I am?" she said. "You're a very interesting man and I'd like to know more about you, Giles. I think we may have a lot in common. We've plenty of time."

Giles looked up at the wooden clock. Only ten past eleven but it seemed that he'd been here much longer. He couldn't remember telling her about Sandra. It isn't the sort of thing he'd usually tell anyone about. As part of an attitude and performance assessment, all of his team at work had to spend time with a psychologist and even then he managed to skirt around questions about his relationship with Sandra.

"Well, I met her on a course from work… " he started.

Suzie interrupted "Oh, Giles, the strawberry wine must be going to your head. You met her when you were on a course fifty miles away from where you live and you can't remember what it's about. You left the other students to have some food and a cuppa. You found a bistro nearby called 'The Crescent Moon' which turned out to be very busy. She asked to sit at your table in there, because all the other seats were taken. During a chat it came out that she'd amazingly been offered a job near you. You owned a two-room flat and had been thinking about renting the spare. She said she'll take it before you really offered it and didn't ask the price. What happened next, Giles?"

"Oh yes, I remember," he lied. He didn't remember saying any of that. Another strange blank, he thought.

"Well, she moved in a few weeks later and we were flatmates for a year" he said. "We got on pretty well. Sandra used to go a bit quiet; if she found out I had a date. She'd go away for a short break every couple of months and that's when I'd sometimes plan stuff. Something always went wrong to spoil any romance, like the oven would stop working or the toilet wouldn't flush. Once I got to base camp and just about to unhook a date's bra, when the fire brigade turned up. The officer volunteered to finish the job and the girl took down his phone number!"

"I used to joke that she masterminded my misfortunes, until one evening after we'd shared some wine, she pounced. Woke up in the morning in her bed and we got engaged that week. It just seemed right. Never did remember much about that night but she always said we were good together," he said.

"We were engaged for ages and she'd always avoid marriage talk or anything to do with children. Suddenly on February the twenty-ninth, seven years ago, she proposed. She said it would keep me out of trouble. There was a funny little ceremony arranged by her, north of the border in Scotland, I've never seen the certificate. She bought me a ring. This one..." He held his fingers out towards her.

Suzie looked a little worried, "Oh yes, I've noticed that. Do you ever take it off?"

"Not normally. Bit tight and Sandra goes all funny if she catches me. I can see that it's second-hand but Sandra says it's very old and special," he replied.

"I'm sure she's right." Suzie gazed at his outstretched fingers. Her head rolled from one side to the other as she scanned the ring closely. "Do you know anything about the pattern?"

"Just some random symbols from the mind of the maker, I guess," Giles answered. "Why, do you like it?" He peered at the slightly tarnished, brassy gold-coloured ring with its oddly marked surround.

"Yes... may I try it on, please? I'd really like to," Suzie said eagerly.

"Well alright, if I can get it off," Giles started twisting the ring around his finger, in order to work it over his knuckle.

"Ouch," he cried, waving his hand vigorously at his side. "I just had an electric shock or something." He looked at his hand and his throbbing ring finger. Suzie had taken two steps back.

"It's okay," he grinned, "Probably just the Sandra effect." They both started laughing.

"Is she a jealous one then, Giles?" Suzie queried, or was it a statement, he wondered?

"Sort of... Maybe more like my protector sometimes?" he responded.

"How do you mean, Giles?" Suzie had moved her chair closer. Her big brown eyes were wide open and gazing at him.

"Well, she seems to sense a rival female and soon drags me away. There's always some excuse if I'm chatting to a nice lady, even at a supermarket checkout. I get the idea that she's trying to save me from someone, maybe even myself?" he explained, wondering why she got up.

"Maybe it's the seven-year itch?" Suzie smiled and sat down again astride her pine chair, with her back towards him.

"I also have one, right between my shoulder blades where I can't reach. Would you mind, Giles?"

Giles couldn't believe his luck. He loved backs. Suzie wore a cream T-shirt with the thinnest of straps over her shoulders. The back cut deeply away from her neck. He could make out the individual vertebrae showing under the skin.

Suzie put both hands behind her head and gathered up her brown hair with her thumbs, holding it against the back of her skull. With her neck now fully exposed, he could smell the soft warm flesh as he leaned closer. A little star tattoo in a fainter circle on the back of her neck caught his eye. He hadn't seen it before on her, because of her long hair but it looked familiar.

"Just rub me in the middle above the edge of my blouse," she reminded him.

Giles obeyed and lightly stroked the vertebrae in the ordered area, with his first two fingers.

"A little harder, bigger circles... " she said and wriggled her shoulders, pressing back against his fingers as he responded.

Getting more confident, he put a hand lightly on the top of each of her shoulders. He gently pressed the tips of his fingers and thumbs into the soft tissue of both trapezius muscles. Suzie lifted her head back and let out a low growl. "Oh... that's good Giles. Please carry on..."

He flattened his palms on her shoulders and curled his fingers to touch her clavicles, with his thumbs on her shoulder blades. He gently brought his digits together rolling the skin against the bone.

Suzie let go of her hair and her locks fell down and partly covered his fingers. She partly rolled her head, stretching her neck muscles and he heard and felt several clicks.

"Sounds like I'm getting the knots out," he said.

"Makes my old bones feel young again," she replied.

She wriggled her shoulders even more now, in parallel with him at first, as he rubbed both simultaneously. Then as he alternated his squeezes, she lowered each shoulder in turn to match his touch, making a gyrating motion with the top of her arm. "Oh...Giles, harder and deeper, pleeeease..."

He found the closeness of her skin and her curious but attractive perfume mesmerising. The soft, almost flawless flesh could have been on a twenty-year-old. He so much enjoyed watching the bones and muscles move under the skin, seeing her agile body dance under his touch.

Giles remembered the tattoo and gently moved her hair up by pretending to rub the nape of her neck between his right fingers and thumb. He loved seeing a girl's anatomy here. Longer, thicker hairs running out to fine short ones that you couldn't pick up if you tried. He tried to twirl some of the short ones around his fingers, deliberately failing to catch them and pressed his fingertips against her neck muscles as he did so. She sighed and nodded her head up and down in response to his actions.

"I've seen that tattoo shape somewhere before, Suzie," he said, looking at the little star as he twiddled.

"Really?" she answered and brushed each strap from her shoulders down to the top of her arms. She lifted the hair back off her neck with her right hand and said "Is that any better?" and placed her left hand gently on his knee.

Giles could feel himself trembling slightly. The little star in a circle seemed to be pulling him closer.

"Go on, you know you want to," the soft female voice encouraged, for the third time. He could hear her breathing slowly and deeply.

Giles placed both hands on her shoulders and with one swift movement, like a bird of prey taking its victim, he kissed the tattoo. Soft and warm, yet somehow cold, he kissed again, more firmly the second time and Suzie wriggled underneath him. He licked along the line of her neck vertebrae up to the tiny hairs and could taste the sexy saltiness of her skin.

Chapter 5

He woke up lying in bed. It had gone dark. Panicking, he touched the back of the woman spooned up in front of him. "What's the time, Suzie?" he whispered. The woman's head turned slightly towards the bedside clock and said "four o'clock and who's Suzie?" in Sandra's voice. "Are you having a dream?"

Giles froze, if that's possible, when you're lying still in bed anyway.

"You okay, honey, or are you after a bit more?" Sandra's warm ample behind pressed back into him and wriggled.

He hadn't spooned up and slept with Sandra for absolutely years. What was he doing? Hadn't he been kissing Suzie's neck, what seemed just a minute ago? What had happened to him?

Sandra started gently snoring again but Giles couldn't go back to sleep as his brain went over everything it could remember about yesterday. He licked his lips. They still tasted salty, Suzie salty. He gently moved his fingers to his nose and could still smell her hair on them.

He finally nodded off after an hour or so and had vivid dreams about tuna fish flying in clouds with Suzie riding one of them. An alarm began ringing and a large cooker door opened. A slightly burnt gingerbread man came running out, shouting "Don't go near the chef," and he woke up to find Sandra shaking him.

"That stupid fire alarm's beeping again. I thought you'd changed the battery," she shouted over the loud annoying sound. "I'll check but if the house is not burning down, you're in trouble."

Giles just lay there on his back looking up at the crack in the bedroom ceiling. What is going on, he wondered? I've forgotten another day. Am I going senile? I came home fine and Sandra seemed okay about it apart from the Suzie word. Then he remembered he'd been drinking Suzie's wine again. Is he hypersensitive or something? He felt okay. A little tired maybe and he'd eaten some bread there. Had he developed a strange gluten allergy?

A black spider with an ill-matching white leg came to the edge of the lampshade to watch him. He'd seen it there and wondered if he ought to tell Sandra about it. She prided herself on her tidy organised house and it seemed a little surprising that she'd missed it. Live and let live, he thought and waved at the insect. It raised a tentative leg in the air before scuttling back inside the shade. Did it wave back, he mused? He rubbed his eyes hoping that everything would be alright.

The chinking noise grew louder and Giles knew that Sandra's Kenyan run had begun. She appeared in a short silky nightie carrying a tray, dressed quite unSandra-like.

"Sorry about snapping, the alarm woke me up. Here's a nice cuppa best African tea for you as I promised last night, if you were a good boy," she said. "And you were a verrry good boy, weren't you?"

Sandra put the tray down on the dressing table, deliberately bending over and showing her bottom under the short silky garment. Keeping the pose, she turned her head towards him and wiggled. "This Suzie you dream of. Can she do this?" Her bum looked a little overweight and it did a little extra wobble after she stopped.

Giles hoped that she'd forgotten and her little performance was quite unexpected.

"That's very nice dear, she's not at all like you," and he forced a laugh, hoping she'd forget it.

"Sex twice this month, Giles; it takes me back." They both laughed, genuinely, at the comment.

"We make a good team and I think the best is yet to come," she giggled, "if you pardon the pun." She lifted the front of her nightie up and flashed him.

"You can have a lie-in if you want, but make sure you fix that battery before I'm home."

"Okay." Giles rolled over and pulled the duvet up tighter. He heard her turn on the shower in the bathroom and started wondering what to do about Suzie or even what she did to him to make him 'engage' with his wife after many years. Life seemed to be getting stranger by the day.

Chapter 6

Giles decided to lay low for a while. He'd really enjoyed his little rendezvous with Suzie but the small gaps in his memory caused him concern. His past few years seemed to have run into one another with no really special memories or achievements to be proud of. This thing with Suzie felt so nice; it gave him a lovely feeling inside. It seemed like a hole had slowly formed inside him and she'd come along with a spade and shovelled lots of conversation and attention into it. By just thinking about the pale skin on her back, he really felt that he could smell her again. Thoughts of her kept popping into his head and distracted him, from his mundane tasks. He only compare with being young again. Vague memories of his first girlfriends, combined with his youthful hormones and those feelings of being in love. Wanting to finish whatever you were doing and go around and see the lady. Yes, that's the feeling. How odd that it should have resurfaced after all these years. It's almost as if someone had been inside his mind, dug out an old record, dusted it down and said listen to this again…it's really good…and that person is Suzie.

He remembered to change the beeping smoke alarm battery, this time. The fitting sat on the landing ceiling in the void above the stairs. Giles hated doing this. He didn't like heights and it could only be reached by leaning over at a crazy angle, whilst standing with one leg on a chair and the other on the landing bannister. As usual, the white plastic clip on cover resisted his first attempt to pop it open. He nipped downstairs and came back with a dinner knife and resumed the stretching posture. With a twist of the blade, the flap flipped open suddenly. He lost his balance and ended up in a heap on the landing. "Shit," he announced and pulled up his sleeve to look at his right forearm which had collided with the top rail on the way down. The soft under-surface throbbed and he poked the offending area. "Ow," he said and then gently rubbed it. The area turning red already told him where his body had switched on its knock-repair mechanism.

He continued with the job, successfully extricating the battery and replacing it with a new nine-volt cell. After pressing the red button for a test beep, he called it a difficult job, well done and time for a cup of tea.

After putting the chair back in the spare room and looking out the front window, he could see his friend Pete, chatting to someone who'd pulled in opposite his drive, a few doors away. Pete is the eyes and ears of the street. He is always in his front garden, tending his plants or if not, is washing his car. Not really nosey but always after a chat. Giles had bonded with him because neither got on particularly well with their respective partners. In fact, Giles seemed to get on better with Pete's wife and vice versa. They both knew this, and would get one another to make an excuse, for each other's wife to go to the pub, or bookies or to get out of a mother-in-law visit. They didn't know that the two wives knew about this or that the girls often swopped stories and had a good laugh at the gents' ruses. Pete's wife had run off with a toy-boy, a couple of years ago and they'd divorced. Pete shrugged off the separation, by saying it happened after he tossed a coin in a wishing well. "Didn't know they worked," he said…

The very black car with darkened windows that looked like the Torchwood Range Rover, revved its engine before driving slowly away past Giles' house. He just started to pour the water in his mug when the doorbell rang. Wondering who it might be, he stopped his brewing, nipped to the door and opened it.

Pete stood there. "Hey, Giles, got a minute?"

"Come in, I'm just making a brew. How are they hanging?"

"Like a donkey on anabolic steroids," Pete replied.

Giles laughed and Pete joined in. He watched his neighbour do a John Wayne-like walk into the kitchen and carefully sit on a stool.

"All this so I'm firing blanks. I'm sure my latest girlfriend just wants me in pain rather than having safe sex," said Pete. "They look like two beetroot in an old colour supplement."

Giles and Pete often had this descriptive competition thing, to try and catch one another out.

"Black and blue and read all over," he added because Giles didn't get that one at first.

They both laugh out aloud at this point.

"Give over, it hurts," said Pete trying to speak. "Make the tea before I do myself an injury."

"One lump or is it two in your case?" relied Giles to continued hilarity.

Giles made the tea and after plonking two mugs down and joining Pete on another stool asked, "So what brings you here, cowboy?"

Pete noted the reference to his gait and replied "Well pardner, some hombre just stopped over at the Big Nuts Coral and asked about you," in a Southern drawl.

"Oh really, what did he want?"

"He'd seen your car and liked it, didn't want to ask you directly. Asking how long you'd had it and were you originally from around here, for some reason. He thought he'd seen the number plate somewhere else," said Pete.

"Well the car's fairly common. Probably fancied the number plate for himself or maybe he's a dealer?" replied Giles. "He can have it for twenty thousand pounds if he comes back."

"Hardly worth two thousand?" said Pete surprised.

"I know but maybe it's a seller's market?" Giles laughed. "It looked like he had a posh car so maybe he had a bit of money. What did he look like?"

"He dressed a bit odd, sort of old style countryman clothes. I wouldn't be surprised if he had a deerstalker hat and a retriever in the back. Anyhow, what have you been up to? Haven't seen you around for a few days," Pete said.

"Well, if I tell you, you'd better keep it quiet," Giles warned him.

"Cool," said Pete "It's either a murder mystery or another woman."

"Ha, pretty close, a bit of both."

"You've murdered Kylie Minogue? Just a wild guess," asked Pete.

"No, stupid, met this gorgeous brunette who's moved in recently down into Yew Tree Avenue. She's into gardening and winemaking, a great conversationalist. Must be about forty but looks much younger. Think she fancies herself as a witch. Is it the white witches that are the trendy ones nowadays, making good spells?"

"Married, Giles? Be careful. You could have Sandra and an angry bloke after you," Pete warned.

"Said she had a husband but I haven't seen any man stuff lying around. Think he works away," replied Giles.

"Bet she's got big tits, Giles, I know your sort. Leggy as well," said Pete, fishing for dirt.

"Actually she's got a really nice small bust and they hold up well for her age," said Giles, pretending to have breasts and cupping them with both hands. "And no, I haven't held them," he quickly added.

A vision of a naked Suzie flashed into his head. She seemed to be actually there.

In fact, he could swear that he could feel the warmth of her breasts in his hands, at that moment. He wriggled his fingers and rubbed his hands together because of the odd feeling.

"Is that how you warmed your hands up before the dirty deed?" asked Pete.

"Chance would be a fine thing," replied Giles, although he reckoned that he had more than a fifty/fifty and liked a bet, hmm…

Chapter 7

It had been over a week since Giles had seen Suzie.

He had dreamt about her every night. Boy, he thought, have I got it bad.

In the fun dreams, he and Suzie had been king and queen together, ruling a small European country, travelling the Sahara desert by moonlight before sleeping by day in a Bedouin tent and picking apples in a French orchard. Crazy ones had been Suzie dressed as a nurse taking pints of blood from him, Suzie forcing him to eat huge biscuits and Suzie putting him in an oven on a giant baking tray.

Giles woke up in a sweat after that last one. He actually felt hot, as though he'd been in an oven and had to have a cold shower to cool him down. After two nights of weird dreams in a row, he became a little bothered about going to sleep so he avoided things that were supposed to give you bad dream such as cheese, chocolate, red wine and strong curry. He would sup a creamy hot drink and scoff a bland pizza before bed because he'd read that milk and carbs help a restful sleep.

It seemed to have worked and at last, he had a sound night's kip. Sandra had actually managed to stay all night in the marital bed, whereas for the last week, she had been forced to get up and sleep in the spare room because of Giles' tossing and turning. Giles asked her if he'd said anything because sometimes he muttered in his sleep. He didn't want her getting any hints about Suzie but all he seemed do is roll about on the bed.

He went down to the breakfast table to find Sandra leaning her elbows on the table and reading the paper. Yesterday's Daily Express to be exact. On the front page, the headlines read 'Witch-hunt for Clinic Whistle-blower'. She lowered the paper and looked at him over the top of her glasses, as he pulled a T-shirt over his naked torso. She made a low wolf whistle.

"Is everything alright, honey? You seemed a bit hot last night.

Not going down with anything are you?" she queried.

Giles read the headline and tried to think of a comment on the whistle headline when he suddenly had a vision of him and a naked Suzie in a lift. She kissed him and he could see her reaching to the control buttons and pressing the down arrow.

What did Sandra say? Going down with Suzie? The Suzie in the vision pulled his head down towards her nether regions. Giles looked away from Sandra feeling like she could read his thoughts. He shook his head and mumbled "I'm alright, dear, just a little tired. Maybe lack of sleep."

"You seem to daydream enough to make up for it," she said. "Don't forget house-husband, to put the recycling out for the bin men. Please check the meter and ring the gas company with the real number because I'm sure they're estimating too much. The greenhouse still needs repainting and don't forget to put the cat in the oven."

She picked up her handbag before walking to the door. She opened it and turned back and waited.

Giles looked at her, "Goodbye, dear, I've got all that in here," and tapped his head.

She frowned.

"What temp should I do the cat at?" he sniggered.

"Alright, you were listening, cheerio, Giles, and be good," she smiled and softly closed the door.

Giles felt like a naughty kid waiting for the parents to go away. He listened for the hatchback to start up and zoom off into the distance.

"Free," he said and changed the radio to the local station. Sandra always had radio four on. She seemed almost obsessive about news. Giles used to ask her what did she listen for in particular and she'd just reply "Someday it may be useful."

When Giles first started his latest job, house-husband as Sandra termed it, he used to enjoy every minute of it, running around cleaning stuff, putting things away and getting Sandra's tea-time meal ready. He'd take the car to the shops, make a list, buy the food and plan the meals for the week ahead.

It seemed such a change from his previous management job in a small building supplies firm, he answered the telephone, filled in orders, chased up suppliers…the list went on almost without end. He couldn't really remember how he had landed the position but it certainly kept him busy. The firm virtually collapsed with the death of the owner and the abrupt slow-down in the industry on the back of the banking crisis.

When the unexpected happened, it turned out that the canny deceased owner had for years been insuring against such a situation and pension schemes had been set up for named trusted employees. He had no relatives and left all his assets, which were a considerable penny, to the pension fund. This allowed several, Giles included, to take early retirement and receive a fixed income almost at the level of their final year's pay.

This seemed a great idea at the time but the novelty started to wear off after a year or so and sometimes Giles had difficulty filling up his spare time. There were only so many times you can clean the bath in a week. He'd tried a few hobbies and settled on cooking, drinking and chatting especially to the fairer sex. There remained, of course, the obligatory flutter at the betting shop.

Sandra had warned him that he might be a target for some of the twenty-year-old to middle-age gold diggers that inhabited the local area. "They exist in all English towns," she said, "and although you can be an arrogant pig at times, you're pretty handsome for your age and would be a nice catch. Wouldn't want a posh pram being pushed around the local high street subsidised by your little pension, would we, Giles?" She knew that he had an eye for the ladies but didn't want him to stay inside the house all the time. He thought that she acted a little overprotective but could also be right after recent events, not to trust him one hundred per cent.

Giles sat in the kitchen wondering what to do. He made

himself a mug of Earl Grey. He liked this particular fragrant tea because he felt it helped him relax. As he took his second hot sip and tried to empty his mind, another Suzie vision came into his head. He started getting used to this new 'being in love feeling' and closed his eyes to let it flow over him. There seemed a fine line between a daydream with which he had control over the action and an image seemingly running the show and telling him what to do.

Suzie wore an orange bikini as she ran towards him, from the silvery waves on a long white sandy beach. Like something from Baywatch, she moved in slow motion as her graceful feet skipped over the sand with her tanned fit body, looking every inch a surfing boy's wet dream. Pert boobs gently bounced with the rhythm of her steps.

She stopped a couple of yards away from him with her hands on her hips, panting slightly. He couldn't help noticing how the seawater had made her cossie go slightly transparent. He could see the circles of her breasts' dark areolae plainly visible through the material, with their bullet hard points trying to burst through the restraining fabric.

"Hard work running across the sand at my age," she said.

"You look fantastic, Suzie," said Giles as she flung her arms around his neck and kissed him on the cheek with her full pink lips.

He realised that he'd started to daydream and focused on his cup of tea again. His right cheek tingled again where the virtual lips had touched. He put his fingers to his face and it felt moist as though it had really been kissed. Suzie's curious perfume entered his nostrils. What an amazing vision, he thought. Better than going to the cinema.

"I think she's telling me it's time for a visit," he said out aloud, then looking around guiltily in case anyone had heard him. No one around, he thought, thankfully. He hadn't noticed the black spider with the white leg that had been watching him for the last thirty minutes. It retired from the lampshade to the upstairs bedroom, through the crack in the corner of the ceiling.

Giles went upstairs and changed his shirt and trousers. He seemed to remember Suzie saying she liked men in jeans, so he found his best pair and the shirt that she'd had given him. It had gone through the wash and Sandra hadn't commented. He often bought himself a new shirt, long- or short-sleeved, so she probably hadn't noticed anything, even though it looked an unusual style.

He did up the shirt and looked in the mirror. He stroked his chin, a nice smooth shave, turned his head this way and that. Giles looked a bit grey now, his receding hairline partly disguised by the short haircut but he still appeared a good-looking devil for his age. He dropped his old leather wallet as he tried to pick it up from the dresser. It fell open at a photo of Sandra behind a stained plastic cover. "Sorry, old girl, duty calls," he said, as he popped it into his back pocket. Then he realised that Suzie might be older than Sandra but everything about her; the look, body, clothes and attitude all seemed so much younger and fresher.

Giles almost ran down the drive and then remembered in his haste that he'd forgotten his keys. He hardly noticed the magpie that watched him from the roof ridge tiles. The bird flew off as he came back up the drive, in the direction of the town. If he'd been looking up he'd have noticed that the magpie didn't sport the usual black and white colours but wore an unusual spotty, almost leopard-like pattern.

Armed with his keys, he strode off down towards the town. He didn't notice Pete's garage door open and his neighbour clocking him as he walked past in his tidy clothes. Pete whispered, "Dirty dog," from the back of his den. His Labrador looked up at him worried. "Not you, mate," and patted the golden pooch.

Giles wondered what to say, as an excuse to see Suzie.

Nearing the corner of her street he noticed an odd-coloured magpie settling on the roof of the corner house. He still looked up at it as he rounded the bend.

"Well there you are," came a cheery familiar voice, "I wondered if I'd ever see you again."

He looked back down from the rooftops and smiled at that lovely face. "H-Hello" he stammered.

"Just going out to get some supplies, but now you're here, come in for a cup of tea and tell me what you've been up to for a week. I've hardly spoken to a soul," she said, looking deeply into his eyes without blinking, her head cocked slightly to one side.

She looked even younger than the last time he saw her about a week ago. A delighted Giles beamed at the fact that such a pretty lady took an interest in him and a sexy one to boot. She linked arms and almost dragged him, to the house door.

Giles felt a bit embarrassed at this and looked around to see if anyone had seen them. An old couple struggling along with shopping bags, on the other side of the road and he wondered if they were looking.

"Don't worry, Giles, I've made sure no one will spot us," she said, and true to her word, the retired pair didn't take a blind bit of notice of the brown-haired woman, almost bundling a fully grown man, up her garden path.

She closed the front door and stood with her back leaning against it. She held her arms wide open silhouetted against the glass in the top half of the door. The sun came out in the front garden and streamed in through the window. Her pretty face disappeared against the brightness of the light. She became a contrasting dark, cut-out figure against a brilliant white background. She swung her body from side to side, arms outstretched. An artist could not have pencilled in a more attractive outline in a hundred years. Wide hips and a wasp-like waist, firm pointy boobs and fine hair that swung like a shampoo advert.

"Come and hug me, Giles," she ordered.

He obeyed and put his hands on her waist. He suddenly noticed that she had no blouse on and as he moved his hands up her back found no trace of a bra either. He wondered how she could have taken them off without him noticing, when her soft lips latched onto his and her arms locked around his neck in a surprisingly strong grip.

She tasted of wine. Sweet and strong but Suzie hadn't been drinking. It felt just like the lovely intoxicating high that alcohol can give you. He allowed the feeling to flow over him and bathed in its splendour.

Giles wondered what to do next but Suzie decided for him.

She loosened her vice like grip and uttered that Suzie saying he'd heard before… "Go on, you know you want to," and took both his hands and placed them on her naked shoulders.

"Lower, Giles," she whispered and said something else that he didn't catch.

He couldn't move. He hadn't been in a situation like this for years. The sun still hid Suzie's face from his view. She could have been any woman but he could hear her breathing, almost urgently and recognised the smell of her skin. Before he could answer, she guided his arms by the elbows so that his fingers rested on the top of her boobs and he could feel the hardness of her nipples on his palms.

Her arms pulled his head down for another strong Suzie kiss.

Giles woke up with a headache and heard the bedroom door close. He looked around. Seven am, own bedroom, no Suzie…here we go again…

Chapter 8

Giles could hear Sandra whistling downstairs. A bit of a tuneless whistle meant happiness, unless the radio played a track known to her and she would badly join in.

No sign of her coming upstairs with a cup of tea so he got up, jumped in the shower and had a long warm dousing which helped clear his fuzzy head. He still couldn't remember anything after Suzie kissed him. Whilst trying to recall what happened, he visualised Suzie standing with her arms outstretched in front of the sunlit glass. He thought how stunning she looked, when he heard a call outside the en-suite door.

"Giles, I'm ready." Sandra's voice made him jump.

He quickly rubbed his hair with a soft, bright pink towel, wished Sandra would buy some blue ones, wrapped it around his waist and stepped into the bedroom.

"Towel really suits you, Giles. Does this suit me?"

He turned around to the wardrobe and found Sandra leaning with her back to it, arms outstretched and totally naked. "You've been in there a long time. What were you thinking about, me maybe?" She did a little twisting and arm swinging with the top half of her body, as though exercising. Then she cupped both boobs in her hands, pressed them together and advanced towards him.

He'd started to forget how attractive Sandra could look. They'd drifted apart over the years like many couples. They'd do their own thing in the evening and go to bed at different times, she worked now and he didn't. Several things all seemed to contribute to them not really touching or being affectionate any more.

This all seemed to have changed recently since he'd been seeing Suzie and he now had two women after him, even if he had a job remembering what he did to them.

Giles looked at her as she came closer. Her figure looked quite different to svelte Suzie. Sandra's at least a couple of inches taller, with darker skin, no wasp-waist like Suzie and a slightly saggy tummy. Her thighs looked too wide for her legs and she had wide rounded hips. The best description is pear shaped with an ample bosom and that very item proffered itself at the moment.

She flung her arms around his shoulders and pressed her boobs against his chest. She smelt nice, she smelt, well… a bit like Suzie, he thought, as she kissed him.

"Is this just a lump in this pink towel or are you happy to see me?" and she squeezed it.

Giles hadn't realised that he'd been getting interested and before he could answer, she whipped the towel off him.

"I'm a girl cat and you're a randy ginger tom," she said.

"Pardon?" he answered.

"Look, I've got a tail." She swung about. He could see her wearing a slim cord around her waist with a long black furry tail attached, hanging between her buttocks.

"And ears," she produced some velvet clip on feline-style and put them on. "Meow," she mewed.

Sandra climbed on the bed on all fours with her back arched and wiggled her bum at him. The furry tail swung about enticingly. "Meow, does the big bad ginger cat want some fun with this lost little pussy?" and she reached back and twirled the black appendage.

The double entendre didn't get lost on Giles. He walked to the corner of the bed, lifted the tail aside, pulled Sandra's hips towards him and whilst standing up, made kitty love.

"Be an animal, Giles."

"Rroargh."

He almost collapsed on top of her laughing and she joined in.

"Funny bloody cat, that is," she laughed.

"Sabre toothed tiger, my dear, Rroargh," and resumed pounding.

Sandra's skin smelt wonderful and they both moved together as a well-oiled machine just like the old days.

With the cat job completed, Giles stood there feeling very proud of himself.

Sandra had rolled onto her right side, twirling the tail with her left hand. Her breasts were larger and droopier than Suzie's and the pose made her thighs look even bigger. Even so, Giles thought that she still looked pretty hot.

"Why thank you, Giles," she said.

Did she mean thanks for the job or is she reading his mind? Giles thought for a split second. "That perfume, what is it?"

"It's just pure sexy Sandra. Why, do I remind you of someone?" she asked inquisitively.

She senses something, thought Giles. "The sex felt good. Something about you today, Sandra, the cat thing, being close to your skin and seeing you naked when I least expected, helped me keep my pecker up."

"Oh good, because I'm beginning to think that you'd been a bad old tiger and maybe had been practising elsewhere. Alright, get dressed then stripy because I've got a day off and you're taking me shopping."

Payback time for the action, Giles thought. Oh, well, he'd enjoyed himself, so time to pay the price and as he went over to the wardrobe, Sandra whacked his behind with her cat-tail.

"Ow,"

As he turned around to look at her, she got off the bed and said "Don't spurn this little kitty because she has sharp claws," before heading into the en-suite.

Giles took this as a guarded warning. Better watch his step with this Suzie thing. Her face appeared in front of his eyes, blew him a kiss and disappeared. He shook his head. He now felt like he'd just cheated on Suzie with Sandra. What the heck is happened in his mixed-up mind?

Sandra whistled something in the shower, a tune from an old

TV programme. He couldn't place it as he sang to himself, "La, la, la, la… La, la, la, lalalah…"

Giles had a spooky feeling about the catchy tune and had a little shiver.

The shopping trip turned out uneventful. Giles did his bit and played chauffer. He followed her in and out of clothes shops, stood dutifully at the changing room door and gave opinions as she twirled in different outfits. He even presented his debit card each time at the till, without being asked.

"You see, Giles, you don't have to be grumpy whilst shopping with me. It's pretty easy, isn't it?" she enthused on the way back.

"Very enjoyable, dear," he lied.

As they got out of Giles' car, Sandra spoke. "Anyway, thanks for my birthday presents, especially in the bedroom. I'm delighted," and she beamed at him.

"Aw shit, Sandra, I clean forgot." He looked at her, very embarrassed.

"Giles, my little tiger, I can wrap you around my little black tail anytime I like, so don't worry about it," and she skipped happily into the house whistling that song again.

Later that day Giles decided to go for a walk to get a paper. The bedroom antics and the shopping had put his usual routine out of kilter. He said cheerio to Sandra who had settled down to watch some afternoon TV with a large packet of chocolate biscuits. She passed one to him as he walked past her to go. "Better have one now, Giles, because their days are numbered. About thirty minutes at the outside," and she laughed before patting her tummy. "You don't mind me being a little curvy, do you?"

Giles had a quick vision of Suzie lying on a sunbed, in a one-piece red bathing costume which tightly encompassed her slender waist. She cheerily acknowledged him with her hand, as a wave came over the sand underneath her and retreated, leaving a line of chocolate digestives in the sand.

"Erm… no dear," He answered and the odd tricks that his mind had played, made him smile to himself. Giles left the house and felt safer to have the front door between him and Sandra's questions.

"Off to see Wanda again, Giles? My girlfriend's left me. Don't suppose yours has a mate?"

Pete, spraying water on his car in the drive, winked at him. Giles, focused intently on getting his paper, hadn't even noticed his friend as he walked along the street.

Who?" replied completely mystified Giles.

"Has her magic wand bewitched the unsuspecting victim?" Pete teased. "Never see her when I pass. Place looks empty to me."

"Ah, Suzie, gonna go around Friday when Sandra's off early on an all-day course. Sorry about your lady. Suzie said she'll go through a few recipes with me over a brew," replied Giles.

"Using a big black cauldron?" Pete asked, mischievously.

Giles frowned then laughed.

Suddenly something that Pete had said, clicked in his mind; Sandra's tune, the programme is *Bewitched,* an old sitcom about a pretty lady sorceress.

The frown returned to his face, those missing moments really started nagging him…

Chapter 9

The last week had been pretty busy for him. Giles had completely forgotten that Sandra had booked a coach-trip to Ireland. This mode of travel didn't suit Giles. It seemed to take ages to get anywhere. All those numerous pick-ups, scheduled lunch breaks, rest time for the driver and so on. Sandra liked them. She said that you get to meet people and can relax with a book, while someone else does the driving. She also pointed out the saving in time compared to waiting at the airport, whilst eating overpriced food, undergoing luggage checks, body frisks and queues.

They were picked up a few hundred yards away from their house at three in the morning. That ungodly hour where normal beings are fast asleep, thought Giles. The only things stirring were a few bats and the call of some weird unidentifiable bird. The street lamps had packed in, on that stretch of the road. The cloud cover and lack of moonlight made Giles uneasy. If man is made to be up this hour, he'd have x-ray vision.

"Stop pacing about, Giles. The bus always picks up here," said Sandra sitting on her suitcase.

"More chance of finding us on the moon," he replied.

A dog did a good impersonation of a wolf in the distance. "Hear that? It's calling his mates. We're dinner."

"Giles, you're such a prick sometimes. You know we're going to Ireland. Didn't you put on the combined leprechaun-and-wolf repellent?" she retorted.

"Ha-ha. Listen, I can hear an engine, something big," he shouted.

The trees lit up in the distance and two bright white eyes came around the corner on full beam, partly blinding them.

They both held their hands partly over their eyes, as the coach flew past.

"Stop you prat!" shouted Sandra, waving ferociously.

The bright red lights on the rear of the bus showed them that they had been noticed. The coach quickly stopped and began reversing back towards them. They grabbed their wheelie cases and trundled towards the vehicle.

The passenger entry door opened and the driver got out. "Don't you lot pay your electric bill around here? I could hardly see you. I'm Jim. I'm afraid my list says you're the Morons."

"That's just a description of how I feel," said Giles.

Sandra whacked him. "It's Morton actually, Giles and Sandy."

He opened the side luggage door and Giles helped him stow the cases in the hold under the seats. The dog-wolf howled much closer and louder this time.

"Bloody hell," said Jim "Let's get out of here, quick."

They climbed on as he shouted, "Seats twelve and thirteen please."

"You hardly ever call yourself Sandy," said Giles, as he sat down next to the window.

"I'm on holiday. Could call you Gilly if you want? Sandy and Gilly go on holiday. Sounds like an Enid Blyton book," and they both laughed.

Sandra grabbed hold of Giles' arm and snuggled into his shoulder. "You keep a lookout for werewolves and witches while I have a little sleep," and quickly nodded off.

Giles thought silently to himself. A relationship with a witch is one thing but he'd draw the line at a werewolf, and sniggered quietly.

"What's that, Giles?" she said opening one eye.

"Just a bumpy road, sweet dreams, dear."

The coach picked up at several more places before making it to the M4 motorway. He could see the lights of a few planes in the sky, as they lined up to land at Heathrow. He gazed at one taking off, seemingly going the same way as the coach. Probably off to Mexico or Cuba for two weeks and I'm on a slowcoach to Ireland, he thought. Hope the Guinness makes up for it.

They stopped at a motorway service station for an early breakfast. Sandra had achieved a few hours' sleep whilst Giles felt like death warmed up. He could never sleep on buses or trains. The constant movement, bumping and vibration kept him awake.

Giles surveyed the contents of his plate. The all-day breakfast looked like it had been left out all day. The egg seemed to be made of white and yellow rubber, he could have used the beans for plastering and the toast might have been made out of bread, but he'd only give fifty/fifty odds. The bacon shattered into shrapnel as he tried to stab it and a piece landed in Sandra's lap opposite.

"Nice breakfast here," she said as she tucked into her soft fresh croissant. "How's yours?"

"I don't think I can manage it all." He demonstrated by turning the plate upside down and only the toast fell off. "I may save it for later, if I can think of a reason," and he just drank the black unidentifiable liquid with coffee written on the plastic cup.

Sandra laughed. "Cheer up, Giles. If the ferry ride's not too rough, we can pig out there."

They climbed back on the coach with several other bleary-eyed travellers that they had got to know. Sandra seemed to have the knack of talking to the oddest people that she could find and they all seemed to want to be Giles' friends.

One couple behind had got on the bus before them. They were in their early fifties. Chris and Angie, both from up north and sounded like it. He designed planes and she had a business selling toys. They promised to show them some of their stuff on the laptop, when they arrived at the hotel. The woman kept giving Giles funny looks and smiling at him in the motorway cafe. When they got back on the bus, he felt quite happy to see that they were sat right at the back, far away from them. Nearby, sat a little old lady, who kept leaning over the aisle in the bus and offering him sweets and biscuits. The young couple directly in front of them were either wearing headphones making a low thud-thud noise or snogging.

This became his life for the several hours and he wondered how many more it would be.

Giles gazed into the waters as the coach glided over the Severn, wondering how on earth the engineers built the pillars that supported the bridge in the river. He could see the old bridge from the new one that they were travelling on. No doubt, there would be a third one eventually. Would one be renamed the ancient bridge and the other, the not so new one, he mused?

The coach belted on past Newport and signs for the Rhondda. He remembered going out with a Welsh valley girl once; an author, part-time amazon and granddaughter of a coal miner. Possessed a fabulous body but absolutely loopy. He put it down to all the coal dust in the Welsh air.

Unusually he nodded off at this point. He awoke with a start to find Sandra with her nose in a book and the coach no longer on the motorway. The road had shrunk down to A-road size and the hard shoulder replaced by green countryside. He spotted a sign for Fishguard, the home of the ferry port. That means we're well into Pembrokeshire, he thought and about to change horses.

On his only holiday in Wales, he stayed with Sandra in a caravan, near a little village called something like Atishoo. He remembered a wide sandy bay, just a few miles away and an evening in a pub just across from the shore. On their final night, the locals tried to teach them Welsh swear words and different uses for a sheep. A bad case of eating too many leeks and inter-breeding, Giles and Sandra concluded, the next day, on the way home.

At Fishguard, after a bit of a queue, the coach carefully manoeuvred into a parking position in the bowels of the ferry and they escaped onto the upper decks of the boat. It looked a nice clear day with no real wind or other nasty weather, forecast. Giles actually looked forward to the trip.

He realised at this point that he hadn't thought of Suzie for a while. Wonder if it's because I'm further away, he mused, looking out to sea?

"Penny for your thoughts, Giles?" came Sandra's voice, "or a quid if they're dirty."

"Just wondering what I'm going to do when I get home," he said almost truthfully.

"How about the greenhouse?" she hinted.

"Okay, okay, I'll remember," wondering how much longer, he could put it off.

"And don't ruin any clothes," she reminded him. "You can stay here if you like. I'm going for a wander," and she left him leaning against the side rail on deck, watching the waves.

Giles eventually found his way downstairs to the saloon bar and decided like if he had a couple of pints, he could take anything that Ireland may throw at him, unless their breakfasts were tougher than the motorway café.

The crossing passed fairly smoothly. Giles had his two drinks and after Sandra joined him, settled down for a boozy sleep in a comfy high-backed chair, in a quiet corner of the bar. Feeling rather refreshed afterwards, he went to the shop and bought a pack of sandwiches, which he ate outside on the viewing deck, watching the waves. Seasickness usually came with even the slightest swell, so Giles usually avoided eating but today he felt so different.

The Irish coastline came into view and he could swear that he smelt Guinness in the fishy windy sea air. The little seaport of Rosslaire came into view and excited children ran around in front of them on the deck, pointing at their destination.

As they climbed back onto the coach in the depths of the ship, amongst the mad revving of engines and smell of diesel fumes, they were accosted by Chris and Angie.

"Lovely voyage over, this can be quite a choppy crossing. You two okay?" said Chris.

"Giles looks like he's seen a Welsh mermaid or two," said Angie winking at him.

Angie had nice big blue eyes and looked good for her age. He followed them onto the bus admiring her curvy behind just in front of him. She half turned around, as she passed Giles and Sandra's seats and grinned, before following her husband to the back of the bus.

"She fancies you, Giles," said Sandra as they sat down. "Don't go getting any ideas."

"Chris gave you the once over as well, I noticed," replied Giles.

"I'd rather read the paper, anyway, I have you for all that stuff, my little cat-stud," and she snuggled up next to him.

The coach eventually reached their destination. They clambered off, found their cases and were soon in their room, in the little Dublin hotel, after a welcome speech from the owner.

The hotel sat about a mile and a half from the city centre. Sandra planned to descend on Grafton Street, the main shopping area and Giles felt pleased to be able to see the Guinness Factory with its viewpoint tower looking over the Dublin, from the bedroom window. Within easy walking distance, he thought. He could see some silver trams zooming along rails cut into the road. It seemed more modern than he expected, especially the transport system, compared to their old buses. In fact, it looked quite pleasing, so far.

There were coach trips organised the next two days into the green Irish countryside and various tourist spots that he'd heard of. The time passed quickly but every now and then he felt a little twinge of guilt inside him and wondered about Suzie. He hadn't told her about the trip. He tried to do so, the day before he left and went to her gate but the house seemed empty and he couldn't get it open anyway.

That evening after their day out, he got dressed for dinner. He'd brought the shirt that Suzie had given him, in his luggage.

He looked at it, thinking of the gooseberries and for some reason held it up to his face. It had been washed but surprisingly he could detect a faint trace of her perfume. Well, possibly not perfume because she didn't seem to wear any, maybe just her lovely womanly smell, a bit like warm sexy bare skin. He inhaled deeply. He could vaguely see her in his mind but she seemed so far away.

Giles put the shirt on as Sandra came in the room door. She'd been downstairs to ask about that night's menu.

"Hey, sexy!" and she tweaked his nipples. "I'm going to have a quick shower and I'll be with you." She walked over to the bed and pulled off her T-shirt, unhooked her bra and dropped them both to the floor. Then she dropped her jeans and stepped out of them. "I need to paint my toenails again," she added, as she bent over to inspect her tootsies.

Giles stood quietly, appreciating the rounded curves of her bare behind and without even looking, she said, "I can read your mind," and turned around to tease him with her hands cupping her boobs.

"A woman in her prime," she boasted, before running into the shower.

Giles became a little frustrated by this. He changed his trousers and wondered whether to tuck the Suzie shirt in or leave the tail hanging out, so he went over to the mirror to decide.

He looked at his reflection and it morphed into Suzie, half bending over and dropping her trousers as Sandra had done. She had a short yellow T-shirt on and slowly wiggled her slim behind as if to show that her butt looked sexier than Sandra's. He could clearly see the witch on a broomstick tattoo, advertising something, a bit out of the ordinary.

Suzie parted her bare legs and bent over further until she could look at him through the gap. She took hold of her ankles, "Go on, you know that you want to."

"Stop daydreaming, Giles, and pass me that flowery dress in the wardrobe." Sandra had reappeared, now washed and putting on her bra. How long had he been staring at the mirror, he wondered?

He passed her the dress and she gave him a suspicious look. He knew when she knew that something was afoot.

"Thinking about the lovely Angie? You'll see her tonight, lover boy," she laughed. "They said they'd meet us for dinner."

"And show us buckets of Lego bricks and designs for jet engines afterwards. I can't wait. Better have a few pints first," he laughed. "Is there anything interesting for dinner tonight?"

"Chicken, fish, pork and yet more chicken. I thought we were in the home of Irish Beef. Haven't had a sniff of stew and I don't think the cow sausages for breakfast had ever been in a farmyard. Anyway this isn't an expensive holiday. You get what you pay for, as the mistress said to her client." Sandra then lifted up the back of her dress to show a knicker-less behind and wiggled as she walked to the door.

"You're not wearing pants," Giles pointed out and she just laughed.

It's like Sandra and Suzie are competing against one another, Giles thought, as he locked the room door.

They met Chris and Angie downstairs in the foyer, went into the dining room and sat at a table laid out for four.

Chris had spruced himself up somewhat from before by putting gel on his greying hair and wearing a neat shirt and tie. "You sit opposite to Angie, Giles and I'll sit opposite Sandy," he encouraged.

Sandra winked at Giles, "Fine by me. I've been looking at him all day."

The couples ordered bottles of red and white wine. When they arrived on the table, they looked at them and all agreed that the brands were pretty obscure.

"Some guy in a warehouse just makes random made-up

vineyard labels on his printer, licks them and sticks them on," said Chris. Angie poured Giles some red and did a slow rather provocative lick at the bottle neck whilst looking at him which the other two didn't seem to notice.

Meals were ordered. They all had the scallop starter because it sounded so much better then pate with toast or melon. The menu had little more variation in the main course, where the apparent disappearance of Irish cows caused some suspicion amongst the diners, after the first glass of wine.

"Maybe they don't like the grass here?" suggested Angie.

"I think the IRA has sold them to the Mafia," said Chris a bit too loudly.

"Shh...Chris. I have it from a higher authority that an Irish McDonalds on Mars is doing great business," said Sandra.

The table erupted with laughter at this point with comments about bulls in spaceships, Ronald McDonald ray guns and green, three-eyed cows. Captain Kirk of the Enterprise became Captain Cowpat of the Prize-Cow with First Officer Steak and Medical Officer T Bones, flying into space on their never ending quest for more grass. Giles had tears in his eyes as the starter arrived. They ordered another two bottles at this point.

They settled down to eat the scallop starter which consisted of an absolutely delicious combination of the aforementioned shellfish, cooked in a large flat Portobello mushroom, with melted blue Brie on top and drizzled with balsamic vinegar.

"Wow!" said Chris after the first bite.

"Amazing," said Angie and Sandra almost simultaneously.

"Bloody hell," said Giles almost rising off his seat then settling "That is good..."

Angie smiled at him and wiggled her stocking clad toes in his crotch a little more.

"I can't wait for the main course. Hope it's the same standard," enthused Sandra.

Giles surreptitiously imprisoned the invading nylon-wrapped digits under the tablecloth with his right hand whilst drinking with the left. He found that he could make the obviously ticklish Angie laugh at will.

The main course arrived courtesy of two waiters and they were all able to survey their meals simultaneously.

They carried two Cajun Chickens for Giles and Chris, who both commented on the fact that their meals were actually sizzling on a hot black metal dish. The servers placed two silver-lidded, oval plates in front of the ladies. Several dishes of veg and sauces made up the food.

A waiter stood by the shoulder of Giles' wife and raised the shiny lid in a theatrical fashion.

"Fish on Friday, is it Friday? I'm tiddly," shouted Angie and giggled as Giles squeezed her toes.

"I love a bit of pork," said Sandra and the rest of the table looked at her and burst out laughing. "No, I mean I like to eat meat," which only added to the merriment and Angie even had to put both stocking-clad feet on the floor, to stop herself falling off her chair.

"Please stop, I'm hungry," said Sandra, trying to control her shaking comedy fork.

"Let me help," said Chris and reached out to steady her hand.

Sandra seemed to jump a bit and answered "Oh…thank you, Chris. Giles wouldn't have done that," looking over at her husband and winking.

Three of them dived into their mains, whilst Chris topped up their glasses and called over a waiter for two more bottles. He joined their chomping with an "Absolutely gorgeous." Giles noticed that Sandra beamed back at him as he spoke.

The bottles emptied into a conversation about sport, cars and red wine versus white. Women's Lib won as after Sandra insisted on taking the bottle off Chris, to top everyone up. Angie said that she hated wearing bras and had undergone breast surgery to uplift her chest.

"Look Giles." As she stood up, she leaned over to him and pulled the centre of her low-cut top out towards him. "They stand up on their own now. Looks like I wear a permanent balcony bra. I've also had fat taken from my tummy and re-injected to give me a Beyonce Bum as well." She walked to the side of the table and bent over to give him an eyeful of her firm rounded buttocks.

"I'd never have guessed, Chris," Giles lied, thinking about following her ass onto the bus, earlier.

"Alright chaps, we promised to show you our work, so if you like, you can pop up to our room before we retire and go to bed," said Chris, in a matter-of-fact way.

"Okay," said Giles, maybe just a little disappointed that the Angie show had ended. "Coach leaves at ten tomorrow so we can't be late."

Once inside the room Angie told Giles and Sandra to sit on the bed whilst Chris started up the computer.

"Forgive me while I get my dongle out, Sandy," and he sat on the edge of the bed next to Sandra and nudged her.

"I dream of a man with a big dongle" Sandra replied, watching the computer screen whilst leaning on Chris' shoulder.

Giles felt a little left out as Angie had gone into the bedroom and hadn't returned.

"Here we are. Some of the designs for the aircraft," Chris said proudly.

Sandra began to laugh and Giles, who couldn't quite see the technical-looking drawings on the screen asked, "What's funny about jets, Sandra?"

"You design toy planes, don't you Chris?" she replied.

"Oh yes, I worked on the Airfix Sopwith Camel at my peak," he announced, causing much merriment. "Anyway, Angie's bringing in some stuff from her toyshop to show you."

They turned around to see Angie reappear in a short purple nightie, carrying a small suitcase which she placed on the bed saying, "Some of these are quite expensive. I have some customers who have the whole set."

Giles waited for the lid to open and reveal rare Steif Teddy Bears or Victorian porcelain dolls.

Yet again, Sandra saw the promised items first.

"Oh my god, they're beautiful," she said, with her hands quickly reaching into the case.

"Gold or chrome-plated, all based on actual ones," Angie explained.

Giles moved over to peer into the case.

Dildoes.

"Anatomically correct, try one if you like, Giles," Angie went on.

Giles stood speechless as Angie placed the eight-inch long silver and black plastic object in his palm. As he read the 'Black Attack' on the side, it started buzzing and he nearly dropped it.

"Have a go, Giles. If Sandy's too shy, Angie won't mind," Chris encouraged.

Sandra creased up on the bed with a fit of the giggles, as Angie came closer to Giles and lifted up her nightie to expose her tanned naked torso.

"Chris likes to watch," Angie explained.

"I gotta be dreaming," said a genuinely shocked Giles, still gripping the upright dildo, as Sandra ran over, wrapped her arms around him as the advancing leggy pelvis was covered up.

"My poor Giles, stage-fright it is. How much is the orange one, Angie? It looks fearsomely gorgeous."

"It's called the Sensuous Suzie and it costs fifty-six pounds in the internet catalogue but call it fifty quid cash."

Sandra reached around to Giles' back pocket and deftly took out his wallet out. She passed the notes to Chris. "It's been worth it to see his face."

Giles saw the funny side of it now and joined in the laughter.

"I've never been refused before. I must be losing my touch," said Angie cuddling up to Chris. "Are you sure that neither of you want to spend the night with us? We could swop if you prefer?"

"We're so grateful for the offer," Sandra replied. "You're a lovely couple but I don't think my husband's heart is ready for this kind of thing yet. Give us your card tomorrow and we'll keep in touch and who knows?"

"Splendid," said Chris squeezing Sandra's bum as he took them to the door. Angie lifted her top off, wrapped her arms around Giles neck and then kissed him slowly. "I'll miss you."

Giles looked back at her firm shapely breasts. "Am I allowed to change my mind, Sandra?"

"Come on, Giles, cheerio both," and she dragged him away.

"How ridiculous did that get?" said Giles to Sandra, sitting in their hotel bed-room. "There's no way I could use a vibrator on you, let alone on another girl, with you sitting on the bed watching."

"Don't make out you're innocent, Giles. I could see you stroking her nylons under the table. Chris is good with his toes as well," she added.

"But you had no pants on, Sandra."

"He found just the right spot. Oh, Giles, you're such a prude sometimes. You're so funny. I don't think that I'll be able to look at them on the way home," and they both climbed into bed to sleep off the crazy night.

Chapter 10

"How about next time, Sandra, we go abroad for a holiday?" suggested Giles. "The coach trip to Ireland was a laugh but I'd really like some sun. We've been to Spain a couple of times so I don't need to go back there. What about Cyprus? I know that you stayed there, as a student but I quite fancy it. Every time I look through these holiday brochures, the place just jumps out at me. Look at this hotel here; it's called 'The Palace'." He passed the magazine across the table to her.

Sandra picked it up and leafed through the pages. "Cyprus again, Giles… Every year, you get this urge to go there. What's brought it on now? I'm sure that Italy, or Malta are both much cheaper and we haven't been to any of those."

"Anyone would think that you're trying to stop me going to Cyprus. Read the advert; quality Mediterranean food, private beach, old ruins. Did you know that the island has a history, going back thousands of years? 'Be treated like a king and queen at The Palace', it says, I quite like the sound of that," he said.

"Well as you know, Giles, I spend a few years at college in the south of the island. I'd like to think that one day we could go there. There are definitely some buildings that would fascinate you and I'd be happy to show you around, but maybe next year?" she replied.

"I'd buy you a new swimsuit, Sandra… " he offered and his eyes glazed over. Suzie appeared in an orange bikini, sunning herself on a beach-lounger and holding a golden crown. "You'll never take it from me, Giles," she shouted and ran off across the sand. "But I should be king," replied Giles and gave chase. He cornered her, laughing, against some rocks and grabbed her by the waist. "Caught between a rock and a hard place," said Suzie, sliding her warm hand down his trouser front…

Sandra's voice made him jump, "Why do you fancy The Palace, anyway, Giles?"

Giles replied without thinking, "I should be king, no, I mean hard, no..."

Sandra looked him in the eye, as though she was trying to read his thoughts. "I'll have a bikini, if you're offering. What colour does the king fancy? ..."

"Erm, blue, red, anything but orange," he quickly answered, trying to eliminate the latter colour from his mental spectrum.

"Well, maybe we'll try Cyprus next year. I don't think they're ready, to be ruled by Giles, just yet," said Sandra, biting her lip, deep in thought.

Giles watched her tidying up the breakfast things. He had a strange feeling about Cyprus. Suddenly Suzie's orange bikini appeared in his mind, tied to his fingers.

"Any orange?" shouted Sandra, holding up a carton and glass. She gave a wry smile as she watched Giles staring at his hands.

"Erm…no thanks Sandra, I'll do the washing up. You'd better finish getting ready for work," he replied.

"Thank you my Cypriot trainee prince," she laughed.

Giles' thoughts were in a quandary after she left the room.

Over the last few weeks, his life had gone from mundane to absolutely mental. This had started off as a little gentle flirt with a pretty lady, had left him with weird dreams, memory loss plus a closet-swinger partner.

He decided to take it easy for a bit and try to get back into his usual routine. He thought that if he did bump into Suzie, he would play it cool and say that he'd been away to think his life over. After all, he didn't really want a divorce. Sandra seemed alright at times and had been quite fun recently. He just wanted a little extra-curricular activity in the bedroom. He thought Suzie would understand. She had a husband apparently, after all.

Giles went out into the garden after Sandra had gone off to work.

"Beware of strange ladies selling toys," she joked as she left.

He wandered around the back yard, hardly noticing the dragonfly that had settled on the greenhouse roof.

The sun came out so he thought it would be a good idea to do something outside. He absentmindedly chipped a large piece of flaking green paint away from the side of the greenhouse, picked it up from the floor and said, "White it is then."

Into the shed, he went and emerged with two tins of paint. One said 'white primer/undercoat' and the other said 'one coat white gloss', on the label. Maybe not quite the right combination, he thought but saves going to the shop. He prized the lids off both tins, with an old chisel and poked the contents with his finger. The gloss looked fine in its fairly new container. The primer appeared another story. He used the chisel to chop around the inside of the tin, lifted out a circle of hard skin and carefully put it to one side on an old chair. The paint inside looked a bit thick, so he fetched some white spirit from the shed and stirred a small amount of the solvent in. Still a bit lumpy, he thought, a minute later. He stood there thinking.

"I have a plan," he said under his breath and went back to the house up to their bedroom. He rummaged through the drawers when there he heard a knock on the door. He went downstairs to find Pete standing there.

"Are we robbing banks or just doing kinky stuff today?" Pete asked.

Giles looked at the object in his hands.

"Oh…the tights, I'm going to strain some old paint. I saw it on a DIY programme."

"Won't the missus object to lumpy legs? I've always liked women in black tights. Your Sandra has nice pins," Pete replied.

"Erm…yes," Giles replied, carefully. Does everyone fancy her, he thought?

"I've done it before, give 'em to me," his neighbour said and after Giles passed them over, he pulled them over his face.

"I once acted as an extra in The Sweeny. Make a good villain,

I do."

Giles laughed "You hadn't even checked if they'd been worn, Pete."

"This is the best way, mate," he answered and the bank-robber and his accomplice both laughed their way to the paint tins.

Pete went in the shed and emerged with a small bucket and wiped the dust from inside it. He stretched the black nylons over the rim and gently slopped the paint into the top.

Giles sat down to watch the thick gloopy mass sinking through the fine mesh.

"You know that you just sat on the old paint skin, don't you?"

"Shit," said Giles and jumped up. The painty chisel clattered to the floor and he looked to see the wet white hard circle that he'd dug out earlier, firmly stuck to the thigh of his shorts.

"They're new," he said "Sandra will go potty."

"Not to mention her best nylons," said Pete as he held the tight clad primer lumps in the air above the tin. "Got a newspaper?"

"I'll never clean my trousers with a paper," Giles replied.

"No, stupid, it's for the old paint. Maybe you can get that off with some of the white spirit?"

Giles found an old carrier bag and got Pete to plop the mass inside. He looked down at his shorts. "How worse can my day get?"

Pete held some kitchen roll soaked in spirit, "Bend over old boy and I'll give you a rub."

"It's burning my leg Pete. I'll have to take them off."

Giles somehow knew that this is wrong…

"Oh… What you two up to then?"

Mrs Parker from next door looked over the fence at the two of them; Giles with his shorts around his ankles and Pete standing just behind him with a tissue in his hand.

"Do your wives know about this? I know it's sunny but

someone might call the police," the old lady asked.

"Just spilt some paint, Nora. Not what it looks," said a red-faced Giles.

"It's dripping down the crack," said Pete, not helping matters.

Giles spun around showing his half-mast underpants to Nora Parker, who promptly covered her eyes.

"Look, the bottle's damaged at the neck and it's leaking," Pete explained, "and you loosened your cacks when you pulled your shorts down."

"I feel faint," said Nora's voice.

Giles looked down to see his blue boxers around his ankles, then realised and bent down to grab them.

Another shriek followed from over the fence.

In his rush, Giles knocked over the strained paint bucket onto the grass and onto one of his trainers.

Pete leant on the house wall trying to stop laughing. "Think I'd better go Giles before Nosey calls the police. Have you got another stocking that I can wear as a disguise?"

"Get them, Tyson."

They looked around and saw Nora lifting her annoying little terrier over the fence, onto a dustbin.

"Yap, yap, yap," barked the terrier and jumped down.

Giles regretted teasing the creature in the Parker front garden now. Tyson had revenge in his eyes.

It came at them like a small Exocet missile. Nipped them both on the ankle and ran through the paint, leaving white doggy paw prints on the patio, before jumping back onto the top of the dustbin.

"Good boy, Tyson, that'll teach those gay boys," shouted the mad old lady.

Giles and Pete legged it into the house and slammed the door before Nora sent the pooch out on another sortie.

"This has to be the best day ever," laughed Pete. "It's like being a kid again."

"You haven't got a mark on you. I've ruined my clothes, wrecked the patio and Nosey will tell Sandra tonight that I'm queer. It's like being in a Norman bloody Wisdom film," Giles replied, seriously.

"I'm sorry, Mr Grimsdale," said Pete in squeaky Norman impersonation which defrosted Giles and made him laugh.

"Just go. I'll see you in a few days, Pete" he ordered, watching him as he turned his peaked cap to one side, pulled up his trouser legs and did a crazy Wisdom-like walk down the drive.

He put the kettle on and looked through the kitchen window. He didn't really worried about Nora Parker or Nosey Parker as the Mortons fondly called her. She forgot all sorts of things sometimes and at others, acted as mad as a box of frogs. Even if she said something to Sandra, the wife would probably just say 'yes, yes, Mrs Parker, nice day isn't it?'

A bigger problem seemed the trail of destruction that he could see from the window. After a cup of tea and a quick check that the garden looked terrier free, he spent the next two hours paint stripping the patio with the power washer, mowed the longish grass which removed almost all of the white paint and even found time to scrape some of the loose paint off the greenhouse.

Whilst this went on he emptied the contents of the white spirit into a washing up bowl and left the painty shorts soaking. When the other jobs were done, he stood on one leg of the pants and blasted the painty mark with the water jet. He then hung them up in the shed to dry, out of Sandra's view.

He heard Tyson yapping in the garden so he looked over for any sign of Nora then let the pooch have it right between the eyes. "Touché, Tyson," and put the machine away laughing to himself.

Odd morning but at least it had ended, he thought, whilst devouring a tomato and cheese sandwich.

He realised that he hadn't shaved yet. He got the razor out of his bedroom drawer and walked around the house thinking and buzzing at the same time. After stroking his chin, he looked in the lounge mirror. Suzie looked back, dressed in a smart Sandra like business suit. She drank from a glass of wine, turned to him and waved. Then she beckoned to him and blew him a kiss. His right cheek started to feel warm and tingly just like before.

I get the message, he thought. I've done my work for the day. A boy has to have a little relaxation. Anyway, he did want to talk to her.

One quick shower and a change of clothes later, he strolled down the drive despite his earlier decision to play it cool. She's so pretty he thought, as he walked along, almost mesmerised by the vision he had earlier, in the mirror.

Suzie stood in her garden so he didn't bother attempting the gate. She shouted "Hello, Giles!" ran over and used her usual sleight of hand to undo the annoying latch.

"You must have been away. We've all missed you."

He looked around for the other people but there were only two cats and a couple of birds on a bush.

"Come in, I'll fix you up with a beer or a tea. You want to ask me something?" she said.

How did she know that? Must be the look on my face, he decided.

"There's something that's been bugging me, Suzie. Sometimes I wake up and I can't remember what I've done. It seems to be after I've seen you. I'm pretty sure I've had a good time and things do come back to me later. I get lovely thoughts about you. I was wondering if you'd had anything like that feeling, maybe that wine of yours has some bad alcohol in it or something? I know that I sound silly, sorry."

"Oh… You poor thing, Giles, I haven't had anything like that. I'm sure it's okay. I made it from the fruits of mother-nature. It's greener than a green frog, sitting on a green lily-pad, in a green pond, in a green jungle and whistling *Greensleeves*." She laughed.

"I made up the whistling bit, though."

Giles laughed as well, his memory fears forgotten as he looked into those deep brown eyes. The little lines crinkled up at the sides of her eyes and her smile seemed to go from ear to ear.

"Frogs don't drink wine," he pointed out.

"Of course they do," she replied, "and they speak French."

Giles took a second to get the joke and burst out laughing at her clever humour. She wrapped her arms around his neck and gave him a long juicy kiss.

She let go to let him come up for air. "Well I'm very sorry if you can't remember the good bits, Giles," and took hold of his hand. "Come upstairs with me now and I'll try to cure your forgetfulness."

Chapter 11

As she leaned over him, her 'Witch' necklace dangled close to his face. She moved her hips from side to side, grinding her mound against him. As she did so, the letters moved hypnotically in front of him. His eyes started to close in pleasure and he could smell her curious perfume more strongly.

He suddenly jumped, when she tweaked both his nipples simultaneously and just a bit too hard.

Suzie laughed, "Just checking if you're under yet."

"Under paid and under you at the moment," he replied.

"Under my control," she added.

Suzie moved forcefully up and down on him. She had deftly slipped him inside her, a few seconds ago and he'd hardly noticed. Her fingers were skilfully rubbing his nipples. Her moist inner grip felt like a tight hand. Maybe she did regular pelvic floor exercises, he wondered? The ends of her dark locks were tickling his face. He could hardly see her face for the dangling hair. He heard her say something above the noise of their movements and the creaks of the mattress, stressing the bed. It sounded foreign but not in any familiar language. Softy repeating, it sounded almost like a chant.

After several minutes of this he neared the final act and said "Better slow down, Suzie, don't want any little accidents." She replied "You cannot harm me, Giles, you will only make me stronger," and carried on with her sexy movements.

He put his hand on her hips and could feel the curve of the bones moving under the soft skin as she wriggled on top of him. Usually, Giles did the work, all the grunting and thrusting. It felt so different to be underneath, almost like being milked…

Giles climaxed like never before in his life. Suzie had moved down wide-mouthed to kiss him and seemed to draw all the air from his lungs. At the same time, it felt like every vital sperm he possessed sprayed out of him into her, like a giant magnet would attract iron filings.

He lay there motionless, unable to breathe at first even though the vacuum kiss had ended and Suzie had now sat upright, shaking her hair from side. He couldn't see her face at first and felt a little faint from lack of air. For a split second her face looked much older but when the hair settled the attractive smiling visage returned and dare he say it, looking even prettier and younger.

As usual, he woke in bed the next day, with missing memories, to a smiling wife. "I'll bring you breakfast in bed, old man. You need to rebuild your strength after last night's exertion."

"Thanks," he mumbled, whilst trying to remember the bit from one bed to another. Looks like he scored with his wife again… How strange, he thought.

He heard her coming upstairs. Not her slipper-clad feet but an on/off rattle of a teaspoon, badly balanced on a saucer.

As he started to sit up, he felt a large twinge in his back. "Ow, that hurts," he said to Sandra and struggled to get a pillow behind his back. She put the tray down on the bed and passed one of her pillows behind him, in addition to his.

"Feeling your age, now? Eat up. I'm going to see mother today, remember? And do some shopping, do you want to come?"

Sandra's real mother had apparently died years ago. She met this other similarly titled woman through a friend. That person had gone away and Sandra had continued seeing the old bat. She read tarot cards and practised fortune telling. She had once looked Giles in the eye and said "You smell different. I don't think you're human," and also told Sandra, "Trouble will follow him around, he is not of this world yet he is the father of another."

"Who's the mother, eh?" asked Giles, laughing but feeling a little uncomfortable.

Load of crap, he thought. He looked at his breakfast tray and took great pleasure in visualising the boiled egg as 'mother' and then decapitating it. As he forced a bread soldier into her chopped-off head, he started thinking that maybe she isn't so bad, compared to being boiled alive or forced to drink acid. Whilst eating his toast, he wondered what to wear and to do that day.

As he did so, Suzie flashed into his head, sitting topless in the kind of big pot that cannibals would use and waving him to join her. He shook his head to get rid of the odd vision and thought Suzie would know what to put on.

After a quick shower, a rummage through the wardrobe and drawers for clothing, he nipped downstairs, hoping Sandra would have popped to the shops so he could read the paper in peace.

She had. Giles made a coffee and sat down at the big wooden kitchen table, his favourite seat, where he could spread the Daily Telegraph out in front of him. He flicked through the myriad of free magazines until he spotted a picture of a woman in an advert that looked just like Suzie. She had the same big brown eyes and wide smile. The model seemed to be winking at him from the page. A tapping by the window, drew his attention so he closed the papers and got up for a look. A black crow sitting on the old greenhouse looked back at him.

He'd never liked crows, since one pecked his foot when as a nipper, in a pushchair years ago. He opened the back door, to shoo it way. As it flew off with a loud "rack", he could see a flash of white feathers on its left wingtip. Unusual, he thought, being a crow shooing regular, not seen that before.

He went back to look for that picture of Suzie and couldn't find it anywhere. After going through all the magazines, he even looked in the bin, just in case he'd absentmindedly put part of the paper in it but to no avail.

Never mind, on to the sports pages. Giles could never jump or throw very far and didn't get on well with any team games. He ran quite well, a trial and a season at a local running club had ensued but he struggled to motivate himself enough to go to regular training. He always enjoyed reading about football and athletics. When young at school, he dreamt about being a top hurdler or javelin thrower rather than the Kevin Keegan of his mates. They used to say you'll never get the girls by thinking about athletics, they want footballers. He wondered what they'd say now about him and Suzie, eh?

Sandra eventually came back and plonked two shopping bags on the table. "I've bought some nice wine here for tomorrow night. South Australian merlot, good price, Giles," and handed one to him.

The label had a bird on the front, 'White Feather Vineyard'. He nearly dropped the bottle. "Lemme see the other one, Sandra." He looked, South Australian, 'As the Crow Flies Vinery'.

The colour drained from his face. He stared out of the window. The crow on the fence looked back at him. He pointed at the picture on the first bottle. "That's the crow in the picture…on the fence. It has white tipped feathers on one of its wings."

"There are a lot of crows in England," she said and then added, "bet there's a few in Australia as well. What other birds have you been bird watching again, then?"

Giles froze. She's sensing something, he thought. Suzie dressed only in a leather thong flashed into his head.

Sandra came closer and put her hand on his forehead. "You seem a little hot recently, Giles," looking deep into his eyes.

Suzie slowly danced across his vision between him and Sandra now. He felt sure that his wife would see her there. He tried to blot her out by thinking about something else. Giles tried a can of tuna but the lid peeled back, Suzie climbed out and blew him a kiss.

"Giles, you're up to something fishy. I just know it. What's her name?" she said softly, biting her lip gently.

Did her woman's intuition pick up the tuna can, he thought? "Don't be silly, Sandra. At my age?" he answered and forced a laugh.

"Well you be careful then and if any nasty ladies bully you, come and fetch Sandra to sort them out," she said, still in her softest voice.

She must know something, Giles thought. Maybe it's the sex. Getting ideas elsewhere?

"Anyway let's have a glass of wine. I need you in bed later, Tiger," and she made a growling sound.

Giles gratefully took the glass of wine that she handed to him.

He sipped, half expecting it to taste of old crow but thankfully the fruity white settled his nerves. "Not bad at all, Sandra," and he took another close stare at the 'As the Crow Flies' bottle, before checking out of the window, to see if it looked like the same one.

The white-tipped crow had gone. A magpie landed to take its place and hopped along the hedge before settling on the grass.

"I reckon that one's watching me now," said Giles.

"When I offered to sort out your birds, I wasn't referring to the feathered kind, Giles," Sandra replied. She rattled the door handle and the bird flew off. "I suppose that you're going to tell me that the black cat on the fence is in league with them as well."

Giles glanced over. "With any luck, Tyson will have a go. I guess I feel like everyone's got it in for me today. I'm a bit tired."

"You have been looking rather rough around the edges at times, the last couple of weeks. I think the sex has worn you out. I think Mr Tiger had better have a few early nights. Mrs Blacktail will just have to be patient." She leaned over and kissed him on the forehead.

"Have another glass. I have to go back to the shop because I forgot the milk. I might get some other stuff there, as well. Couple of birthdays coming up and there's a Co-Op offer on boxes of chocolates. Mother never eats the ones we give her, just passes them back a few months later. You like Black Magic don't you, Giles?" she asked.

Suzie popped into Giles' head, jumping across the top of a box of giant chocolates. She leapt from the top of one dark sweet to the next. One of them cracked and she slid halfway in. She pulled herself out, her lower half all pink and sticky. Suzie pushed the straps of her short dress off her shoulders and dropped the sugary garment to the floor. She looked as though she wore thick pink tights. She bent over and flashed her behind before doing an athletic hop, skip and jump over the next three chocolates. A wave and she disappeared.

"Magic it is then, being as you haven't answered," said Sandra impatiently.

"Oh erm...yes, my fave. Especially strawberry," he replied, thinking about the pink lady.

"Why don't you scrape some more paint off the greenhouse while I'm away? Should keep you out of mischief for a bit?" she suggested.

Giles finished off his glass. "I might just do that. An easy afternoon is what I feel like. I might even be nice to Nora if I see her."

True to his word, Giles did a bit of scraping, before tuning the radio into an easy-listening station and lolling on a sunbed that he had pulled out from the shed.

To tell the truth, he had spent more time cleaning up the old sunbed than on paint removal duty. He even found a can of spray oil and gave the joints a squirt. Works like magic, he read on the label and with one more press, the top broke off. The remaining contents whooshed down his arm and onto his newly cleaned resting place.

"Balls," he said as he carried the still-dripping can to the dustbin. He went inside and emerged with a kitchen roll and mopped the now shiny plastic surface of the sunbed.

'Balls' was not as bad as 'Shit' in Giles' repertoire. It meant frustration at something that should go smoothly. Giles had got fairly used to having a 'B' category life but his recent flirtation with the 'S' category had pissed him off a bit. "Suzie begins with S," he said out aloud, "Oh dear…"

Giles wondered if he should adopt a new profanity in case things became worse.

"Double shit," he tried.

He looked up to see if the devil would appear or to be struck down by lightning.

"Did you call me, Mr Morton?" shouted a voice from over the fence.

"Well, in an odd sort of way, Nora. How are you?"

"I'm fine apart from my joints, you know," she replied.

"I'm afraid that I've just used up all my oil." He attempted humour.

"You can have the rest of mine then dear, I've done Tyson. Don't want him getting sunburn," and she passed Giles a bottle of factor fifty over the fence.

Giles could see the strangely spikey mutt rolling around in the grass. The dog appeared to be frothing slightly at the mouth and generally not enjoying life.

"I've given him some of my constipation tablets because I accidently bought him the wrong food, last week. I wondered why there the tin had a cat picture on it," she explained.

"But I couldn't remember if those were to slow you down or speed you up, Mr Morton so I've given him some diarrhoea pills as well. That should sort him out, don't you think?"

Tyson now bolted up and down the garden path.

"I gave him some of those blue pills that my old Arthur used to take to perk himself up".

Giles now waited for the punchline.

"But he kept chasing after that bitch over the road," she said, shaking her head.

Giles' straight face started to crack. He almost felt sorry for Tyson, until the blue pills.

"Have you got many of the blue ones left?" he enquired wondering.

"Oh, there are lots. Would you and your friend with the stockings like to try some? Arthur used to go racing with Bert and his two daughters. Always dressed up, those two girls did. They wore stockings as well… Arthur always said they used to make his old dog perform better."

"Don't suppose that you ever found out where the dog track existed, Nora?"

"Well no, he'd always say an old lady like me shouldn't go to such places. He never won any money. I'd sometimes check in his wallet afterwards and he'd spent a couple of hundred. He always seemed happy when he came back though, so I didn't mind. He's the best husband in the whole world, my Arthur."

A loud yowl from Tyson interrupted her, closely followed by the sound of a massive fart. Another yowl and the oily sun-proofed dog shot off under the bushes.

"I detect something in the wind," smiled Giles.

"Rain? Oh no, it's been such a nice day," said Nora. "I'd better get in now. It's been good to get Tyson running because I can't take him out nowadays. He won't be the same old dog after this."

"He'll certainly remember this day," Giles laughed.

"I didn't waste the cat food. I made a nice pasty with some left over crust. I'll pass it over the fence with the rest of the blue pills later for you and Pat," she said.

"Sandra will be pleased," he corrected.

"Oh, does your friend use a women's name as well? How modern. Well, I hope the two of you are very happy. Goodbye Pat." She disappeared into her back door.

Giles lay down the sunbed to contemplate the last few minutes.

"Double Shit," he tried again.

No devil appeared like last time. He decided to have a more seriously bad life category 'DS' on the grounds that some of the recent happenings were fairly crazy. He then spent a few minutes wondering what a 'TS' or Triple Shit day would be like and decided that could be the day Sandra found out about Suzie.

Once again he found himself making a promise to stay away from Suzie for a few days and then see her to try to slow things down a bit. Life in this house isn't too bad now. The affair with Suzie is marvellous fun but maybe the devil you know is safer.

Even, if she does make cat-food pasties…he laughed to himself.

The next day he remembered the magic trick book he'd bought from the newsagents, a few weeks ago. He rummaged around and also looked out an old pack of cards.

Some of the ideas required construction of props varying from elaborate to simply childish. He leafed through the book looking out for card tricks, which had always been his favourite and started practising.

Giles had been encouraged by Sandra to go to a few neighbouring kids' parties as part of the entertainment. He'd had mixed results that varied from being pelted with ice cream and trifle to being asked to make one woman's husband disappear permanently. Sandra reckoned Giles' black suit looked a bit mafia-like and he'd worn sunglasses to the party doorstep.

He could shuffle the cards in clever ways, spreading them out fan like and whipping them back together. He could make people pick a card and find it again. This book had some more difficult ones, where the card would reappear in a sealed envelope in someone's pocket. Required a lot of pick pocketing skills. May come in useful one day, if he ever loses his pension, he thought.

The mental effort and practising helped fill up Giles' next few days. The weather had been a bit wet so he'd had an excuse to leave the greenhouse painting. When Sandra came home, he usually roped her in to help him practice, even if she did quickly work out how each particular trick worked.

"Oh, I see, that's how you did it," the words that a magician hates to hear.

The reason why he tried so hard is to impress Suzie. He had enough of her pretend witchy little tricks and decided to show her how a man did some real magic. So good that you couldn't guess how it works. Not that he knew how she did some of her stuff but he would make out that he did.

"That last one is really very good, Giles. We've done it three times now and I'm none the wiser." At last Sandra uttered the words that he wanted to here. He would try that one out on Suzie later.

"Are you going to do parties again, Giles? Don't think that the kids would like that one much."

"Maybe, Sandra. Just get my confidence back first. I might have a go on Pete first."

"And how is your bosom buddy? Forgot to tell you that Nora had left a Sellotaped-up tin, saying 'Mr Morton and friend' on top of the dustbin a couple of days ago. That black cat that you saw before ate a funny-looking pie, also put there. Your tin's in the drawer over there and god only knows what is in the pie. I suspect you're involved somewhere in this but I'd rather not know. I've got to be in work, very early for a meeting tomorrow, so I'm having a bath straight after supper and off to bed. I might be back at lunch so maybe I'll see you then. If not, I don't want to hear that you and Pete have been playing tricks on Nora. Got it?" she said sternly. "Oh and don't forget that we're having a barbeque tomorrow evening."

"Okay Kommandant," he saluted. She forced a smile and left him to sort out the dinner.

The next day, Sandra had gone by seven o'clock as promised.

Giles would usually have a lie in when this occurred but today he'd started on a mission, a magical mission. After a quick shower, shave and toilet, he sat downstairs practising his masterpiece. Beans on toast followed and he felt ready for his audience of one, or three if the cats were present.

He went off down the street feeling very confident, going to show this pretend witch some real magic and she would have to do something really special, to top him.

Somewhere, though, at the back of his mind, he had a feeling that she might do just that but he tried really hard to squash the tiny thought.

Suzie stood in the garden and the wide open gate beckoned him in.

"I guessed you'd be coming so I opened up for you. I see you have something for me," she said, looking down at his carrier bag.

"I'm going to play a trick on you. Conjuring actually," he said.

"Oh, I adore magic, Giles," she smiled, and he could see her twiddling with her 'Witch' necklace. "Come into the hall. I bet you do cards because you haven't got a saw to cut me in half with."

Giles laughed at the saw joke and then had a quick vision of a gingerbread man on a plate being cut in half. She led him into the house to a small table in the hall that he hadn't noticed before.

He performed the trick in the garden.

"Bravo, Giles," she said as she opened the envelope. "It's a Jack and you're nearly right," she added. "But this is Hearts."

"Can't be," said Giles "Should be diamonds," and stared disbelievingly at the held out card.

"Do it again, please," she said.

He did it again with a similar result and looked mystified.

"Never mind, Giles, tricks don't work on me. Come in the house and I'll cheer you up. You look quite disappointed."

He did as she told him. Turning into another 'B' category day, it seemed.

Chapter 12

"I know," Suzie exclaimed as he stood in the hallway. "I'll try to do a trick".

"Hold out both your arms, Giles," she ordered.

Suzie placed both hands over his left wrist so that he couldn't see the watch. He felt a warm feeling in his arm. She withdrew her hands slowly, whilst he looked and the watch had gone. He didn't hear or feel anything apart from the slight heat and a touch of her red-nailed fingertips on his skin.

She opened her hands triumphantly to show the watch.

Giles looked at it open mouthed. "I didn't feel you undo it at all." He looked closer. "Actually it's still done up. It would never slide off. How'd you do it?"

"Hold out your right arm," she ordered.

Giles did so and watched her hands pass slowly over his right hand with the clasped watch out of sight. The same warm feeling occurred and as the soft female hands left his arm, the timepiece reappeared on his right wrist.

The heart-shaped brown mole on his right wrist near the watch strap tingled a little and a quick scratch soon sorted that out. He held up both forearms near his face, marvelling at the illusion.

"You really should be on TV or the stage, Suzie. That is amazing. My tricks are like kid's stuff. It's like you can really do magic."

"Can't I just?" she replied and came closer and put her arms around his neck. She gave him a moist full kiss and backed away.

"Nice necklace, Giles."

He looked down towards his chest.

He wore a sparkly necklace. "You put your 'Witch' jewellery on me. I didn't see you take… oh; you've still got yours on… " He lifted it and tried to look at it upside down. It seemed to have more letters on than hers.

"B.E.W… " He spoke out aloud, "Bewitched."

"Wow! I'm only borrowing this, aren't I? It's lovely but I don't think Sandra would like it," as he struggled to find the clasp.

"Wear it while you are with me today, to show that you are mine," and she put her arms back around his neck. Thoughts of taking off Bewitched disappeared, as her tongue entered his mouth.

When he finally got away from her mouth, Giles said, "I can't stay too long today, Suzie because Sandra's coming home early today. The weather's nice so she's asked a couple from work around for a barbeque."

"Are you looking forward to it? Your face doesn't say so. I hoped that we could do some cooking together. I planned something tarty."

Giles had to grab at his trousers which had suddenly started to slip down.

"Looks like you want to stay and play, darling," she teased.

Giles looked at her standing there, swinging his belt in her right hand. She turned around and ran further into the house.

He followed her, yanking up his trousers. "Aw, come on, Suzie. I can't hang around."

He cornered her in the kitchen.

"I've met them before but don't get on with them much. Now just give me the belt before you get me into trouble." He tried to grab her with one arm and reach behind her to the hidden belt. This only led to his trousers dropping to his ankles.

Suzie grabbed him by his privates, just tight enough to get his instant attention.

"I just know that the weathers going to take a turn for the worse, the barbecue's off and Suzie's on. Trust me." Her face came very close to his. Giles couldn't answer. She had fire in her eyes.

She stroked his manhood through the material and resumed her tight grip. "Sometimes you have to have a little pain before some pleasure."

Whack...

Giles jumped. "Shit, Suzie," He had focused on her grip around his bits and didn't notice that she'd folded the belt with the other hand, until she'd caught him squarely on the behind.

"Let me rub it better," she said dropping the belt and sliding both hands down the back of his boxers.

A warm glow replaced the stinging from the leather strap. Her hands were cold yet made him feel warm. She pressed her crotch tightly against him and moved it about.

"It will rain soon and then you can ring Sandra to say there's not much point in a barbeque."

"The forecast said fine all afternoon in this area. I saw it earlier," he replied.

"Today it's wrong," she said confidently. "Come have a glass of wine and watch the clouds build up."

"Okay then." Just have a glass and then go home, he thought. It's never going to rain. He bent down to pick up his belt.

Whack...

Suzie delivered a stinging hand-slap on his butt. "Oh yes, it will rain," as though she'd read his mind.

He put his belt and trousers back on and then sat at the kitchen table. Suzie bent over, looking in a kitchen cupboard. He admired the curves of her behind as she spoke.

"See anything that you fancy?" she asked...

Reading my mind again, he thought? But she quickly got up and placed three bottles on the table.

"The choice is Parsnip, Melon or Tomato? You can have me later," she giggled.

He heard a noise at the window. Giles turned around to look. It had started to rain outside.

Rain very hard...

He went over to look, "I don't believe it."

"Told you," said Suzie. "Better ring the little lady."

Giles did as she suggested. No point in asking how she knew

it would rain. A lucky wild guess, maybe?

He came off his mobile. "She says it's off. The visitors have just texted her, anyway. She's going to stay on for some overtime."

"How nice, now you're all mine," and she beamed from ear to ear.

Suzie poured out two glasses from the first bottle after she'd popped the cork out. "You're too slow so I've picked the melon. Drink up while I get a snack."

"You should have been a waiter, the way that you took that cork out," he said, looking at the simple corking device that she'd left on the table. He picked it up and examined it, wondering how it could remove the plug so easily. "It's a bit like you and that gate. You have a knack with opening."

"I have a way with some things. I like to get what I want."

Giles first sipped, then took a long quaff of the light golden liquid. Delicately sweet with a fruity smell, the tipple gently massaged his nostrils in a most unusual way.

"I think that the experts would say this wine has a very nice nose," he mused, wiggling his conk with his finger and thumb.

Suzie came back with some dry-looking biscuits. "Have some of these before you try the next one."

Giles did not look impressed at the unappetising-looking plate but picked out one anyway. He bit into it. The most lemony sensation he had ever tasted, flooded into his mouth.

"That's amazing." Giles had another two mouthfuls of wine then reached out for another biscuit, incised out a chunk and waited for another lemon hit.

Raspberry… He looked at the last piece of biscuit, bemused.

"I call them clever biscuits. All different flavours even though they almost look the same," she explained. "Some of them even have more than one taste…"

She picked up another bottle and with a single movement removed the cork.

"Now you're showing off," he said. "Which wine next?"

"Tomato," she replied.

"Hmm, thought you might say that," he said, sounding a little concerned.

"This one's nothing like the name. Not a bit of sauce about it, unlike me," and she struck a model pose and pursed her lips.

Giles took a tiny sip and then a larger one. Not a strong taste but as he swallowed it, he could feel a warm glow in his throat similar to drinking spirit. He smelt it and couldn't detect any real odour. "It's like whisky but it's not, sort of weird but still lovely." He reached for another biscuit.

"Oh erm…now it tastes like tomato." He pulled a face.

"Can't be, let me check it," and she took it off him and had a bite. "Hmm…it should be fine now," and handed the remaining piece back with two missing semicircles.

He took another bite.

"It's honey now. What did you do? You switched it, didn't you?" He looked at the two different-sized bite marks and found that one fitted his top front teeth.

"I don't understand," and he took another couple of gulps of the tomato wine. "Excellent," he said, referring to the wine.

"Excellent," repeated Suzie. Giles wondered if she meant the wine or the sudden biscuit taste change. "I do hope you are enjoying yourself, Giles. I'm having a lovely time." She smiled and took a big bite of another biscuit whilst staring at him.

How can someone look so sexy, eating a biscuit, Giles wondered?

She wiped away a crumb from her cheek. He watched her pick up the third bottle and magic the cork out. It's the only way his slightly tipsy mind could describe it. He remembered his Bewitched necklace, reached down and twiddled with it.

She noticed. "Is it true? Am I getting to you?" and half turned before wiggling her behind.

"And finally the parsnip," she announced, passing over a third glass. Giles still had a little left in each of the first two but eagerly took the third from her outstretched hand.

Giles noticed a pair of red knickers on the table as he put the glass to his lips. He hadn't seen her take them off. He closed his eyes and without sipping this time, took a large mouthful and swallowed deeply.

It tasted quite different again from the other two with a strong flavour and very dry. A sort of full bouquet, almost thick feeling, a bit like a heavy red wine but looking nothing like it. He took another gulp and started to feel a little drunk. In fact, more than a little tipsy, it was time for another biscuit.

"What next, Suzie? Chocolate?" he laughed.

"If you want," and she seemed to wave at the biscuit.

Giles took a chunk out of the dry-looking object and awaited the taste…

"It is chocolate. You knew. It must be marked," and he turned the cookie over several times and then looked at the surfaces of the remaining biscuits sitting on the plate.

The kitchen window rattled as a low growl of thunder rumbled overhead.

"Wait for the flash," she said.

Craakk.

The room lit up with as the lightning streaked across the sky. Just for a second, Suzie suddenly looked much older in the bright light. Giles blinked with the intensity. He refocused on Suzie, to find she'd moved closer and had unbuttoned most of her blouse.

"And here's a softer flash," she purred, undid the final fixing and dropped the cotton garment to the floor.

She pressed her left boob against his face. His mouth was already open with surprise anyway. A hard nipple pressed against the end of his tongue. The soft flesh squashed against his nose and cheeks. That lovely curious Suzie scent, filled his nostrils and he breathed in deeply and slowly.

"Very good, Giles," she said like a school teacher. "Now suck my nipple."

He did as she ordered. As soon as he pursed his lips around the hard centre and started to create a vacuum in his mouth, he became aware of a pleasant flavour. The feeling grew to fill his mouth. Only a small drop had emanated from the tip but it tasted so powerful. He rolled his tongue around his mouth and over his lips.

The wonderful feeling spread out from his oral cavity and ran up inside his nostrils. It even seemed to go into his ears. His head went all tingly. He didn't feel drunk and neither was it like cannabis; only slightly light-headed but not about to faint. Just a great feeling; as though he turned into Superman and could do anything in the world, he also noticed that he felt very randy.

Her other boob came into view, "And this too one, please," she ordered and the process repeated itself.

Giles sucked and a similar feeling hit him, only this time it was more intense.

"Stand up, Giles." He had his eyes closed, enjoying the moment and felt himself being pulled up.

She grabbed his crotch. "Come to mama," and he felt his trousers falling to the floor and being pushed back onto the chair.

Before he could comment on his treatment, she sat on his lap, legs astride him and tore at his shirt buttons. Pulling it down off his shoulders, she left it up to him to extricate his arms. Suzie bounced excitedly, up and down and all of a sudden, he realised that they were one.

She still had her skirt on and he reached down under the material, to hold the sides of her thighs. He could feel the muscles and sinews working, expanding and contracting, as she rode him.

The nipple condiment had put him in the mood and he started pushing upwards, to meet her downward motion.

'Bewitched' met 'Witch' as their necklaces clattered together. The collision between the two items of jewellery seemed to spur them both on, with renewed energy.

"Do it, Giles," and she started firmly rubbing his nipples.

He noticed that her breathing had become faster and faster, harder and harder...and couldn't help but follow. Giles didn't feel like himself. Sex is never this good... No love here, just pure lust.

She knew just how to move, just where to touch and rub him. He felt her wrapped around him but also inside, reading his mind, walking through his pleasure cortex, searching for the orgasm switch.

Suzie screamed seconds after she'd pressed his special button.

Giles opened his eyes to check on her.

He had really sweated. It dripped down from his forehead. Her face seemed a mass of tousled hair but he could see the top of her boobs were glistening. He reached out to pull back her hair and she knocked his hand away.

"Don't look at me just yet," she said sharply before saying something that Giles didn't understand but it seemed familiar from his distant past.

"Incredible, Suzie, are you okay, what's that you're saying?"

She ignored him and carried on babbling and started moving up and down again, on his now very sensitive manhood.

"Ah... Suzie, no more..."

"Pleasure and pain, Giles..."

"Ahhh...please stop."

She finally hopped off, her face still covered in wild hair and reached for a brush that seemed to have appeared on the kitchen table. Giles hadn't noticed it earlier. She turned around from him and he watched her bare back and shoulders as she combed in hair-control.

"Incredible," said Giles.

"Aren't you going to cover yourself up, stud?" she asked, when she turned around, looking faultless.

Giles looked down and realised he still sat naked on the kitchen chair surrounded by his clothes. "Oh yes, of course. That sex was incredible," he repeated. "You're just so good at it," and he bend down to collect his trousers.

He put on his trousers and gazed at her. The fully dressed Suzie looked radiant. In fact somehow, she looked even younger than a few minutes ago.

"Wow, you look just great. I feel really tired," he said.

She came over, picked up his shirt and tossed it to him. "You must be hungry. I have another biscuit for you to try and you still have a little wine left, anyhow."

"Okay then," he replied and put on his shirt watching her.

She poured the remains of the three glasses into one and stirred them with a little stick. He walked to the kitchen top and she passed it to him. The stick had sprouted a little umbrella and the wine now turned red.

"Melon, tomato and parsnip make red wine? They were all clear before. Good trick," he said and gently sipped it. He noticed that she had put a couple more plain-looking biscuits on the plate.

"Hey, this tastes like blackcurrant liqueur but I saw you pouring the old glasses together." Giles looked confused.

"Clever wine, clever biscuits and a very clever girl," she said as an explanation. "Try one of these. I've put together the recipe just for you." She placed a biscuit in his palm and put her hand over it.

Giles felt a little tingle in his fingers, like a tiny electric shock. Similar to when he'd tried to last take off his ring. He took a bite out of the biscuit. "Gingerbread, haven't had one for ages. It's absolutely gorgeous."

He could see she stared at something in her hand. "What is that language that you were speaking in earlier, Suzie?"

"Oh, just saying thanks for everything that you have given me, Giles," she replied. "What do you think of the ring?" and she held up the back of her left hand towards him.

"That's just like mine," and he held out his hand to show her his ring-less fingers. "That is mine. You took it off. That must have been the little tingly shock that I felt earlier."

"You said that I could borrow it before. I trust that the offer still stands?" she inquired.

"Well, I said that you could try it on. Sandra would probably notice if it didn't end up back on my finger."

"Don't be a spoilsport, Giles. I'll be extra nice to you next time," she said, batting those wonderful natural eyelashes at him. "I've taken off your necklace as well, so she'll never guess what we've been up to, my sweet."

He could see the Bewitched necklace on the table next to her discarded red knickers. He hadn't noticed her take it away. In fact, he felt sure that the hairbrush sat there a few seconds ago.

"You'd better be off now, Giles," and she led him to the front door. "Till the next time," and gave him the usual tingly kiss on the cheek.

He stumbled after taking two steps out of the door. His trouser leg had got caught in one of his shoes.

"You might be missing this?" and she tossed him his belt. "Not very good at magic are you, Giles?"

"But I know I put it on," he exclaimed.

"And this…" She tossed him his wallet.

"Ha-ha, very funny." He looked at his wrist for the time and his watch had disappeared. He looked at her accusingly.

"Don't blame me. Other hand, remember?" and she laughed and closed the door.

Giles checked his clock and hurried down the path, glad to see the awkward gate still stood open. A dragonfly hovered above the wet hedge as he went past. Its wings shining in the sun that had replaced the thunderstorm but he hardly noticed.

Have to get home and tidy up before Sandra gets back, he was thinking. He'd had a great time but there was so much to take in. Giles didn't know whether to laugh or cry. Must get back to the house and have a strong cup of tea because I'm feeling so tired, he thought, as he hurried along the pavement home.

Chapter 13

"Hi, Giles, been out for a little exercise?"

Pete stood behind him. He seemed to spring out from behind the hedge, as Giles passed.

"Oh, hello, Pete, just had a little wander to stretch the old legs." Giles answered.

"Wouldn't be stretching anyone else's, would you?" Pete pointed to something red, just peeping out of Giles' trouser pocket. He pulled it out.

"Ah, these knickers, Erm…Sandra likes these so I thought I'd get some similar for her birthday," he lied badly, as he realised that Suzie must have put them in his pocket for a joke.

"Oh, is that true? So there you are, looking like a gigolo who's been dragged through a hedge backwards, shirt buttons torn, smelling of booze with some red muff-covers in your pocket and you say you've been shopping?

"Not good, is it, Giles?" Pete continued. "Better get your story straight before you're home."

The dragonfly fluttering near Pete's shoulder seemed to look at him and agree.

"What is it with those creatures? There are either loads around or they must be following me," Giles said, admiring the pretty insect that had settled on a bush in Pete's garden.

"They're clever little things, really. So unusual," Pete said. "Anyway, Sandra's bum would never get into those skimpies so I think that you'd better leave them here with me. We wouldn't want Nora seeing you walking up the drive with women's knickers in your hand, either. You'd be getting another visit from Tyson."

Giles handed over the underwear. Pete held them stretched up to the light. "Marks & Spencer brand? She's girl of fine quality. Unusual smell as well, quite nice though."

"Can't believe you're sniffing Suzie's knickers," Giles

laughed, "And you put Sandra's tights over your head. What are up to?"

"Don't tell Nosey Nora about my underwear fetish," he whispered, deliberately loud.

"I've actually got a very sensitive nose and I swear that your two women smell similar. Have you noticed, Giles?"

"Well, funny you should mention it. I got that feeling the other day. It can't be perfume because Sandra rarely bothers and Suzie doesn't seem to even use makeup, only red nail-varnish," Giles replied.

"Hmm, a mystery," said Pete. "See ya, then." He turned and walked back to his open garage door twirling the red underwear singing the *Beatles'* Magical Mystery Tour. "Roll up, roll up for the mystery tour…"

Giles went back to his house and headed straight for the shower. He couldn't stop singing Pete's song in his head. Some of the lyrics seemed so apt. He appeared to be on a magical voyage of discovery with Suzie. 'Hoping to take you away, take you today', he hummed under the warm blast of water, as he soaped himself. Wonder if Suzie wants to run away with me, he thought?

"Dying to take you away, take you today," he sang, as he dripped onto the bathroom floor, looking at his reflection in the steamy mirror. He wiped it with a towel and looked at the tired, wet grey-haired man staring back. "Dying is the right word. This fun with Suzie seems to be wearing me out," he said out aloud as he twisted to dry himself with a fluffy towel. "Shit," he uttered and flinched as his back clicked.

Giles picked up his clothes from the floor and had nearly put them into the laundry bin, when he had an idea. He rummaged in the bin and took out an item and pressed it to his face. He then did the same with his dirty shirt.

How weird… Sandra's blouse and Suzie do smell very similar. Pete had a good nose…

He padded over into the bedroom to get some clothes, deep in thought.

Other things were bothering him as well. The more that he thought about it, the bigger the list grew. First, the missing moments, the sudden rain shower, the visions and his failed card trick. Secondly, the Suzie things like the gate-lock which only she could work, the clever biscuits, her tricks with his belt and watch. Then there were the 'Witch' necklaces, black cats and tattoos.

Giles alcoholic head started come around a bit and for a minute, he thought about the little tattoo on her neck, just under her hair. A star in a circle, He went into the lounge, turned on the laptop and Googled the phrase 'Star in a Circle Tattoo', the first four results showed five pointed stars just like hers. Should have guessed, he thought, another witchcraft symbol.

Okay, so there's a load of weird coincidences, some body art with a nice smell thrown in. Hardly a guilty verdict with the key thrown away, is it, he mused?

Wondering about the time, he looked down at his watch. For some reason, he stared at it more closely. Since Suzie had played that trick of moving it from one wrist to the other, it didn't quite look or seem right.

He wriggled his left arm and wrist. Not strained or injured but something looked wrong and he couldn't work out what it was. The numbers looked the same. He pulled both sleeves back and held his hands in front of him. Everything looked normal…but then it didn't…

He took the watch off for a closer inspection. It seemed alright. It still told the correct time and the strap hadn't been twisted or damaged when Suzie had swopped it over. With a little trouble, he put it on his right wrist, like Suzie had done and again held out his hands.

"Double Shit."

Giles dived for the computer. Like a mad thing, he looked at the old photo files stored on the hard disk, only slowing down when he found the holiday folder. He scanned through the small icons, opening several pictures of himself at the beach. Several times, he upped the magnification on two pictures in particular, arranging them side by side on the screen. He stared at them, motionless apart from his lips…

"Triple Shit."

A cold shudder ran over him. He felt scared, really scared.

He slowly held his arms together again and looked at the back of his wrists. He put the watch back on the correct left wrist but one thing stayed very wrong. He tried scratching it but it made no difference.

Next to his watch, the dark brown, slightly raised mole stayed on his right wrist, even though the photos showed it clearly on his left…

Suzie is a clever girl indeed, to move a watch and a melanin patch.

"Guilty triple shit verdict," he muttered.

Giles decided that he had to go and see Suzie, confront her and find out who or what she is. Had she done anything else to him? How did she do this stuff?

He started to change his clothes and then thought better of it. Sandra would be back in a couple of hours. Don't want to be back late and have her asking questions so he decided to have a normal night in with Sandra then go over to see Suzie, first thing tomorrow. Try not to worry he thought, looking down at the migrant mole.

"You look worried, Giles. Is everything alright?" Sandra asked later, after tea. "You haven't crashed the car or got anyone pregnant, have you, darling?" she asked. "Would you like a glass of wine with me?"

"Not really in the mood, Sandra. I've a few things on my mind. Nothing to worry about," he lied.

She pulled a face. "Be like that then. I'm going to watch the soaps in the lounge and leave you to your misery. Hope you're cured by tomorrow."

Makes two of us, Giles thought. "Sorry dear. I'm going to have a bath and an early night."

She pulled an even worse face, "Goodnight then."

The next day, Giles rose before Sandra. He hadn't slept much because he just wanted to get a certain task over with.

He went through the usual morning routine with Sandra. The usual list of things to do, he nodded, said yes and even kissed her goodbye. The fastest shower and shave in the world ever followed, he skipped breakfast, grabbed some clothes and was out the front door.

Being as he got up earlier than usual, Giles wondered if Suzie would be around. He didn't really know the hours that she normally kept. Perhaps she went out all night dancing with werewolves? He shuddered at the thought.

He needn't have worried about the time. The gate and front door were open at Suzie's house. He ran up the path, gave a knock and stood there for a couple of seconds before he noticed that his hands were trembling.

"Suzie, are you there? It's me, Giles." He grasped his hands tightly together to contain the shaking.

"The cats told me someone arrived when they ran inside. How are you, Giles? I'm in the kitchen. Do come in."

He walked into the hall and towards the two black cats standing in the kitchen doorway. They almost seemed to be guarding the entrance and only scattered at the last second, one shooting outside between his legs and one scooting into the kitchen.

Giles stood there looking at her.

"Cat got your tongue, Giles?" she enquired and raised pretend claws at him.

"You moved my mole," he said.

"Does that make me a clever gardener?" she replied and giggled before around towards the stove.

"Are you a real witch?" he asked and noticed a smell of ginger biscuits in the air.

Suzie adjusted the cooker control and then carried on stirring a bowl on the worktop.

She turned her head to face him and smiled.

"Why do you say that, Giles? Surely you don't believe in fairies or goblins? Come and hug me again." She pushed her pert boobs out at him, provocatively.

He noticed that she still held the wooden spoon in one hand and watched a brown sticky liquid drip slowly to the floor. The two cats were now both in the room and stood either side of her, like guards. They stared menacingly at him, tails in the air.

"That's not my question, Suzie. All your clothes, tattoos, black cats…are you really a witch?"

She smiled at him. "Just between you and me, witch with a capital W."

This smile looked different to the usual welcoming ones though.

This is a hungry smile, the smile on the face of a crocodile…

"Let me show you some more magic," she said.

He noticed that the hairs had stood up on the back of his arms and he felt more than a little concerned.

"I really want you, Giles." She tasted the sticky contents of the spoon and then blew a kiss at him.

Giles felt a tingle in his spine. Nervously he bluffed, "That's a spell?" He paused and nothing else happened. "Wow, really hurt… "

He used to act tough at school with the bullies. There were boys much bigger than himself that he used to stand up to, whereas Suzie was a lot shorter. He decided to grab and restrain her in case she really could do sinister stuff.

Giles took a step forward. In fact he tried to take a step forward. His feet were rooted to the floor. He looked down in disbelief. His shoes were covered in brown stuff, glue maybe…

No, it's the same sticky matter from the spoon.

He looked at Suzie. She turned around and spooned the mixture into moulds on the melamine kitchen top. They were body-shaped. She talked as she dolloped and gently smoothed the brown mixture. He strained to hear and caught something like, "Make me a ginger man, as fast as you can…and cover him from head to toe, down below he…will go…?"

"What the hell are you playing at Suzie? This isn't funny."

"Oh, Giles, you're such a sweet yummy man. I could eat you all up," she pointed at his feet.

He could smell cooking. Maybe a cake…no…it was biscuits, definitely ginger biscuits.

His legs began to feel stiff. Giles looked down to where she had pointed. His trousers…no…his legs were brown… No, they were ginger. The brown sticky stuff started climbing quickly. It went up to his thighs and advanced. His knees started gently bubbling… As though they were cooking and his feet and toes had the colour and texture of ginger biscuits.

Absolutely gobsmacked is a phrase Giles used to consider overused slang but if ever he'd seen a tailor-made situation for it, well, here it is…

He watched the sticky biscuit mixture rise up his torso and looked back at Suzie unable to speak. She still pointed but higher up than before, now at his midriff. Then he realised…

Giles found his voice, "Your finger…you're cooking me…"

"Doesn't it just take the biscuit," she quipped. "Actually I think you look a little fitter now," and laughed, showing those cute laughter lines around her eyes before she slowly licked her lips.

Giles looked back down at his body. He now had a ginger-biscuit tummy. In fact, not the usual sticky out tummy of a fifty-year-old man, instead he had a ginger-biscuit six-pack. He noted his ginger muscular legs. His clothes had gone and he had morphed into the gingerbread man equivalent of a Chippendale strongman.

"Giles, I really liked your grey hair but I just know now, you're going to look irresistible as a red head…"

The sticky mass crept up his neck and over the top of his head, tickling his ears as it spread.

He screwed his eyes tight, took a deep breath and tightly closed his mouth waiting for the end. I'm about to die, he thought. An unexpected image of a blue-uniformed woman riding a horse flashed into his head.

The vision shouted "I'm coming, I'll help." The horse galloped towards him and seemed about a hundred yards away. The rider held a small sword in her right hand, pointing it upwards and skilfully steering the reins with her other hand.

"No!" shouted a voice. He opened his eyes. Suzie looking perturbed.

"You cannot stop me, you not powerful enough, Giles. Anyway, you are nearly baked now."

He opened his eyes and was thankful to find himself still alive. Giles watched her turn back to the worktop. Suzie continued with her biscuit moulds. His eyesight had an orange tinge like some of those fancy sunglasses, something to do with the ginger, he surmised.

Giles attempted to move his limbs, one at a time but apart from the neck up there he had no feeling. He looked down at his biscuity muscle rippled body. He even had a ginger willy, small, but it existed.

This seemed a funny detail in a crazy situation but it made him smile.

"Fully functional." came a voice. He looked up and Suzie again pointed at his nether regions.

He felt a surge of pleasure tingle through his body from his midriff, through to his fingertips.

His willy started to grow and slowly point further to the horizontal position. It finally stopped at about forty five degrees to the vertical and appeared about eight inches long.

"What you've always wanted," she giggled.

"Not too keen on the colour," he replied, then realised that he could still talk.

She came closer and took hold of it by the shank. A glorious feeling raced through his body. His sensory nerves obviously worked well but the motor control to his muscles had been turned off below his neck.

"Thought you'd like that," Suzie said. "Wonder what happens if I do this?"

She leaned closer to his chest with the tip of her tongue sticking out.

For the first time, he noticed that he had gingerbread nipples. Her tongue gently lapped firstly at one and then the other. He felt waves of pleasure across his chest just like he'd felt with Suzie before. Having his nipples fondled was one of Giles' favourite secrets. Suzie already knew this and had somehow kept this pleasure in his new biscuit body.

"Listen, Suzie; stop it, I believe you now. Please turn me back to normal. I'll go away and won't tell a soul about you, I promise," he pleaded.

"I've got other plans for you, my sweet. You're insurance. I'm off to get more cooking ingredients," and she opened a tall cupboard door to take out a long-handled brush with twiggy ends. The kind that you would sweep leaves up from the patio.

"You have to be joking?" he asked, visualising her astride the cleaning instrument, streaking across a moonlit sky, with stars twinkling in the background.

She threw back her head with laughter and used the brush to chase together ginger crumbs off the floor, "No, my little biscuit, just removing evidence." A black cat came along and lapped up all the little pieces.

She carried on "Tried it once for fun, uncomfortable to balance on. Left it leaning against the bike rack by *Sainsbury's*, after all, I couldn't make it disappear in front of a load of Saturday shoppers, could I?"

"Came out to see a kid in a hoody, riding a bike and making off with it," she laughed. "He still lives nearby."

Suzie came closer and looked him square in the eye. "In a pond," she added and grinned.

"Anyway, you be a good boy and wait here. Beelzebub will keep you company," and she smiled at the black cat. "Little devil, he can be sometime."

Giles could swear that the cat smiled back at her.

She reached for the back door handle and again Giles noticed that she hardly seemed to touch it, yet it opened. She walked through with a sexy wiggle of her hips and disappeared.

Chapter 14

Beelzebub walked up and down in front of Giles. His long black tail waved high in the air behind him, making him look as though he was proud to be in charge.

This went on for a few minutes with the cat suddenly turning his head towards him as though trying to catch him moving and then looking away.

Giles tried to flex his muscles again. No joy. Not a trace of movement or feeling. What happens if he gets cold, he wondered, because he appeared to have no clothes on, just his crunchy covering? Is ginger biscuit a good insulator?

The cat had scampered over to the corner; its attention being drawn away by something higher up on the wall. It seemed to be some kind of insect that looked like a small dragonfly. It hovered just out of reach of the cat, almost teasing it. Beelzebub jumped up and down, trying to swat the insect with an outstretched black hairy paw.

The insect moved away from the wall. He could see its colours now. There were many shimmering pigments and it looked beautiful. It fluttered above the kitchen units and Beelzebub jumped up onto the worktop, scattering condiments and spoons. They clattered noisily to the floor and Giles closed his eyes, as with a leap and a swipe, the feline just caught the wingtip of the beautiful creature as it attempted to get away.

When he opened them the dragonfly had flown directly over his head. Beelzebub leapt from the worktop directly at him. Giles had a quick premonition that this might hurt as the fur-ball flew towards him with claws outstretched.

The cat made a clumsy landing, front paws on his left shoulder, rear paws on his tummy. He felt the impact and then the claws…

"Shit," he yelled and saw that the front claws had taken crumbs out of his shoulder which fell to the floor. The cat scaled up him like a mountaineer with crampons and ice-pick. Giles felt every puncture mark.

The cat continued with its swiping and batting, leaning out at crazy angles as the insect circled just out of reach, safely anchored by its rear claws in Giles' shoulder and neck.

The pain grew intense and Giles racked his brain what to do. He wanted the clawing agony to stop but for some reason, didn't want the feline to win and reach the dragonfly.

The insect swooped down in front of his face and the cat leapt towards it with its paws out.

Without thinking, Giles used the only 'weapon' he had. He spat at the cat and caught it square on the butt as it left his shoulder.

Why did I bother, he thought for a second? That evil cat's going to come back and claw me.

He watched the feline just miss the dragonfly and produce a quite un-catlike final landing on the floor. In fact, crash landing was a better description. It sort of laid there with its tail stretched out, seemingly immobile. He wondered if it had been concussed or had a broken neck.

Then he noticed a weird thing…

Something moved on the cat, growing…a ginger patch. What's more, it seemed to be where he scored a direct salivary hit on the feline. In an identical way to how the sticky substance had spread over his body, it enveloped Beelzebub.

He watched disbelievingly as it spread over most of its body and crept along the tail of the prostrate cat. As he looked, he realised that the cat wasn't dead because its ears could move. It seemed to be only paralysed from the neck down, just like him.

He watched the ginger coating form over the cats head and up to the tip of the ears and felt a twang of guilt that he'd apparently caused this. He'd always liked cats, not only good cats but also the naughty ones with attitude. Maybe Beelzebub had just fallen in with the wrong crowd?

Giles had forgotten about the dragonfly. It fluttered and twinkled back into his vision and came close. It almost seemed to be looking at him.

Nearer and nearer it came. Giles didn't like things too close to his face, especially insects. He automatically shook his head and said, "Get away."

The unimpressed dragonfly settled on the tip of his nose. He decided it would be better to just keep still and wait for it to fly away. Being long sighted, he couldn't really see the coloured insect properly. The vision of the blue-uniformed woman riding a horse suddenly came into his head again and seemed to merge with the shape of the dragonfly.

Then he remembered the uniform from the favourite cowboy films of his youth, U.S. cavalry. Her clothes looked similar. He could make out crossed swords in the shape of an M on her wide-brimmed hat and some insignia like an officer's. The object in her hand, which earlier looked like a sword became clearly visible. He could see a long metallic stick. It shimmered with the colours of the dragonfly as she pointed the item at him.

For a split second, he flinched as though about to duck, then realised the impossibility of avoiding something that's already sitting on the end of his nose.

Nothing happened and the lady officer reared up on her horse which span around and rode away. The vision merged seamlessly into the dragonfly which had fluttered away towards the cat. It landed on the tail for a second before leaving the kitchen through an open window.

Giles wondered if he might be lucky to feel paralysed watching all this, as otherwise he'd probably have fallen over with disbelief.

The cooking smell had returned and he noticed now that Beelzebub was gently bubbling, as he had earlier. The cat cover mixture had looked still sticky until the dragonfly sat on its tail…

He reached up to scratch his right temple. Giles always did

this when thinking or confused. It made a not too pleasant crunchy sound in his skull, so he stopped it to look at his fingers and then realised something…

"I can move my arm," he said, out aloud.

He quickly put it back down and stopped talking to himself, remembering that Suzie may come back at any second. He tried to move his legs. They would move a little, a bit stiff at first and so would his waist. He could virtually do that nineteen sixties dance, The Twist, but his feet were stuck solidly to the floor.

Giles looked around. He stood just within range of the kitchen units and managed to lean over and open a drawer. It revealed a bowl of stones, some dull, others sparkly. Some clear plastic pots of dust or sand and a couple of clothes pegs.

He tried the next one. Better luck, some wooden spoons, long knives and a fish-slice. He took out a knife and started hacking at his ginger feet when he remembered the pain from the cat's claws.

Thinking twice about it, he said to himself, "I'm a cooked biscuit stuck to the baking tray, it's obvious..."

Taking the fish-slice from the drawer and gently pushing the end in between his right big toe and the tiled floor he released it with no discomfort. He worked around past the heel and within two minutes he had freed both his ginger feet leaving only a few crumbs stuck to the floor. He looked at the remains closely and back to his feet. When he satisfied himself that there were no important bits of him left on the floor, he put the fish-slice back and closed the drawer.

What the heck should I do now, he wondered?

Chapter 15

Giles slowly walked around the kitchen testing out his new legs. It felt like walking with a thick pair of trousers on at first but he quickly became used to it. He did a few stretching exercises, like back in the days before he went for a run and everything seemed to be alright. In fact, his body felt much more flexible and fitter than it used to. Must be the new muscles, he thought, as he patted his ginger six-pack.

He turned around and inadvertently stepped on Beelzebub's tail, which promptly snapped in half. The cat let out a low yowl, its ears flicking back and forth.

"Sorry, old chap," he said to the prostrate feline. "Suppose that makes us even now."

He picked up the tail end. "Hmm…I wonder…" he said and licked the fractured piece, kneeled down and pressed the ends together.

Giles waited a minute then flicked the tail gently with his finger. It stayed in one piece. "Right, you owe me one now, cat."

Whilst kneeling down, he again became aware of his ginger nakedness. His tackle appeared in full view and looked pretty wrinkly at the best of times. Combine this with a ginger-creviced crust and it became an acquired taste only. Have to find some clothes and get away, he thought.

He'd only been upstairs once before, to a bedroom and couldn't really remember much about the house because he'd had a drink. He climbed the steps to the landing. The house here looked like it hadn't been decorated for years, unlike the downstairs with its fancy kitchen and marble-tiled floors. He opened the first door, a nineteen twenties bathroom complete with black and white chequered tiles on the walls. Looked like something out of the London Underground. The next door turned out to be a large bedroom with old furniture. All the cupboards were empty. The other two landing doors were locked or jammed. He barged the second closed one with his shoulder. He heard a crunch. Did it move, he thought? He tried again, another crunch and this time he realised his shoulder had chipped and ginger crumbs were falling onto the threadbare landing carpet.

"Ow," he rubbed his arm and dusted some bits to the floor. "Not good."

He had an idea and peeped out of the rear bedroom window after sweeping a mass of cobwebs aside. He scanned the neighbouring gardens to be rewarded by a line of washing, blowing in the breeze a couple of doors away.

Giles nipped downstairs into the rear garden. The border hedges were pretty overgrown, a mixture of privet and laurel. He found a gap, through which he could see his prize. A three-foot-high fence stood just the other side of the hedge. The windswept clothes were in the adjoining garden over another similar fence and some bushes.

Climbing through a hedge is not easy at the best of times but attempting in your ginger birthday suit is sheer madness, he thought. The branches scraped and prodded his outer skin. His tackle got a nasty whack from a swinging branch which made him flinch and feel slightly sick.

"Shit," he said under his breath. Once through, he took a quick glance in both directions and could only see a rabbit hutch on the lawn and no one about. He sprinted across to the next fence feeling like an outsider at the Grand National.

To his dismay, the bushes he had seen over the hedge turned out to be hawthorn, the hedge of the devil with its spiny thorns, waiting to impale anyone foolish enough, to attempt to cross.

He looked around in a panic. His ginger nakedness could easily be seen from any of the half-dozen houses around.

Giles spotted the wheels of a barbeque sticking out from under a small tarpaulin-like cover. He yanked the fabric off the outdoor cooker and folded it in two. He placed it over the lowest, thinnest part of the fence-cum-hedge and scrambled over. He got pricked a couple of times in his hand and leg but seemed otherwise unscathed. He scanned his tackle. "Well at least I haven't pricked my prick," he said quietly and looked at his fingers, where he had been impaled.

"Aw no!" he said, as he surveyed the small dripping blobs of ginger coloured blood.

He heard a noise and quickly looked down near his feet. A fluffy pet white rabbit had bobbed over to see him and sniffed at his feet.

He leant down and pushed it away with his hand. "Go away now, bunny. I've come to take the washing in."

Giles stood up and took the two steps to the washing line hardly noticing the two spots of blood he'd left on the pristine white fur.

He yanked an armful of men's clothes, socks and pants off the line and looked for a way out.

The wooden side gate which looked like it led to the main road. As he made for it, he stumbled over something. He couldn't see down properly because of the size of the pile of washing he carried. He held it to one side and looked down. "Aw shit!" This phrase usually got used only once a month but this had turned out to be a very bad-shit day.

A stiff ginger rabbit lay on its side, still sticky and bubbling slightly in the hot summer sun.

With thoughts somewhere in between 'maybe I can fix it later' and 'hide the evidence' he stuffed the washing underneath one arm and grabbed the bunny with the other hand.

After just managing to open the gate-latch with his nose, Giles headed down the side of the house for the front gateway, to a chorus of voices.

"Oi! What you're doing?" shouted a woman's voice.

"Bloody students!" shouted a man's voice, joining in with the first.

"He's dressed up, Mummy, my rabbit will escape, the door's open," shouted a little girl.

Giles went into top gear dropping clothes behind him as he ran in his bare feet. He darted down the side road, passed the laundrette and bank, then down an alley which led to a covered area where the shops' bins were kept.

He'd covered a fair distance and surprised himself at how quickly he caught his breath back. This new body must be pretty fit. This thought was immediately followed by; well, anyone who would dress like this would have to be quick, to avoid being arrested.

He looked at the booty in his hands, one hard orange rabbit and one under garment.

"Could be worse," he muttered, stepping into the one he could wear and hiding the poor rabbit in a large blue skip of bottles. Painted on the side of the skip, a sign said *Hoppers of Bisque Warren*. He had to read this twice to believe it, closed his eyes and tried pinching his hard biscuity butt.

Upon opening his eyes, everything seemed the same apart from the piece of ginger biscuit in his fingers. "Shit!"

He wondered if there might be suitable clothes in the laundrette that he'd passed and sneaked to the end of the alley. He peeped around the corner to meet a policeman's gaze.

Giles froze. The blue tall-helmeted officer walked closer and looked him up and down.

"Great outfit dude," the law officer said. Then walked back to the short-skirted nurse accompanying him and rattled a bucket.

Giles then realised that they were students and more than a little drunk. The nurse turned her head towards him and blew a goodbye kiss, before strutting after the policeman in her fishnet tights. The policeman wore a pair of Spiderman knee length shorts and red heels. Maybe I don't look too bad, thought Giles, for a second?

He looked up and down the street for inspiration. A couple

passed, pointed and smiled. Feeling braver, he smiled back and a dragonfly fluttered by. Must be the season, he thought and then his prayers were answered. That car approaching, he knew the owner but this would take some explaining…

The street looked like there had been some parade passing through earlier. Pieces of coloured paper on the floor, litter, crisp packets, several coins lying here and there, pennies, fifty pence…

Then he remembered something happening at the local college. It's collecting for charity today, under the guise of getting drunk or the other way round. He also remembered doing some crazy stuff when he'd been a student and had smoked pot a few times. There had been some weird dreams but today is something else.

Giles straightened his pants, clenched his ginger buttocks, gritted his teeth and ran out into the road, waving madly…and praying.

Chapter 16

"Strange goings on, at a major supermarket near Garton on Thames, occurred early this afternoon," reported the voice over the local radio. "The police have appealed for witnesses to a potential kidnapping which took place in the car park just after dinnertime."

The voice went on, "A dark-haired lady shopper in blue jeans left the store and to be met outside by three adults on horseback. They appeared to be wearing uniforms similar to those worn during the American Civil War. A struggle developed and according to eyewitnesses, there were bangs or explosions and smoke but no weapons were seen or have been found."

Sandra had come home unexpectedly for dinner and listened to the local news. She wondered where Giles had got to. Maybe he gone to this shop, where this had happened and got held up?

"The woman appeared to be lifted onto the back of one of the horses and all four persons left the scene. The police state that no one has been reported missing or injured and are unsure if this is a student rag-week stunt or something more serious."

Sandra laughed to herself. "Bloody students," and carried on making her-self a cheese and ham sandwich. She wondered if she should make one for Giles as she'd opened his favourite Cheshire cheese.

She made a cup of tea and looked in the cupboard for some biscuits. Sandra had a choice of digestives or ginger nuts. She heard something at the window. A silly dragonfly flapped at the glass. She really liked digestives but for some reason, the ginger nuts drew her attention. She held one between her teeth, while a couple were wrapped in a tissue for the afternoon tea-break at work. She looked for her handbag and with it not being to hand put the little round package in her suit pocket.

The radio carried on about some other curious local incidents, a small whirlwind or tornado had knocked off some chimney pots, a sudden storm-cloud had flooded a park depositing a load of frogs and a student had been seen streaking in a street, near the shops dressed as a gingerbread man.

She laughed at the last one. Where the hell is Giles, she thought again? She wanted to ask him about dinner next week with the neighbours. A sort of *Come Dine with Me* competition being organised in the street and she knew Giles fancied himself as an amateur chef. No point in her cooking the food, as she'd always been a working woman. The waste bin had been littered with 'can't go wrong 'and 'easy cook recipes' over the years. Marks and Spencer's microwave dinners were her crowning glories. Giles did a natty line in spicy pastas and fragrant Thai dishes. Her mouth started watering at the thought. He once did some tasty home-made biscuits, mmm...

As she went out the front door, two police cars and a third black car roared past the front gate with multicolour roof lights flashing and heading towards the main shopping area. A large black cloud hung ominously in the distance over the town centre and she noticed the shimmering dragonfly still around, sitting on the bird-box. It fluttered up into the air higher and higher until it disappeared from view, against the dark cloudy background.

She walked towards her car. A Japanese hatchback, new but oh so bland... She then looked over at Giles' much older but still sexy Triumph Stag convertible, its age hidden by the private number plate. She wanted a personal reg but couldn't find one that she liked. Giles had bought his at early retirement.

It then struck her that if Giles had gone shopping to the town, he would have taken the car. Probably means that he walked to some of the smaller shops nearby and got waylaid by one of those odd friends of his. Better not be talking to any strange women, she thought.

She started the little black car and drove down to the end of the drive. Another police car drove past on the road at speed. The men in the back seemed to be carrying guns. To get to the clinic, she had to turn left but Sandra had a funny feeling that something was very wrong. She hesitated for a second, gunned the engine, waited for a space and turned right to follow the police cars. The black cloud sat there ominously in the distance. It seemed to have increased in size.

She passed a few students dressed up and carrying buckets, collecting change from passers-by. Then she took a left down the side street that Giles liked to use as a short cut to the local shops. She laughed as a muscular kid in a tight orange suit wearing red underpants, superman style, came out of an old gate and started waving.

Sandra slowed down to a halt and reached out for her handbag. To her surprise, the orange super hunk ran around to the passenger door and opened it. Okay, she thought, dangerous to stand in the road. The student sat in the front seat.

"Ha ha, the jokes over, I'm going somewhere," Sandra said.

"Just drive, Sandra," the ginger superman said in Giles' voice. "Someone's after me."

A dragonfly landed on the car bonnet. Spot on the midline of the car nose. It sat still, resembling an old-fashioned car mascot.

His calming voice stopped her from screaming and leaping out.

"It's you, shit, erm...okay, Giles," said a shocked Sandra. "This is a really weird dream. Hope I remember it when I wake up. Like the muscles by the way. Did a pretty girl student do your make up?" she asked with an enquiring voice.

As she drove off she reached out to feel his forearm. "You feel like a biscuit…wow! This is real special effects stuff. And from experience, I see those pants you're wearing are women's," she giggled. "Who's chasing you. Did you nick the knickers?" They both laughed at the unintended pun.

"Listen, Sandra, this suit you think I'm wearing…"

"Get down, Giles, it's a policeman."

He ducked down as she ordered...

"A policeman with stilettos and crazy shorts," Sandra burst out laughing "Had you!"

Giles put his head above the door edge and the policeman saw him and waved. Giles held up a ginger paw in reply.

"Don't scare me like that, I mean there's some really odd stuff going on. I think I've found a real witch and she's turned me into a biscuit. Pull over into that cul-de-sac and look at me," he said.

Sandra turned, in as instructed. She stopped the engine, looked straight ahead and asked, "Suzie maybe?"

"You mean that you believe me? You haven't even looked."

She had her head in her hands. "Giles, it's starting now, and I wasn't there to protect you. I'm sorry." She faced him as he sat there open-mouthed and reached out to touch the biscuity skin on his cheek.

"She sure did a good job on you. Anyway, we now have to get you to remember," and she started driving out of the cul-de-sac onto the main road.

Giles had never seen Sandra drive like this. Her hands were almost a blur as she changed from gear to gear, scooting past slower traffic, slotting into gaps without annoying others and making fast progress. "Where did you learn to drive like this?" he asked, hands gripping onto the seat fabric, "And where are we going?"

She answered, "Just hang on tight. We're going somewhere safe for a long chat. Is there anybody following us?"

"Like a woman on a broomstick? No and I can't see any stiletto cops either. Do you know what's going on, Sandra? You've got a funny look on your face. What do you mean, get me to remember?" Giles said, "I know I'm forgetting things recently. What's happened to me?"

"It's a long story, Giles. I'm forgetting some of it myself to be honest. I'll go over to the car park at the lake and we can have a talk there, if no one's about. You probably won't believe what I tell you at first but just look at your new birthday suit and pinch yourself. Guess you know it's pretty serious already," and she carried on weaving skilfully through traffic.

Giles did as instructed and attempted to pinch the ginger skin on the back of his right hand. A large crumb broke off and he sat there holding out his hand, contemplating.

Sandra laughed and reached over and grabbed it. "Waste not, want not," as she popped it into her mouth. "You're pretty tasty, Giles."

"Apart from that seeming slightly cannibalistic, isn't there a risk that you might catch it?" he said.

"I would say the hard bits are well-cooked. It's the stuff inside you that we'd better be careful of," she replied.

"Like that ginger rabbit biscuit, I accidentally made," he admitted. "Then I put it in a skip that said Hoppers on the side…"

"You didn't? Aw no, poor little thing," and she burst out laughing.

"Right, here's the car park. Let's go sit on that bench. There's no one around. Look, there are still some clothes of yours in the boot, from when we went walking a month ago. Put them on." She went around to the back of the car, opened the hatch and tossed two carrier bags to him over the back seat.

Feeling like a contortionist, he pulled on a pair of jeans, T-shirt and thin waterproof hooded jacket inside the small car. He also found a pair of trainers. Lucky Sandra's the organised type, he thought. If they went walking she'd always put in spare stuff, in case they got muddy shoes or it rained.

She looked him up and down. "Put this on," and tossed him a peaked cap from the car which said Benidorm on it.

"How do I look?" he said.

"You've changed from Super Biscuitman to chav gingerbread man on holiday," she giggled. "Very sexy," and kissed him on his crunchy cheek. "Come and sit down by the river and prepare yourself for a shock."

They sat down on the bench and Giles picked up a stone and tossed it into the lake. It plopped in and he watched the ripples spread out twenty yards from the point of impact to the shore.

Sandra watched him, "Some people have that effect, Giles. A seemingly small action may affect all around… You're one of them."

"What do you mean, Sandra?" He looked around him. Something seemed familiar about this lake.

"Your father brought you here many years ago."

"My father died years ago but I seem to remember this place, even the shapes of the trees. It's like they haven't grown much. How do you know that? He died before you were born, Sandra."

"There are constants in this world, sort of fixed laws and places," she answered.

"Laws… Alright, like gravity. By places, do you mean planets or suns?"

"Smaller than that, this lake is a fixed place. The area nearby has hardly changed for centuries and is kept like this by something special, something that you are part of, Selig."

Giles stood very still. That word… Selig, it meant nothing to him, yet everything…

He could feel the blood coursing through his veins, his heart starting to pound.

A crow circled overhead. Rraaack it called and swooped down in front of them skimming the water. Giles caught a glimpse of white wingtip feathers as it shot past.

The sky darkened as though it might rain. He heard a splash and looked into the lake, wondering if a fish had jumped and saw a vision of Suzie swimming under the surface. She waved at him, blew a kiss then pretended to throw something underarm to him.

Giles instinctively held out both hands as if to catch something.

A small ripple appeared in the surface of the water, which grew and grew. The water pulled back away from the bank, leaving a muddy shoreline and an unlucky silver perch flapping on its side.

"What have you done, Selig?" shouted Sandra urgently.

"I haven't done anything. Why are you calling me that?" said Giles, taking a few steps back from the water's edge.

"Eizus has found us!" Sandra shouted and grabbed a stunned Giles who gazed at the rising wave of water, now two foot high. The sky continued to darken.

"Get behind the tree!" and she half dragged the flummoxed Giles towards a nearby oak tree.

He started to run and glanced behind him. The wave had grown to six foot high and was flying towards them like a mini tsunami.

He made it to the tree and Sandra clamped him against it, grabbing onto two low-lying branches.

The impact shook the tree and knocked the breath out of Giles. Sandra had taken the brunt of the wave and had almost held on but lost her grip as the water receded and ended up lying ten foot away on the wet grass.

Giles looked over at the lake and the water had returned to almost something like its original calmness. He leapt over to Sandra who looked like a bedraggled mermaid. He pulled a large piece of algae of her face and hair, "Sandra, are you alright?" and reached inside his old coat pocket. He found some tissue and wiped her face. He put his ear to her mouth. She'd stopped breathing.

Panicking, Giles desperately tried remembering his first aid courses from work; he opened her mouth, looked inside and then took a deep breath. He placed his lips against hers, to give the kiss of life.

Hands reached behind his shoulders and held him there. Those lifeless lips pressed back in a soft embrace. He pulled away and they said, "Fooled you again."

Sandra's eyes opened and they both started to stand up.

"Shit, don't mess about, woman. Listen, I saw Suzie in the river, I think she knows I'm here," he said.

Giles looked at his clothes. "How come you're soaking and I'm bone dry?" and added "and I'm supposed to be the man and the hero to protect the lady but you covered me. How'd you keep me dry?"

"If you want to know I created a protective envelope around you. Like a curtain of rigid air. I got worried that your biscuit skin could go soggy with water and that'll be the end of you," she said. "Oh, and Selig is your real name. It's Giles backwards."

Something stirred in the back of Giles' mind. He followed Sandra back to the car. She got there first opened the boot took out the spare clothes, still in bags from that walk a month ago. She stripped naked and Giles looked around to see if anyone watched.

"I'm not bothered," she said as she cuddled him and looked up into his eyes.

"I didn't say anything but I think you answered?" he said raising one eyebrow.

"Kind of telepathy, that's unless you guard your thoughts. You used to be able to do it too. It'll come back. Remember anything yet, Selig? How about your father?" she asked.

He watched her as she dressed. Orange blouse first. Did up a few buttons, then bent down to pick up her trousers off the floor. Her undergarments were thrown on the floor and she didn't have any others to put on. As she put one leg into her trousers, Giles or possibly Selig took hold of both cheeks and squeezed. Her pale buttocks felt so warm and soft to his ginger paws.

"Selig, don't you know you're twice my age?" Sandra laughed. "You Magi men, all the same."

"The Magi? The men who followed the wandering star in the Bible stories?" he said "I'm one of them aren't I? Well not one of those three but from the same…tribe?"

Sandra had dressed just out of his reach. "That book story's a bit mixed up. Your memory may take a while to recover, but in a nutshell, do you visualise a man descended from an ape-like creature when you think of humans?"

Giles nodded.

"Well, along the way there were several branches of Hominin leading to chimps, gorillas and the like that you will know of. There were also branches that died out through competition or disease and occasionally the scientists dig up something that starts, ends or clarifies a line."

"You're saying that the Magi are an undiscovered link living alongside twenty-first-century society?" Giles asked.

"Not saying exactly. You just read my mind, just testing and could feel you there," she answered.

"So I'm the notorious 'Missing Link' that the scientists have been looking for? Are you a Mrs Magi?" he asked, looking slightly worried.

"Sort of, did you like mind reading?" Sandra just stared at him.

"You didn't move your lips, just then. Wow, and I heard you. So just how can you tell the difference between a Magi and shall we say human?" Giles asked.

"Well, just quickly because that dark cloud is worrying me. We Magi regard us all as humans. They could be termed Homo sapiens, Homsap to us and we are Homo magi or Homag for short. We have four toes on each foot, a single larger kidney, twenty-four teeth and a differently wired brain. It's the latter that can in rare circumstances cause hurt or harm to either human type," she said sadly and held her head down.

"You mean, Suzie? You shouted out something before the wave, Easy has found us? Is there another name for Suzie? Do you know her?"

Sandra nodded and looked very worried.

"If my name's Giles backwards, then Suzie is E I Z U S. That's what you shouted, Eizus."

"Spot on, Giles, and I wish you were wrong. Anyway, get in the car and show me where she lives."

He obeyed after entering, "Head for Maple Avenue, then," and began to think about ape-men and wondered why Sandra had said he is twice her age…

Sandra said "If you don't want me to hear your thinking, just do it 'quietly'. Yes, we do live for a long time. You're one hundred and twenty years old and I'm fifty-nine so you are twice my age but you're not a dirty old Magi because we can live to be two hundred. We have a far better immune system and cell-repair biology. It's all in the genes."

Chapter 17

They parked opposite the house.

All appeared quiet. The house seemed deserted. In fact it hardly looked like the same house. It had deteriorated badly in the few hours since he had run away from it. An overgrown, weed-infested jungle had replaced the green bushy garden. The front gutter flapped in the wind. Ivy had partly covered the front and two panes of glass were broken in the upper windows.

"Look at the house. What's happened to it, Sandra?" and before she could answer, "Your backwards name, is it really Ardnas? Sounds like Hardnuts. You can be a bit bossy," and he laughed.

"Ha ha. Well almost. It's a Magi tradition to reverse the name to fit into the local language. Sometimes it doesn't work so a slight variation is allowed. It's really Ardnax. Some of the most common Homsap names are reversed Magi."

She went on, "Helen of Troy, reputedly the most beautiful woman in the ancient Greek world is really Neleh, a Magi. She had the ability to hypnotise and could keep men thinking she looked as young as eighteen, even up to her death at a hundred and forty years old. Several, of what the English Homsap would think are upper class names, such as Charles, George, Nigel and their female variations are Magi. More common names such as John, Peter and Chris are pure Homsap," she explained.

"Suzie had hypnotic ability like Helen. She could make those around her see things that weren't there. I guess she conjured up a mask of a newer house over the old one."

"So you mean that if I actually looked in a drawer and took something out, there really is an old drawer in front of me but I would see and feel a new one?" asked Giles.

"More or less, we've never worked out exactly what goes on in hypnotised people's minds. Some Homsaps can hypnotise but Magi do it at different levels in the brain. Magi can use it on

Homsaps but I don't know if it works the other way around. Let's go in and have a look, Selig," said Sandra.

"Can you call me Giles until I feel like I'm actually Selig?"

"Sorry, Giles. It is just so nice to use your real name. I haven't seen a Magi officially for twenty years," she said and added "or spoken about them. It seems so long ago." She had a tear, at the corner of her eye.

"We cry like Homsaps then?" he asked noticing her.

"Oh yes… " and she hugged him.

"Some of this seems vaguely familiar. Does that mean the Magi are all witches and wizards casting spells and suchlike?" he queried.

"There's no such thing as a 'spell'. That's just kid's talk. Newton's Laws about conservation of matter and energy being converted from one form to another all apply. He's a Magi by the way. Over the centuries many of us have risen to well-known positions. We are not competitors and don't generally recognise Homo sapiens as our lesser brethren." Suzie explained.

"What about my skin and that wave?" he asked.

"Our talents, if that's the right word, vary. Eizus or Suzie as you knew her became very good at the energy/matter conversion side of things and using it for her own aims. She cannot do magic as you may have thought but can make materials do strange things that even other Magi cannot understand. Do you remember what your father did for a living, Selig?"

"I believe he was a lawyer. Had a practice in London somewhere, as a partner?" Giles stated, "Or at least that's what someone told me, I think."

"More or less, he used to be the Magi equivalent of a judge. Those who stray too far away from our code and hurt others are usually found and punished, if necessary, unless they can thoroughly explain their behaviour. It's all carried out in a sort of court with witnesses called, if necessary. Homsap witnesses may be 'borrowed' sometimes, under deep hypnosis, and then returned to their rightful place. The Court's situated on an island off Greece."

"Eizus had been warned to mend her behaviour on previous occasions. She had been involved in African slave trading to America, many years ago. The infamous sinking of the Titanic ocean liner is down to her. The Magi spread the word that an iceberg caused the disaster but you've seen her at close hand controlling waves. The ship carried enough gold to have made her queen of a small country. She's always craved power."

"She disappeared for a few years after that and resurfaced in South America, masquerading as a deity, living among a little known jungle tribe. We captured and brought her to trial on the island. After listening to the overwhelming evidence, the Elders curbed her powers and sealed her in an old salt mine with enough rations for a hundred years, in South Africa. She should have spent the remainder of her life imprisoned underground."

"I assume she escaped then. What's it got to do with me?" Giles asked.

Sandra answered with a sad face, "Three judges presided over her trial and your father gave the majority judgement. Eizus cursed him, declared that no prison would hold her and that she would return to destroy your father plus you, his only child. Your father died naturally before she escaped and so that leaves you, Giles, in mortal danger…"

"You were hypnotised against your will, under your father's orders. He became gravely ill. You now have a Homsap mind full of fuzzy memories and thus became a little part of England, in order to hide away. My job as a member of the original court security team is to keep an eye on you for as long as it takes. Your father convinced everyone that your Suzie would return and hunt you down. How right he is."

"So you're assigned to be my minder?" he asked, already knowing the answer.

"Yes, in Homsap slang. I'm your Terry McCann. Bet you

thought that you looked after me, all these years. Long time to keep a secret, eh?" she laughed.

"Enjoyed every minute," he lied and laughed with her. "How are you going to keep Giles Arthur Daley alive then, guvnor, because my old Dick Emeries aren't coming back? If I've got any superpowers, they aren't working."

"You've got a bit of telepathy back. I didn't know you before we came here so I don't know your powers, as you term them. Knowing our luck you haven't got anything useful," and she laughed. "I've noticed your familiarity with the opposite sex so maybe it's purely in the bedroom," and winked at him.

Giles didn't know whether to be disappointed or not with the comment. They walked across to the rusty gate and as usual it resisted opening. Sandra held both hands over the catch and the metal barrier made its usual creak but it opened easily enough.

"How'd you do that?" he asked.

"Just kind of applied mental heat through my hands, a little trick, not magic of course. The heat has come from the food I eat. Makes me hungry doing it," she replied. "I can't do fancy stuff like Suzie."

The front door looked closed. Whenever he had seen Suzie outside, it stood open. He wondered if it might be locked but it opened easily enough with no spooky noises or obvious booby traps. He looked inside first. The house seemed like it had been abandoned for years. Dust and cobwebs everywhere in the hall and a couple of old coats hanging on the wall. He looked into the front room as he passed. He not been in there before and it turned out to be a large bay-windowed room, still furnished but with everything covered in dust. It was as though someone had closed the door fifty years ago and hadn't come back.

Sandra rubbed a finger along the wall. "Don't think much to your girlfriend's taste in décor, Giles."

They walked through the door at the end of the corridor into the kitchen. Giles wondered what it would be like. Sandra had been correct. The kitchen layout, even down to the position of the drawers and cupboard doors, looked identical to what he remembered. The main difference being that everything here was dusty painted wood whereas Suzie cooked in a pristine melamine-wrapped designer item. She most certainly had used some kind of mental overlay to fool him.

Sandra bent down over something, "Your handiwork, Giles?"

He looked down at the ginger cat, stiff as a board "Afraid so. That's Beelzebub. We use the same hairdresser," and laughed.

"All is not lost, little cat. Maybe you can tell us something about Eizus and her plans," she stroked the cat's head slowly and repeatedly.

The ginger feline's ears started to twitch followed by a flick of its tail. Sandra started stroking the body and saying something, just like Suzie's special talk.

Giles couldn't understand a word. "Is that Magi?" he asked. "Are you waking him up?"

"The language of the ancients and our forefathers, it doesn't seem to have any magical properties apart from helping us to concentrate our mental energies on a task. Ginger here is telling me a story," she said.

"You can talk to cats?" he said amazed.

"Almost any creature, some are very limited. They don't have words as such but they have memories and feelings. Beelzebub here is a clever cat, a bit sly and will live with whoever gives him the most. His job is Suzie's guard-cat, it seems. A noisy dog living in this abandoned house would have attracted attention but a quiet black cat creeping around could belong to anyone. He would let her know if anyone entered in the garden and patrolled around the neighbouring area, keeping an eye out for anything that may have led to someone visiting the house. It was the cat, who spotted you passing, the first time. Suzie had implanted a mental picture in his mind of you and aged it. She somehow knew that you were around this area and it's just a waiting game, before you were found. Seems she had other animals on the lookout for you as well; a crow and a magpie."

"Maybe that's the crow with the white feathers?" Giles queried.

"Indeed, it could be." Sandra answered. "Did Bez here have any markings before you gingerised him?"

"White paw, I think," Giles replied.

"Makes sense," she said. "Convicted Magi criminals undergo deep thought manipulation. Some may mend their ways through this. Some are very resistant and Eizus undoubtedly is. The aim is to get them to leave a mark or a signal to tell others of their presence or danger."

"A kind of warning sign?" he asked. "Suzie had a witch on a broom tattoo and a necklace."

"So you weren't at all suspicious, duh," and she laughed. "She won't understand why she had them. Probably, she finds them amusing. She won't understand either why she picked perfectly black animals with a white flaw."

They heard a noise from the front room that sounded like something falling over. They both looked urgently into the hall and a black cat shot out of the room and straight out of the open front door. It's white tipped tail flailing behind it.

"That made me jump," exclaimed Sandra, "One of the nosey neighbours."

Giles said "Double Shit."

"What's wrong, Giles?"

"Suzie had two black cats. I didn't get a good look at the other one but Felix there definitely had a white tail and you know what you said about warnings?"

He ran to the room and looked inside. Everything seemed as before. Then he spotted a couple of things knocked over on the old oak sideboard; a porcelain figurine and a couple of dusty picture frames.

Giles looked at the figure, a lady in a red dress and stood it back in the dustless circle where it obviously came from. The first frame contained an old photograph. He blew on it first and then wiped it with a ginger hand to see it properly; an old couple standing by a nineteen forties car. He stood it back up. He didn't know why he tidied up. After all it isn't even his house but it seemed to be respectful towards whoever had owned it in the past.

He picked up the other frame. The glass front appeared much dirtier. He gave it a rub but couldn't see the figure on it properly. He thought for a second then licked his fingertip. Even if he shouldn't get wet, surely he couldn't harm his own fingertip. His damp digit looked fine so he rubbed the mucky surface of the picture and wiped it with the side of his hand.

Giles could see Suzie. She smiled at him from the glass surface. He froze. She beckoned to him and suddenly he couldn't move or talk. He could just see the top half of her, naked and moving provocatively from side to side. She put her fingers to her mouth in a Marilyn Monroe impression, his fear of her drifted away and he really wanted to see her gorgeous body again…

A sudden slap knocked the frame out of his hand and it crashed to the floor. Sandra stood there, "What are you doing, Giles? What did you see in the mirror?"

"Suzie... She must know we're here. I think she tried to hypnotise me, again. How can she see through a mirror? I could see her in the lake earlier. It must be something to do with reflections and light," he said, looking startled.

"Shit, Giles. That's very worrying on both counts. I didn't know she could do anything like that and it also means that she'll be on her way here soon. Maybe she sent the other cat earlier to check the house out?" Sandra replied.

"I don't understand why she hasn't been back already. After she turned me into a biscuit, she said that she needed to go to the supermarket to get some more ingredients, whatever that means. Shouldn't take this amount of time," said Giles. "Hadn't we better get out of here, Sandra?"

"I'll just have one more look around the house. I can't see anything that tells me what she's up to apart from turning you ginger. Now why did she do that, when she said she'd end your life?"

"Thanks for reminding me about the imminent death bit. I don't know. Just toying with me?" he replied.

"It's more than that. She could have just run you down with a car but for some reason or other had to capture you first and make you drink wine," she said. "Strange."

Three minutes later they were heading out the door and across the front garden. Giles said "Maybe I should pick some gooseberries and strawberries to examine?" He headed to where he'd harvested the fruit before, only to return quite disappointed.

"Only a few very small gooseberries, from an old bush, I can't even see the strawberries." Giles handed them over to Sandra who put them in her plastic carrier bag with a few other nick-knacks she'd picked up from the house.

They opened the gate and looked up and down the street before running over to the car and quickly jumping in. Sandra drove off at speed with Giles checking behind, in front, to the side and even opening the window, poking his head out and looking up for birds.

"It doesn't look like we're being watched. That dark cloud seems to have gone away. Where shall we go now?"

"Back to our house, Giles, we have to pick up some clothes and money. For the time being, we are on the run. I have no real weapons to fight Suzie. We don't even know what she's capable of. You have yet to recover your memory which may help us or not. I haven't had the chance to go through everything in detail, that's happened to you the last few weeks. There may be some clues there."

"Don't you know someone we could turn to? Where are the nearest Magi? Have you seen any nearby?" he asked.

"When we moved in together, as it were, I had to avoid any contact with Magi. This area had checked out as being one where no known Magi resided," she replied. "As you know, we look similar to Homsaps and if we guard our thoughts, which most do in public, I could stand next to one of us and not know. I had to give up my friends, colleagues and family to watch over you."

"Well, I'm really very grateful and sorry to have taken you for granted all these years," he said, "although I'm wondering at this speed how much longer I've got left." Giles flinched as Sandra narrowly avoided a rabbit in the road.

"One rabbit corpse is enough for today, just doing my job. There existed a risk that either my whereabouts or yours could be exposed and believe it or not, Eizus did have followers. I don't know how she found you but my job is only really starting. Time to earn my pay packet," Sandra said.

"I never thought of it like that. I know you get paid at the clinic but will you get something if Eizus is defeated or recaptured?" he asked. "I hope so."

"You bet. I'm not stupid, Giles. A small private island off Rhodes and a pick of husbands, maybe? Who knows? Just be lucky to survive this," she smiled.

"Thought you were married to me?"

"A Homsap marriage of convenience, I'm afraid that, Giles, doesn't count. Because of our longer Magi lives, we don't usually pick partners until sixty or seventy years old. Traditionally, even later is the norm as most women waited for their children to grow and leave home. Quite different to Homsap," she stated. Sorry, Selig, I do fancy you but you're not the one for me."

"It sounds so strange, as though we're getting divorced after all these years. Suppose I just judge things by Homsap standards?" he said, noting that at last, the car had reached their house drive.

"English standards," she interjected. "Other countries do things differently. We're home now. Remember, no time-wasting looking at stuff. Just fetch the cases from the loft and grab your clothes. I'll find some food, map and the sat nav. My laptop's in the car already. Find that dongle thing, you used it last. Oh, get the binoculars as well, think you had them. You can put the stuff in the car while I find my clothes."

Typical organised Sandra. She makes the lists, barks the orders and he gets to pack the stuff in the car. No change there then. He wondered what to say to his neighbours, if they returned home and asked why he looked like a McVities reject but all looked quiet in their street.

Chapter 18

The old man out walking his dog couldn't believe it. He had enough of the student rag chaos in the town and decided to stretch his legs in the nearby countryside. He crossed a stile after encouraging his Dalmatian to hop up the crossed planked structure first and heard voices from the other end of the field. Excited voices, quite loud but he couldn't understand a word. He looked over and could see some horses and figures. Two animals, no three; a couple riding, one horse being walked by the reins and he noted one horse had two passengers. They all seemed to be wearing uniform. He stood by the stile and watched for a minute as they approached. The group had entered the field through a farm gate. There looked to be another similar one at the other end of the field and they seemed to be heading in that direction. He walked on an official path and wondered why the group were going through the fields because it's not marked as a bridleway.

Then he remembered a few months ago, some travellers stayed for a couple of weeks illegally, nearby. They had horses that they rode without saddles, leaving a mess before being moved on by the police after a court order. By all accounts, the plod just accompanied them to the end of their patch and then they were someone else's problem. He hoped that the next county hadn't dumped them back...

As they got closer he decided that couldn't be the case. They were too well-dressed. The men had cavalry uniforms on. Old-fashioned American ones. The single woman wore jeans and a blouse and didn't quite fit in. He wondered if a circus had come to town, maybe a Wild-West show with trick horses. That's it, he though, they're here to practise and the woman is the ring master in civvies. He decided to watch and get a free show. He clipped the lead on the Dalmatian and whispered "Sit," in the dog's ear. The dog obeyed, with its ears pricked up, as far as its black and white lugs would go and waited, tongue hanging out. "You just stay still, Spot and let Dave watch the circus." The group didn't seem to have noticed them on the edge of the field.

Dave heard the sound of an engine. The other gate had been opened and a large black car drove through the gap in the hedge. He could make out a Range Rover with blacked out side windows. The V8 engine throbbed and burbled as it slowly approached the group. He laughed and wondered if Torchwood had arrived to solve a Sci-Fi mystery? The riders had dismounted. He could see that the woman wore a metal headband or possibly a tiara? She looked very pretty from this distance, probably why she'd been picked to be in charge in the ring. The lady seemed to be holding something in each hand in front of her joined by a short shiny cord.

The vehicle stopped about twenty yards from the horses and maybe the farmer had driven his car over to ask what they were doing on the farm? One of the horses seemed a bit jittery so the rider stroked its snout and said something to the animal. There seemed a pause of about a minute before the front passenger door opened.

A man dressed in tweed climbed out. He put on a large hat and slowly walked a few yards towards the others then stopped and leant on his cane.

Two cavalry men started walking towards Tweedy. One of them took hold of the cord that the lady held and she followed although she seemed to be resisting. The other man started pushing her. Dave realised then that she wasn't holding the cord, actually her hands were tied by it. The rope shone in the sunlight. Maybe the material could be metal and not shiny fabric as he had first thought? There's something wrong here, he decided, as he turned his collar up against the breeze. The wind had risen and it had turned cloudy. Rain in the air maybe, the weather had been a bit funny today.

Spot whimpered and Dave looked down at him. "Shush,

they'll hear us. Something's up here." He crouched down remembering his army training and hoping not to get mud on his newish trousers. He didn't want to be seen while he sussed out the situation.

The woman shouted something in a foreign language holding her corded hands up to the sky. One of the cavalrymen shouted at her to stop. He noticed some black birds had started to circle overhead and their numbers seemed to quickly increase. They were either rooks or crows. Dave didn't do feathered identification very well.

Suddenly the birds started dive-bombing the group. They knocked off a couple of hats, the men were waving their arms around like windmills trying to shoo them off. They didn't seem to be bothering the woman and whilst one man bent down to pick up his hat, she slipped her cord under his chin and pulled him to his feet. She half dragged, half turned him to face the others and shouted "Take it off or I will finish him. I won't warn you again."

He heard a rumble of thunder from the now darkening sky. The men looked up and seemed worried. The birds had turned their attention to Tweedy and he flailed his cane around, trying unsuccessfully to fight them off. A collision from two crows simultaneously to his head knocked him off his feet, he let go of his cane and the wind seemed to catch and blow it closer to the woman.

One of the men came over to the lady and her hostage. Dave thought the woman would be released from the cord but he appeared to just touch the tiara headband first and it dropped to the ground. The man stepped away quickly.

"Loosen my wrist binding quickly. I think your boss is having difficulty breathing," she shouted. The hostage was on his knees, his face turned purple and grasping desperately at the cord around his neck.

The cavalryman obeyed and went over to her, once more. He

noted the other two had backed away, one holding the side of his face which dripped blood. The crows continued their pecking attack on Tweedy, forcing him to roll and crawl back to the car. A slim blonde woman had opened the driver's door and shouted at him to get back in.

The woman driver got thrown to the floor as a bolt of lightning hit the roof of the Range Rover. It seemed to light up the whole car and he could see inside through the darkened windows. There were two other passengers in the back seats.

The car went dark again and Dave's attention went back to the first struggle where the cavalryman had untied the woman's hand and she immediately dived to her side towards the cane. The three uniformed men were now legging it towards the first gate. Their horses had scattered and were running crazily around the field.

The woman had got up with the cane and waved it at the birds and for some reason she managed to scare them off. She ran over to Tweedy on the ground and waved the cane in a threatening way at him. She placed her hand on his forehead and he kept still on his hands and knees.

Another rumble of thunder and the rain came down. Almost the heaviest he had seen. As he let go of the dog to rummage in his pocket, another flash of brilliant lightning streaked across the sky and hit a tree very close to them, near the stile.

The woman swivelled around and looked in their direction. He wondered if they'd been spotted. The Dalmatian barked and ran towards the woman who had held both arms up in the air.

"Come to me!" she shouted.

Dave couldn't tell if she called the dog or both of them. He didn't fancy meeting her anyway. "Spot, come back here!" The dog ignored him and went straight to her. He saw her pick up the lead and pat the dog on the head.

She started walking towards him, cane in one hand, dog lead in the other. The wind had gone down now and the rain had stopped. The woman and dog looked made for one another as they strutted over the field towards him. He didn't know what to do. Should he have helped earlier? She had a smile on her face. She didn't look about to tell him off. He looked over her shoulder. The Range Rover had no activity in it and Tweedy still struggled on his hands and knees.

"Are you okay, what is this all about? Thanks for holding onto Spot," he shouted.

"Spot, what a lovely name, those men were trying to kidnap and sell me but I think they've changed their minds now," and she giggled.

She looked so pretty and had beautiful deep brown eyes. He couldn't help looking into them.

"Hi, I'm Suzie. I hope it's fine if I keep your dog. I rather like him and I think I've just lost one of my cats. I'm sure you'll understand."

Dave now had fallen soundly asleep on the wet grass by the stile.

"Must be the silent type," said Suzie and she turned around and leant on her new cane as the Range Rover roared into life and headed off at speed through the second gate.

"I wonder where they'll go?" she said looking at a crow in a nearby field.

With a flash of white, the almost black bird soared into the air and over the hedge out of sight.

She looked at Dave on the floor and tapped his head with her stick, "A day to forget, young man."

Spot licked him on the face and the lady with her new dotty black and white dog, walked away across the field.

Dave woke up with a headache and covered in mud an hour later. Must have fallen off the stile as I climbed over it, he thought. Spot must have walked home. Hope he's alright crossing that main road...

Chapter 19

They grabbed their stuff as planned. Giles found a couple of rucksacks in the loft, to put some of the things in. Whilst up there, Sandra called up to him to get an item from one of the eaves, a dusty carrier bag with a box inside.

"What's in here?" he said, as he fiddled unsuccessfully with the lock after bringing it down. "Is this where you hide your jewels?"

"Don't mess about with it, Giles. Tell you later," came back the reply from downstairs. Giles shrugged his shoulders and put the box in one of the bags.

He'd banged his leg climbing down the loft ladder and rubbed his knee. As he did so a pile of ginger crumbs fell out of the bottom of his trouser leg, over his trainer and scattered onto the floor. He quickly rolled the material up to have a look and picked off the loose bits. He expected it to hurt and quite unexpectedly discovered pink skin underneath.

"Sandra, come look at this quickly," he shouted.

She ran up the stairs half expecting to be greeted by a monster and felt a little disappointed to find a bare leg.

"Look, Sandra. It's me. I'm underneath!" he said excitedly.

Sandra took a closer look. "Well, well. I wondered if it could be permanent."

"Do you think that the spell is wearing off?" said Giles.

"What she did to you, which is not a spell by the way, appears to be reverting back to normal. Maybe her work is not perfect or your body and mind are strong and are fighting it. I hope it's a bit of both," said Sandra.

"I'd happily settle for the mind and body bit. Any ideas yet why she did it?" he said poking at the edges and finding that it hurt him. "Ow."

"Don't pick, Giles," she said. "I guess it'll come off when it's ready. You'll probably have a bad case of ginger dandruff and crumbs in your knickers," she laughed, thinking of him in the red lady pants.

"As for why she did it to you, I've got two theories. After she received her sentence she went through the usual psychological and hypnotic mind treatment in an attempt to get her to mend her ways. This appears to have failed on the surface but there would have been several specialists working with her at different levels using different techniques. I think that something worked. She's marking herself, the tattoos for instance and she's picking animal friends with odd markings. I think that someone has planted a block to stop her eliminating you straight away. For some reason, she can't do it," she said. "Another factor is you, Selig, and your own mind." You were treated by the same people. I know that some Magi have a sort of aura around them, which can be sensed by others unconsciously and affect their behaviour. You may have something that protects you."

"You mean that I have a force field like in Star Trek? Beam me up, Sandra," he replied.

"Ha ha, and no you haven't. You can be hurt just like me, Spock. I meant a mind-block that affects Eizus," said Sandra.

"Maybe covering my skin with ginger biscuit stopped it working?"

"Quite possibly, anyway you haven't told me exactly what you got up to with sensual Suzie yet, have you?"

Giles had dreading this moment. He'd been keeping this little chapter away from Sandra, filed under fun – access for Giles and mates only. Now he had to open it up for the wife and he felt like a kid having to explain his stash of porn.

"I guess that you were up to no good with Suzie. Do you think she suspected me at all?" she asked.

"She did ask a few questions about you and now that reminds me. On one occasion she seemed to be telling me things that I don't think I actually said. Like she read my mind," Giles replied. "Oh, and once, she seemed to infer that I read her mind, a bit like

I did to you although I didn't feel anything."

"You're not supposed to," she laughed. "I guess you got intimate?"

"That's bad isn't it, judging by the look on your face?" he said, feeling very guilty.

"I'm not bothered by the sanctity of Homsap marriage, Giles," she said. "If you swopped bodily fluids of any description, she had the opportunity to A infect you, and B obtain bits of you. Come to think of it, you've been looking noticeably greyer, the last week or two."

"You mean take bits to sample? Maybe analyse to find weaknesses? I'm definitely greyer. I've noticed and I often feel tired for no reason. If I'm supposed to live a couple of centuries, isn't that a bit odd? I'm a spring chicken, relatively speaking," he replied.

Another vision started. Suzie put a chicken in the oven. She turned around and smiled at him as she bent down in front of the cooker dressed in a skimpy bikini. The chicken morphed into a miniature Giles on the baking tray. He had a crinkly Sunday-roast skin. Suzie ladled the fat over his torso.

Giles screamed, "Shit, that's hot!" and snapped out of the day dream. He ran to the bathroom undoing his shirt as he went.

"What did you see, Giles?" asked Sandra guessing correctly that he'd had a nasty vision.

Giles stood at the sink splashing cold water on his ginger chest. He filled the sink and placed a soaking cold flannel to his tummy and held it there. "She tried to scold me. Poured hot fat over me like a chicken."

"You just said spring chicken, Giles. She must know we're here," said Sandra and ran to the window looking out to the road.

The spider up above them, moved further out of the crack in the ceiling where it had been watching them for five minutes.

"Does she know that we live here?" Sandra asked again.

"Actually, don't bother answering. She may have read your mind or sent one of her birds. Of course, those birds have been in the garden before. Come on and let's get away from here."

"Oh my God," she said. Giles had lifted the wet flannel from his tummy.

His gorgeous six-pack had gone soggy, turned into a small saggy beer belly. He poked it gently and made a small indentation which remained after he removed his digit.

"I told you not to get wet. If that doesn't dry out quick, it could flop off and your guts will be hanging out," she warned.

"And I did it myself. Don't you see, Sandra? If she can't hurt me, she'll trick me or others to do so. Get to know me, find the weaknesses, by using the kissing, the sex, whoa..." and he ducked.

"You little bastard," Sandra had lifted her arm and took a swipe.

Giles flinched. Sex payback, he thought, ducked and waited for the slap to connect, eyes closed.

"Got you. Oh get up, Giles, and don't be stupid."

He opened his eyes to see Sandra examining a squashed spider on the wall, to the side of where he'd been standing.

"First blood to us, or maybe second blood because you got the cat. This black spider had a white leg. Suzie's been watching us for a few minutes," said Sandra.

"Erm...hate to tell you but that spider's probably been in the house for a couple of weeks. It's got a web by the bedroom lampshade. I stuck some of your coco pops to it and the spider wrapped them up like flies. Sorry," he said.

"Selig, you are such a daehbonk sometimes."

He thought for a second, reversed the spelling in his head... "Correct." They both burst out laughing.

"On the subject of bonking, I'm really not concerned about you seeing Suzie," she said.

"That's rather kind of you. What's the catch?"

"Well, I knocked off that mate Pete, of yours, a couple of years ago," she replied with a grin.

"Little bastard," he said.

"No, that's the spider remember?" and she started laughing. "You called Pete, the eyes and ears of the street. It should be more like hands and tongues. He always smelt of oil and animals."

"That's because he's a slippery old dog," said Giles trying to imagine the two of them together and ending up with a hairy and tailed Pete, between Sandra's outstretched legs.

"Giving me a bone, I suppose?" she answered, with a knowing look on her face.

"You read my mind," Giles said and they both started laughing again.

When they calmed down, she said "Actually you sent that thought to me. You're getting better. Let's go."

Giles put the bags by the side of the car and looked nervously up and down the street. He opened the boot.

"What the heck?" and took a few steps back as he saw something move.

"Oh, I'm sorry Giles, forgot to tell you, he's on our side now," said Sandra.

"Hmm..." Giles pushed the purring ginger Beelzebub to one side and loaded up before taking the co-driver's seat.

Sandra got in. She turned into Ardnax the rally driver and the three of them shot off down the street.

Chapter 20

The little hatchback carved through the traffic heading southwards.

Giles asked where they were going.

Sandra replied "I guess it may be better not to tell you, just in case Suzie gets into your head and can track us. We're on the run, Giles, from a powerful woman, we need to see if you can recover and we need to make a plan of attack."

"Can't we just hide and she'll get bored?" he said hopefully.

"No chance. She wants to dispose of you, period. You'll have to just trust me for the moment."

Their little vehicle diced with the lorries and coaches, on the A roads down to Brighton and parked up in a car park not far from the promenade.

"Time for a bracing walk by the sea, I assume, Sandra, or should I call you Sandy?"

"Pebbly might be better because there's not a lot of sand here," she replied.

"Let's settle on Pablo then," he replied with a laugh.

"You can be Picasso then, Ass for short," she said, "or Short Arse even."

"Fine, you win. Sandra it is," he replied.

"Let's just forget this stuff for a bit and have an ice cream. You stay here, Ginger, because I don't think the world is ready for you yet. Be back soon."

After a few minutes he got bored and decided to get out and stretch his legs. He had a quick look around first and then got out. He could smell the sea air, could hear the sound of fairground-style music in the distance and also see the seagulls circling overhead.

Around and around they flew, their circles seemed to be ever decreasing.

Then Giles started being dive-bombed from behind and

crumbs flew out of his bonce.

"Shit, I'm a biscuit!" he exclaimed.

"Look out, Giles," shouted Sandra from behind him.

He ducked at the warning and felt gull feet scratch the back of his neck. Running to the car, he managed to open the door and enter in one seamless movement.

Sandra came to the driver's door, laughing her head off and pointing at him through the window.

She got in and passed him an ice cream with a flaky chocolate sticking out of it. "That's the funniest thing that I ever saw. Man-eating seagulls."

"Do you think Suzie sent them?" Giles said as he rubbed the dents in his head. "That hurts."

"No, they were white and just plain hungry," she said. "You're bleeding ginger blood from your scalp. Hold on I've got an idea."

She remembered something that she'd popped in her handbag. A quick rummage and she took out a folded tissue and handed it to Giles.

"Thanks, Sandra," and pressed the wad to his head. "There's something in it".

"Open it up, stupid," she encouraged and he did so to find two ginger biscuits.

"Ah, a do it yourself gingerbread man repair kit?" he laughed.

"Crunch up some crumbs and rub them in your head, maybe?" she suggested.

Giles did as she suggested. "That feels really good, most weird."

"It's stopped bleeding now." She placed her hands on the top of his head and he felt a warm feeling.

"Should be set now," she said. "That made me hungry. I saw a chip shop around the corner. I'll buy you a disguise as well. Don't move from the car this time."

When Sandra arrived back, she rewarded Giles with the most

delicious fish and chips that he could remember in his life. "I'm so hungry," he said and scratched his cheek which promptly fell off.

As he looked at the bits on his lap, Sandra said "That's probably related. You'll need energy to recover your normal skin as the gingerness wears off."

"Cool, I follow. I guess we're staying here. How are you going to sneak me into a hotel?" he asked.

"With this…" She produced a clown mask and blond curly wig. "There's a fairground down near the prom."

"And I'm a visiting clown who needs somewhere to stay?"

"You said it," and they both laughed.

Beelzebub purred from the back seat. Sandra said "Haven't forgotten about you, mate," passing a chunk of her fish over to the back seat.

"Can't take him into a hotel," Giles pointed out

"No problem. He's used to being outside. We can always open a window for him to climb in. I'll talk to him," she said.

"You can talk to cats now?"

"Sort of make them understand. They'll be plenty of other town cats about to keep him company," she said.

"Like in the Topcat cartoon where they all meet up in and alley and plan heists on fish factories? Remember, we are in Brighton, gay capital of the UK. Tell him to watch out for Toms with pink collars and limp tails that meow with a lisp," he laughed and looked Beelzebub in the eye.

Beelzebub cocked his head and appeared to wink at Giles.

"Guess that means he already bats for the other side," Sandra replied laughing.

Beelzebub purred and climbed over onto Sandra's lap. She started to stroke his head slowly and the cat looked up at her transfixed.

After a minute of this, she said "He understands. I'll let him go now. We'll be in a hotel around the corner. They had a vacancy sign up. He'll find us. Off you go then, puss," and she opened the door so the cat shot out.

"Put your stuff on, Giles, and we'll go and book in," she said.

Giles felt past caring at this point and duly put on the mask followed by the blond wig. He got out of the car, went around to the boot and took out the cases.

"There's someone coming, Sandra," he whispered.

"Act naturally, Giles," she replied.

The couple with a young girl came closer and were looking at them. Giles smiled, then realised that he wore a mask and had wasted his time.

"Alright, mate," the young chap said to Giles.

"Is that really a clown, mummy?" said the little girl.

"It's his day off," said Sandra and they passed by, laughing.

"Let's get to the room before I die of embarrassment, Sandra," he said to her. "Which way is it?"

At the reception desk, the smartly suited young man looked at the pair over the top of his glasses. "Mr and Mrs Mor-Morton. Here for a few days' work. I see you're still dressed up after yesterday's performance, Mr Morton."

"He likes to stay in character," said Sandra smiling.

"My life is just one big pantomime… " added Giles.

"Indeed it is, sir. Breakfast is served in the Spellbound Dining Room from seven am and the main meal from six pm in the Witches' Lair. Feel free to use the Wizard Bar in the evening. Do you need help with your cases?"

"We'll be fine, thanks. Let's go up straight away, dear," said Giles, now conscious of crumbs in his shoes.

"Oh…and sir? The management would be grateful if you've been on the beach to shake any sand out of your footwear by the door. I'll get the maid to sweep up by the desk."

"Sorry about that," Giles shouted through the closing lift doors.

"Witches' Bloody Lair, are you having a joke, Sandra?" as he steadied himself in the rapidly ascending lift.

"I didn't know we'd come to a themed place, honestly, Giles. I thought Fairytale Hotel sounded fine."

"Fine? I'm a Gingerbread Man dressed as Crusty the Clown with a Gay Devil Cat and I'm on the run from The Wicked Witch and her Enchanted Animals. Nightmare Hotel would be more suitable," and they both creased up laughing, for a minute.

Finally Giles stopped and reached out to hold Sandra's hand.

"This is really bad isn't it, Sandra? We could die." The reality of the crazy situation began to hit Giles.

"I wish I could have warned you years ago but no one knew what to expect. I'm here to protect you ginger-nut and Suzie's gotta get past me first... " replied Sandra, giving his hand the firm squeeze of a Minder.

Once they'd worked out how to use the key-card to open the door and get the electric on, Giles looked in the mirror. He hadn't seen his disguise properly yet.

"Oh, my God," he exclaimed. As he took off his mask, another bit of his face fell off and shattered on the floor "Shit." He looked back in the mirror. "Phantom of The Opera, eat your heart out." His face looked half uncovered now and he could see one of his cheeks and eye properly. "Welcome back, face," and he tried a few smiles to remind himself just what he looked like. More pieces fell off.

"You're making a mess, Giles," said Sandra "If you're going to pull faces, hold this towel to catch the crumbs. I'll open the window for Beelzebub."

Their room faced the rear courtyard, on the second floor. Sandra looked out and felt happy that the feline would make it. A flat roof extension stuck out just below and there existed enough ornate mouldings and drainpipes on the back of the building for a three-legged cat in a wheelchair to get up.

"I'll go and put the hotel parking voucher on the car and bring us back some food and drink. We'd better stay in this evening," and she left him sitting on the end of the bed, feeling totally exhausted.

Chapter 21

Giles woke up in bed. Someone's hair tickled his face. He opened his eyes to see a black tail on the pillow. His first thought is that Sandra's feeling playful again then he recognised the item. "Get off, cat," and saw Beelzebub's purring face come into view.

"Thought you'd never wake up," said Sandra's voice. He rolled over to see her sitting in a small black leather arm chair. "I've got some sandwiches here for you. I'll make a cup of tea. I bought something for you to tidy up with," and she tossed him a lurid green dustpan and brush.

He pushed himself up and looked at the pillow. "I see what you mean".

"Brings a new meaning to that film *Face off,* doesn't it," she chuckled. "I can nearly recognise you again. You remind me of someone…"

He rubbed his head and a generous portion of ginger dandruff fell onto the pillow.

"Let me wipe your face with a damp flannel and then you can have a look in the mirror. It's breaking off your fingers and hands as well," she added.

He rubbed his hands together and exposed his pink skinny palms. "Cool."

After a quick wipe he stood up and looked down at his body. His hands and feet were almost visible and there were many fissures in the surface of his ginger legs and torso. His ginger tackle still looked back at him. "With all these cracks, how deep do they go? I'm thinking of my manhood here," he said looking down.

"I'll still love you even if your knob drops off Giles. Look in the dressing table mirror and tell me who you look like," she said.

Giles did as ordered "I'm as bald as a coot. You mean that American hard man actor, Yule Brynner?"

"I'm thinking more Little Britain. We are in the capital of Gay Country, remember?" she replied.

"Ha ha, I'm the baldest gingerbread man in the village. I guess the hair will take longer to grow back. I've got no eyebrows as well," he noted.

"I could pencil some in," she said reaching for her handbag.

"Wear make-up in Brighton? No way," he said, backing away. Beelzebub purred. "And I don't need your opinion, either, because it may be biased."

"I think you'll be alright to go downstairs for a drink with me. Just keep your shirt buttoned up," Sandra suggested.

"If you're sure, I really could do with a stiff drink," he said.

"Maybe you could keep something stiff for me later?" she laughed and raised an eyebrow.

"Wouldn't it be too weird to do it with a ginger willy?" he asked.

"Oh, I don't know. I've got some odd-shaped ones that I hide in the wardrobe from you. A girl's got to relax sometime," and she winked at him.

"Hmm…let's get dressed and see if I can have a drink without getting arrested first.

They took the lift back down to the ground floor and soon found the Wizard Bar. The place seemed totally empty. They sat on two bar stools and looked around. The black ceiling twinkled with little lights. The walls were cream with dark material draped across them, in flouncy shapes. There were paintings and drawings of bubbling jars and pots over the walls. The word Abracadaver had been written in gold letters above the bar and weird shaped glassware stood behind the bar, where the optics usually resided.

"It reminds me of my school chemistry lab. Shouldn't that read abracadabra?" Giles commented.

"Boo!"

Giles nearly jumped out of rest of his ginger skin, as a pale face in a pointy hat jumped up from behind the bar.

"Don't be so uptight, Giles," she said laughing before addressing the new face. "I suppose you're the Wizard?"

"The boss is off so technically I'm the Sorcerer's Apprentice," the pointy hat said. "I usually work as a Gremlin in the Witches' Lair but he asked me to cover tonight."

There followed an impression of a snarling gremlin. "I'm Snake, what can I get you? The spelling on the sign is wrong as you spotted. Dyslexic painter, bet you don't believe me?"

"Trust me, Snake, I do, I do… " Giles replied.

"I fancy a cocktail," said Sandra, reaching under the bar and giving Giles' privates a gentle squeeze.

"My pleasure, Madam," and Snake turned around to the counter behind and passed over two laminated drinks menus.

"Should have bought my glasses, it's a bit gloomy in here. You pick for me, Giles."

Giles scanned the list.

He read them out to Sandra: Black Magic, Moon Dust, Turn to Stone, Hair of Dog, Mesmer-eyes, Bat out of Brighton, Jaw Dropper, Spell it Right and Magi Magic.

"The last one Snake, what's that?" she asked and looked at Giles.

Snake looked at a recipe list behind the bar. "That's new. A lady staying two weeks ago gave us the recipe. The boss liked it so it stayed. I think she may have been Greek or Cypriot. Said her countrymen would like it. We get a few folks from the Med staying here. You fancy one?"

"I'll have one," said Sandra, "and you, Giles?"

"How about you drop the twist of lime in the Turn to Stone and replace it with a splash of ginger ale. I'll call it Turn to Ginger?" he suggested.

"Right on, man," replied Snake and gave him a high five. "You're one cool cookie".

"Yeah, yeah," he replied. "Full on biscuit," to which Sandra nearly fell off her stool with laughter.

The evening passed quickly with one cocktail after another and the alcohol helped Giles to forget the gravity of their situation.

Snake turned out to be a highly intelligent university drop out, computer geek, gremlin and part-time gravedigger. He told them that he could get them a discount with any Brighton and Hove funeral director, if they ever needed. "I do Co-operative funeral plans but would waive my commission because you're such nice guys." He then told them that the Fairytale had run a vampire convention a month ago and he'd sold loads."

"I thought vampires were the un-dead. They shouldn't need to be buried?" queried Sandra.

Snake informed her that the bloodsuckers had all ordered coffins with internal handles so they could open up the lids themselves, rather than being screwed down. "The coffin carpenters will make anything you want," he smiled.

At this point, Giles decided that the craziness had to end for the night. Another young couple had joined them and were absolutely pissing themselves at the banter between Giles and the Barman. "See you tomorrow Ginger Giles and Magic Sandra," Snake shouted as they staggered somewhat unsteadily, to the lift.

They got back to their room to find Beelzebub sitting on the bed.

"Bez" said Sandra, "Come to mummy," and put her hands on his head.

She let go after a couple of minutes and the cat jumped up and climbed out of the window.

"He's been keeping an eye on the hotel and room. The other cats reckon there have been some strange goings on here, over the years. They're always wary of the Greek Cypriot visitors. Let's sleep and discuss it in the morning," she said.

Giles had already thrown his clothes plus a pile of crumbs

onto the floor and climbed into bed. “Okay dear,” he mumbled and started to snore.

Sandra was looking out of the window gazing up at the sky. She saw a shooting star.

“The Magi have been here. How did they know?” she said quietly and smiled before retiring to bed…

Chapter 22

Giles slept soundly. He woke at about seven, the next morning, still in the middle of a dream. The window had been left part open and the calls of the nearby seagulls woke him up.

"I had the weirdest dream, Sandra," he said to the person hiding under a pillow and moved it to one side.

He heard a moan.

"Just checking that you weren't Suzie," he carried on, glad to see her face.

"Giles, you were rolling about all night and even talking at one point. You kept waking me up," she said grumpily.

"Sorry, Sandra." He rubbed his eyes and more of his face fell off, onto her.

She pulled the pillow back over her face, saying, "Tell me about the dream," in a muffled voice.

"Well, I remember being chased by a dragon or something and ended up in a cellar full of gingerbread men. The dragon got scared away by some ladies in uniform, who wanted to take me away. We were just leaving on horses when the dragon came back breathing fire. They battled the dragon with little silver swords that seemed to shoot light. The dragon's tail knocked me off the horse. We were flying at the time. I could see an island underneath and I fell into a lake there, a very salty lake, ended up being pulled out by pink flamingos," he recalled, "Weird, eh?"

Sandra came out from under her cover and shook ginger crumbs out of her hair.

"Actually, Selig, quite comforting, it just confirms that we're not on our own," she replied.

"I know. You're going to tell me that Beelzebub has gathered a feline army to protect us," he laughed.

"Better than that, the Magi have drawn us to this place," she replied.

"Hmm, are you referring to the misspelt Magic Magic cocktail last night? It looked like a typo. You mean it really should have said Magi Magic?" he asked.

"Correct Giles, you need a history lesson. Get yourself cleaned up in the bathroom first. Looks like you can wash the top half of your body, at least." She lifted the sheets. "Your todger has reappeared but his two mates are still biscuity though. I guess that makes them genuine Ginger Nuts," she giggled.

Giles managed to have a shower, half in and out of the cubicle. His ankles and calves were reappearing much to his satisfaction and as he'd noticed with his head, they were hairless. When he came out of the shower, he found his clothes for the day neatly set out on the bed. Typical Sandra, he thought.

"Typical eh?" she imitated as she walked towards him, naked, on her way into the shower.

He slapped her on the bum as she walked past. She retaliated in the same way causing part of his derriere to come away leaving fresh pink skin.

"LMAO, Giles," she said giggling and pointing at the biscuit debris on the carpet.

"Pardon?" said Giles raising an eyebrow.

"Laughed my arse off," she explained. "It's text-speak, Giles."

"We gingerbread men get too much hassle from the public, although I'm not looking forward to becoming a slaphead either," he replied, appearing a bit fed up.

"I'll have a quick shower and tell you some more stuff after. Turn the little kettle on and make us both a coffee after you've dressed," she said.

While she showered, Beelzebub came in through the open window and jumped up onto the bed next to him.

"Meow, meow and meeooww," the cat said looking at him and cocking its head to one side.

"Sorry, old boy. We'll have to wait for the translator, she's having a shower."

Beelzebub cocked his head to one side and stared at him.

"Come here," and he put his hands either side of the cats head imitating Sandra before. He didn't say anything but thought his loudest thoughts and then let go.

Beelzebub shot under the bed and wouldn't come out for him.

"Maybe cat-speak isn't my thing," he said quietly as he made the drinks. He poured some of the long-life milk from a little plastic tub into a saucer and placed it on the carpet. The cat's head emerged and it started lapping just as Sandra emerged from the shower.

He watched her curvy body walk over to the wardrobe and take out some clothes. He could still see a red mark on her behind where he'd slapped her earlier. He quite enjoyed that slap; it felt quite nice, when he did it. His eyes followed her long legs down to her slim ankles…

"I know what you're thinking but we have some work to do, so just behave, Giles. You can watch me dress and that's all." She laughed and deliberately performed a reverse striptease.

"Very nice," said Giles. "I tried to get Beelzebub to talk to me but I haven't got the knack like you."

"Meow," answered the feline.

She dressed and went over to the cat and sat on the bed next to him. A hands-on silent conversation followed.

"First thing, Selig, you shouted and frightened him. He couldn't follow your loud thoughts; it sounded just like noise to him but he picked up a few things from your mind. Secondly his new mates have told him about a place that the Greek Cypriot visitors frequent. I think we'd better pay it a visit. Thirdly, and I should have noticed, he said you gave your ring to Suzie. Tell me the last one isn't true."

"Well, we were sort of comparing conjuring tricks and she came out on top, so to speak… " he replied.

"Yes and I can guess what she was doing on top of you, as well. The trouble is the ring is an ancient Magi relic. It belonged to your father and he passed it on to you. To some Magi, it has great significance and power but to others, it brings misery and oppression," she explained.

"I usually wore it; couldn't understand the language written on it. I thought that you gave it to me, another false memory? It hasn't bought me much luck," he replied.

"It protected you, Giles. Suzie couldn't make you into the gingerbread man until she had taken it off you. All the stuff before, aimed to soften you up and weaken your defences. Those samples, for want of a better word, that you gave her during sex, have enabled her to use your inherent Magi energy to boost her own, at the expense of yours. The ring may help her to harness this energy even more. It's worrying..."

"She put it on and kept it. I noticed that she sometimes seemed to look even younger after sex and I seemed to be going greyer quicker. Suzie drained me, didn't she, Sandra?" he asked.

"I'm afraid so, Giles, just building herself up, we never knew the extent of her powers but I guess from that wave in the park that they are pretty far reaching. We're going to war, Giles, so remember this... Whatever strange things that she may to do to us, it's not magic. If it's physical, then she will be manipulating something that already exists. It may be only in the mind. She can give you visions, as you know and mask things," Sandra warned. "She's not a witch, even if she thinks she is. We will have to outwit her. Your father's gift had been foresight and intelligence. Hopefully, you will have inherited some of his genes."

"What did you mean earlier by the ring having significance to others, especially the misery bit?" Giles asked.

"Many years ago, the Ruler of the Magi used to wear it as a sign of office. Some were good and people flourished, others were oppressive tyrants and left a sea of misery. Either way, the people worshipped the ring and the wearer," Sandra answered.

Giles frowned "So how did I end up with it? I'm no king."

"Merely in hiding, unrecognised as it were. Your father acted as our ruler until he died. Traditionally, the ruler chooses his successor, sometimes his child or sometimes a friend. If the ring is taken away by force or trickery, the wearer may appeal to the Elders and accede to the position," she explained.

Giles repeated, "Trickery," in a soft voice.

"Your father chose his son, but being as you were in hiding when he died, things are still in limbo. If Eizus appeals and finds favour with the Council of Elders, your claim may be dismissed. There would be some who would support her, if they thought they could get something out of it. It's pure politics."

"Why should I want to lead a tribe scattered all over the world, Sandra? My semi-retired life isn't too bad… " Giles replied, looking quite fed up. Beelzebub snuggled up to him.

"Well firstly, she promised to do away with you, at her trial. Secondly, if she does, then she wears the ring and has no rival and thirdly, this is what your father predicted may happen. You need to overcome her, where he and others failed. You are the chosen one," and she took a deep bow.

Sandra rose and grinned. "I know I don't really have to bow, sire," she laughed "but like it or not, you are our leader so you'd better get used to it."

"Looks like I don't have much choice, minion. But what's the significance of the Greeks?" Giles asked.

"More history and geography, then, our ancient civilisation existed in the Med, centred in Northern Crete. A volcano further north in Santorini erupted, causing a tsunami which destroyed the city and decimated the population. Birth rates were declining badly prior to the disaster. The remaining Elders decided to split the survivors but keep a small 'Magi capital' hometown on an island at a reasonable distance, just in case Santorini let go again," she explained.

"Where did the rest go?" he asked "Some of this seems vaguely familiar but it just won't click."

"All over the world, singly or in groups," she said. "We've left our mark on human development, discovered things, invented things, led countries, gained empires and started wars. We've been in the thick of it but now we're on the decline. Our numbers decrease every year. The males have lost their fertility and we females are only fertile once a year."

"Double shit," said Giles. "Do we breed with the others, erm…? Homsaps…is that possible? Maybe there'll be a hybrid?"

"There have been many so we'll live on effectively. They usually know nothing about their ancestry. The Homsap genes are very dominant so any Magi traits are much reduced. You haven't asked where the Magi town is set up, Giles, or have you guessed?"

"Hang on. A while back you said Magi have four toes on each foot. I know that I've got four toes but I'm sure your feet have five. Let me see?" he asked her.

She took off her short socks and splayed out her toes on the bedroom carpet.

"One, two, three, four and… the same on the other, how come that I haven't noticed?" he asked.

"Because, Giles I've been very careful for years about it. What men really look at women's feet and count their toes? Although thinking about it, I suppose there are some and perhaps a website called Toecounters.com," she laughed.

"While we're talking toe to toe as it were, I have a confession to make. I haven't told you the complete truth about one important fact. In my defence, I've been told not to do so initially and wait for a suitable moment later," she said.

"This is a dream and I'm not a Magi?" he suggested.

"Hmm, along the right lines, I think that you must have been picking up on some of my thoughts even though I guarded them. Take off your shoes and socks, Giles."

He did as ordered and splayed out his toes as Sandra had done. "Eight," he announced.

"Which is the missing one compared to a Homsap?" she

asked.

"The little one, I guess, the side one that gets tucked under a bit. Why?" he replied.

"Rub the side of my foot and then yours. I'm not being kinky," she grinned.

He did as told, starting with both of her feet. "Yours are perfectly smooth and one of my feet has a bump, like a bony lump under the skin." He rubbed his other foot to compare "But this one's smooth."

"Any ideas?" she asked. "Look more closely at the skin over the bump."

"Sounds stupid but it looks like a little scar. Not noticed that before," he answered and then the awful truth dawned on him.

"Someone's cut my toe off, haven't they, Sandra? Who am I really?" He looked worried.

Her reply hung in the air for a few seconds, "Some would say, the best of both worlds and possibly our future... Your father took a Homsap wife. Hardly anyone knew. As you asked before, sometimes the genes match and you were the product. Years ago, such a child would have been banished from the royal palace along with its mother. Not long after you were born, a sharp scalpel severed the fifth toe from your tiny foot and the doctor, and midwife sworn to secrecy. Your mother died when you were young and only your father plus a few close friends knew about your past. You had a minor dental operation, as a boy, to remove the extra developing tooth germs because Magi never have wisdom teeth. There you have it," she explained.

"Am I allowed to be the ruler? Me, a half cast?" he asked.

"That's a good question and it will be up to the Elders to decide. A couple of them were told by your father and sworn to secrecy until such time as you may make a claim. Hybrid is a better term or even Homo sapmag as your father used to say. In his later years, he spent a lot of time trying to get our race's heads out of the sand. We are dying out and the only option is a merger.

What better way, than to have a SapMag Ruler? We are a silent part and parcel of human history and surely that is better way than to just slowly disappear?" Sandra said, adding, "There could be a fight with the Elders…"

"So after fighting Eizus, we fight the Elders? Not cool. Do they have powers as well?" he asked.

"They are honourable men, a verbal fight. We will have to have a good argument ready. An advocate at Suzie's trial that I met, a friend of your father, did agree to act when the time came. Unusual dress sense but he is a good Magi who believes in integration. I hope he's still alive," she said, pulling a concerned face.

"Alright, I get it," said Giles "So we have to get to this place to make my claim at the Court of Elders or whatever you called it, get them to lower their ancient accepted standards, rubberstamp a SapMag race and somewhere along the way defeat the Wicked Witch of the East. No pressure then? I think I'm going to need two organised Sandras to help me on this one."

"I'll see what I can do," he said and winked. "You still haven't asked where the Magi hometown is, Giles."

"Well thinking back to that night with Snake, Magi Magic? Greek Cypriots? It has to be in Southern Cyprus, Sandra," he replied.

"Spot-on Giles, that's where we're going to be heading but we have to check out this place where the cats say that the Greek Cypriots go. We may get help or learn something useful," she said.

"At last some fun. A holiday in the sun, I think I've earned it," he laughed, "but maybe our battle's just beginning?"

Chapter 23

They decided to skip breakfast and headed into town. Their main delay had been tidying up the crumbs that Giles had left everywhere. The cascade definitely seemed to diminish and as Sandra put it, "Wahay…you're in the pink now, Giles," when she saw him coming out of the bathroom.

As they left the hotel, a couple of dragonflies fluttered in front of them and their wings twinkled in the sun.

"Aren't they pretty, Giles?" said Sandra.

"They're okay for bugs," he replied. "There were loads back home in Garton. It must be their mating season or something."

"I might have seen one but not a lot of them. Maybe they were following you around?" she suggested.

"You mean secretly filming me? Real bug bugs. I remember Beelzebub trying to swipe one in Suzie's kitchen. The thing landed on his tail, just after I spat, to make him stiff and ginger. It was almost as though it started the process of setting the biscuit stuff? Bit like a cat-catalyst, I suppose." Giles said.

"Bug bugs and cat cats. What's next, Giles?" she asked.

"What about spotty spots?" he suggested and bent down to pat the four-legged creature that had walked up to them.

The Dalmatian dog allowed himself to be stroked and sniffed Giles trousers. It then walked around to Sandra and rubbed his nose against her legs.

"Looks like he's lost," she said. "I can't see anyone around," and she too greeted the obedient pooch by rubbing its ear.

"He's probably escaped from one of the houses nearby. Better not fuss him too much or he'll be following us," he replied.

"Alright, Giles, shoo boy, go home," she shouted at the pooch.

The startled dog backed away and walked to the front of the next hotel where it sat on the steps.

"There we are, Giles. It probably lives there."

The animal sat still and watched them walk off in the other

direction.

"It looks just like the Dalmatian, back home, owned by that the old bloke in the next street," remarked Giles.

"You mean Dave? It's just a spotty dog. They're quite common, Giles."

"A bit like dragonflies..." and he pointed out one on a nearby wall. "Let's get going then."

They were both keen to see the Greek place that Beelzebub had discovered so they had picked up a basic town map from the hotel foyer.

With the help of the feline instructions; over those three roofs, along that gutter and under that fence etc. plus the quips of a few passers-by; "Can't stand all those olives," and "By Greek do you mean Turkish?" they eventually came to the front of a possible building.

The façade consisted of narrow columns supporting complicated horizontal beams. They were decorated with egg and dart mouldings. Vine leaves wrapped around the structure, which appeared to be plastic from a distance and even more plastic in close up.

Giles picked off an imitation leaf. "Perhaps they won't grow in our climate? Or maybe the Magi just like vinyl?"

"Don't be rude, Giles. If it makes money, then it's fine. It's obviously all closed up. I can't see any one inside. It says that it opens at twelve for lunch so we'd better come back then."

Giles looked up at the sign written in Greek-style English letters on the window; Orphanides Bistro and Greek Pub. "I thought bistro came from France and pub is English?" he asked.

"We're in Europe now. It's all interchangeable. You can have Polish cheddar and Swedish wine now," she answered.

Giles laughed. "Okay, I won't argue being as I'm only half human or something like that. Let's go for a walk around the shops and sit down for a coffee somewhere. You can carry on with my Magi education, if you like."

"So long as we keep a look out for anything suspicious, Eizus is bound to be looking for us. She may know about the Magi presence in Brighton. We don't know how well they hid themselves. Obviously most Greek or Cypriot places will have absolutely no links to the Magi, so hopefully she'll be looking at London first where there's a much larger community," said Sandra.

"Alright, let's head for this area where there's loads of antique shops," said Giles pointing at the map. "You always liked to rummage through those places. Give our minds a bit of a rest?" he suggested.

"Sometimes Giles, you are quite sensitive and clever" she said, then added "Most of the time though, you're a traftew."

He thought for a few seconds, put the back of his hand to his mouth then did a rasping impersonation of himself.

"You blow off like a true leader. Plenty of meaningless hot air," she said.

Giles and Sandra walked along several streets following the little map. They engaged in a bit of window shopping, going inside a few places but every time they emerged into the open, they looked around warily for any of Suzie's hench-creatures.

"I'm sure that security guard, over by the door, thinks we're shoplifters. He used his radio when we went into the second shop and now he's walked into this place. He keeps looking at me," said Giles. We must appear suspicious when we keep turning around. Can I plead Magi diplomatic immunity if the police pick me up?"

"If you travelled to North Wales… The Chief Constable there is one of us so please behave. The prisons of Brighton are not the place for a pretty boy like you. Maybe the guard just fancies you? He might want to handcuff you and show you his truncheon." She placed a stick of Brighton rock against her nether regions and did a thrusting action…

He laughed. "Think you'll have to buy that now," he paused,

"The tills over... Ow."

Sandra cracked him over the head and snapped the rock.

When they got to the till, the little old lady noticed the break and said that she'd get another for them. "No, no," said Giles "I know exactly where this one's been. A good lick and it'll be happy."

Sandra trod on his toe. "Forgive my boss; he always likes to give me something, when we go away on business together. I do enjoy a suck in the evening." And she gave an innocent smile to the woman.

"I've had a stick or two in my time, dear," said granny behind the till. "I don't like the hard ones that leave a salty taste in your mouth," and she pulled a face.

When they got outside, Giles asked if he heard correctly. "You did, Giles. She must be related to Nora," and she giggled. "Would you like to give the broken piece to your friend over there?" Sandra nodded her head to one side.

He looked over. The security guard watched him from the exit. Giles waved the rock at him. "Let's go before he asks for a civil partnership."

They found the street with the antique shops. "Mostly old junk," commented Giles after the first two. "Beats me how someone decides what's collectable or not."

After an hour of this, he felt bored. Sandra always enjoyed herself, chatting to shop owners, trying on old necklaces and discussing porcelain.

They found a place to sit down for a coffee. Sandra quietly told him a few more facts about Magi tradition and when the cups were empty asked him, "How about we split up for an hour and a half? I fancy looking at some clothes. If we're going to Cyprus, we'll need something thinner for the warmer weather. I'll meet you back at the bistro. I know you've been feigning interest. Just be careful, keep your eyes open and ring me if you see or sense anything odd."

Giles got up and didn't argue. "Okay dear. I'll easily find it. I'll just wander around in a big circle and end up in that general area. See you again in about ninety minutes. Don't buy too much stuff."

He paid the bill and walked off down the street. He'd decided that Brighton seemed quite a pretty place. The old buildings fitted in well with the modern cars even though some were well over a century old or two.

Twice he thought he saw a flash of a black and white dog at the end of the street and behind a car. The second time he crossed the road to look and found a sheepdog-cross weeing on the wheel of a posh white BMW series one sports car.

"Good boy," he said. "Now go do that Mini Cooper over there." He laughed as the dog walked over the road towards its next victim.

He had a good look at the items in a fishing tackle shop, an old-fashioned tobacconist and a music shop full of vinyl records. He looked at the many pictured sleeves and thought how small and insignificant CD covers looked. In fact nowadays, hundreds of tracks could be contained on a device a few inches big with only a title list. Hmm…progress?

A newsagent's window caught his attention. A book signing should take place later that afternoon. He wandered in and found the area where the little event would be. He leafed through the book, a first novel which is apparently taking the local area by storm. First stop Brighton, next stop Hollywood, he thought. Maybe someone would be interested in his experiences as a living, breathing, gingerbread man, he wondered? He looked at his watch. Better hurry up. Sandra's always on time. He looked again to see if the mole had reappeared by the strap and this is all a bad dream. No mole. Bistro it is then, he decided and hurried along.

The sun shone from well up in the sky now and he felt quite warm. He had his jacket over his shoulder and was quite looking forward to a cold pint at the Greek pub bar.

The blinds were open when he arrived there, a few minutes after twelve. He opened the old wooden door and a small bell dinged above him, as he went inside.

His eyes took a few seconds, to become accustomed to the difference from the bright sunlight outside. There were a few people around the wooden tables and he could see Sandra already sitting at the bar with a drink. She glanced at him then renewed her conversation with the barman. He noticed that she'd tied her hair back.

Giles walked up to the bar. A customer nodded at him as he went past and said, "Hello."

Giles replied "Hi, looks like a nice place. It's my first time here."

A waitress said "Can I get you a table, sir?"

He replied "Soon, I'll just have a drink at the bar first."

As he approached the counter at the back of the bistro, he could see that Sandra was dressed differently to before. Obviously she had been shopping because she was wearing leather trousers and a black sleeveless top. She looked like the girl in Tomb Raider, he thought. She perched on a bar stool and as he closed in, she shifted position slightly and leaned over to say something to the barman. As she did so, the arched angle of her back made her muscular buttocks stretch the soft leather of her trousers into a glorious peach shape.

This was more than he could resist, so he sat down on the stool to her left and grabbed her right bum cheek. Her flesh felt gorgeously firm through the pliant leather.

"I'll have whatever she's drinking," he said to the barman.

"That'll be a Magi Magic then, sir. Good choice," said the barman. She nodded and placed her right hand tightly over his.

"I am honoured by your greeting. I would not let any other man, sit with me like this," she said and half turned towards him.

"I like your new outfit and the way you've done your hair."

He couldn't get his hand back because of her grip so he gave her derriere another squeeze.

The barman plonked a Magi Magic in front of him, "Anything for your other lady friend?"

He looked down puzzled at her almost full drink and back up to the bartender.

"Having fun, Giles?" he heard.

"You spoke without moving your mouth. It didn't quite feel like how you sent your thoughts earlier, my darling," he replied to her.

She turned further around to look past his right shoulder, whilst he kept a firm grip on her posterior. "Long time, no see, Sandra," she said to a newly arrived customer, smiling broadly.

The new woman behind him surprisingly kissed Giles on his left cheek, before whispering in his ear, "Let go of her arse before I break your hand," in Sandra's voice…

He smartly turned to the kiss side, to see the old Sandra that he'd left shopping. A quick double-take to his right side produced the Tomb Raider Sandra, complete with his hand on her tight leather behind.

Someone else's large hand grabbed him by the right shoulder. "We don't want any trouble, sir."

Giles turned to see the security guard from the shops.

"I'm sorry. It must be mistaken identity. She put my hand there…well no, she kept it there," he stammered.

Raider Sandra said "Shall I break his arm?"

Shopper Sandra replied "Better not, he is your ruler, after all."

"Is my butt firmer than hers?" Raider Sandra asked Giles.

Shopper Sandra kissed Raider Sandra on the lips, giggled and then placed Giles' left hand on her own behind.

"Now, now girls, I take it that none of you want to make a complaint," said the guard releasing his grip.

"Well, Giles, who has the best bum?" asked Shopper Sandra, adding, "Me or my sis?"

The penny dropped, "Double shit. She's your twin..."

The whole bistro roared with laughter. Giles turned around and took a bow.

"You never told me," he complained.

Raider Sandra kissed him on his right cheek and said "I'm Xena. You have strong hands, Selig," and winked.

Giles realised that he had let go of Sandra but still held Xena's bum flesh.

"Oh no...sorry, erm...Xena," he stammered and released his grasp.

"And I'm Pinky," said the guard, holding out his hand. Giles shook it, expecting a light touch after hearing his name but he had a surprising firm grip. "My army comrades christened me that because my surname's Perkins," Pinky explained to Giles' confused face.

Xena had got up and embraced Sandra a few feet away, with her back to him. She looked a little shorter than Sandra with a slimmer more muscular build. She looked like she worked out regularly. He admired her tight trousers when Sandra spoke to him over her shoulder. "Just remember Xena can read what you're thinking as well."

"Thank you, Selig." Xena had turned around. "I am proud of my body and try to take care of it. I see that I will have to give Sandra some training. She is a little flabby." She grabbed Sandra's tummy and the two of them erupted into a fit of giggles.

"I'm sorry that I'm late, Giles, but I met someone on the way," said the real Sandra.

"Three more Magi Magic please," shouted a voice behind him that he recognised. He turned around and Snake stood there with his hand raised in anticipation. He gave him a high five.

"Are you a Magi as well, Snake?" Giles asked.

"Like you, Selig, half and half. My mother got sent here after my Magi father had been promoted to one of the pre-Elders. They're a group being groomed as possible future Elders. I left

Cyprus when I reached two years old. It wasn't deemed correct for an Elder to have Homsap offspring even though your father actively promoted the idea. There's a group of us here, keen to move things into the twenty first century and we're behind you all the way," said Snake. "I'm your computer guru."

"Similar story to mine," said Pinky, "sixteen when my mother told me. I had a hard time accepting it. I joined the army to get away but ended up being stationed in Cyprus where I'd spent some of my childhood. I rooted around and made a few Magi contacts and got told about this place so I came to Brighton after my tour. I'm not the cleverest of blokes but I'm strong and have army training to help your cause."

"Well I appreciate the help. You'll have to forgive my lack of leadership because the cause, as you call it, is very new to me and all a bit confusing. There are people appearing out of the woodwork who seem to know me and keep telling me that I'm their new ruler," Giles said.

"We must apologise for the secrecy. I'm sure that you appreciate most of it is necessary because of the unknown extent of Eizus' power," said an older-sounding man's voice from a doorway leading off behind the bar.

"And we're not all strangers, mate," came a familiar voice.

The two men emerged through a gap in a multi-coloured beaded curtain across the doorway.

Pete walked in and a strangely dressed old-fashioned man who looked familiar. Giles recognised him as the man he'd christened Tweedy from that odd day with Christina at the newsagents.

"Edgar," shouted Sandra and rushed over to him before flinging her arms around his neck. Pete came over to Giles, reached out and shook his hand.

"Bit of a mess that your girlfriend Suzie has got us all in," Pete said to Giles.

"So you're a Magi as well, Pete? How come Sandra didn't

know?" Giles asked.

"I'm no weirdo superhuman," he replied. "I'm just plain English."

"I wish this is really plain English. I'm glad to see you but what are you doing here, Pete?" inquired Giles.

"Well, the story is that I went out for a walk with my dog down the fields. We were sheltering from a sudden rain storm under some trees and had just emerged, when this Range Rover came haring across the fields. It just missed the dog. It stopped, I thought, maybe to apologise or something but instead two blokes dragged out Edgar here and Rula. They were both looking pretty battered and upset but the men drove away in the car and left them. I offered to take them back to my house to tidy up which they accepted. On the way back, we met Dave from the next street who thought he'd fallen over a stile and got covered in mud. He'd lost his dog. I got them into my car, dropped off Dave and brought Edgar and Rula back to my gaff. After a bit of a wash and a couple of whiskies, they started telling me a cock and bull story, I thought. He gave me his number and I dropped them off in the town, thinking that they were a pair of escaped loonies. I contacted him a short while later, when I saw a pretty little dark-haired lady open your front door with a bolt of lightning."

"Sounds like Suzie. Has a thing for the weather, it seems," said Giles.

"Edgar explained that I might be in danger, if Suzie got hold of me to ask questions about you and Sandra. He reckoned that she would be desperate to find you. We decided that it would be better if we stuck together, so I put the dog in the kennels and gave them a lift to Blighty. Edgar somehow guessed that you'd find this place, some kind of Magi homing instinct, maybe?" Pete explained. "By the way, I secured your front door before I left. It looked like Suzie had gone through a few drawers but no damage."

"Maybe she needed the address book? We don't know anyone

in Brighton, luckily," replied Giles.

Sandra and Tweedy had come over to him.

"This is Edgar," said Sandra and he shook hands with Giles.

"He's the old friend of my father that I told you about, an advocate who has practiced in both London and Nicosia. He saw Suzie's trial and will act for you in your leadership claim," she explained and the old man smiled.

"I think that I saw you in the newsagents recently, back home. Shouldn't I ask to see a list of his charges before I accept?" joked Giles.

They all laughed. Pete said, "You'll say yes when you see his assistant," and winked.

"Rula," shouted Pete towards the curtain. "Giles wants to meet you."

The beaded blinds were parted by the tips of a pair of hands, their fingernails resplendent in shiny chocolate-brown nail-polish. The brown arms were followed by a pair of pointy boobs in a close-fitting sleeveless top. Blonde hair in a long bob and matching blue eyes completed the vision.

"I'm coming," she said as she glided towards him.

Giles' alternative meaning of her first words, were compounded by her short black skirt and long brown legs.

"Guard your thoughts, Giles," warned Sandra.

Giles reached out and kissed the hand proffered to him.

"Rula McDonald at your service, sir, ten years' experience in litigation and business law," she said in a soft accent. Also adding, "I'm a full blood Magi and not married."

"Did she have to say the last bit?" asked Xena, as her and Sandra looked on enviously at her entrance.

"As is the Magi tradition, I am also known as Allure," said Rula. "I don't mind it either way."

"She's definitely on the case, isn't she, Giles?" said Pete's voice cutting into his dream.

"Oh... erm yes, no problem." Giles recovered. "What

happened to you in the field, Edgar?"

"An error of judgement, dear boy," answered Edgar.

"Typical men at work?" suggested Xena

Edgar explained. "We got wind of where Suzie lived from a team who had been searching for her since her escape."

"A male team," said Xena, "Bounty hunters."

"There is, as you say, a price on her head. A considerable sum and there were several people out there, looking for her. Somehow they tracked her down and subdued her. They then contacted me and I came to arrange her transfer and imprisonment. The meeting in the field should have been to prove that they held her and agree on terms of payment. They may also have passed her onto more sinister persons who could have used her or joined with her for their own ends. They surprised her in a supermarket car park and placed a device on her head to neutralise her telepathic skills," said Edgar.

"But they didn't tie her up very well and she got loose," said Rula.

"Typical men, half a job," added Xena who noticed Giles' puzzled look.

"Magi women make better police, security, prison guards etc. We have an attention to detail, sneakiness and are better planners. We may not be as strong as some males but we apply ourselves better. To think that a group of men could successfully hold Eizus as a prisoner for long is laughable," explained Xena.

"Anyway, she got loose, had the security device removed and ordered in the bad weather. I received the tail end of a lightning bolt that knocked me out. Edgar here also got splattered and she attempted to read his mind. Our two ex-military minders that we'd hired were useless and just wanted to get out of there. They dumped us at what they thought seemed a safe distance away from here and took the car. I woke up to see Pete's face. You weren't about to give me the kiss of life, were you, Pete?" said Rula.

"Wouldn't dream of it," Pete lied, with a straight face.

"I think that I heard about the supermarket kidnapping on the radio before I picked you up as a gingerbread man, Giles," said Sandra.

They all looked at Giles apart from Xena. "It's a long story. You'll have to wait for the book to come out on Kindle," said Giles, noting Xena's lack of interest.

"It said that one was dressed as an old soldier on horseback?" queried Sandra.

"Daehbonk," said Xena. "The US cavalry get-up is similar to the ceremonial uniform of the Women Magi Security from over a century ago. They dressed up to prove a point and failed… "

'I've had little dreams or visions of similar women on horseback," said Giles.

"Really…" said Edgar, "Probably just some telepathic neural feedback from my pets."

"In English, please," said Giles.

"Haven't you seen Eddy's dragonflies flitting about? He can watch you with them," translated Pete.

"I knew you were an amateur entomologist years ago and very interested in how I could communicate with cats. You obviously managed to do that with insects," said Sandra.

"Only with the aid of modern electronics and the mobile phone network, Ardnax, I worked with some engineers to link in with their limited thought patterns and amplify them, over long distances," Edgar explained.

"It's really easy to use. Just put on the headphones and close your eyes," said Xena.

"You must have been seeing the lady cavalry when Xena watched you. As I said, feedback over the mobile signal; a conversation can work both ways," said Edgar. "I thought it undetectable by Magi but obviously the system still needs work."

"That means that you probably saw me being made into a

gingerbread man by Suzie," said Giles to Xena, "because you were that dragonfly," said Giles, "and you knew where her house was."

"I missed the first bit but saw Eizus pointing her finger at you and guessed she directed energy in your direction to cook the ginger transformation. I saw you later stuck to the floor and when you spat ginger at the cat, I landed on it to see if the transmitter energy could do the same thing and it did. You ended up with a stiff cat instead of a sticky one," said Xena.

"We were watching the house but wasn't sure that Eizus was Suzie until too late, I'm sorry," said Edgar.

"The cat's name is Beelzebub and he's on our side now. How come he recovered from his gingerness in a few hours in the back of the car and Giles took days?" Sandra asked.

"One cooked by an expert and one partly done by a man. A ginger one at that," explained Rula and they all laughed.

"The management have prepared some food. Let's eat and relax for an hour and plan our trip to Cyprus later," said Edgar as Snake and a waiter started bringing plates to the tables.

Chapter 24

The meal consisted of a variety of cold meats, olives and salad. Accompanying it were many bottles of Keo, one of the famous Cypriot beers.

"Do Magi eat the same kind of food as us humans?" Pete asked Xena over their wooden table. The food had been spread out over three tables and everyone sat down, in no particular order.

Xena laughed "We're all humans. I'm no biologist but I think that our insides work in a very similar way. I suppose the Magi in China eat Chinese food and those in Mexico eat Mexican."

"I can see we eat in the same way because you have cream cheese all over your cheek just like a human would do," and after she failed to find it, Pete leaned over with a napkin to complete the task.

"I think my twin just blushed," said Sandra from the next table.

A well-aimed olive hit her square on the forehead with a flick of Xena's fork.

"Don't listen to her, girl. I haven't listened for years," laughed Giles.

"I think food is the answer to all the world's problems," said Edgar demolishing a huge plateful of meat and pickle. "Pass me some of that bread, Pete and fetch some more beers, Snake." Giles looked at him. The rotund tweed man seemed to be getting bigger by the second.

Edgar read his mind. "When you are in court, Selig, it pays dividends to have a large presence; Intimidates the opposition, as it were. No judge listens to a skinny lawyer."

"They seem to listen to me," beamed Rula sitting opposite Giles.

"You're a special case Allure, you wear a short skirt," shouted Edgar over the rising volume of the conversation and they all laughed.

"Hey look, guys," said Snake. "Rula and Ruler sitting together, it's like being at school. What's that word for two things that sound the same with different meanings?"

"Twat," shouted Pete and the hilarity continued to much scoffing and drinking.

"If this is what it's like to be a ruler, then I'm all for it," said Giles as Sandra came over and sat on his lap to reach the last black olives on the table.

"Better not get carried away yet with too much debauchery. We have to plan our escape," said Sandra.

The American couple who had taken a table by the window for lunch couldn't make head or tail of the conversation. "Crazy Limeys," the man said to his partner as they went outside having finished their food. Edgar beckoned to the waiter who started clearing the tables. The barman went over to the door to pull the blind down and lock it.

"Right, get the computer out, Snake, and let's look at some flight times," said Edgar.

"Surely there's a risk that Eizus will be able to track us with some of his crows or other birds? There are probably not many airports that fly from the UK to Cyprus. She could bring the plane down by a bird strike to an engine on take-off or bad weather over southern England," said Giles.

"We're aware of that. Her power and reach seem to be increasing. That is why we have decided that you will be travel by boat to the continent. From there you will fly by plane to Cyprus," replied Edgar. "I have devised a plan to move you so that even if her aerial spies found you now, they wouldn't be able to track you."

"We think that once you are in France that you will be safe to travel without being spotted. That won't help you at the other end in Cyprus though, because she will have already guessed that you are heading there. She will undoubtedly be going there as well, to make her leadership claim but chasing after your shadow here, will slow her down and hopefully give you an extra day or two in Cyprus to make contact with the Elders," said Xena.

"I agree with my sister," said Sandra. "The sooner we get there and make our case, the better. There were people who didn't like your father and would be happy if you never returned. If Suzie gets there first, they may drum up some support for her. Guess that's the first time I've agreed with sis for twenty years."

Xena laughed. "We used to fight so much but today we stand together. Sisters rock," and she and Sandra engaged in a high five.

"Wouldn't want to take you two on, that's for sure," said Pinky looking at the two defiant women still clasping one another's hand in the air.

"I dunno about that," said Pete admiring Xena's strong buttocks in her tight leather trousers.

Within seconds he'd been pinned to the wall by the neck and Xena pointed a pencil straight at his left eyeball.

"What were you thinking about my bottom, Homsap?" she shouted.

Pete's tongue wouldn't move. His body scared rigid and he turned cross-eyed looking at the pencil.

Xena dropped the pencil and with her free hand grabbed his privates. His eyes bulged.

"This is how Magi warrior women agree to make love. Prove yourself in battle, Etep and I will be yours," and she put him down.

Edgar and Sandra were laughing. She said, "I think sis fancies you, Pete."

"She is a fine woman and has already given you a Magi name, as is the tradition prior to marriage," explained Pinky.

"Marry her? I only looked at her arse," he replied.

"Could do worse," replied Giles smiling at the two girls.

"Is it legal for twins to do what he's thinking?" said Xena looking at Sandra.

"Don't know sis but knowing Giles, if he becomes king, he'd make it part of the coronation ceremony," laughed Sandra.

Xena picked up the pencil and pointed it in turn at Giles and Pete. "No trouble from both of you until this is over. My ass is out of bounds, got it?" she said and everyone laughed.

"Don't bother putting your hands over your eyes because she can still read you through your fingers" added Sandra to the self-blinkered Pete.

"What did you mean Xena, by chasing after my shadow?" Giles asked.

"We have arranged for the barman here, to act as a body double. He is about your size and will wear your clothes to travel in a different direction. I will accompany him dressed as Sandra," she replied.

"He might get caught or killed. That's a pretty dangerous job being Giles' double," said Pete.

"I will protect him for two days. By then Eizus will have guessed our ruse. I will then return to Cyprus to protect you, Etep," and she smiled at him.

"She's got the hots for you, mate, any chance that you could protect me a bit as well?" Giles asked.

"Of course, I will, Selig," winking at him, "it will be an honour."

"There are seats from Paris, the day after tomorrow to Larnaca. Paphos is nearer but there are no seats available for a week," said Snake looking up from his computer.

"Alright then, we have to get busy" said Edgar. "If you two change into some other clothes that we have upstairs, the doubles can then go back to the hotel and sort out the bills and your stuff."

"What about Beelzebub the cat?" asked Giles.

"He'll probably be back in the room when they get back. Xena will be able to communicate with him like I do. He'll have to come and live at the bistro for a bit. He'll be fine," replied Sandra. Giles and Sandra went up to a room upstairs and found a pile of brand new clothes still with labels attached lying on the bed.

Giles picked up a shirt. "Cool and it's my size as well."

"Someone's been doing some clever shopping. It doesn't seem to be Xena's style. Probably Rula," she replied and picked out some outfits for herself and Giles.

Suitably attired, they went back downstairs. Giles felt like he'd attended a fashion show. Worse to come, Rula waited downstairs with a wig for him and a stick on moustache. He reluctantly put them on and walked over to a mirror behind the bar.

"I look like an extra from a nineteen seventies American TV series," Giles said.

"You look lovely," said Sandra, having her hair made into a little bun by Rula. She never wore that style and it made a big difference to her appearance.

"No moustache for you then, Sandra?" said a familiar woman's voice from behind him.

Giles turned around to look and saw Giles and Sandra looking back at him.

The Sandra copy really looked good. The Giles appeared passable.

"You've even cut his hair off," said Giles laughing "and Xena has done her hair like Sandra's, very good."

"I only shaved his head" said XenaSandra. "He didn't want me to go any further."

BarmanGiles looked a little embarrassed as XenaSandra rubbed his bald bonce.

"Give them the keys to your hotel, car and house. They can be off now and we'll wait a couple of hours until you two leave," ordered Edgar and they went through their pockets looking for the items.

"I'll just check that the coast is clear," said Snake unlocking the door and peering outside.

"No one around, apart from some seagulls and a dog," he reported back.

"What kind of dog?" asked Sandra suspiciously and looked at Giles.

"Dalmatian," said Snake.

"Must have followed us," said Giles. He turned to Pete. "You said Dave lost his dog in the field where Suzie got away. She likes black and white things."

Snake peeped out of the door. "It's still there, sitting over the road."

Pete looked out. "I'm good at dogs and that one looks a dead ringer for Dave's Spot. Shall I call it?"

"Shout out a few other names first," said Edgar.

"Tyson!" Giles smiled.

"Dog!"

"Imaginative," whispered Sandra.

"Ben!"

"Pooch!" Giles desperately tried not to laugh.

"Spot!"

The dog stood up and looked around then sat back down.

"It could be," said Edgar having a look. "Anyway, if it's a Suzie spy we could use it to our advantage. Go back to their hotel, Xena and see if it follows you. Don't interfere with it. Just get yourself sorted there and drive back to Giles' house. Leave the car there and come back in a hire car as we agreed."

Xena and BarmanGiles walked out of the door and went arm in arm down the street. As predicted the dog got up and came over to the pavement near the bistro. It sniffed at the ground and then trotted off after the pair.

"Hope they're okay," said Rula watching the dog go around

the corner out of sight.

"Xena will look after him. She'll be good at this kind of thing," reassured Sandra. "Tell us how we're getting to Paris then, Edgar."

"There's a friend of mine who has a small fishing vessel down at the harbour. He's done a few jobs before for me. For the right fee, he'll get you over the Channel safely and drop you off near Calais. You'll be able to get a hire car there and get to the airport," said Edgar.

"My French isn't up to much," said Giles.

"Or mine," added Sandra.

"Don't worry. Snake and I will accompany you to the airport. I will deal with any language and paperwork plus pay the bills. Snake can do the driving so that you two can get some rest. We'll be travelling during the night," said Rula.

"What happens in Cyprus?" asked Giles.

"You'll be put up in a safe Magi house and wait for the rest of us to travel there. It'll be dependent on when we can get flights," said Edgar.

"When you say 'the rest of us', who do you mean?" queried Giles.

"Well, there'll be you and Sandra, Rula and myself, Zena, Snake, Pete and Pinky," Edgar replied.

"Eight of us then," said Pete "and you've got a bald head."

"Yul Brynner and the Magnificent Eight go to Cyprus. Cool!" shouted Snake and gave Giles a high five.

They all laughed especially when Sandra added, "More like Little Britain on tour."

Chapter 25

A few hours later, Edgar received a phone call from Xena.

They had reached Giles' house with no real problems. The Dalmatian had followed them back to the hotel, waited for them to check out and then trailed them to the car park. Just as they were leaving in their hatchback, a slim woman with dark hair came running around the corner and the dog went to her. They didn't wait around to see who it might be.

"What about Beelzebub?" asked Giles, when she'd had finished her report.

"Oh, she said that the cat had been told to wait and watch as they left and that someone would pick him up from the car park" said Edgar. "Pinky, will you go and get him quickly so that Sandra can talk to him before they go?"

"Okay, and the name again, Bezzyzel?" he asked.

"Just shout Bez. He'll come," said Sandra.

"No problem," and Pinky hurried out of the door.

"That probably means that Eizus knows about this place now. Maybe she'll come here," said Giles with a worried look on his face.

"I would hope that our doubles tricked her and that she is on her way back to your house. The scent of your clothes would have fooled the dog and I think Eizus would trust Spot's nose. Keep an eye open outside, Snake and when Pinky gets back, set up a guard rota," ordered Edgar. "Pete, you stay close to Sandra and Giles inside."

"More likely that I'll be looking after the menfolk," said Sandra laughing.

"Put the kettle on and let's have a cuppa while we wait for Pinky. He should only be five minutes," said Giles.

They all sat down slightly nervously with cups of tea and coffee, apart from Snake who watched the street outside from the partly open door. They all looked up twice when he started to speak until they realised that it's only potential customers, asking when the bistro would be open. Private party he told the first one and run out of olives to the second man.

"What's he going to tell the next one? A secret witches' coven?" whispered Pete as the second man went away.

They didn't find out because Pinky came in straight away, cradling Beelzebub in his arms.

"What a friendly kitty," said the big man as he gently lowered the cat to the floor.

Sandra had sat down on a wooden chair. She opened her arms towards the cat. It ran over and jumped on her lap. She put her hands on the feline's head and everyone went quiet and watched her. Her eyes were closed and the cat sat very still. When Sandra frowned, Pete looked at Giles and pulled a questioning face. Giles shrugged.

Sandra let go after a couple of minutes. The cat meowed and jumped down.

"He's starving. Will someone get him some food?" asked Sandra.

"We sent the staff home earlier but I'll knock up something for him. Won't be long" replied Rula as she went into the kitchen. Beelzebub seemed to understand and followed her.

"I think he'll like living here with all this food" said Sandra smiling.

"Any good news?" asked an impatient Giles.

"Good and bad, I think. Suzie is unlikely to be coming here but is probably chasing after Xena this very moment. Beelzebub said that Xena communicated with him. He told her that after we left the hotel this morning, a man looked at our car and attached something underneath. Bez walked underneath and saw a small black box. Xena told him to keep an eye open, so as they left he climbed over the roofs to watch the car park. He saw Xena just look underneath but not remove anything. The spotty dog watched them and Suzie turned up just as they were leaving. She saw them go in their hatchback. Beelzebub followed Suzie and the dog to another car, a couple of blocks away. Suzie got a grey box out of the boot and attached it to what Beelzebub calls the clever, folding, black picture box. I guess that's cat-speak for a laptop. She got in and a man drove off after a couple of minutes in the same direction as Xena," Sandra said.

"Could be a bomb but Xena wouldn't have left it?" suggested a worried Pete.

"Exactly, Suzie's abandoned all her clever matter manipulation skills for a simple vehicle tracker," replied Sandra.

"She can't be far behind Xena if she left straight away. Rula, better give her a ring to let her know that she may have company soon," said Edgar.

"Xena can be a bit headstrong at times. I hope that she doesn't have a go at trapping Suzie on her own," said Sandra.

"Not after she heard about us in that field," replied Edgar. "She's under strict instructions to just be a decoy and if life gets too hot to disappear. The barman Giles just needs a change of clothes and he has a wig in his pocket. Xena will have to use her wits if cornered. She's good. Don't worry."

Rula came back into the room. "I've told her. She realised about the tracker. They've decided to go on a trip to London straight away and leave some clues to their destination in the car that they'll leave unlocked. That should keep Eizus busy for a day at least."

"Good work. Well, my friend with the boat is moored up, and the tide will be suitable to leave at seven pm. Get your things, you two. Snake will drive you over. Pinky, have another walk around the block to make sure no person, or animal even, is watching this place," ordered Edgar.

By the time they had put on their new clothes and some food in some bags, Snake had a car waiting around the front of the bistro. Edgar ran through a checklist of things with them. Sandra had been carrying their passports in her handbag, since they had left the house. Rula gave them several hundred Euros each and computer printed details of their airline tickets. She also produced two toothbrushes and a mini tube of toothpaste which Sandra popped into handbag.

Rula carried two big bags and squeezed through the door. Snake got out of the car to help. "This is our stuff," she explained.

"Cool," said Snake "I thought that I'd have no clothes," and he laughed. "I'll get the laptop and power cord. Have we got a French adaptor?"

"In the side of the brown case," replied Rula pointing. "Put your bags in, Giles."

Giles did as instructed, then after a few goodbyes and good lucks, the car drove off with Sandra and Giles in the back, Rula and Snake in the front.

A fifteen-minute drive took them to a small quay. Snake parked the car and they grabbed their stuff and followed him to small open speedboat tied to the side.

"This is Andre," said Snake.

"Hi," said Giles. We're not going over the channel in this little thing are we?"

"I will be taking you to my skipper's boat just off shore," laughed Andre. "The sea is a little choppy tonight so I hope the ride is not too bumpy." He climbed onto the quay and loosened the ropes holding the boat to the side and with Snake steadying the boat, he jumped in. The engine started at the first turn of the key and with a few blips of the throttle and turns of the wheel, the little craft left the safety of the small harbour and headed out into the open sea. Andre opened the throttle and the boat rapidly accelerated, skimming the tops of the waves but occasionally dropping into a trough which made Giles cling on very tightly to the chrome handrail.

"Yee haa!" shouted Sandra standing up behind Andre at the

wheel, holding on to his shoulders. "How fast will she go?"

Andre pulled the lever further back and the engine revs behind Giles, rose to a point where he could hardly think. The boat went even faster and crashed up and down even more.

"Go man!" shouted Snake and stood up behind Sandra, his hair streaming in the breeze.

Giles looked towards the stern of the boat and could see a large V-shaped, white-edged furrow growing in the ocean behind them. The wind whipped into his face with occasion splats of salty seawater leaving a taste on his lips.

Rula had just slumped down in the bottom of the hull with her hands over her eyes and kept very quiet.

It began to get dark and Giles noticed some lights not far away. He quickly made out the shape of a boat, which rapidly grew into a small trawler. Andre slowed the boat down and pulled alongside. A rope dropped down unexpectedly into Giles' lap. "Tie it up, man," shouted a deep voice from above.

Giles found some metal hooks on the top edge of the boat, wrapped the rope in and out of them and knotted it off. "Is that alright?" he shouted to Andre.

"It will do. I will change your knots later. You are no sailor, *Monsieur*," he replied and grabbed a small rope ladder that had been dropped down. "Be careful climbing up. Only move one hand or foot at a time. I will bring the bags up last."

Giles liked the last bit about the luggage. The two craft were moving independently of one another. One moment they were both going up and down together, the next in opposite directions. It had the effect of making the short rope ladder either rigid or very floppy.

Sandra scrambled up like a mountain goat. "Easy," she shouted down to them.

Rula looked as green as a frog. She managed the first two rungs and Andre had to climb up behind her, pushing up with one hand on her derriere. He came back down and wiggled his fingers in front of the two remaining men. "Very soft," he smiled.

They laughed. "Here goes," said Giles.

As he expected, he missed his footing several times and at one point almost had his leg through two rungs of the ladder. Sandra grabbed him by the shoulders and dragged him over the side from the last step and he ended up in a bundle on the floor.

"I thought you were looking after me," he said, trying to stand up.

"You're doing fine, Giles. I will take Rula into the cabin because she's not feeling well. You help get the luggage," she replied.

Snake leapt over with the first bag and leant over the side as Andre passed them up one by one. He gave them to Giles and straight afterwards he heard the speedboat start up again.

"Is he going?" asked Giles.

"No, he's tying it up to this boat in a better position, to tow it with us. We'll need it the other side to land in France," he explained. "You go inside, I'll help here."

"Okay," said Giles, glad to get away from the sight of the waves. As Andre said earlier, he's no sailor and although he wasn't feeling ill, he didn't feel like eating anything for a long time, just in case.

He went inside. "Is this the cabin or the wheelhouse?" He asked as he entered.

"*C'est centre de mission*...mission control to you English. I'm Marcel, the captain," said a bearded man with a French accent. He held out a grubby hand which Giles grasped. You will be on French soil within two hours, *mes amies*."

"Can't be soon enough," said Rula, sitting in the corner holding her tummy.

Andre came in. "All secure skipper, shall I weigh anchor?"

"Yes, let's go." He turned to Giles. "We will be crossing the tanker lanes in the channel so we have to be on the look-out. Please do not disturb the crew."

Giles didn't know how many men were on the boat. He'd noticed two others apart from Marcel and Andre.

The diesel engine clonked into life and he could hear the rattling of a chain which he assumed to be the anchor being raised. He noticed the ship started to turn to the right, no…to starboard, he corrected himself and the ship started its short journey across the channel.

It soon started to get really dark as he leant on the rusty safety rail outside and looked into the twilight. There were a few stars twinkling in the sky. He wondered to himself, how on earth would he achieve his next goal? To become ruler of a tribe that he hadn't even heard of a few days ago.

Sandra came out and joined him. She put her arm around him. "Poor Rula's regretting volunteering for this. She says she's taking a plane back. Snake loves it; he was watching the engineer tinkering with the engine. What are you thinking about? You've been staring at the horizon for a few minutes."

"Looking at the stars actually, Sandra, if you look over there, just above the horizon, you can see a moving light, probably on an aircraft."

She peered into the sky. "I can see it. Aircraft landing lights usually flash, I think. That one's steady, just like a star. Maybe it's a shooting star?"

"Far too slow, they pass quickly and this one's almost going sideways," he replied.

"Only one answer then," she said. "We are Magi following a wandering star." She leant over and kissed him on the cheek. "We must keep following it to find our new saviour," and she put her arm around him. "Whatever the cost," she added.

"I just don't know what to do," he admitted.

"It's your destiny, Giles. We are with you to help. You survived being a gingerbread man didn't you? You have hidden strengths."

"Why doesn't more of my Magi past returning to me, Sandra?

It's like I don't want to remember but just stay being retired Giles."

"I don't know. Maybe the hypnotism went too deep? Can I see lights over there apart from the flashing lighthouse?" she said.

"Yes, you can. It's France. They must be some streetlights or something. Better tell Rula. She'll be pleased," and he watched Sandra go back inside leaving him alone with his thoughts.

The moon had risen now. The reflection sparkled on the sea and contrasted with the yellow lamps of the land on the horizon. The moonlight scattered from the crests of the waves, fitting in perfectly with the knocking soundtrack of the throbbing engine. The combined smell of fish mixed with diesel filled his nostrils. He tasted the salt on his lips and rubbed his hand along the rusty rail to complete the sensory feast. He closed his eyes for a minute to relax and enjoy the moment.

The dream shattered when someone pushed past him. "Look out," shouted a woman's voice.

He opened his eyes startled.

"Bleuggh!"

Rula threw up over the side.

"Why did I agree to this?" she gasped and took the tissue that Giles offered her. "Thanks, feeling a bit better now. Oh, I can see the lights of France over there. Is that Calais? Hope so."

"They are. It won't be long before we can take the speedboat," said Andre, joining them on deck.

"Oh good, my second favourite after this boat," lied Rula. "Well at least it doesn't stink of fish. Couldn't you have sprayed some air freshener over this trawler before we got on?"

The two men looked at one another.

"Les femmes," said Andre and laughed.

"Keep your hands off my bum as well, when I get into the boat, please. I will smell of fish," she said.

They both looked at her lower half.

"I can read your minds. That's disgusting," and she stomped

off inside, with her nose in the air to their renewed laughter.

Three quarters of an hour later, with the land looming a few hundred yards away, they found themselves clambering down into the repositioned speed boat. Marcel tossed the bags down to Andre who skilfully caught each one with no drama. Giles had visions each time, of one going overboard but minutes later, the little fully loaded boat zoomed off towards the coast. It still remained quite dark and Giles wondered how Andre knew the way.

"Must be difficult doing this in the dark, Andre?" he asked.

"*Non monsieur*, I have carried goods many time along this path in the moonlight. I have friends in the coastguard who turn a blind eye in exchange for some Scotch," he answered.

"Aren't we illegal immigrants?" Sandra asked.

"Technically not, we all have European Union passports and may travel freely. We're just not going through the correct gate. A mere oversight," said Rula, and they all laughed.

They got to within a hundred yards of a rocky beach and Snake asked "Are we going to have to wade ashore?"

"No worries, *mes amies*. Be patient," replied Andre slowing down the boat to a crawl. He turned the boat carefully around a fearsome looking rock and a small wooden jetty appeared. He blipped the throttle and moved alongside as Snake climbed out with a rope and tied up.

"There is a step path cut into the stones at the end of the jetty. Climb to the top. It leads to a small field. Cross diagonally and you will come to a road by the field gate. Take a left and the town is half a kilometre. Bon voyage," instructed Andre.

Sandra gave him a hug. "Thank you."

Snake shouted from the jetty, "Cheers, mate."

Rula looked back after alighting from the boat. "Forgive me if I don't recommend this voyage or your vessel on Trip Advisor.com due to extreme fishiness. However you have done a fine job and hopefully we will never meet again."

Andre answered, "My pleasure, madam, and good luck to you, Giles, with your quest. *Bon voyage*"

"Cheers, Andre. Say thanks to your skipper for aiding and abetting us. Goodbye," replied Giles.

Snake tossed the line back and Andre reversed the boat back out of sight with a final cheery wave.

"Okay chaps. We've landed safely. Now we march on the enemy," said Snake in a posh officer's voice.

"I'd rather drive," said Rula struggling to get the strap of a large hold-all over her shoulder.

"Don't be a wimp," replied Sandra. "Let's get going." She led the invasion team over the field, followed by Snake and Giles with Rula lagging at the rear. They waited for her to catch up at the field gate. Giles looked across the road as they stood there. "Look, that sign says Calais. We're on the outskirts."

"Excellent. It shouldn't take long for us to walk in but it's still early morning and there's not much chance of anywhere being open, to hire us a car," said Sandra.

"There's a bus stop over there with some long seats. Let's wait there for a bit. Maybe get some sleep," suggested Snake.

They wandered over and Rula slumped on a seat. "Funny place for a big bus stop," she said.

"Looks like that field over there, with the empty buildings got used for something recently. Didn't the French used to have loads of illegals camping near some ports trying to get into Britain?" asked Giles.

"Quite appropriate then," said Rula having extricated herself from the large bag and then lying down. "I will sleep first," she said.

"You try as well because you're driving, Snake," ordered Sandra and he clambered onto the other bench with a "Yes miss."

"We'll keep a look out then," said Giles to Sandra who nodded in agreement.

Rula had started snoring already.

A dog wolf howled in the distance.

"Bloody hell, let's get on the coach" said Giles being reminded of a trip that seemed years ago.

"Ha ha, might be a long night," replied Sandra.

Chapter 26

Sandra woke the sleeping beauties just at dawn. The sky commenced to redden on the Eastern side as the Lady Dawn awoke from her deeper slumber. Snake stood and had a long stretch. Rula said, "That's the most uncomfortable bench that I've slept on in my life," and couldn't work out at first why everyone laughed. "I don't usually stay out all night," she explained.

"We've got to get into town now and find transport," said Sandra. "Take some stuff out of your bag, Rula, and put it into Snake's because you were struggling a bit carrying it."

She unzipped her bag and started handing tins of hairspray, shampoo, conditioner, fake tan, mouthwash etc. to Snake.

After the first two, Snake looked at Giles and started chucking them over his head into the field behind and she didn't notice whilst rummaging.

"That's all the heavy stuff. Thanks, Snake. I probably didn't need to bring most of them, anyway. I hope your bag's not too heavy now," she said.

"I can hardly feel the difference," he said truthfully, lifting it up by the straps. "Let's hope that you don't need much of it on the way back because it might be difficult to get out."

Rula gave him a puzzled look and then turned to Sandra "Wouldn't it be wonderful if we could find a *'petite boulangerie'*, selling fresh croissants for breakfast?"

"We'll see. We might just have to find a shop for food," replied Sandra.

It turned lighter quickly now and after a few minutes of walking, a few houses came into view. Nothing of interest though, until, "Look over there, a bakery," shouted an excited Rula. Hold my bag, Snake," and she ran on ahead a couple of hundred yards. By the time they had got to the shop, she was emerging with their breakfast and handing out the tasty curved sweet horns that she had craved earlier. "They're making us some coffee as well. It'll be three minutes."

"Can I have cocoa?" asked Sandra. Rula rushed back into the shop and re-emerged quickly with some butter sachets and a knife. "They are doing you a hot chocolate, Sandra. Isn't this good?"

"Pretty cool, considering it's not seven am yet," said Snake.

Suitably fed and watered, they resumed their walk. The baker had said there were two places that hired cars to tourists, and they found the first one still closed but the second one just opening up. They piled in and Rula started speaking quickly in French and filled in a few forms. The owner asked Snake for his driving licence and passport, passed him some papers and told him to sign. Ten minutes later, they were sitting in an almost new red Renault hatchback.

She unfolded a map that came with the car. "Listen, Snake, turn left out of here onto the main road and along to the next roundabout. Keep your eyes open for signs to Paris. We don't need to go deeper into Calais."

Snake did as instructed. Giles marvelled at how quickly he became accustomed to driving on the 'wrong' side of the road. "Are you used to driving in France, Snake? I hate it," said Giles.

"Never driven on the wrong side of the road before, in my life," Snake replied as he nipped out and overtook a dawdling lorry. "Played loads of rally computer games where the driver's in the left seat though," as he sped past a Citroen and through a light on red. Giles frowned and gripped the sides of his seat a little tighter.

"Plenty of time to get to the airport," said Rula, reaching over to grab his hand on the gear lever, to try and make him slow down.

"Sorry guys," came back the reply. "Just keen to get the job done," he replied.

"Well, so am I. We can do some shopping afterwards. I think we'll spend the night here in Paris, Snake. Separate beds of course" said Rula.

"And I'd highly recommend that you used the French hotel free shampoo and soap. Much better than the stuff you buy in British bottles," said Giles from the back seat.

"Much better," repeated Snake looking at Giles in the rearview mirror.

"Do you really think so? I can't wait to try them then," replied Rula.

"Giles and Sandra, you may as well try to get some sleep now," said Snake.

"Yeah, I'm pretty tired at the moment," replied Sandra.

"Ditto," agreed Giles and leant his head back on the headrest. Sandra snuggled up to him. He dreamt of dragons breathing fire and boys turning into kings. Going fishing with his father and being watched by sinister-looking crows.

They were woken a couple of hours later.

"Anyone know any good lady psychologists? I have to get my dreams analysed sooner rather than later. They're getting crazier than the ones Suzie gave me," asked Giles.

"It might be your Magi self, fighting the deep hypnosis," said Rula. "I've been to a Magi woman in Hove."

"If she's blonde like you, I'll go as well," added Snake.

"I can't help being blonde and intelligent. Women like me are special. Did I tell you that I'm not married, Giles?" she replied.

Sandra nudged Giles and smiled.

"I can't tell what these French airport signs mean. Talk to me Rula, babe," said Snake.

"Charles de Gaulle airport is straight ahead. Now take that left. This road is going to the drop off point." Rula turned around. Forgive us if we do not wait, I have shopping on my mind. I want to stand on the steps of the Sacre Coeur in Montmartre and look at the Eiffel tower."

"That's no problem, Rula. We're really grateful to you and Snake for getting us here," thanked Giles.

Sandra checked that she still had the printed airline tickets, money and passports in her bag. All looked okay and Snake pulled into an empty space in the drop off lane, directly under the gaze of an armed police officer. The black uniformed man just looked them up and down as Giles said a cheery "Bonjour," and didn't answer back.

"Doesn't know royalty when he sees it," Snake said to Giles as he popped his head back in the car to say goodbye. "See you soon, man" and held his hand out of the window for a high five.

"Bye," shouted Rula as the guard looked on disapprovingly.

"Definitely not as friendly as Pinky," said Sandra as they went through the sliding doors into the foyer of the departure area.

The scene inside the room resembled organised chaos. The Spanish air-traffic controllers had gone on strike leading to long delays for some planes and a build-up of passengers waiting to board. Every available seat had been taken and many people sitting on their cases or even on the floor.

"Let's hope our flight is on time," said Sandra after finding out the reason for so many people. "We're going in the opposite direction and if we're lucky our plane will have come straight from Cyprus and just need refuelling."

Their check in desk lit up shortly afterwards and they were able to rid themselves of the holdalls. They walked into the departure lounge with its maze of shops and Giles managed to find two seats to sit down on.

"You keep mine warm and I'm going to look in the bag shops. Won't be long," said Sandra wandering off, leaving Giles to look at the newspaper that he'd just bought.

He turned a few pages of the tabloid and an article about his local area drew his attention. The headline read 'Dawn Raid on Fort Tesco' and described a student stunt where cavalrymen kidnapped Lady Godiva from inside the supermarket. A police spokesman said that no one got hurt or actually seemed to be missing and that the whole thing wasted expensive police time.

The student union spokesperson denied any involvement. The article went on to say that several students dressed as gingerbread men had been scaring local residents during the rag parade. A little girl had reported that "one biscuit man let my rabbit loose by opening the gate. I think that he should be made to clean the cage out for a month." The paper had provided a new white rabbit and offered one thousand pounds for the identity of any of the gingerbread students.

Giles pointed out the article to Sandra when she came back.

"Cool. You have a price on your head now, Giles," she said. "You'd better watch these police guards with the guns here. I bet you're on their wanted list," and they both laughed.

Giles then took a stroll around the shops. He had no intention of buying anything until he saw a T-shirt shop. He purchased two of them and then decided to get two sun hats as well. It had to be hot whilst they were in Cyprus and he couldn't remember seeing any in the clothes that they packed. They might not have a camera, he thought, but after looking at the bewildering, complicated shelves of image capturing equipment on display, he decided it would be better to ask Sandra's opinion first. There were also packets of some of his favourite sweets in the newsagents so he stocked up on jelly babies and bonbons. Happy with his little shopping spree, he walked back to Sandra to report the camera shop situation.

He needn't have bothered. As he approached, Sandra said, "I saw you looking in the camera shop. I have one fully powered up in my handbag and the charger is in the luggage."

"I knew that," he lied. "I just wondered if the time had arrived to upgrade."

Before she could answer, he said "Got you a present" and passed her a bag.

She opened it to reveal a black, women's T-shirt with the words 'Security' on the back and 'Woman' on the front.

"Very good, Giles, and what does yours say?" she asked,

"Daehbonk?"

He held up a ginger-colour shirt to his chest which read 'I am your leader' on the front. "Good eh?" he asked.

"What does it say on the back then?" she asked.

"I didn't look, actually." He turned it around.

"I Need Therapy."

"How appropriate," she said, and laughed as Giles pulled a face.

"Look, Sandra, I think our plane has come up on the boarding screen," said Giles peering at the monitor screen hanging from the ceiling. They got up and went closer for a better view, Boarding Gate Twelve.

They grabbed their things and headed off looking for the signs giving directions in French and often English to the awaiting plane.

After a short walk, they finally came to a row of exits and found a seat in the section twelve. The rest of the seats quickly filled up and many passengers ended up standing.

"We have got booked seats, haven't we, Sandra?" Giles asked.

"Yes, but at opposite ends of the plane, Giles," she answered.

He looked worriedly at her.

"Only joking, Giles. We're together. Better than that, we have priority boarding," and she smiled.

Ten minutes later and they were sitting side by side in their comfy aircraft seats. It wasn't a large plane having two pairs of seats either side, and three in the middle.

"Glad that we didn't have to go in the three seats," said Giles. "Going to the loo is always a pain."

Twenty minutes later after the pretty girls had checked their safety belts, they were forced back into their seats as the Rolls Royce engines sucked in air mixed with kerosene at full throttle. After a short bump, bump, bumpity ride down the runway followed by the roar of the jets, they gained altitude. Looking through the aircraft's porthole window, Giles saw the buildings quickly shrink in size. He had a great view of the area surrounding the airport as the plan banked and turned towards his side before carrying on a straight climb to cruising height.

He realised that he had been squeezing Sandra's hand as the plane took off.

"Sorry, darling," he said and she laughed.

"Let's get some more sleep before they come around with food," Sandra said.

"Alright, I'll try. Never very good on planes and buses though," and he leant back and closed his eyes wondering what awaited the man in the leader T-shirt.

Chapter 27

The flight took about five hours. Add on a couple of hours lost because of the time zones and it always seemed much longer.

Giles hated flying. In theory, it seemed a great way of travelling long distances but the sensation of being cooped up with a load of unknown people always bothered him. It seemed a bit like going on a bus or a train where he always seemed to end up sitting next to the crazy man or the smelly baby.

This flight isn't so bad, he thought. The two blokes behind went to the loo as soon as the plane took off. Presumably they had to relieve themselves of vast quantities of beer that they had consumed prior to boarding. They'd settled down and slept a lot of the flight. The smell of their initial farting competition had long since disappeared and the stain on his trousers from the orange juice that the steward had spilt onto him had almost dried. He bought headphones to listen to the film showing on the monitor in the seat back. Of course, only one of the ear pieces worked and after swopping with Sandra, he decided it looked like the fault of the seat socket and had to listen in mono.

Halfway through the flight, the girl in front told her boyfriend that she wanted a nap. She then kept moving her seat backwards and forwards, trying to get comfortable. Giles, behind, was attempting to watch a Shrek film but it kept moving in unison. One second; she'd lean over to whisper to her boyfriend, the next; she'd sit back sharply and the seat would jolt again. Over and over, this happened. She had long hair and sometimes after stretching her back, it flipped over the headrest onto his viewing screen.

Giles had looked at Sandra, in annoyance, several times but being mild mannered he put up with the distraction. Sandra however noticed that with one particular head flop, masses of long brown hair came within her reach. Sandra looked around, before placing her hand over the stray hair and closing her eyes in concentration.

About twenty seconds later, the girl sat up quickly. "Flipping heck, I've just had an electric shock from that seat, my heads on fire. Ow," she said as she rubbed her fingers all over her head.

Her boyfriend tried to calm her down. "It's only fabric. You must have fallen asleep and had a dream."

The girl held strands of her hair under her nose. "I can smell it. It's burnt. Don't you tell me I'm dreaming," and whacked him on the arm. "I want to change seats, now."

The steward had noticed the commotion and came over to calm things down. After asking what's wrong, he turned to Sandra and Giles and asked if they had any problems. "Did the screens work okay in the back of the seats?"

"Absolutely fine," said Giles "And my trousers are nearly dry now," he added because this chap had orange juiced him, earlier.

"Oh, good to hear that, sir," and he turned back to the couple saying "There are two empty seats near the front if you are unhappy."

They took up the offer and followed the steward down the aisle with their hand luggage.

He returned with a small bottle of vodka and handed it to Giles. "I trust your trousers will be fine, sir."

"They're feeling just right now," replied Giles, grabbing the bottle. "Better not put anyone in this seat in front until it's checked out, eh?"

"Indeed not, sir. I've never seen anything like it," said the steward leaning forward and running his hands over both headrests.

After he went, Giles asked Sandra what she did.

Sandra replied "Just something that I used to do to annoy the girls in school. I'm not sure but I think that I can build up static in long hair until it sort of heats it up, if I concentrate."

"She said her hair is burning," Giles said.

"Maybe I overdid it a bit. It's been a long time since I used to tease that ginger girl in school," she laughed. "You can enjoy the rest of the Shrek film in peace."

"There's a gingerbread man in this flick who's a bit scared but comes good in the end. Hope that's a good omen," said Giles.

"Maybe you'll pick up some witch-fighting tips from it," and Sandra held his hand.

The rest of the flight passed quickly enough. As usual, Giles bought a scratch card lottery ticket and as usual, he didn't win anything.

The co-pilot announced that they were very close to their destination and that the island could be seen from one side of the plane. Several people on the opposite side began pointing through the planes' portholes.

"I'm always on the wrong side," said Giles, a little disappointed.

"Don't worry" said Sandra and smiled.

The plane took a long banking turn and the engines' noise slowed right down. The angle of the plane suddenly filled half of Giles' window with land. He could see it covered with lots of various-sized little buildings, set against a dry dusty yellow looking background, with blobs of green trees here and there.

Giles noticed a feature on the landscape.

"That's the lake that I saw in my dream. The one with flamingos in, I can't see any birds from this height though, Sandra," he said.

"That's the Hala Sultan lake. It's a salt lake. There are all kinds of migratory birds there," replied Sandra.

"I think flamingos like salty water so maybe I dreamt correctly. I saw a funny-looking building in my dream as well," he said.

"How curious is that? There is a mosque on the bank of the lake which gives it the name. It's very important to Islam. Some important lady buried there and a place of pilgrimage" she replied. "Maybe you went there as a child and remembered it in your dreams?"

"I don't feel like I've ever been there. It's like a vision that's just come true," he explained.

The plane approached the short runway from the sea side and made a steep descent which quickly blocked Giles' ears and made talking a waste of time. He could see Sandra's lips moving but couldn't make out the words. He pointed his fingers at his ears and shook his head. She laughed.

He could make out the roar of the engines using reverse thrust to slow the plane down and felt a rather vicious bump and screech as the fat tyres landed on Cypriot concrete. His ears started to come back to life as the aircraft taxied along towards the terminal building.

Giles felt an eerie shiver spread over his body. There was something familiar about this landscape that he could see out of the window; the dusty concrete, the sparse vegetation that grew on the other side of the runway fence, the cloudless azure blue sky, he was coming home…

"After we get in the main building, I want you to go straight to the loo and put your wig back on. Pop your new sunhat over the top. Look like you're keen to be on holiday. Don't bother with the moustache," said Sandra.

The plane came to a halt. The chief stewardess asked everyone to remain seated and they watched out of the window as a little lorry that looked like a cross between an escalator and a giant golf cart headed towards the plane. The machine nudged its higher-most parts against the fuselage with a clonk and the male steward opened the door and started allowing passengers off.

"We're nowhere near the terminal," said Giles looking out the window and turning around to see that Sandra had already grabbed her bag and stood in the queue to vacate.

He snatched his rucksack and put his sunglasses on. He needn't have worried about walking because there a small bus waited for them at the foot of the stairs. They were herded on like sheep and had to squeeze in to let the last two passengers on.

"I paid extra for more room" complained an old lady, sitting down and holding back a standing youth's rucksack perilously close to her nose. "Be quiet, Gran," said another voice, "or we'll leave you at the lost luggage."

Giles smiled to Sandra and clung on to the strap hanging from the ceiling. The driver seemed to be trying to get as many weaves in, as possible, on the short journey and Giles could hear "Sorry," "Sorry," "Pardon," as the passengers lurched into one another.

They all emerged from the bus like a can of decanted sardines. Granny said, "Cypriot bleeding drivers," straightened her sunhat and stuck her middle finger up at the driver as he zoomed off.

"Feels pretty warm," Giles said as he took his first deliberate inhalation of Cypriot air outside the terminal door. "Better get inside and changed then." He followed Sandra through the already open sliding doors and headed to the toilets.

Giles did as previously instructed and emerged looking like a nineteen seventies porn film director, complete with sunglasses. They were of the variable lens type so didn't look too suspicious.

"Well done, Giles. Give me my hat and you follow me through. No clever comments, now," she instructed.

They joined the EU passport queue and Sandra walked straight through. When Giles walked up, the security officer looked at him, then closely at his passport. He said something in Greek, which Giles didn't understand. He then took his own glasses off and motioned Giles to do the same.

Giles got the message and removed the glasses. The officer nodded and handed his passport back. He put his glasses back on and went through with a thank you.

Sandra didn't say anything for several yards, until, "He really looked at you closely then. I got a bit worried."

"Me too, I thought he would ask me take my wig off as well." He opened his passport at the picture page. "It's not a bad likeness. Heaven knows how they deal with some women who are forever changing their hair."

"I'm bothered that Suzie may have all the airports watched. She will have supporters here on the island and we don't know how big her network is. There were several gentlemen here on the plane with shaved heads and I could see that officer giving them all a good looking over. Let's get our luggage quickly and see what happens to them on the way out," Sandra said.

"Surely they'd have been told to just look out for a Giles Morton passport?" he asked.

"I'm hoping that they'd think we have false passports and just concentrate on a couple, one being a bald man. We have to be careful because they couldn't just stop us, in front of other people. More a case of spotting us and finding out where we are heading," she explained.

They found their luggage carousel and stood back while other passengers jostled for the best positions. It took several minutes until the cases started to appear. Theirs were some of the first ones coming around on the belt.

"Excuse me," said Sandra elbowing in. She grabbed hers and dragged it to Giles then dived back in as his came past and reached that one as well. They pulled the holdalls to one side. Giles put the big strap over his shoulder and said "Let's go, Sandra."

"Hang on a minute, Giles," she said, watching a bald man getting his own and partner's cases. "Let's follow them through customs."

Giles did as instructed and held Sandra back when he spotted another bald man, stroke, dark-haired women combo. They followed the quartet towards down the 'Nothing to Declare' aisle and walked through directly behind them.

As Sandra feared, the two bald men were instructed to take their cases into a side room, leaving one surprised woman to say to the other "I've been here five times and never seen anyone stopped." The other replied, "Well, we have a villa here. I'm going to complain to the mayor if they find our scotch."

Giles looked straight ahead and followed Sandra past the lady officer who had pulled in the two men, trying to think of nothing at all, because she may be a Magi but they sailed through. They didn't talk or look back for a hundred yards.

"Phew, got out then. What do we do now? How do we know where to go?" he asked.

"Edgar said that we would be greeted. Look out for a message at the exit," replied Sandra.

They scanned the various awaiting family members, holiday reps and taxi drivers standing at the exit. Several of them were holding up cards with things written on them.

"Can't see anything for us, Sandra," said Giles.

"It'll probably be cryptic," she said. "Hang on; look at that blonde with the sign over by the door."

'Mr D. Aehbonk U.K.'

"Guess that's me," Giles laughed.

The woman spotted them and waved. They went over to her.

"Follow me quickly to the car," she ordered. She waved the card at him, then added, "Rula's joke."

"Fine," replied Sandra and they hurried after her.

The heat hit Giles as he walked into the Cypriot afternoon sun.

"Whoo, that's hot," he said. "I need to put my shorts on soon."

"I'm Maria," she said. "I am honoured to meet you, Giles. I wish you good luck. You must be his guardian, Ardnax."

"Hello," they both said in unison. "Better call me Sandra. I'm more used to it," said Sandra. "We seem to be in a hurry. Is there anything wrong?"

"I am told to get you away from the airport as quickly as possible. Once we are moving, we will be harder to find," Maria answered.

"I don't know where we are going but I saw a building from the air, near the lake and wondered if we could have a quick look, if it doesn't upset our schedule? It seemed sort of familiar to me," Giles asked.

"You must mean the Hala Sultan Mosque. I can take you past there. It is not much of a detour. We shouldn't spend too long there though. We have a long way to travel now," she warned.

"Thank you. If you know it, maybe you can tell me something about it on the way there?" replied Giles.

They made their way to a large Suzuki 4x4 parked in the staff section of the airport car park. Giles and Sandra sat in the back of the vehicle in the sumptuous black squeaky leather seats.

"Wow, these are so much better than the plane seats," said Sandra.

"This vehicle belongs to your friend, Edgar. It is strong and reliable. Designed by a Japanese Magi woman, of course," explained Maria.

"Of course," echoed Sandra.

They all laughed. Both Giles and Sandra were beginning to look forward to their Cyprus adventure, but in their enthusiasm they didn't see the lone figure of the lady security guard who had let them pass, watching the vehicle from an upper floor window. Neither did they see her making a mobile phone call.

Chapter 28

As they left the airport, Maria started to explain where they were heading.

"Firstly, we need to get out of the Lanarca area. I will use a few back roads and stop a few times to see if anyone is following us. We will be heading for the Paphos area eventually. How familiar are you with Cyprus, Giles? I know that the Mindbenders got inside your head."

"Is that what you call them? That's a good description of what they did to me. I very vaguely recall some bits but they seem unreal, as though I read them in a book. Sometimes, something triggers them off, like seeing that Mosque from the air. I think Paphos is in the West and Lanarca, where we landed, is in the South," he replied.

"Your geography is accurate. We have over one hundred and twenty kilometres to travel," she said.

"Probably more than that," replied Sandra. "Are we using the motorway or the old coast road?"

"We'll visit the mosque first. Then we can use the side tracks and the coast road for about thirty kilometres. The car will be changed at a stop off point. You may have some food there and there is a place nearby which Edgar wants you to see, Giles. It may help stimulate your memory," said Maria.

"Does anyone know if the Mindbenders treatment is reversible? It's been a while since you spilled the beans about my past and I'm not very hopeful?" asked Giles.

"Sandra has probably already told you that there are different levels of treatment and it all depends on the skill of the operator and the mind of the individual. It is not normally carried out with the idea of reversal. It's used mostly on criminals. Occasionally it's used on Homsaps, if they get too close to the Magi secret and they just don't recover, full stop," said Maria as she busily negotiated side roads and junctions.

"I'm sure that we have come up this road," said Giles, "unless there are two donkeys with three legs in this area?"

Maria laughed. "Well spotted, Giles. I have just doubled back to check behind us. Happily it's all clear, there's no one following."

"You'd make extra money in the UK as a taxi driver doing that and there aren't any tripod donkeys to give it away, either," Giles joked.

"The Hala Sultan Mosque is just along here. There is a car park soon," announced Maria and before long a building partly hidden behind some foliage, mainly palm trees, came into view.

Giles gazed out of the window with a frown on his face.

"What's wrong, Giles?" asked Sandra, sitting next to him.

"There's something not good here. I don't mean the building. It's obviously a place of worship. I think some of my therapy went on here or nearby. There's some deep unhappy memory at the back of my mind. I don't know what religion the Magi are. I just assumed that the wandering star stuff meant that we are Christian," answered Giles.

"There is no fixed religion; just like Homsaps, we have several. Various ones have come in and out of fashion. Those Magi living for years, either solitary or in small groups frequently take to the local beliefs. Those that marry Homsaps nearly always do," said Sandra.

"What about the Mindbenders?" he asked.

"They live on the edge of Magi society. They are not always trusted for obvious reasons. Some of them have used their abilities to hypnotise or get into people's minds, for their own ends over the centuries. A lot of them seem to go crazy, as though they cannot handle the sounds and visions that they apparently receive inside their heads," Maria said.

"A lot of them are priests of various religions. I think that the beliefs of others coming to them, helps calm their strained thoughts and emotions," said Sandra.

"So there's not a Mindbender society that you just ring up if you need one, then? It's more recommendation and finding one who's happily focused?" Giles replied.

"More or less, it helps as well if you pay in cash," added Sandra and they all laughed.

"Right," said Giles getting out of the vehicle. I'll have a quick nosey around and you two watch the car."

"Correction," said Sandra. "Maria will watch the car and I'll keep an eye on you. It's what I'm paid for, don't forget."

Giles looked over to the mosque, with its domed top, shining in the sun. A tall minaret next to a smaller dome pointed skywards at one side, looking like a designer missile. There were several tourists and worshippers wandering around outside and pointing. It looked a beautiful building, in a wonderful setting by the side of the salt lake. He walked past the edifice to the shore and looked across to the other side, over the glistening silvery blue surface. A squadron of large birds in tight formation came in and landed on the lake surface. He scanned the area for the flamingos in his dream but found no trace of pink. Sandra or Maria had said migratory birds so maybe the time of year is wrong, he thought. The current avian population looked pretty enough.

Sandra had come over to him. "This building appeared when the Turks controlled Cyprus, centuries ago. The Magi have seen many countries and empires running their slide rules over the island and eventually invading. It's been part of the Greek and Roman empires. The Venetians were here, the French and the Ottoman Turks. They've all left a mark on Magi culture and vice versa."

"All long gone into history as well," Giles remarked, touching the buff rendered side of the building and looking at the dust on his finger. "From what you've told me about our birth-rate, the Magi will soon be following them. The only difference being that history will not remember this secretive race."

"Everyone leaves a footprint on their own little moon," said Sandra putting her arm around his waist.

"Or a fingerprint in time," said Giles wiping his dusty finger on the end of her nose. "Where did you get that saying?"

"It just came out of nowhere," admitted Sandra, holding him still as she got revenge by wiping her palm on the wall and deliberately leaving a white handprint on his behind.

"I suppose, though, parts of all those empires live on, by being assimilated into the local areas, buildings, traditions and religions. That is how the Magi will survive. This interbreeding with Homsaps, my late father is right. It is the future," Giles said. "I am the future," he added emphatically.

"Well done, Giles. You're beginning to sound like your father. That's fighting talk. Let's get back to the Suzuki and get on to the next stop. I think this visit has helped you," and she pulled him by the arm, back towards Maria watching from the waiting vehicle.

Giles took one last lingering look at the mosque, feeling certain that he had been here, under none-too-pleasant circumstances but his father, being a clever man had maybe made this part of a reawakening of his consciousness? What better way to become a leader than to have no preconceived ideas. To just learn about a society from scratch and not make judgements based on old ideas. Surely the reasons why the old empires perished were by clinging to old-fashioned ways and being unwilling to advance into a more modern world, it had made them vulnerable. History has taught that sometimes an alliance with a rival or an old enemy can usher in a new era. Giles climbed into the back of the car, deep in thought. The Homsaps are the way forward, he concluded.

Maria drove the Suzuki slowly across the car park and all their heads were bobbing back and forth looking for imaginary enemies. With none forthcoming, they went along a few short side streets and were soon onto the coast road. This used to be the main road, linking Lanarca and Limassol but European money allowed the construction of a very British-style motorway about three miles further north.

This way seemed a nicer route to drive, especially for passengers as there were many attractive views of the sea and the coast as they travelled along. Their movements were slowed several times by ancient tractors hauling improbably large loads. They were usually driven by wizened dark-haired old men who had probably been travelling the same route since they were boys. Tomatoes, potatoes and cabbages piled carefully into large open side slatted boxes. All of this tasty mobile food had made Giles realise that his last morsel of food, entered his stomach a long time ago on the plane and tasted pretty bland, at that. "Did you say we were eating soon?" he asked.

"Soon, Giles," replied Maria. "There is a service station that is run by a relative of mine. We won't eat off the menu because it's pretty awful. They live in the house behind and always keep something special in the pot for relations and friends. They make the best Cyprus coffee in the south."

Giles watched the signs. He worked out that the road is the B4. They were passing a few houses and the odd red-tiled villa but not really going through any villages. The sea view to his left looked very attractive at first but he soon began to wish for something more to see. On top of that, he had been getting even hungrier. They passed several Tavernas, little roadside shacks advertising food and drink. He noted that most were offering fish as the headline meal. He asked and Maria told him it is very popular with the tourists in the area. A fish meze consisting of many small dishes of all things seafood, caught locally from mussels to squid. Giles didn't know if he could take a whole meal of such creatures and asked, "It won't be a fish special at your relatives', by any chance?"

He felt relieved by the answer. "That's for the holidaymakers. You will have a warming Cypriot home-cooked lamb and a locally brewed beer," said Maria.

Giles mouth started watering.

"We're just passing under the motorway," announced Maria. "Fuel stop in four kilometres with food."

"Lovely," said Sandra. "Is the place near here, where you said you would show Giles something?"

"It is. It's just a bit of history but may be useful," Maria replied.

Giles saw the sign for the restaurant cum petrol station. 'Last chance to fill up before the motorway' it said and 'One kilometre ahead' written in two languages, followed by 'Choirocoitia (Khirokitia)'.

"Why are there so many ways of spelling the names?" Giles asked.

"Well there's old Greek, then the English version and a more modern interpretation by the tourist people. Sometimes signs are also written in actual Greek which has different symbols to your English," replied Maria.

"I heard Suzie saying stuff that sounded like a foreign language. Would that have been Greek?" Giles asked.

"More likely ancient Magi, there are some similarities with Greek and Latin. If she used incantations, then old Magi would most likely be the one. Probably helped her to focus her energies," Sandra answered.

"We're here now," said Maria, bouncing the car into a pot holed dusty parking area, leaving a cloud in their wake.

Giles coughed as he got out of the car. "They don't get much rain here, do they?"

"Alas the amount has been falling on a regular basis for several years. It may be global warming. We rely on the rain falling in the mountains to fill the reservoirs and it's been unreliable. We're an island surrounded by water so have started building desalination plants. They use so much electricity, though, to run and we have to import all the fuel oil. It's all run by men. They allowed storage of confiscated ammunition recently near the main power station which blew it up. Caused island power cuts for months, typical men. Magi women would not let this happen," replied Maria and led them inside the unassuming-looking building covered in Coca Cola and Keo adverts.

They sat down at a wooden plastic topped table and Giles fiddled with the multi-lingual packets of sugar in a paper cup, whilst Maria waited at the empty counter.

She rang a little brass bell on the top.

"Maria," shouted a voice and a little dark haired lady, dressed in black, came out and hugged her. "These are your friends, yes? Is he the special one?" and she walked over to their table after Maria replied "Yes, Alexa."

"My English not good. Happy to see you. My husband. He is dead. He Magi. I am just a little woman making tea now. I wear black in his, how you say, Maria?"

"In honour of him," filled in Giles. "What did he do?"

"He in work with your papa. In the court. A judge. He believe in Magi and Homsap. He fought to keep me." A tear started at the corner of Alexa's eye. "I go to the house to get real food," and she wobbled off, with the walk that only older rotund Greek women can do.

"Does that mean she's wearing black because her husband has just died? I didn't know what to say," asked Giles. "I've seen several women in black on the way here."

"Passed away several years ago," explained Maria. "It's traditional Greek mourning attire worn by the surviving woman. They sometimes wear the black for years."

Several truckers left and a couple of German tourists peered through the door checking out the facilities. They said "*Guten morgen*" as they passed and sat down in the far corner. The guy was overweight and going prematurely bald. The woman had a sexy walk, very short shorts and long legs. The waitress went over to them and spoiled his view as she took their order.

Alexa returned quickly with three steaming plates. She placed one in front of each of them and put her hand to her head. "Cutlery," she shouted over to the waitress, then something fast in Greek.

Maria laughed. "She cannot get good staff these days, she said in a roundabout way."

The waitress came over quickly with a red face and deposited knives, forks, spoons and napkins.

"This is my best *Kleftiko,*" explained Alexa. "Baahhh," she said, doing a sheep impression, in case Giles didn't recognise the food.

"Lamb on the bone actually, cooked in a clay oven," added Sandra. "Remember this as a boy, Giles?"

"Not really," remarked Giles, attacking the joint first with a knife and then marvelling at how he only needed a fork to pick the gorgeously soft meat from the bone. He spoke after the first mouthful.

"This is amazing. It's so succulent and soft. Lamb is usually a dry chop in my experience. The clay oven that you mentioned, must keep the natural juices in."

It came with a bevy of locally grown vegetables all cooked to the same standard. They were fresh with a bit of a crunch and just as he liked them.

The waitress came over with two beers plus a bottle of spring water and placed the beers in front of Giles and Sandra. "I'm driving," explained Maria.

The glasses said Keo on the side in big letters.

"That's the same as we had in Brighton," said Giles taking a large mouthful. "Mmm."

"It's brewed in Greece and here on the island," said Sandra. "Believe it or not the factory is run by the church," she said.

"Bet they get a good deal on the communion wine," he laughed. "It tastes better here than in the bottle back home or maybe it is because we're on holiday."

They greedily gobbled up the remainder of the food leaving immaculate plates. Maria called Alexa over, thanked her and pressed a roll of Euros into her hand. The little lady came around to Giles and stood on tip toe to kiss both his cheeks.

"I will come to your corporation, Giles," she said.

"Coronation," said Maria.

"Yes, that as well, we will do both," and Alexa waved to them as they walked to the door.

The German tourists were just leaving and the man held the door open for Giles as they left. He watched them as they walked over to their car arguing and the woman took a map out of the car and spread it out over the bonnet of their Mercedes.

They climbed in the Suzuki and Maria said, "We're only going a kilometre to some ruins then back to the motorway." She put the car in gear and drove off down a side road in the direction of a tourist sign.

As they drove up to the Germans' car, the couple were still debating. The woman wore tight khaki shorts and her derriere looked very attractive as she leaned over the bonnet, pointing at a place on the map. In fact the shorts were so short that Giles could almost describe them as hot pants. Her legs were slim but gloriously muscled. The gym bunny looked at Giles as they passed and gave him a quick smile

Giles tried to 'guard' his thoughts because something about a tight ass and fit legs always appealed to him. After a few seconds, he looked sideways at Sandra and Maria but there were no comments.

"Sandra. When you read minds or hear thoughts, how long do they stay in the air for you to listen or grab them?" he asked.

"Good question, Giles. They're only around a split second, just like a spoken word and easily missed. It's much easier to listen or communicate with someone you know, than a complete stranger. There's a degree of tuning in, necessary," she explained.

"As I've said before, the ability of individual Magi to do this varies considerably. You cannot be trained to do it, if the ability is not there. Some can guard their thoughts but not read and vice versa. We call guarding your thoughts 'mentguarding'. Do you remember that phrase?"

"No, but I have another question. Is it possible to have echoes, like shouting across a valley?" he asked.

"It has been claimed by some Magi. Others have said that even objects can hold words for a long time and may release the echo years later. I find that impossible to believe," Sandra answered. "Why do you ask, Giles?"

"I don't know, it's strange, the question just popped into my head. Are those the ruins over there?" he asked as Maria pulled the car into a small car park.

"Yes, they are. These are evidence of the earliest occupation of the Island of Cyprus by a human. The Homsap archaeologists have pinned it on cavemen but your father thought the Magi are responsible. Let's see what you think, Giles," said Maria.

As they got out of the car, Giles noticed the German Mercedes trundling into the car park. Good, he thought, he'll be able to check her out again and quickly mentguarded.

As he got out of the vehicle a gust of wind came from nowhere and stirred up the dust from the floor. For a split second, he thought he heard a voice in his head say Selig. He looked around. No one had said anything. Sandra and Maria were walking towards the site entrance and so were the Germans who had parked behind. The woman acknowledged him with her hand. Giles turned and read the sign, 'Khirokitia Neolithic Settlement'. He walked in and shivered as an ominous feeling descended over him.

Chapter 29

Giles jogged for a few seconds and soon caught up with Sandra and Maria.

On the nearby hillside, he came across something that looked like an old quarry. As he walked closer, he could see that the area consisted of many stone walls. There stood a larger outer one with several smaller ones built inside, some of them in the shape of round buildings.

After paying the entrance fee to the uniformed security guard, who looked extremely bored, they walked through the tall wooden-slatted gate and Giles started to look around. There was a large sign nearby. He walked up to it and could see that it explained about the area in several languages.

Japanese wasn't his strong point so he settled on the English, which contained several spelling mistakes and Americanisms. Apparently occupied over seven thousand years BC, maybe as much as ten, the settlement contained the earliest evidence found of humans living on Cyprus. They had developed a farming way of life and kept animals such as pigs and goats. They also grew crops and lived on nearby wild fruit and nuts, when in season. There were protective walls built around the village, home to a population estimated from several hundred to over a thousand.

Sandra pointed to the phrase 'The complex design of the buildings and arrangement in small streets combined with the isolated position of the village and its strong protective walls indicates a well-organised society'.

Giles looked at her. "Organised society ten thousand years BC? I've heard of the Romans and Greeks. There were the Phoenicians and Corinthians as well but they were years later."

"Indeed Giles. Civilisation is a controversial term. To some it means fancy cities and to others, it means a sustained gathering of a group of humans dependent on one another and relatively free of barbaric in-fighting. Your father reckoned that there were

Homsap humans here, living side by side with early Magi. The more intelligent Magi were running the show, of course," she added.

"Using the Homsaps as slaves?" he asked.

"Absolutely no evidence of that, archaeologists have found plenty of sites around the Mediterranean area, some in nearby Turkey for instance, of so-called early civilisation but not as convincing to your father as here. Around us exist big houses and smaller ones and each seemed to have a use, such as for living in or storage of food. There has been no evidence found of weapons, wounds or traumatic fractures to the bones that have been dug up," Maria explained.

"So how do you know there's a complex society? I take it to mean that some of the cleverer or more skilled artisans were better off and owned the bigger houses?" Giles asked, as they turned away from the sign to look at the ruins. He noticed that the German couple, who had been talking to the guard for a few minutes, were in the site. The guard had closed the gate and walked back to the car park.

"Typical Cypriot," said Maria. "No business, so off for an early lunch or a sleep."

She went on, "The people strangely buried their dead under the earthen floor of their individual houses. The archaeologists have found hundreds of bodies. The male adults seemed to have been between five foot and five foot four. That's not great by today's standards. Some of them were carbon dated and this has given an indication of the time of occupation."

Sandra joined in. "A young Magi who had joined the research team as an archaeologist approached your father. Being familiar with Magi anatomy, he took a little more interest in the recovered skeletons that seemed to have lost their insignificant little toes."

"Okay, but what makes this site special to the Magi?" asked Giles.

"He dug deeper in the bigger houses and consistently

brought up four-toed individuals, two to four inches taller than the recorded average," replied Maria.

"Wow," said Giles. "You think that the Magi were probably the village brains and bosses so they lived in the mansion house. I'm assuming that the young man kept the information secret?"

"Later, yes but the deeper bones were smuggled away by the Magi researcher and stored. What is so interesting is that some were also carbon dated and predate the earliest Homsap items by at least a thousand years" said Maria.

"In other words, the Magi were probably here first and absorbed the Homsaps into their society?" suggested Giles.

"Exactly, Giles, they appeared to have their own small society and as the Homsaps spread, they joined. They would have lived, worked and it seems slept, side by side. There would probably have been a noticeable height difference at first and one of intelligence. Their genetic structure would have been closer, thousands of years ago and they probably interbred with successful results," said Sandra.

"An early blueprint of what should happen now, by the sound of it," said Giles smiling. "Which is the head Magi house? I'd like to see it."

"It's the one with the blue flag next to it, but it is closed," said a man's voice behind them with a German accent. "In fact, the whole site is now closed."

They turned around to see the burly German tourist standing ten foot away pointing a gun at them.

"Eizus would like to meet you again, Selig. She says that I am to shoot you only a little bit, if you resist," said the gunman.

"Triple shit," said Giles, frozen to the spot.

"She didn't say that I couldn't shoot them, Herman," and Giles turned his head to see the German lady with the nice ass, holding a large vicious looking gun.

"It won't help Eizus' cause if you kill us," said Sandra.

"We know," said Herman. "We will lock you away until Eizus

is crowned and then she can decide."

"Probably a trial and then hanging, I hope I get to watch," said the rifle-girl.

"Just be quiet, Ingrid, and stop pointing that thing at me. They're the prisoners," replied Herman. "Now move slowly one at a time, in front of me and walk up that path to the house with the blue flag."

Sandra went first, followed by Maria and then Giles. Ingrid pushed past and ran forward to the flag post a hundred yards away. She turned around by the stony building and pointed the gun, which she held down by her waist at them. "Anyone who moves, I shoot," she said.

"They have to move, you dolt," shouted Herman. "Hurry up, in front."

As Sandra went in through the old fashioned stone doorway, she said "Be careful, Giles."

Maria followed and then Giles.

"Pretty short people in those days," he said ducking his head.

"Stop talking," barked Herman and prodded him in the back with his gun.

Giles walked in and could hear voices. There must be other tourists in here, he thought. They could raise the alarm or maybe confuse Herman.

He looked around and as his eyes became accustomed to the gloom, he found no extra visitors. He looked at his companions and his smiling captors. No mouths were in motion but still there were voices.

Giles started to panic then he remembered Sandra's conversation. His father said that stones could hold words...

Sandra looked at him closely, almost inquisitively. She winked.

Giles sat down on a wooden bench and the other captives did the same.

"What now, Gerry?" Sandra said to the German.

"We will wait here until Eizus arrives. Go and phone her. Say that we have captured the traitors, Ingrid," said Herman.

"Traitors?" said Maria standing up.

Giles pulled her back down.

"Maria here is just our taxi driver. She knows nothing about the Magi. Let her go and she will not tell anyone about this day," he pleaded.

"Really?" asked Ingrid, who turned back, just as she ducked through the doorway, "Does that mean if I take her shoes off and count her toes, then I won't have to shoot her?"

Maria kept still and carried on looking down at the floor.

"Thought so," said Ingrid taking her mobile phone out of her pocket and walking outside.

Herman watched them like a hawk for the next two minutes, alternately pointing his gun at each of them.

Ingrid came back in. "I cannot get a signal on this phone. This stupid island, nothing works."

"Go back to the car and get mine. It is on the local network," ordered Herman.

Giles had his back to the rocky wall and leant his head on a large boulder. The walls were made of many various sized stones interlaced together. The taller ones seemed to be many feet thick and he couldn't see evidence of any mortar, to cement the stones together. The circular building seemed to rely on the position of each stone to stay intact. Even the stony roof seemed to hang magically in the air.

He closed his eyes in order to concentrate on the voices. People quickly came into focus in his mind. He couldn't understand a word. Men and women were moving around. They were carrying pieces of stone and constructing a small dwelling. He watched for a few seconds before realising that he'd become imprisoned in the same building.

A man and woman directed the stone carriers, they were taller than the workers and dressed differently. They all seemed excited and it appeared that an important final few stones were being placed. Two men were sweating and using large pieces of wood as levers, to hold up part of the roof. The last stone was raised up next to the remaining space and two workers alternately hit it with large wooden club hammers until it slid into place.

The labourers retired to the door opening whilst the taller man and woman remained in the centre of the room looking around. Dust hung in the air of the room from the stone-hammering and the woman used her hand to brush some of it from the man's shoulder.

She bent down to pick up a club hammer from the floor. In doing so, Giles noticed that she had bare feet. He focused on the toes. Four, both people had Magi feet. She passed the handle of the tool to the man and kissed him. He smiled and said something back to her.

A large wooden post, stood from the floor to the centre of the roof. The tall man swung the hammer at the base and the post moved an inch. The woman steadied the post. He hit it again and it came loose. They both looked up at the circular flat stoned roof which hadn't moved and smiled at one another.

The ex-stone carriers came back through the doorway and cheered excitedly, in an unknown language. Giles could see for definite now, that they were shorter. He looked at the nearest worker who was around five feet tall and each of his bare feet sported five toes. The tall man raised his right arm in triumph as the workers took the weight of the centre steady post from the woman and carried it away.

The two Magi turned towards Giles and looked in his direction. In fact, they seemed to be staring straight at him. The woman reached forwards with her hand and said something. The man came closer.

The woman looked a bit like Sandra but darker skinned. She seemed to reach out towards the wall just to the left of Giles. He felt like he was watching a 3D movie. She moved her hand from side to side in the air almost like she felt for something in the dark.

She said something that sounded like, "Gil-es…"

He felt her fingertips touch his cheek and her hand passed through his face with a sharp tingle that made all the hair on his body stand on end.

"Triple shit," he uttered and sat upright, opening his eyes.

Herman came over, pointing the gun at him.

"No tricks. You move from there. Go over to the other wall away from the women," and he beckoned with his gun.

"You alright, Giles?" asked Sandra.

"Think that I just met your great, great granny," he replied.

"Be quiet," said Herman. "Face away from them towards the wall."

Giles did as he'd been told.

"Hands against the wall, Eizus said that you might be trouble," said Herman.

Giles put his hands against the stones. He noticed straight away that the pattern looked like the same area where the last stone had fitted in his vision. He placed both hands on that same large stone and closed his eyes.

The room came into focus again. Fully furnished and occupied by several different people, now. They were putting something in the wall. A stone had taken out from the wall and two people were now replacing it. Another two were in a panic and desperately trying to close the wooden door of the building. Someone banged outside on the door. The wooden frame then repeatedly shook from a battering by something heavy. After the replacement of the stone, three of the four occupants huddled at the far side of the building. The fourth taller man stood in front of them, holding a small silver stick and watched the door.

The door splintered apart and a bearded man with a sword burst in and headed straight for the taller man. He ran to within four feet of him, before the tall man pointed his stick and he flew backwards through the air like a ragdoll, knocking over the two men following him.

Another three men charged in, the first receiving the same greeting and ending up in the pile of groaning males. The tall man ran past them towards the door. The next intruder swung his sword at him and just missed, hitting a stone near where the four occupants had been hiding something. Sparks flew from the wall. The outnumbered man looked around to the wall where they had replaced the stone, as if to check if it had been found. This, unfortunately, turned out to be his last action. The final invader dealt the tall man a crashing blow to the neck with his sword.

As the tall man went down, Giles could see what he expected. Four toes on each foot, a Magi.

The three shorter men were dragged up by their clothes and roughly pushed from the room outside. The first dazed man staggered to his feet to be helped out by two other bearded men.

Giles thought that the show had ended but discovered that he could move about the room by 'thinking' about it. A bit jerky at first, but after he inadvertently mentally moved into a wall, he managed to make his way slowly through the door and looked in the direction of some shouting.

He could see down the hillside and make out the sails of ships at the coast nearby. The only movement seemed further down the hill, where he could see the three men from the building, now obviously prisoners, following others towards the ships. There were a couple of bodies of villagers lying on the floor. Apart from that the settlement looked deserted.

Giles remembered seeing on the notice board that the village had been suddenly abandoned for unknown reasons. It said that an unexplained gap occurred in human occupation of Cyprus, for maybe several thousand years. This explained it. The population of this site and other areas were probably taken off to another land, put into slavery and the tree-covered island abandoned.

Herman prodded him in the back. “Wake up. Take this rope and tie the women up.”

Giles walked over to Sandra and Maria and did as he had been told.

Herman then produced a second rope. “Turn around. Hands behind your back,” he ordered and wrapped one loose end around Giles’ arms with one hand whilst holding the gun at his temple with the other. A few threads in and out, finishing with a pull and they were secured.

“In the boy scouts, were you?” asked Giles, getting unexpectedly brave.

“Hitler Youth more like,” joined in Sandra.

“Silence,” shouted Herman. “Hitler’s an amateur. The real master race will return as the Magi. Eizus has promised. I have to see where Ingrid is, stay here and no tricks.”

He went out and closed the wooden door. They heard the click of a key in the lock.

The footsteps disappeared.

“Get these ropes off, Sandra,” said Giles.

“You’re the magician, Giles,” she replied. “I thought you could do rope tricks.”

“I can” said Giles. “I kept my hands tense while Herman tied us up, to give some slack but he still pulled it too tight.”

“I can try and warm it up,” replied Sandra and put her fingers on the knot of the blue nylon rope.

She closed her eyes and after thirty seconds, Giles could feel the warmth. The heat made the nylon slightly softer. Giles started pulling his wrists apart with all his might. His face reddened with the effort. The rope started to slide apart. He rested for ten seconds and Sandra did her work again.

Another pull from Giles and the rope slid free. He quickly turned around to loosen Sandra and Maria.

“There’s something hidden in the wall. Help me get a stone

out," he said as he untied them.

"How do you know?" asked Maria.

"The stones were talking to me. Don't laugh, Sandra. I saw the opening ceremony for this house and also when the place became abandoned. My father must have seen or sensed some of this too. The last Magi were hiding something here." He scrabbled at the stones looking for the right one.

Giles then noticed a stone with an almost vertical cut-like scar in the side. He ran his fingers over it and remembered one of the invaders hitting the area with his sword. The previously loosened stone sat just to the side of it.

Giles wiggled his fingers in the gaps around the stone. There seemed to be a little bit of movement and by pulling and pushing, the stone started to slide out of the space.

Maria fiddled with the door. "This is securely locked. We'll never knock this down."

"Herman will be back soon anyway, so he'll open it," said Sandra as she helped Giles remove the stone. It turned out to be larger than Giles expected and quite weighty. It sat at head height, up on the wall and just underneath the last big stone that he had seen the builders inserting.

Sandra stood on tip toes and reached into the cavity. After a few seconds, she smiled and withdrew a light brown flat parcel about three inches long, bound with some string.

"I can hear someone coming," said Maria urgently from the door.

Giles looked back at the opening in the wall.

"No time to fix it. You two get back over there and I'll loosely tie you," he ordered.

After a few loops, he passed the end to Sandra. "Hold this and if they pull it, the rope will seem tight. I'll pretend I've done the digging," and he ran back to the wall.

They waited silently as the door unlocked. Herman came in, gun first and noticed Giles over by the wall straight away.

Giles raised his hands. "Sorry, Hermy, can't blame a king for trying."

"You will never be king. What are you doing? You cannot tunnel out. The wall is half a metre thick. Answer or I will shoot you in the leg," and pointed his gun at Giles' nether regions.

Ingrid came in. "Shoot him anyway. He annoys me."

"Search the women and check the rope in case they've been up to something as well," ordered Herman. "I will give you three seconds to answer, Selig. One, Two…"

"Alright, alright, there's a treasure map hidden in the wall. Some Magi stolen gold is hidden nearby and we came here to pick it up," replied Giles quickly, eyeing up the gun.

"And you expect us to believe that?" asked Ingrid, after giving Sandra and Maria a quick pat down. She yanked on the end of the rope and Maria said "Ow."

"They're secure," she said. "I should go back to the car because that's where the mobile signal is. I will have to direct Eizus to where we are. She won't be long."

"Good you go," replied Herman. "Eizus will be pleased to see you again, Selig, even if you do have a hole or two in you. Find me that map," he ordered.

Giles started fumbling around in the wall pretending to find a loose stone. He worked his fingers around the one adjacent to the removed stone. He managed to get a hold and wiggled it free. The rock was half the size of the previous one and he reached up to lift it down to the floor.

"How much further?" asked an impatient Herman.

"We don't know exactly but our contacts assured us, it was just within eighteen inches," Giles said. "I'll try the next one," and he probed around the next stone. Two minutes later, he wiggled out the rock.

"What do I say if Eizus turns up?" asked Giles, probing.

"She won't be here yet. Just hurry up," answered Herman.

"Maybe we could do a deal," asked Giles. "You look like a

businessman. Perhaps Eizus is paying you?"

"I believe in the cause of Eizus. The Elders are leading the Magi in the wrong direction. Their temporary leadership is destroying us. Eizus will make us great again. I do not think that you will be able to offer anything greater than victory. Keep digging," he answered.

Giles started pulling at the big stone above the existing hole. He managed to get it moving.

"There is an old parchment buried behind this large one. It shows where the village gold is hidden. I can't move it on my own. I am not interested in being ruler. If you can help me get it out, I will share it with you, Herman," suggested Giles.

Herman went closer and looked at the stone.

"Move over to the women, Selig, and let a real German man finish the job. The trouble with you British is that you have no strength."

"That's not really fair," said Giles.

"Move," said Herman, pointing the gun at his face,

Giles quickly obeyed and took a place next to Sandra and Maria with his hands in the air.

"No tricks," said Herman. "I can pick up this gun in a second," and he laid the gun down on the floor.

He raised his arms to try to move the stone that Giles had indicated.

The three captives watched as he took hold of the stone. He got a grip with his fingers, just like Giles and started working the rock backwards in the same way.

Giles indicated to Sandra to loosen her pretend bondage with Maria, whilst Herman became distracted. Sandra motioned as if to run but Giles held her back.

The big guy Herman grunted as he pulled back and forth.

"It's behind that stone, if you want a partnership with me," encouraged Giles.

"The heavens would have to fall in before I join with you,"

Herman shouted at the point of finally extracting the remaining edge of the jammed in stone.

"Okay then," replied Giles…

A mass of stone suddenly collapsed onto the hapless gunman. One large stone cracked him on the head and he went down like the tall Magi man, years before.

Sandra got over and kicked him in the nuts.

"Whoops." She bent down to grab his fallen gun.

"Let's get to the car before he comes around," said Maria heading for the door.

"Fine," answered Sandra, "But watch for Ingrid, she's armed."

They headed for the car park with Sandra in the lead, holding the gun.

They walked to a point near the entrance where the vehicles could be seen. Sandra peeped around a post.

"She's not by the Merc. Where the hell is she?" she said

"Shall we run for the jeep? I've still got the keys," asked Maria.

"Too risky, she could be nearby and come out shooting. Her rifle will have a good range. We need to find and neutralise her quickly," said Sandra, taking command. "I want Maria to wait here, ready to run to the car. I'm afraid that you, Giles, will have to walk around unarmed as a decoy. She won't kill you because you are too valuable. Get ready to surrender and put your hands up, the instant she sees you. I'll follow nearby and pounce on her," Sandra said.

"Hmm, I don't suppose there's a plan B? No? Didn't think so," replied Giles, looking worried.

"As soon as you hear any noise or shots, get the car and I want it left running at the entrance. We'll be leaving in a hurry, Maria," instructed Sandra.

Maria nodded. Her hands were visibly shaking.

"Go, Giles," urged Sandra.

Giles moved out of cover and started walking hesitantly along one of the paths. His legs felt as wobbly as Maria's hands. He noticed Sandra sneaking off in another direction, gun in hand.

He went around a couple of corners and could see no sign of Ingrid. The weather was hot and he perspired heavily in the Cypriot sun. Giles wanted to get this over with, as soon as possible. He wiped the sweat and dust from his brow with a tissue and then had an idea. If he blew his nose, maybe Ingrid would hear?

Giles gave a loud honk and cleared his throat noisily for good measure. He heard footsteps and a shuffling sound from what seemed around the next corner, then silence.

He slowly moved to the end of the building and looked down the next alley. A high overhead trellis, partly covered with a spreading vine, provided some shade and Giles felt grateful to get underneath to cool down.

Giles looked from side to side and in the open entrance of the adjacent ancient building. Where the hell is she, he thought, as he turned around and came back out of the doorway?

He thought about blowing his nose again, when suddenly everything went dark and a great weight landed on his shoulders. His face felt like it had been put in a vice.

"Going anywhere, Selig?" asked a muffled Ingrid's voice.

He realised now what had happened. Ingrid had climbed up on the roof and dropped down on him from the trellis. He had his head trapped between her thighs and she held onto the wooden framework with her hands, so that Giles couldn't throw her off or walk anywhere.

Giles couldn't answer her because of the firm flesh of her thigh pressing against his face. In fact her tight grip almost stopped him breathing.

Ingrid squeezed harder. Giles tried to pull at her muscular thighs, for air but to no avail.

"I used to do this to my customers in Hamburg," Ingrid explained. "Apparently you can have a bigger orgasm if you suffocate someone," and the blonde clamped her powerful legs even tighter around Giles face. "*Mein Gott*, this feels wonderful," she exclaimed and closed her eyes to enjoy the dominant grip as Giles started to buckle.

Under different circumstances he might have agreed to a session between a pair of soft Aryan legs but this particular oxygen-depleted position, left a bit to be desired and his last confused thoughts were, 'What's *soixante-neuf*, in German?' Ingrid let go of the trellis and Giles went down, but not in a way that he usually enjoyed...

Chapter 30

Giles woke up on the floor to find Sandra gently shaking him.

"Sorry that I couldn't whack Ingrid sooner. I had to wait until she'd dropped down to reach her. You must have blacked out, Giles."

Giles' spinning head started to clear. He looked to his side to see an unconscious Ingrid impersonating a splattered starfish on the floor.

"Shit, Sandra," coughed Giles, as he staggered to his feet. "I'm not playing decoy duck again."

"Your lady must have been working in some Bavarian dungeon before. It's the kind of stuff that would give a bloke 'wood' as they say. Last thing she expected is for me to whack her on the head with a lump of it," laughed Sandra.

Giles then noticed the small fence post that was lying next to Ingrid.

"By the sound of it, she probably enjoyed being knocked out," said Giles shakily getting up. "Where's her gun? She had a rifle. Is it on the roof?"

Sandra climbed up and retrieved it, from where Ingrid had put it before attacking Giles. She took it over to the door of the building and jammed the gun barrel in the hinge side of the door.

"Is she a Magi?" asked Giles. "I thought the women were educated and sensible. She's got a big screw loose."

"Pull off her shoes and see, then," replied Sandra, shoving hard on the butt of the rifle.

Giles did as suggested. "Full blood," he said after the second shoe.

"There are good and bad Magi, clever and crazy, just like Homsaps. No wonder we can blend in for centuries. Fancy shooting around corners?" she asked, showing the bent muzzle of the rifle.

Giles laughed, "She'll be pissed now."

"Maria should be fetching the car. Let's get to the entrance quickly," ordered Sandra chucking the useless metal to one side.

They half ran, half jogged down to the exit but no vehicle awaited them. Giles looked across at the car park. The Suzuki sat in the same place where it had been parked and the bonnet had been raised.

They hurried over and Maria's head popped out from under the lid.

"Ingrid has pulled out the spark leads. I've just found them in the bushes. They're back in the right order now but she broke off part of the coil and two lead ends keep popping out," she shouted, as they approached.

"What about the Merc?" Giles asked.

"It's locked and even if we broke in, it would have an immobiliser," answered Maria.

"Let me see," said Sandra so Maria stepped aside.

She fiddled with the two loose leads. "Have you tried starting it, Maria, before we waste any time?"

"Yes it runs fine but shakes the loose lead ends out, after running for a few seconds," answered Maria.

"Well then, we need something to tie them in with. Are you wearing knickers, Maria?" asked Sandra.

"Of course, why didn't I think of that?" she answered.

Maria pulled up her skirt and Giles could see that she wore a thong. She pulled the thin side straps down and Giles watched as the partly trapped centre strap pinged out from between her buttocks. She bent down and stepped out of it, showing a nice firm rump in the process. She passed the red thong to Sandra and then wiggled her tight skirt back down into place.

"Brilliant," said Sandra and knotted the stringy elastic around the loose leads and broken coil-housing.

"Fire her up, Maria," shouted Sandra.

Maria already sat in the driver's seat. A turn of the key and the engine ran smoothly. "Get in. We're out of here."

Sandra took the front passenger seat and Giles climbed into the rear.

Giles looked back as they drove off. "I can see Ingrid by the gate. She's woken up and seen us. The girl's alone. No, erm…shit, Herman's there as well, now. They're going to be chasing after us."

"No kidding?" said Sandra coolly, and she knocked the magazine out of the gun. After examining it and clicking it back into place, she said "I'll be waiting…"

"Shall we go back to the café for help?" asked Maria.

"No, we have to get to Edgar," replied Sandra.

"I'll go down the country roads, then. This jeep will have a chance. If we go straight onto the motorway, that Merc will easily overtake us," said Maria, driving the large top-heavy vehicle as fast as she dare, down the winding roads.

The Suzuki soaked up the bumps on the road well. The tarmac had given out to a dusty stony track. Narrow in some places, wide enough for passing at others and very twisty. Giles found himself being flung from one side to another of the back seat, as the vehicle lurched through the corners. He tried to hold on to the top of the back seat, to see through the rear window.

"They're coming. I can see them," shouted Giles over the roar of the engine and crashing of the suspension, as they crested a hill. The Mercedes in the distance was half hidden in a cloud of rapidly rising dust which gave an indication of its speed. Giles could plainly see it go airborne a couple of times, as it hit bumps in the road. "He's driving like a nutcase," he added.

A minute later, Giles said anxiously, "They're really gaining," and turned to the girls in front, leaning through the gap in the seats. "Should we go off road?"

"Before they could answer, the rear window of the Suzuki disappeared in a thousand pieces. There was a metallic Donk, Donk, Donk and an angry wasp buzzed past his ear to embed itself in the headrest. He looked at the smoking insect hole for a split second.

"Shit." He couldn't even think of a prefix. Triple was far too low. This was an absolute cow herd full of shite. "She's got a machine gun…"

As if to answer him, he heard a loud Burrr Burrr from behind again and the Donk Donk sound of bullets entering the metal of the tailgate behind him.

"Stop the car, now!" shouted Sandra leaning through the gap in the seats. "Get your royal head down Selig!"

Giles saw she had the pistol in her hand and ducked.

The jeep screeched to a halt… Krack, krack, krack.

Sandra used a two handed grip on the gun and fired straight through the broken rear window. Krack, krack, krack went a second burst.

"Got them," she shouted.

Giles popped his head up to see the Merc sliding sideways into a tree with a badly crazed laminated front windscreen and coming to a halt. They watched for a couple of seconds, until a large German man's boot started kicking out the opaque screen from inside and straight away, a gun butt bashed out the other side.

"They're not done yet," shouted Sandra. "I'll take over the driving. Maria, climb into the back quickly with Giles, keep out of the way and get your head down," she ordered.

Maria climbed over the gap between the front seats. After a struggle and a ripping noise, as the seam at the side of her short skirt gave way, Giles was treated to the delight of an uncut Magi Cypriot muff.

Under different circumstances, he would have enjoyed the experience but the next gunshot refocused his attention and he pressed his head down next to Maria, who took hold of his hand to squeeze it tightly.

Sandra started the engine and spun the rear wheels as she roared off. In the distance Giles could hear the throb of the

German V8 as it gave chase again.

Thirty seconds later, the road disappeared into some large trees and widened. Sandra slowed down and started reversing at right angles to the road.

"Are we hiding in the trees?" asked Giles hopefully.

Sandra completed a quick three-point turn, to leave the Suzuki facing in the opposite direction and sat there revving the engine.

"Guess not," said Giles, answering his own question.

He could see that Maria had wet herself. "I'm so sorry," she said and Giles noticed that the tears running down her cheeks, matched the rivulets down her legs. He put his arm around her shoulder and held her tight, waiting for Sandra's next move.

"Dratsab. Shoot at me would you? Tnuc!" Sandra spoke softly to herself whilst revving the engine.

The Suzuki suddenly shot off from out of the shelter of the trees. The Merc driver saw it belting towards him and stamped on the brakes, whilst spinning the steering trying to avoid a collision.

Sandra had other ideas and kept her foot on the gas, shouted, "Brace guys," and planted the nose of the jeep firmly in the side of the big saloon.

Giles and Maria still had their bodies down and were flung against the padded back of the front seat. Giles popped his head up again. He could see Ingrid trying and failing to open her bent door, banging at the side window and then climbing into the back with her automatic rifle. The impact of the crash had shattered the rear-door side window.

"She's going to fire at us through the broken window," yelled Giles. Maria had virtually laid on the Suzuki rear floor now.

"All under control," Sandra said executing a smooth three point turn. "Let's play Japanese tow-bar versus German engineering."

She leaned back and looked past Giles at her target, out of the broken rear window.

"Hold on, Selig!"

Giles grabbed hold of the front seat headrest as the rear of the vehicle slammed into the side of the Merc again. He could see the terrified look on Herman's face when they got close. The impact sent Ingrid tumbling to the other side of the car. Sandra kept up the revs and the Merc started sliding sideways.

"And again," said Sandra driving forwards ten feet. This time she put the gearbox into low ratio. "Need more bite, hang on in the back." The Suzuki re-launched itself in reverse, once more at the hapless German couple in the battered saloon. Sandra revved the engine and slipped the clutch. The target continued moving until it was hanging over the ditch by the roadside.

"Just one more tap," and Sandra drove forward to line up again. The jeep smelt badly now of burning clutch.

"They've got their hands up," shouted Giles.

"Whoops, too much dust to see," shouted Sandra back and bashed the jeep into the front wing of the car, this time, sending the Merc sliding upside down into the ditch. "Anyway the Magi never signed the Geneva Convention."

Giles could hear the Germans shouting from inside the roadside wreck.

"Job done, Giles, let's be going," and the Suzuki drove off dragging its prize of the Merc front bumper, impaled and bouncing on the tow-bar for fifty yards, until it flew off into a bush.

Giles watched it disappear. "Looks like the Japanese tow-bar won."

Maria had sat up and stared out of the missing rear window, through mascara stained eyes. "We seem to be leaving a trail of liquid."

Giles looked. "Double Shit; two trails, I reckon."

"Well, we might be walking soon. I've no idea where we're going. Do you know where we are, Maria?" asked Sandra.

"You'll come to a stream soon. The road crosses it. Not usually deep this time of year and a couple of kilometres of track will have us back to a village."

"Not a big hike then," said Giles. "Are you watching the gauges, Sandra?"

"Fuel's definitely dropping. Temp still looks fine," she answered. "Here's the ford now."

The Suzuki strode surefootedly in four wheel drive across the rocky, muddy river bed and climbed up the bank on the other side. It made another half mile before the engine started making hissing noises and exploded in a cloud of steam. The air in the vehicle became filled with a burning smell.

Sandra tapped the temperature gauge. "It says normal but we've definitely overheated. Must have left some of the transmitter in Herman's Heinkel," and they all laughed. Sandra reached under the dash and popped the bonnet catch. "Let's have a look." The strong smell became worse.

Giles lifted the bonnet and Sandra dived in straight away before tossing something onto the track.

"Hot pants," she said.

Giles realised that Maria's thong smouldered by the side of the road.

"You must be packing something pretty fiery between your legs," said Sandra teasing her…

Maria wiped tears of laughter from her mascara streaked eyes with one hand and tied to hold up her badly ripped short skirt with the other. "I think our new king has seen the goods already. I hope he wasn't too shocked."

"You score ten out of ten for natural looks and zero for timing, Maria," he replied.

Maria bowed to him.

"Where's the leathery thing from behind the stone?" asked Giles. "Ingrid didn't find it when she searched you two. Have we lost it in the chase?"

Sandra pulled up her skirt and delved in the front of her knickers. "Lucky I don't wear a G-string like Maria or we definitely have lost it," and passed it to Giles, laughing.

"It'd be covered in pee if I looked after it. Sorry that I'm not a Magi warrior woman like Sandra," said Maria, shyly.

"What's that saying about finding something?" Giles pondered.

He put his arms around both of them. "I remember. Two birds in my arms are worth a map from the bush..."

Sandra whacked him.

"Let's get walking to the village. Probably be about ten minutes. We can phone from there," she said. "Help me get the jeep into the ditch. It won't be seen so easily when Eizus comes looking."

With a bit of grunting from Giles and Maria, doing the shoving, Sandra managed to move the vehicle by using the starter motor in gear and rolled it almost out of sight. She climbed back up the bank clutching her handbag. "Nearly forgot this. Passports and money in here," she grinned.

Giles looked at the battered vehicle. "I hope Edgar has an understanding insurer," and they all laughed.

"Here in Cyprus, it's who you know and who you are related to. It will be fine," Maria reassured them.

"What's in the old packet? Aren't you going to open it?" asked Maria pulling up her skirt, which had nearly fallen down, when pushing the car.

Giles undid the stringy stuff around the folded object and opened it out carefully.

"I thought that it would be really brittle for something so old but it seems intact," he said.

He gently unfolded a yellowed piece of what appeared to be thin animal skin, with symbols or some kind of writing on it.

"That's ancient Magi," said Maria. "I've seen similar shapes before."

"I can speak a little but I don't really understand the writing," said Sandra.

"It looks like it's been torn," said Giles pointing to one edge. "There's probably another part to this."

"Edgar might be able to decipher this or at least know someone who can," said Sandra. "Anyway, wrap it back up and I'll keep it safe in my box."

Giles looked down between her legs…

"Oh, I see," he said, as she scowled at him and produced a make-up kit from her handbag. Sandra tipped the contents back into the bag. The folded parchment turned out to be a perfect fit in the pink plastic container.

"Time for a stroll," Sandra said and started walking off down the track quickly followed by the others.

They travelled at a fairly fast pace to the little village and ten minutes later, Maria went into a little shop, telling Sandra and Giles to stay outside on a bench. She came out after five minutes in a new skirt, with some food in a bag and clutching a set of car keys.

"Who you know and who you are related to," she repeated and laughed.

They made their way around the corner.

"You're joking," said Giles.

There stood an Mercedes identical to Herman and Ingrid's.

"I feel like a traitor to the Japanese tow-bar," said Giles as he climbed into the back and scrunched down into the shaped, cream leather bucket seat.

Sandra got into the front and placed Herman's gun in the glove-box. "A girl has to be prepared." She laughed, noticing that Giles had watched her.

Maria was by now, fully composed and with fresh make up, took the helm.

"You two get some sleep," she said. "Next stop, the Elders," and the V8 burbled towards the motorway and Giles' destiny…

Chapter 31

After a fast luxurious trip in the German limousine; along the Cypriot motorway and dual carriageways, linking the South of the island with the West, Giles awoke sleepily from the comfy seat. It was getting dark when they reached the outskirts of Paphos. The Merc didn't stop in the town but carried on until it reached a small village.

Maria pulled into the driveway of a large villa.

Giles looked out of the window. "Bit posh here."

"This belongs to a Magi friend. They will put you up tonight," explained Maria.

She stopped the car and they knocked at the door to be greeted by a young lady who herded them into the kitchen. "I am Amera. We have food and fresh clothes waiting for you. Bring in the dinner Alexi."

A dark-haired man started bringing in some steaming bowls and said, "Hello," nodding as he did so.

"He is my man and doesn't speak much English. We speak the language of love," and she pinched his bum.

The girls laughed. "Is he expensive to keep, Amera? I might get one," said Sandra.

"He is a Croat. They are trustworthy. Be careful about some of the others. They will leave you with a baby in exchange for their new passport," she laughed.

"Any news of the others?" asked Maria.

"Yes of course. They are flying overnight into Paphos airport. They should be here for breakfast. Edgar and his lovely wife Rula, your sister, will be there bringing a snake. I don't know how it will get through customs but Edgar is a clever man."

Giles and his companions laughed. "Maybe not quite accurate but we get the idea, Amera, thanks."

After food, they were shown to their rooms where they gratefully scrubbed off the dust, sweat and cordite that had built up during the day. They all went to sleep wondering what the next day would hold.

Giles awoke to a welcome voice.

"Get your arse in gear, because Tyson is here. Any spare women, Mr King?"

Pete had arrived, messing about as usual. "Come on, mate, grub's up."

Giles stretched, got up, dressed and became the last one down for breakfast. He wondered from Amera's list of travellers, just who was coming but needn't have worried because everyone sat at the breakfast table.

A tired Edgar saw him first and raised a hand. "I can't take these overnight flights at my age, looks like we're homing in on the throne, Giles."

"Good to see you, man," said Snake running over with the usual high five.

A smartly dressed Rula said, "Hello, and don't think I've forgiven you for letting that ruffian make me use hotel shampoo."

Xena and Pinky shook hands with him. Pinky had a good grip but Xena's mightily impressive grasp clicked his fingers. Giles had to give them a stretch after she let go.

Pete patted him on the back, "Can't wait to try some proper Greek food."

"Work first, then the holiday," reminded Sandra.

"You literally have a mountain to climb," said Edgar.

"Who's going?" asked Pinky.

"Well I'm not well enough to be tramping around. Rula will stay here with me while I go over some technicalities of your leadership claim with her. I'd like Xena here as security in case Eizus finds this place and pays us a visit. Pinky's good with maps so he'll direct you there and Snake's the obvious driver," answered Edgar.

"Do you mean we really are going to climb a mountain?"

asked Giles, suspiciously.

"Not really. Bit of a hill maybe. I'll explain later after we've met the Elders."

"Been practising more video games?" Sandra asked Snake who was pretending to hold a steering wheel.

"You'd have liked our last but one car ride, Snake. Bit like Tomb Raider. The car got wrecked… " Giles' voice tailed off as he realised that Edgar had looked up at him. "I think that Maria knows a good garage, though," he added quickly. Edgar raised an eyebrow and looked at Maria who kept her head down.

After they'd eaten, Edgar took Giles outside.

"By tradition, there are only two of us allowed to meet with the Elders. This will probably be the first meeting. They've undoubtedly spoken about you before, because the old boys have been running the show whilst you've been in hiding. When your father ruled, he curbed their power but they've got it back now. Typical committee men, talk a lot of hot air and want to go back to some version of the good old days. They might give us trouble, so I'll do the talking and you follow my lead. If they don't have us beheaded, we're in with a chance," explained Edgar.

Giles gave him a worried look, "And the mountain trip?"

"Let's see how it goes," answered Edgar.

"Are these going to be a lot of old guys with beards, wearing robes and living in ivory towers?" asked Giles.

"Far from it, a couple are solicitors, ex-estate agent, dog breeder, owner of chain of launderettes etc. There are twelve on the Council. They rarely all turn up for meetings, due to other commitments. We'll be lucky to get six or seven. It's not like picking your next ruler is important," Edgar laughed. "You'll hear stories about the Magi leading the world, in areas from science to politics but most of that has gone now. The birth rate is going against us. We just have to quietly integrate with the Homsaps" said Edgar sadly. Eizus would have a revolution and that could be the end of us. We'd be persecuted and hunted like dogs, I think."

"When are we due there?" asked Giles.

"Just under an hour, we'll leave from here, fifteen minutes before. We can walk there. They actually hire the village hall for their meetings. The janitor thinks we're a weird religious sect," answered Edgar.

Giles laughed, "Fine, see you then," and went back inside for another cup of tea.

When Edgar came back, he took Giles straight to the hall. A young man at the door nodded and took them into the main hall. He asked them to wait in the middle of the room next to a small and tatty red mat.

"What's that for?" asked Giles after the young man had returned to the door.

"That, dear boy, is the Stand of the Ancients," answered Edgar.

Giles looked down at it. "What does it do, fly maybe?"

"You stand on it to talk to the Council. Your voice will not be recognised if you do otherwise," replied Edgar.

"Stops hecklers, I suppose. Looks like it should go in the bin," said Giles toeing it with his shoe.

Bonggg.

A loud gong made Giles jump.

Giles counted the people coming in. All were men, nine of them.

The gong reverberated again and they sat down.

"That's Artis in the fancy high-backed chair," whispered Edgar.

Artis stood up. "We welcome Selig, son of Selig the Great and your trusted adviser Edgar. This is a very important matter and I thank you for your earlier submissions to the Council." He waved a folder at Edgar. "All the members have viewed your evidence."

A dark-haired man stood up.

"Yes, Volt?" asked Artis.

"I ask that the matter is taken no further and rejected at this point in the proceedings" said Volt and sat down.

"Shit" whispered Giles.

Artis ignored him. "Do you have anything else to add to your case, Edgar?"

Edgar stepped onto the mat. "Not at this point, Artis."

Artis the Chairman spoke again. "Very well, in your absence, Selig, we have already debated the situation. The case has been made, that because the throne has been left vacant for years, the position has been forfeited. Succession is important. Continuity of leadership has its place. You are not the only ones who are interested. We have had contact from the escapee, Eizus, who claims to have the Ring of Leadership. How can this be so? She may have made mistakes in the past, but states that she has changed and has ideas to restore the Magi people to their former glory. History will judge whether a ruler is good or bad, not the Council, trying to guess the future."

Edgar answered him back from his red mat "The Ring had been taken from Selig by force and trickery."

Another grey-haired man stood up.

"Yes, Remus?" said Artis.

"Then surely he is not fit to lead, if he loses it so easily," said Remus. "For centuries, we have followed the tradition that the bearer of the Ring is the appointed one. That person and that person alone, has the right to rule and choose the successor."

Volt stood up.

He said, "It cannot be right that a leader may disappear for years. What are others to do? That person may have perished. What would happen then, if they hadn't chosen their heir?"

The Chairman said, "We have considered your case and with no further evidence, have overruled your claim by a majority vote. You may go."

"Better look at this then, before we go, as you put it," said

Edgar. He unwrapped a parcel and passed it to the Chairman.

"It cannot be…" uttered Artis.

The others gathered around the piece of dried animal skin.

"It is the scroll of our forefathers. It had been lost a century ago in the Troodos," said Artis, "but the wording is different to the one that I know about."

"This is the unknown half, lost for generations and rediscovered by Selig after the ancients spoke to him," said Edgar. "You speak of the known half kept by priests and rulers for centuries, awaiting the appearance of the missing piece. Place them together and the history of the Magi will be complete."

"How can it be complete when we haven't seen the known piece for years?" asked Remus. "It's disappeared. This is not a better claim than possession of the Ring."

"Because Selig will bring the other half of the scroll to you with the Ring," Edgar answered. "We know of its whereabouts," answered Edgar. "It is said the Ring picks the wearer. Not the other way around. Eizus has merely stolen it."

The Elders huddled at the back in discussion. Finally Artis came forward and whispered to them.

"If this is so, then we will bow to Selig. There are those not happy and it will be up to Selig to deal with them. They will make trouble. Are you certain that you can achieve this, Selig? We will give you a week," said Artis.

"No problem," lied Giles. "If you'll excuse us, I need to talk urgently to Edgar now."

"Good luck, Selig," said Artis and led his Council out of the chamber.

After the room emptied, Giles said to Edgar, "Where the heck are we going to find the other piece of the scroll and I suppose Suzie is just going send the Ring in the post?"

"Courtroom bluff and exaggeration, Giles, I have an idea of the whereabouts of the scroll but you'll have to work out how to get the Ring. I'm sure that I'll play my part in the latter as well," answered Edgar.

"Someone told you where the scroll is, I suppose?" Giles asked.

"Your father actually, a lot of research and a bit of luck narrowed it down to an old building in the Troodos. It's marked on a map that I took care of after he died," replied Edgar.

"Why didn't he get it himself," said Giles.

"He didn't need it. He became the ruler. I think the idea is that if his successor had any trouble, they could conjure up the pieces and Hey Presto, new king," answered Edgar.

"You never told me that his title was Selig the Great. Another adventure for me then," laughed Giles.

"Indeed he became great. We never mention his name or any other ruler because it is considered very bad luck. A true Magi will only use the name of the ruler when talking directly to him. I think it's linked to us being a secret race within the humans. You will have to take a few members of your team up into the mountains and do a search for the building, because no one will have travelled there for years. The landscape will have changed from the old map that your father obtained. I didn't want to tell the Elders about the other half but I had no choice because of their opposition to you. It turned out stronger than I anticipated," said Edgar.

"No doubt, someone will tell Suzie and she might turn up to the party," Giles said, pulling a face.

"There's going to be a showdown sooner or later. I can't find out where Eizus is. She's in the country because we know that her network of spies is working overtime. It'll be hard to trick her. We won't get away with the Brighton decoy idea again. My advice is to get there as quick as possible," said Edgar.

"I don't think we need to find Suzie. She'll find me. Let's get the others," and they walked back to their villa.

When they got back, everyone sat down around the kitchen tables. Edgar explained the situation and the importance of finding the remaining half of the scroll. He opened out some new maps on the table to compare with an old hand-drawn effort that he had brought out from his briefcase. Pinky pulled them over towards him and started measuring then drawing on one of the new maps.

"Why don't we just use a sat nav, man?" Snake asked Giles.

"I don't know. Do you, Sandra?" he said, turning towards her.

"Because no one has surveyed the mountains, only the four big towns are mapped. It's linked to the Turkish invasion of the North. The government of the southern half are still worried that the info could be used to speed up a new Turkish advance. A few years back, they took down nearly all the signs. You had to be a local, to know where anything was," she replied.

"I'm sorted," said Pinky. "We're heading well north of Limassol to the south side of the Troodos mountain range. We can take the old road past the airport and one of the roads heading North East off that. Looks like the roads get a bit small towards the end of the journey, so we'll need a big 4x4."

"I've obtained you a long wheelbase Mitsubishi Shogun and it's parked outside. All fuelled up with food, coats and compasses," said Rula.

"Why do we need coats?" asked Snake.

"The mountains are a fair bit colder than the coast. You may be alright but take them anyway," she replied.

As they walked over to the vehicle, Snake said, "This is no good for my image, man. This car has pink number plates."

"All the hire cars have these. Pretend it's a cool shade of angry red," suggested Sandra.

"Okay, guys. That's placid," he said and then rapped:

"I'm the angry snake on the bright red plate,
I can't be choosy cos I'm gonna bite Suzie,
Come drive with me in the Mitsi Van,
Giles is king and he's the man."

After he completed a jerky dance, a quick round of applause

followed plus some whistles. They piled in with Snake at the wheel and Pinky on the maps, in the front passenger seat. The others were initially spectators sat on the back seat. Snake tried the radio and all he could find were Greek and Turkish stations so he gave up. "We'll just have to talk, guys," he said.

Giles settled down to enjoy the banter and tried to relax, whilst planning the day ahead.

Find an ancient scroll, in a lost building, climb up a mountain while a crazy woman with gun toting henchman is chasing you, hmm… All in a day's work, Sandra smiled as she read his thoughts…

Chapter 32

Snake swiftly piloted the big vehicle along the old B6 past the airport until Pinky told him to take a left turn. After six miles the road became noticeably narrower. Every three miles or so after, they'd pass through a little village or collection of houses; older cracked properties needing attention, sitting side by side with unfinished and abandoned new builds, casualties of the worldwide credit crunch.

Their path was also lined with olive plantations and hundreds of grape vines, the area providing ideal growing conditions for the green and purple fruits that play an important part in the Mediterranean diet. There were unusual little Greek-style, white-painted Churches, in odd places, in the middle of nowhere.

"This is a beautiful country," said Pinky watching an old Fergy tractor working in a field. "Go straight on at the next cross-roads," he said to Snake.

Giles sniggered at the name of the village off to the right. "Who on earth would buy a villa in a place called Arsos?"

"I bet the locals are called Crackheads," shouted Pete.

Sandra laughed so much that she almost peed herself. "Be quiet you two. All you need is a Cypriot Nora and you'll be arrested."

A sign said that they were over one thousand metres high. Giles could see the big peak ahead. "How tall is that one?"

"That's Mount Olympus, the highest mountain in Cyprus. It's nearly two thousand metres above sea level," Sandra answered.

"How much further, Pinky?" asked Giles.

"We'll be out of tarmac soon and onto dirt roads for a few kilometres. The last couple will have to be walked because you'll be looking for the building. The old map is quite rough. It could be a quarter of a mile; it could be two and a half. Who knows?" he replied.

After ten minutes of bouncing around, Pinky declared, "That's it. You'll have to hoof it now. I know Edgar said for us to wait at the truck in case of trouble but you're really the boss, Giles. Shall I come along?"

"Thanks, Pinky. Sandra's got a mobile. You stay here and buzz us if you see anything of Suzie," Giles replied.

Sandra gave Giles a rucksack to put on, with a few things inside that she said might be useful.

They got out and Giles looked at the steeply rising hillside in front of him, dotted with patches of Cypress pine trees. It was either their genus, Cupressus, that gave Cyprus its name or the old copper mines further down the valley. He slung the rucksack over his shoulders and adjusted the straps. "This looks like a pine needle in a ginger-biscuit haystack job. They've been replanting here a few years ago and these trees grow quickly."

Pinky accompanied them for the first bit because the final part of the rough mountain track had taken Mitsi off course. The path on the old map didn't fully exist anymore. The ex-army man found the overgrown remains and pointed them in the direction of some trees, about half a mile away, before he returned to wait with Snake at the car.

Not long after Giles, Sandra and Pete started walking, a couple of clouds started to form around the mountain. They had left the coats in the car because it had been a sunny day. The temperature remained quite warm when they climbed out but the sky bugged Giles. More fluffy lumps started to blow over from the adjacent peaks, spoiling the otherwise pristine Cypriot blue sky.

"Are you watching what I'm watching, Giles?" asked Sandra when they were three quarters of the way to the trees.

"You mean the clouds? Yeah," he replied, looking up. The sun had gone and it was getting distinctly colder.

"Just bad luck weather or Suzie?" she asked.

"I know what I'm hoping," Giles answered.

"I felt a raindrop then. Damn, we're going to get wet on a sunny day," said Pete.

The wind started to get a bit breezy and the blobs of water increased dramatically.

The rain soon started to come down in torrents. Each large drop stinging Giles, as it landed on his bare arms and hairless head. It became like trying to walk in a waterfall.

"Head for the trees," he shouted over the din of the rain cascading onto his rucksack, cranium and the hard ground.

The dusty soil seemed unable to soak up such a downfall fast enough. Puddles quickly developed which grew into miniature streams and made the surface underfoot difficult to see.

Pete tripped over a hidden tree branch and fell headlong into a three inch deep puddle with a huge splash.

Sandra stopped and hauled him up. Already soaked from the rain, he could get no wetter, just a different colour. "Thanks, Sandy," he coughed, spitting out brown muddy liquid.

"Let's try getting under some cover, quickly," she said, dragging him by his arm as he tried to wipe muddy water out of his eyes.

Giles had gone on ahead, towards the group of trees that were about a hundred yards away from the car. The rain became so hard that the trees were only vertical shapes in the distance. Just getting halfway there ended up being a struggle, he could hardly lift his feet out of the ground that had turned into thick sticky mud. He turned around to check how the others were doing.

"Keep going, Giles, we're okay," shouted Sandra and he turned towards the trees and plodded on.

The wind seemed to have changed direction and commenced to blow the rain horizontally into his face, as though it wanted to stop him reaching the wood. He had to hold his hand partly over his eyes and look through a gap in his fingers, to make progress.

He knew that he had nearly reached his goal when he could feel the sponginess of the layers of pine needles underfoot. Their density had not been disturbed by the mini flood and walking became easier. When he finally reached the first tree, he felt like he could almost hug it. He went past to the further shelter of one of the inner trees, where the heavy rain could not able to penetrate the dense conifer canopy.

A minute later, Sandra and Pete caught up. Pete announced his arrival with a huge sneeze. "Don't tell me Eizus has viruses working for her now," he said, as he wiped his nose with a wet forearm.

Giles looked at his brown and pink mud-streaked, rain-sodden face which now had a horizontal clean wiped mark across his mouth and nose.

"You look like you've had a really dodgy spray on tan," said Giles.

"Thanks, mate, quite a welcome that your girlfriend's giving us. What's next, a plague of frogs?" Pete replied.

The two men laughed. "Don't jest," said Sandra. "I reckon she's only just started."

As they looked out from the shelter of the trees they could see the rain rapidly slowed down and stopped almost as abruptly as it started.

The rain water quickly started to drain away down the hillside. Giles took a step towards the edge of the trees to survey the land and Sandra violently pushed him back so hard that he nearly lost his balance.

"Find a rocky outcrop or stand on something higher off the ground," she ordered. She was stamping on something in the pine needle debris.

Pete pulled his arm "Don't ask. There's a big boulder sticking out over there. Come on, Giles."

They stood on the outcrop. "I feel like a woman who's just seen a mouse in her kitchen," Giles said.

Sandra tossed a piece of rope over to him and then started stamping again. He bent down to pick it up.

"Double Shit, it's a snake," he said moving back from the lifeless object and almost knocking Pete off the rock.

"Viper to be exact," shouted Sandra. "The rain has disturbed them from the grassy shrub land here. I've just killed two. They're heading for higher ground."

"In other words, exactly where we are standing, has Suzie sent them?" asked Pete.

"Wouldn't surprise me, I can see some more moving over there now that the water has receded. They look like grass snakes. Not dangerous," she added.

"Bloody snakes, look dangerous enough to me. It's getting darker out there. Are we in for another downpour?" Pete asked, watching Sandra probing the floor with a fallen stick.

He heard a loud rumble from the sky above.

"Maybe she heard me?" said Pete looking up towards the clouds.

The sky lit up with a bright flash and a loud bang above their heads made him jump. A large branch came crashing down a few yards away which made Giles flinch, a second time.

"Flip. That nearly hit us," he said, looking up through the canopy. They could make out where the lightning struck, from the little smoke trail leading to near the apex of the stricken tree.

"I don't know whether to look up for falling branches or down for vipers," Pete said nervously.

"My money's on the up, Pete," shouted Giles as another spike of lightning lanced across the sky and stuck the pines above. More branches started flying down. Larger ones this time and one of them was in flames.

Pete ran over and kicked out the orangey yellow tongues. "This ground underneath is bone dry despite that rain. It's almost as though the cloud is aiming its rain just outside the trees to drive us in here. Could she do that?"

"I reckon that she could localise it. No idea how… " replied Sandra. Her next words were drowned out by a massive roll of thunder, just overhead, which made the ground shudder underneath their feet.

"That sounded very close," said Pete. "Wait for the encore" and they all looked up.

A minute later, the sky lit up. So much so, that the light penetrated deep into the thick wood where they were sheltering. Giles could see about a hundred yards further into the wood and could make out a small building.

At the same time a huge bang shook the ground.

"Shit," said Giles "What the heck is that?" and they looked around.

A huge rumble of thunder made the tree branches shiver.

"Quiet," hushed Sandra as the noise died down.

They listened. Giles could hear nothing at first but then became aware of a creaking sound. The noise grew and grew then turned into a cracking sound.

"Run!" shouted Sandra and pushed Giles further into the wood. They started running and stumbling over branches. "There's a tree falling!" shouted Pete.

They could hear a very loud craackk and then lots of smaller snapping and grinding sounds. The three of them carried on blundering deeper into the wood, until the ground shook under their feet with a deep muffled thud.

They stopped and turned around looking at each other, to see if everyone had survived unscathed and then surveyed the damage. A sixty-foot conifer had tumbled down behind them, more or less where they were standing.

"We only got out of the way because the side branches of the other trees slowed the fall down. I think Eizus has got over her innate fear of killing you now, Giles," said Sandra.

"Nearly hammered us into the ground like a couple of nails," Pete commented.

"Look, let's keep moving. Surely Suzie can't keep this up? This will be too tiring for her mentally," Giles asked Sandra.

"It's gone quiet now and it looks to be getting lighter outside the wood so I guess you're right, Giles," she replied.

"Good news then and I've got more. During one of those big flashes, I'm sure that I could see a building ahead somewhere over," he hesitated, "over there… " waving his arm.

They looked into the gloom.

"We could easily miss it. Spread out about twenty yards apart and keep looking side to side, as we go forward," ordered Sandra. "Probably won't be any snakes here. They prefer the more open ground."

"Be just my luck to find the one who wouldn't obey his mum's instructions," said Pete toeing the ground in front of him. "Alright then, let's search." They moved apart and advanced. It wasn't too difficult moving forward as the lack of light and the regular dressing of pine needles had kept the undergrowth down.

Giles took the centre, leading in the direction that he thought he'd seen the building. After a couple of minutes, Sandra to his left called out. "It's over to my left, we've nearly passed it. Good directions, Giles," and she laughed.

"My homing instinct works much better, when I'm drunk" he replied. "Probably be just a shepherd's shithouse."

"Do they keep sheep here or is it goats?" Pete pointed out.

"Okay, a goat herder's throne," suggested Giles.

"There were many wild sheep here at one time. The Mouflon they're called, a beautiful animal. The rams were quite fearsome. This stone building ahead looks much bigger than a shelter from years ago even though it's collapsed," said Sandra striding on ahead.

"Do you think that this is it?" asked Pete, kicking at a loose stone. "It doesn't look very 'royal palace', to me."

"I don't think that Edgar meant a ruler owned it. Just an out-of-the-way place that Giles' father had discovered. He did go off exploring regularly," answered Sandra.

"It's been abandoned a long time and these trees have grown around it, since. It looks like there's a wooden door over there," she said pointing.

Giles went over and rattled it. "It's locked," he said. "Shall I try kicking it in?"

"Typical man, let me open your rucksack," and she went around behind him and undid the straps. Sandra looked inside, relieved to find the contents dry, even though the rain had been torrential. She took out a wooden box.

"That's the one from our loft. That's locked as well," Giles said.

"To you, maybe," said Sandra and she held her hands against the side of the box and closed her eyes. The lid popped open. She passed Giles a large black iron key and closed the lid.

"You're telling me that we had a key to the shepherd's bog in our loft for years?" asked Giles, as she placed the box back in his rucksack.

"Your father gave it to me to look after, until a special day. This must be it. Stick it in the hole then," she ordered.

"Bossy, here goes then." The key turned freely and the door moved with a little shove and creaked open.

"Shit!"

Giles jumped back as an unidentifiable bird shot out past his head. "I thought it had been booby-trapped."

They peered inside into the darkness. "I don't suppose that you remembered a light, Sandra?" suggested Giles. He knew that organised Sandra would.

She took a little pencil torch from her pocket and passed it to Giles. He pressed the switch and received a surprise at the amount of light from the small instrument. He could see a small dusty hallway with a fairly flat rocky floor and some stony steps leading off to a lower floor in a circular fashion.

"There's something familiar about this place, Sandra," he said.

"We need to go downstairs, Giles," said Sandra.

"Afraid that you'd say that," and he started down the first step. "What are we looking for exactly? I don't think this is the downstairs loo."

"Probably where they kept the dragons, knowing our luck," said Pete starting to follow them down.

"Pete, I require you to wait upstairs as a look-out. We don't want to be surprised. I will call you if we need you," ordered Sandra.

"Okay, Miss," he answered and he went back to the doorway and peered outside in both directions.

"You don't really think there were dragons here, Sandra?" said Giles.

"No such thing. The Magi used to keep a Minotaur underground in Crete years ago, though. Not sure if it made it here," she answered.

"Rroaghh!"

A loud roar echoed along the passageway.

"Double shit!" shouted a startled Giles who stopped in his tracks. "What the heck is that?" He shone the torch from side to side nervously.

"Sorry, couldn't resist," came Pete's voice from above.

"Daehbonk," shouted Sandra back.

"Pardon?" asked Pete.

"We're looking for evidence left by your father. Edgar said that he used to go to a place in the mountains to escape the hot summer sun," Sandra said quietly to Giles, "Where he did his thinking, his planning and his writing. Away from the people and the crowds, we know that he took you there on more than one occasion. Do you remember this place, Selig?"

"Vaguely, you just stirred something in my head." Giles sniffed the air. "The smell here, the slight dampness and the dust, the mountainside and the big blue sky, I think we used to come up here and he used to read to me. Bits are coming back. There were stories about old civilisations. I guess that may have been true, not Magi history."

Giles spun around and pointed his torch, talking more excitedly. "He would sit on that large boulder over there." He flashed his torch. "I had a little wooden stool. Am I making this up? It feels like I'm trying to remember a dream. Edgar said that father didn't tell him where the building stood. Maybe he kept it a secret from him and drew the map, just to let me know all those years ago."

"Is this your seat?" Sandra had picked up a small three-legged wooden seat and passed it to him.

"Wow!" said Giles, holding the object and closing his eyes.

A vision of a rather angry man towering over him entered his head.

"I seem to remember him getting pretty upset when I marked it," he laughed. Giles shone the light over the top of the seat and a tear started to form at the corner of his left eye.

Sandra looked closely at the wooden surface, carved into it read; Selig Giles, son of Selig the Great.

"Sandra. For some reason I've never asked you the name of my father. Artis said it earlier. Now I remember. This is like a blast from the past..."

Sandra hugged him. He pushed her aside. "And if I'm right, we used to hide things somewhere in here." He started pushing at some stones in the wall.

"One of these stones comes out, Sandra."

She joined him in scrabbling at the wall.

A minute later Sandra said, "Here, Giles." She pulled out a shallow six-inch-square stone.

Giles shone the light inside the cavity. He put his hand in and pulled out a little package bound with string and very similar to the one from the Neolithic site.

"This is it. Time to go," he said and carefully put the stone back in the wall. They locked the door and Sandra reached into his rucksack and put the key and scroll, back in the box.

He had one more look around with the torch and reached out and touched the stone that Sandra had replaced. A vague vision of the upset man, now smiling at him, came into his head.

"He's happy now," said Giles and Sandra hugged him.

They climbed back up the steps to the awaiting Pete.

"Got it," said Giles.

"Good man," said Pete. "Back down the mountain, we go."

With Pete in front, they retraced their steps past the lightning smitten tree and out into the open ground. They were greeted by a perfectly clear sky.

Pete led the way back to the clearing where Mitsi stood parked. The initial muddy ground soon gave way to dry scrubby mountainside and the heat from the sun overhead, quickly started drying their damp clothes.

They didn't say much on the way back. Pete took the front, occasionally whacking the ground ahead of them with a big stick whenever he could 'smell' a snake-trap. He asked if Giles thought that his father had hidden the scroll there, just as they got to the 4x4. Giles answered, "I don't know, supposed to have been lost decades earlier. Maybe he tracked it down and didn't tell anyone at first."

"Hid it away as an insurance policy for you, Giles, something like Edgar suggested," said Sandra. "He'll have been dead right, if this escapade comes off."

Pinky helped them with their stuff and they flopped down in the back seats.

"No sign of Suzie then? It's been nice here. Heard some rumbles though. Mebbe the Turks were having firing practice, up north?" said Snake driving back down the mountain track.

They told him about the storm and the snakes.

"Blimey. That probably means she's waiting further down the valley," said a worried Snake and gripped the steering wheel a bit tighter.

Giles didn't answer. He'd just had a Suzie vision like the ones back home. She had tuned into him.

Their car started being twirled by a whirlwind in the vision. People were flying out the doors screaming and the vehicle is being bombarded with exploding olives.

He shook his head and breathed deeply.

Sandra noticed. "She's here, isn't she?"

Giles just nodded.

Pinky's mobile went off. They heard him utter, "yes, yes and okay."

He turned the phone off. "That's Rula. They're on their way. We must meet them at the Kouris reservoir. Suzie's been identified in Limassol a couple of hours ago. A policeman tried to arrest her and two others for speeding by the new marina. Poor guy got swept out to sea by a huge wave that came from nowhere. She's last seen heading North West towards the Troodos."

"Which way Pinky?" asked Snake, pulling into a passing place.

Pinky got out the map. Thirty seconds later, they were on their way. "Take that road over there," he pointed.

As they turned and passed the crossroads, they all read the warning sign. It said 'Slow, Eight deaths in three years'. There were flowers by the sign and someone had crossed out the eight and added a nine. Underneath a handmade sign said 'Death Valley'.

No one said anything as Snake started driving down the winding road…

Chapter 33

"How far is it to this Query place?" asked Pete, sitting in the back and leaning through the gap in the seats.

"It's spelt K O U R I S and pronounced Kouris," said Sandra. "It's named after a river dammed in the late nineteen eighties. It stores water there for Limassol, which runs down off the Troodos Mountains. It's about fifteen miles or twenty kilometres. It shouldn't take us too long. It'll take Edgar much longer to get there, although most of his journey will be on the motorway," answered Pinky.

"Why does he want us to meet him there?" asked Snake.

"He's obviously got a plan. Do you think he's arranging a meeting with Suzie or some kind of showdown?" suggested Giles.

"Good thinking, Giles. He's a man of words. His profession is fighting with nouns and verbs. He may be thinking of trying to reason with her. Maybe give her a pardon, in exchange for her going quietly away?" suggested Sandra.

"Pardon…a six-letter word and she might go away? More than likely, the response will be a four-letter one," said Snake, trying to look past the rear end of a tourist bus that hindered their progress. The road seemed wide enough on this section to overtake a car but the extra width and length of the coach, made it too dangerous.

"Take your time," said Pete, looking at the dented crash barrier on the next bend and the sudden drop.

"Don't know about anyone else but I'm getting a little peckish," said Pinky.

"Rula said she'd put some food in the car," said Pete, looking around.

"It's in the boot," said Snake. "We looked before, while we were waiting. There are only crisps and bottles of water. I think that Pinky means something more substantial."

"Find a shop then, Snake," said Sandra.

"We just passed a wooden sign, saying food one kilometre," said Snake. "We may as well stop because this Cypriot bus driver isn't going to let us pass." Their car revved in second gear, crawling behind the struggling coach going up a steep short hill, belching black smoke.

"Hope the food is better than their spelling. They have *bakon butts* and *ise crem*," laughed Sandra as they passed another homemade sign, saying '*foode half kilo*'.

"Lay by ahead," said Pinky.

"Amazing," said Pete, as Snake pulled the car in and stopped.

Giles got out and could see why Pete commented. He expected a small tavern but facing them stood a touring coach of the six-wheeled variety, common back in the nineteen sixties. Painted in garish colours, it had been converted to a café.

Someone had decorated the sides of the bus with murals of Cyprus. There were churches, horned sheep, mountains, temples and beach scenes. Aphrodite's Eatery had been painted above a rather buxom version of the Goddess adorning the rear of the vehicle.

To the side of the vehicle fell an unguarded steep drop into the valley, below and the narrow layby left little room for manoeuvre. The rear escape window of the bus hung open and steamy cooking vapours were drifting out.

"I smell burgers," said Pinky.

A car left and two kids waved at them, their mouths stained red with ketchup, from tucking into hotdogs.

Sandra waved back. "Seems the hotdogs at least, are edible."

She turned to the car. "Pete, come with us. You, Snake, stay at the wheel and Pinky, stand outside the car and keep a look out. We'll send Pete back with your food. Tell him what you'd like."

Sandra ran after Giles, already standing by the side of the bus, looking at the menu.

"How about *bakon* and *tato omlet* or maybe the *vogan sosage* and a cup of *tee*?" he asked.

Sandra started laughing and Pete caught up with them.

"It's like that Polish café back home," he said.

"It sounds better English than some of the kids in the UK," added Giles.

"It's cool. Are we dining in, while the guys eat in the car?" asked Sandra.

"We're the privileged class now, dear. Or at least I might be if I get through today," replied Giles.

As he walked around to the entrance, Giles decided that this was obviously an old British bus, because the passenger door opened on the front left and unfortunately next to the drop.

"Nice touch," said Giles as they climbed on, pointing back to the makeshift barrier at the cliff edge behind them, consisting of folded deckchairs and rope.

The driver's seat area looked original and intact. Giles even noticed the keys in the ignition. Most of the front two rows of seats had been removed and replaced by a mixture of plastic and aluminium patio chairs.

They heard a loud double blast of a horn and looked back to see a tourist bus starting to enter the lay by but struggling and getting close to Mitsi. It had driven up the hill and tried completing a U-turn into the rest area.

Snake waved out of his window, started up the car and drove it to the front of the café bus, near the curve of the cliff.

"Never, never," said the chef, behind the rear counter, shaking his head. "New coaches, they are much, much too big…"

The coach continued its toing and froing as they ordered their meals.

"That driver is pretty useless. Must be his first time up the mountain," said Pete.

"Four cheeseburgers and one burger just with onion, two teas and three coffees," ordered Sandra.

The coach pulled alongside. The chef watched it, as he

chucked beefburgers onto the grill in front of him. "They have no passengers, only driver and guide. I make little money from them. They always ask for free burgers, to bring me tourists," and he shrugged his shoulders.

A minute later, Giles turned around to hear voices.

Snake and Pinky were getting on the bus.

"Change of plan, man," said Snake. He could see that Pinky had blood dripping down his temple.

"What's happened?" said Sandra walking towards them as a third person got on.

"We meet again, as you British say. Everyone, stand to the back by the counter."

Ingrid stood there smiling, holding a gun as usual.

"Finish the food, cook," and pointed the gun at the dark, wavy-haired, sweating chef.

The new coach started up and turned almost out of the exit. There were several little crunches as the driver tried to find reverse. When he did the engine roared and the big vehicle continued backwards.

"Mitsi," shouted Snake. The bus whacked into the side of the car and it toppled off the edge. The bumper caught on the makeshift rope barrier and they were treated to a succession of multi-coloured deckchairs flying into the air, before following the vehicle down the slope. A loud crunching and snapping of branches accompanied the car's demise.

"Now we're almost even," said Ingrid. "Two cheeseburgers to take away, cook. Selig is paying…" and she held her hand out.

The chef reluctantly made two burgers with cheese and put them in a bag, then passed them to Giles. He slowly walked forward and passed them to her, under the watchful muzzle of her gun.

"*Danke* Selig, now get back with the others," and she walked slowly backwards towards the steps of the entrance. "Sorry I have to fly but I think that you will fly further. If you get off, I will shoot you…" Ingrid climbed off and waited about ten feet away, pointing her gun at the front of the bus.

The other coach started up again.

"That's Herman driving," said Giles. "I couldn't see before. What are they up to?"

He got his answer when Herman suddenly reversed into the front wing of their café bus, knocking it sideways and sending crockery and tables flying inside the eating area. Only Giles and Sandra were left standing, because they were knocked up against the window, as the bus lurched closer to the edge.

"Aphrodite. She go down," shouted chef, as the bus took another hit and moved again.

For such a fat man, the chef could be very agile when in a panic and climbed up onto the food preparation area and jumped out of the already opened rear window, in the blink of an eye.

"What are we going to do?" asked Giles. He could see that Ingrid had now got back onto the other coach with Herman.

Sandra had run over to the other side of the bus next to the Germans and stood on a chair wrestling the sliding window open. She reached inside her handbag and dropped it to the floor, Herman's Neolithic gun pointing in her hands.

Krackk. Kracck.

Herman's side window exploded in a shower of glass.

"Snake, get Aphrodite started. The keys are in the ignition!" she shouted.

"Man, this bus is ancient and hanging over the edge." He ran to the driver's seat and churned the engine over.

Herman must have stalled his bus because Giles could hear the engine being turned over. Sandra kept her gun pointed out of the window, covering the Germans. "I didn't want to shoot at them… " she shouted.

Snake got the bus going and revved the engine. Anything loose rattled in the bus and plenty of things that weren't originally designed to so, joined in.

He put it into gear, lifted the clutch and revved simultaneously.

"Shit," said Giles grabbing hold of Pete as the bus moved closer to oblivion in first gear.

"Got it now, sorry guys," shouted Snake and revved again.

The rear wheels span for grip at first, slowly scrabbling at the tarmac and the five-wheeler jerkily returned to its natural state of six.

The Teutonic tourists were just leaving now. Sandra had her arm out of the window, holding up her middle finger to them. Ingrid watched her, as the bus turned onto the main road, biting into a burger and obviously laughing.

Giles went to the bus entrance and looked at the cliff edge. A large chunk had broken away and star-like cracks were emanating out through the surrounding road surface.

"Triple shit," he said, as Snake moved the old Bedford crate to a safer position and he watched several pieces of the tarmac disappear over the edge with the vibration.

"What now then?" asked Pete.

"Where's the chef gone? Is he alright?" said Giles.

"He ran off up the hill. Maybe he lives further along or has a car parked there. We passed a couple of places, not far back," answered Snake, leaning back from the driver's seat. "We've got half a tank of diesel, by the way."

"Will it get us to the dam?" asked Pete, picking up a couple of toppled plastic chairs from the bus floor.

"Give it a go," said Giles. "We can't let Edgar face Eizus, all on his own. Better check the brakes first, because there's a lot of downhill stretches yet."

"Okay, boss man," replied Snake and proceeded to do several emergency stops, back and forth in the car park, sending even more things flying around the bus.

"As good as they'll ever be. Sorry about the mess, any chance of a burger on the way?" Snake asked.

Pinky laughed. "I used to work in one of these places. No problem." He went behind the counter and started rearranging the scattered pans and sauces. He lobbed the previously grilled burgers out of the rear window because they'd ended up on the bus floor.

"Those vultures circling up there can have them. I'm not littering," he said and turned the gas grill back on.

Sandra looked out of the window. Four large dark birds were circling overhead.

"They're not vultures. They're black kites. See the slightly forked tail," said Sandra pointing.

As if in response, one of the birds stopped gliding on the thermal and swooped down past the side of the bus. It flapped its magnificent wings and soared back up to join the other three. He noticed a glimpse of white on the tips of the flight feathers as it flew past.

Giles turned to Sandra and they said simultaneously, "Suzie."

"Eizus is watching us through the eyes of those birds, guys," warned Sandra.

Two of them had landed and were eating the discarded burgers.

Pinky bent down to the fridge and chucked out some sausages a minute later.

"We're not supposed to feeding the birds up here," said Giles, just before he noticed the bottle of chilli sauce in Pinky's hand.

"Wouldn't want to be under them when they crap," he said to everyone's amusement. "Burgers all around, then and let's get this charabanc on the road, Snake."

The old six-wheeled Bedford rattled its way out of the lay by, piloted by the long-haired Snake.

Further down the road, Giles looked around at his burger chomping companions, off on another adventure, sitting in patio chairs, trying to stop the sauces and their food disappearing off the tables, each time Snake negotiated a hairpin.

There were worried looks on some of the tomato-stained faces and Giles began to feel that, as their elected leader, he should do something to raise their flagging spirits.

He thought of the crazy adverts on the outside of Aphrodite and became reminded of an old film about a bus. He started to sing and everyone joined in.

"Guys! We're all going on a summer holiday…"

Eat your heart out Cliff, he thought and took another bite of his chilli burger.

Snake finished off the song with:

No magic for Suzie for a year or two,
Cos Chilli Giles is gonna eat you.

Laughter and a round of applause were followed by cooled bottles of Keo that Pinky found in the fridge.

"You'll have to give the old chef a new bus when you're king," said Pete smiling. "I don't think it'll make it back up the mountain." He pointed out the trail of blue smoke that the old diesel left in its wake.

"We've got to sort out Suzie first," said Giles and looked to the front as Snake pointed, shouting "Look boss…"

He slowed down as they passed a tourist bus with a shattered driver's window in a lay by. He couldn't see any sign of Ingrid or Herman but there were two large black-billed raptors on the roof. The birds flapped their wings as they passed.

"Suzie will know where we are again soon, no doubt. I guess news travels fast by air around here. Don't think they're your chilli birds, Pinky," shouted Giles. "They're probably some others sent to watch our progress.

"Chilli birds, great name, that. Sounds like a couple of Turkish slappers," said Pete.

"What about Herman and Ingrid. They may be ahead laying a

trap?" asked Sandra.

"It's probably not too far to the dam now. I bet they've got some other car and headed back to find Suzie," replied Giles.

"Nearly there now," said Pinky looking at the map. "After a few more miles, look out for Alassa."

The others went quiet as thoughts about finally meeting Suzie filled their heads.

The silence is finally broken by Snake. "Sign up ahead. It's here."

"The village is the other side of the reservoir to the dam. Watch out for a car park. People visit this place and go fishing," said Sandra. "Look, you can see it, past the houses" she said pointing to the right side.

Giles looked across. The reservoir looked huge and filled a Y-shaped valley, with the village of Alassa at the top.

Snake turned Aphrodite Val off the main road and drove down a side road that led to the dam. Several people were waving at the gaily decorated venerable old Bedford. Snake waved back as he negotiated the stupidly parked cars, which is a Cypriot custom.

"That's the car park over there and here's a little road that leads alongside the water to the dam at the end. I don't think Aphro will get down the road so I'll pull in here," said Snake, twisting the large chrome and black steering wheel to full lock, as he spun around in the car park to face the entrance and the open surface of the reservoir.

Two young soldiers in a battered army Land Rover, who were having a cigarette, stopped puffing and watched open mouthed as they arrived.

"Ready for a quick getaway, now," he laughed. "Good girl," and he patted the steering wheel, not realising that the horn ring worked and that the chef must have upgraded the original fitting.

Rraaarrh, rraaarh.

The blast of the air horns echoed around the valley.

The soldiers jumped.

"Sorry, man," said the embarrassed Snake and waved.

Several birds fluttered up around them, curious about these noisy invaders of their Cypriot rural roosts.

The party started to climb out of the bus into the bright sun and look around.

Eizus, Herman and Ingrid were watching them through binoculars from the opposite side of the lake.

"They are crazy," said Herman. "They come to battle in a burger van and trumpet their arrival as though they are invincible."

"There are five people but the old man isn't with them," said Ingrid looking through her sights.

"They've made fools of us enough times. Let them know we're here, Ingrid," ordered Eizus.

Ingrid was nearly knocked over by the recoil of the rocket-propelled grenade that blasted out from the metal tube across her shoulder.

"Dolt," said Herman. "I should have done it."

They watched the tail-flame of the projectile heading over the reservoir.

Pinky spotted it first.

"Incoming!" he yelled and knocked Snake and Giles to the floor. The others got the message instantly and dived to the floor, with their hands over their heads.

With a whoosh of sparks as it flew past over their heads, the grenade hit the side of the coach and smashed the large middle window into fragments.

The two soldiers had dropped their cigarettes and were running at speed back to the village.

Giles and friends lay there for twenty seconds.

"Shouldn't something have happened, Pinky?" whispered

Giles.

Pinky got up. "The impact sets these things off. I'll go and look. Keep down."

"Are you sure it's okay? Shouldn't we wait longer?" said Pete.

Pinky ignored him, already walking slowly up the bus steps. He came out with the shell wrapped in a towel, walked slowly to the bank and lowered it into the water.

As he came back, he shouted, "Dud, Chinese or Korean crap. They sell them to anyone but half of them don't work."

"Lucky for us," said Giles, getting up and dusting himself down.

Over on the other side of the lake, Herman had attempted to throttle Ingrid. Eizus had created a mini-waterspout which tossed him into the shallows and had soaked the German girl as well.

"Invincible or simply lucky, Selig… " Eizus spat out. "Take me to the dam, you idiots. I have a meeting," and walked over to a 4x4.

Sandra had pulled a miniature pair of binoculars from her handbag and looked across the lake.

"Eizus, Ingrid and Hermy, they're over there on the hillside," she said to the others.

A wet Herman stared back in the other direction, through his expensive Zeiss binoculars. They gave a perfectly focused view of Sandra as she took one hand off hers and saluted him with one finger.

"Tnuc," she mouthed.

"Bitch," he retorted.

Herman got into the car and with a damp Ingrid in the driving seat, the little jeep trundled along the opposing hillside, on its way towards the dam just over a mile away.

Sandra watched them go.

"The only way out is across by the dam and back this way. They must have driven through here earlier," said Sandra.

"What should we do, Giles? That missile came too close for my liking. They may have more," said Pete.

Giles didn't have to answer. A Merc screeched into the car park and the back doors flung open. Rula ran out and so did Xena. They ran to Giles and Pete respectively before flinging their arms around them. Edgar and Maria got out of the front.

Edgar looked at holed Aphrodite. "I see you decided to part ex the Mitsubishi, good choice," and he walked over to have closer look. "Big girl," he said as he looked at Aphrodite's assets on the rear door.

"Suzie's the other side of the lake. She fired a rocket at us," said Giles, running over to him.

"Calm down. I've had her tracked down and have spoken on the phone to her. We're meeting on the dam for a discussion," said Edgar.

"All on your own?" queried Giles, looking perturbed. "She's been trying to have us killed all day."

"You will all be nearby," he answered.

"We've only got one pistol with hardly any bullets left. They've probably got all sorts of weapons," replied Giles.

He heard Pete laughing behind him. "They haven't got those two though."

Giles turned around. Sandra and Xena were over by the National Guard Land Rover. They were now wearing camouflaged T-shirts and reaching in the back under the canvas flap. They reappeared with black straps tying their hair back and toting semi-automatic rifles.

"Hey, it's the Rambo twins," said Snake, quite serious for once.

"This evens the odds. Anything for me?" asked Pinky.

Sandra passed him a box. "They should fit the pistol. Load it up for us. We'll hang on to the weapons," and took the small gun out of her handbag. "There's a problem, if you want a small war, Edgar. We've only got two bullets each for the rifles, loads of blanks though. The officers don't trust these young guys much."

She went on. "They're driving over to the dam now, I think. We can't all get in the Merc. The boys left the keys in the Land Rover. Let's use that as well."

"Cool, more driving practice," said Snake, going over to the driver's door and opening it.

"Hey, those guys were smoking pot. Here's their stash," and he put it in his pocket. "Get in then," and he started it up.

With a loud crunch, it went into gear. "Needs servicing, man," and revved it. "Look at that smoke, must be running on dope."

The Rambo Security Twins climbed in the back with Pinky, Giles and Snake on the front bench seat.

They pulled off with the Merc following closely.

"I thought that bus drove badly… " said Giles, as he reached up to adjust the passenger sun visor, which came off in his hand. The Land Rover rattled and creaked its way along the rough road alongside the reservoir. The poorly-tethered side canvas flapped in the welcome cooling breeze blowing across the glistening surface of the lake.

"We've got metal seats, so don't flipping complain," shouted Xena from the back.

Giles looked back through the tethered up rear canvas and could see the Merc. Maria waved at him; her face was a lip biting mask of anxiety. She looked scared, no warrior lady, as she said but he felt proud of her, hanging on in there.

He looked ahead. The dam looming clearly visible about five hundred yards in front. A 4x4 had parked on top at the far end and three figures were waiting…

Chapter 34

"I hope there's no one else there. Did you say that guys fished here, Sandra?" asked Giles.

"They can but I reckon that those two National Guard soldiers were stopping people. Sometimes they hold manoeuvres and keep people away from certain areas. This reservoir is very important to Limassol so they may practice here. There may have been a sign that we missed," replied Xena. "One bang and they ran away, typical men."

"Will they fetch others?" asked Snake.

"They were stoned," answered Sandra. "Probably be locked up, back at barracks. Even if any more did come, the National Guard is only part-time conscripts. They won't fight."

"If there are some gunshots, the locals will think it's their army protecting them," said Xena.

"It is, in a Magi sort of way," replied Giles. "Stop over there by that wide bit, Snake."

Snake parked the rattly old Land Rover by the end of the top of the dam and the twins got out and assumed covering positions, pointing their rifles towards Suzie's group at the other end of the dam.

The Mercedes pulled up and Edgar quickly got out.

"Put those down. We're supposed to be negotiating," he said.

The girls walked out of sight behind the dusty vehicle and peeped through gaps in the canvas.

Rula and Maria got out and joined them. Rula had her arm around Maria who started blubbing.

"I'm phoning Eizus. Be quiet please." Edgar had walked a few feet away and Giles couldn't hear what he said.

He came back. "We're meeting in the middle of the dam but first she wants to demonstrate her powers to see if we'd like to surrender. We have agreed to a helper as I will have difficulty walking that far unaided. Come out from behind that truck,

Rula."

"Shouldn't Xena or Sandra go with you? They're...well, tougher," she said and Xena did a dog growl at her.

"I said that we did not want to fight. The war babes will wait by the cars, and no shooting while I'm still here. That includes you, Pinky. Oh and stop crying, Maria. This is all for a reason," Edgar ordered. "Take the Merc back to where the bus is parked, Maria, and stop anyone coming down here. Pretend you're some kind of official. Give her your card, Rula."

Rula ran to the car and got out her case. She gave Maria a folder and an ID card.

"Who's Eleni Elbon and what is the Department of Anomalies?" asked Maria, reading from the card. "This folder is empty by the way."

"Use your imagination. The barcode on that ID outranks a general, so you can do and say what you like," said Rula.

"I have a Magi friend in the village called Eric. He owns a bar. Maybe we should go and ask him for help?" suggested Maria.

"Good idea. Get a message to him and then watch us through Sandra's binoculars," said Edgar. Sandra passed them over. "When it looks like we've finished arguing send someone over to pick us up. Make sure that no police or soldiers come up this way. There'll be too many questions."

They watched Maria drive off in a cloud of dust.

"Pull the Land Rover up on the flat bit here, Snake, to stop them getting past, if they try and run," ordered Edgar.

"We're not allowed to run?" Pete joked.

"And miss Giles finally becoming king? No way," replied Xena, walking behind the Land Rover as Snake repositioned it. She knelt down next to her sister with their two rifles.

Sandra said "Let's put the four bullets in one rifle and blanks in the other. You take the loaded gun because you're a better shot. You may as well have the pistol as well."

Xena smiled "I won't let you down, sis."

"She will give in, Edgar?" asked Snake getting out of the truck. "You were talking a bit strange, earlier."

"What will be, will be, young man. You have yet to learn the true way of the Magi. Selig will guide you towards union with the Homsaps. History will quietly remember this moment," and Edgar turned to the camouflaged twins, "But hopefully not those awful T-shirts."

He began the long walk to the middle of the top of the concrete dam. He managed the first hundred yards unaided but Rula took his left arm from there on. She wore fairly high shoes and strutted fine on her own but now she as she helped Edgar, the blonde looked a bit like Bambi with her legs at crazy angles.

"What's this demonstration of power?" asked Snake. "I've never seen Suzie do anything."

"Did you have to ask that?" replied Pete. "Why is the water rising in the middle of the reservoir? That's impossible."

The wind had got up and the deeper area at the centre of the manmade lake turned into a small version of the North Sea on a bad day, compared to the tranquil blue of the outer edges.

"Better hold on to something," shouted Sandra to the others.

It came at them like an express train…

They were engulfed in a six-foot-high tidal wave which picked up and deposited Rula and Snake about twenty feet away. The others managed to cling onto the Land Rover. They all received a soaking except Giles, who had Sandra's dry bubble trick to thank, again.

"What a ride, man," said Snake, picking himself up and helping Rula from the mud.

Suzie had come forward and stood triumphantly near the middle of the top of the dam, with Edgar and Rula struggling towards her.

She took a bow and they watched as the other two participants of the meeting, came closer.

Edgar stopped and made Rula wait about fifteen foot away

from Suzie. He carried on towards her, limping slightly.

"Eizus looks quite cute for an old witch," said Pete, referring to the fact that she wore gold hot pants and a matching gold lame top. "Well-dressed for the occasion."

"Fancies herself as Queen Kylie of the Magi, she's crazy," said Xena. "I could pick her off from here, Sandra."

"Edgar said no fighting. Anyway, Herman's watching us through his binoculars. I've seen metal glinting so they're armed as well," said Sandra.

A wet and dirty Rula came back over to the truck, followed by Snake in squelching shoes.

"I hope when you're king, you will recompense me with lots of new outfits," she sniffed. Rula's bedraggled hair had been soaked and her cold braless nipples were sticking out through the damp material of her top. Snake looked at them, licking his lips.

"Stop it. I can't help it," she said covering them with her palms. "I don't need to wear a bra," and tossed her wet hair back.

"Wonder what they're talking about?" asked Pinky, watching the meeting over on the concrete.

Edgar and Suzie were in an animated conversation up on the dam. Suzie flung her hands in the air and turned her back to Edgar. He pointed at her with a jabbing finger, as though about to tell off a child.

Suzie turned around and shouted "Never!"

The noise echoed across the now still lake.

"She looks annoyed," said Snake.

"Look. She must be making a wave again," said Pete pointing at the newly swirling waters.

The wind began to rise and it started getting cold up by the dam, very cold.

"What the heck is happening now?" said Giles.

Edgar bent down on his knees to grab Suzie by the hand.

"Selig is the one, not you, Eizus!" he shouted.

"Not the best person to tell that to," whispered Rula, biting her lip.

"A pissed-off witch. Not good," added Pete.

A wave rose up like a giant hand and crashed down on Edgar.

"He'll be soaked," said Snake.

They watched as Edgar staggered to his feet, totally dry.

"The old man can do that dry bubble trick, like you, Sandra," said Giles.

"It takes a lot out of you. I couldn't do it twice in a row. I don't know about Edgar's Magi tricks. Do you, Rula?" asked Sandra.

"No. He used to say that you had to reach inside yourself, to find the glory. Whatever that meant," Rula replied.

Water rose into the air forming a small but ominous cloud. A second wave formed on the lake surface, taller and darker in colour, than the last one. The air felt getting colder and colder. Rula started visibly shivering.

"Look, Edgar's waving at us," shouted Rula, holding her hands in her armpits trying to keep warm. "He must be alright."

"Or saying goodbye," replied Giles quietly.

Sandra looked at him and grabbed his hand, "You don't think…"

The wave came down onto Edgar. Precisely aimed, just like the last one. He stood in a dry six-foot circle, where the previous one had landed around him but the concrete didn't get wet again, even though he hadn't moved.

The wave enveloped him and stopped…

It just hung there in mid-air, like a frozen ice sculpture. Giles could just make out the immobile shape of Edgar at the core.

"Eizus has frozen him with this cold wind," said Xena.

Giles could no longer see Herman and Ingrid in their 4x4 because of completely frosted windows. Their Land Rover's glass had started to mist over as well.

"We've got to help Edgar now, Giles," said Pinky, putting his big arm around Rula who had started to sneeze.

"My wet clothes are starting to freeze solid," she said in a wobbly voice.

"He always has a plan and he said to wait," replied Giles. "Didn't he?"

Before anyone could answer, forked lightning streaked across the sky from the direction of the newly formed cloud.

It struck Edgar's ice statue, which exploded into tiny fragments. The pieces were caught by the wind and disappeared into the valley below.

Suzie staggered on the dam and went down onto her knees, her head down.

"She's tired or hurt," said Sandra.

The valley fell silent for several seconds as every bird, fish, tree, wave and onlooker all held their breath waiting for the next episode...

The wind had died down and the air temperature started rapidly rising. Herman came out of the 4x4 and ran along the dam to help her to her feet. Once standing, she pushed him away.

"Selig!"

Her voice howled across the dam. Giles felt every hair on his body stand on end.

"Edgar has gone. It's my turn now," said Giles standing up and looking over the bonnet of the Land Rover.

"Daehbonk," said Sandra. "Take her out, Xena."

Xena didn't wait for any more instructions. She popped out from behind the rear of the Land Rover and fired off four individual, carefully placed shots.

Kaaracc, kracc, kracc, kracc and she dived back behind the Landie.

"No, Xena..." Giles shouted.

Pinky looked over. "Erm, problem, Xena, you only sort of hit her..."

The well-placed bullets had stopped in mid-air a couple of feet away from Suzie's chest. She moved around to look at them, hanging there and then twirled her finger just above them.

"Didn't have my name on," she shouted across to the astonished onlookers. "You can have them back..."

"Hit the deck," shouted Pinky, diving down to the ground.

"Triple Shit," shouted Giles, following his example.

Two of the bullets whizzed through both sides of the canvas tilt. The other two thudded into the side of the vehicle.

"Giles, there's something dripping out from underneath," said Rula, lying down on the floor.

"Hit the bloody petrol tank," said Pete.

They all looked above the Land Rover, when they heard an engine start.

Herman had started their 4x4 and Ingrid had lifted something from the back.

Pinky and Giles shouted simultaneously, "Run."

Ingrid put the RPG launcher to her shoulder and looked down at her feet. She laughed and moved them further apart, quickly sighted up and pressed the button.

The missile streaked over to the rear of the Land Rover and hit its flank. The Chinese warhead did explode, this time and so did the leaking fuel.

Cypriot nineteen eighties, soft-skinned, army transport versus high explosive, no competition; the rear end rose up completely from the ground in a hellish orange fireball, sending the vehicle spinning and smoking towards the edge of the dam.

The Landie teetered for a few seconds before sliding down the side with a metallic screech and bubbled into the depths, out of sight.

Herman waited for Ingrid to get in the passenger and said something to Suzie who stepped aside to let him drive past. He accelerated along the top of the dam towards Giles' shell-shocked party.

"Scatter," shouted Pinky.

Xena stood her ground. "Behind me, Selig," and she held the

pistol straight out, in a two-handed grip.

Giles had been partly deafened by the impact, but understood her gestures and did as instructed. He watched the others run off in all directions. "Are you sure about this?"

Xena emptied the magazine into the front of the vehicle as it closed in. The windscreen shattered, the bonnet came partly open and a front tyre blew but still it came on, directly at him.

Giles yanked her to one side at the last second and they ended up in a pile on the floor.

The 4x4 careered on into the distance towards the car park, with the burst tyre flapping.

"Double Shit," said Giles, lying on the floor. "I can't take much more of this, so close I could nearly smell his sausage sauerkraut breath."

"Okay, so maybe Sandra is a better shot? I nearly stopped it. Sorry, Giles," Xena said, with her head down.

The others ran over.

"Are you okay? Looks like they're gone," said Sandra, helping Xena up.

"Not quite," said Giles, starting to walk onto the dam.

"Selig," shouted a voice, from half way along the dam…

"Eizus," shouted Giles back, in a croaky voice.

"Wait, Giles," Sandra grabbed her wet battered handbag from the floor and took out the attic wooden box.

"The key's not going to help," he said.

"Your father gave me one more thing from the old building. He said that you'd know what to do with it," she replied and produced a silver stick.

Giles took it just to shut her up.

He turned back to face the dam and put it behind his ear.

"Harry Neolithic-Magi Potter's bloody magic stick, it didn't do him much good," he mumbled as he recalled the tall man in the vision.

"We're behind you all the way, Selig," said Pete using his

Magi name.

"I don't want to be in front of him, it's too dangerous," said Rula.

Sandra retorted, "Be quiet woman. Do this for the Magi, Selig."

"Kick her ass," encouraged Snake.

Giles walked onto the dam until he faced Suzie along the top. He could feel his heart beating fast.

They looked like two gunfighters sizing one another up.

Giles started thinking 'I am Selig' to himself…

Suzie started to walk towards him. She looked tired as she pushed her dishevelled back with both hands and walked towards him wiggling her hips. The sun shone on her gold lame outfit and her legs shimmered gorgeously brown. She smiled at him and held her arms open.

"Come to me, Selig, we will rule this world together," she said.

"She is Eizus. I will not be taken in by her," he muttered under his breath. He looked at his beautiful Suzie-girlfriend's firm bosom and slow-motion hips. He wanted to kiss her nipples one more time…

"What did you say, my lover? We just need to be together for a while. Let me touch you, Selig. I mean no harm. You misunderstand my intentions."

Giles stopped walking as her soft hand touched his shoulder. Maybe everything could be sorted out? Those deep, brown, warm eyes invited him in for a late afternoon swim; yes of course it is okay, if you climb into my head, Suzie…

Before he could say anything, everything went dark…

He woke up standing in a black place with a black floor and a black sky. A voice started talking; Suzie's voice.

"Hello, Giles. It's time to be scared, very scared, scared to death, in fact. I've bought a few people from your past to say hello. Probably won't see you again, so it's goodbye from me and the Magi."

Giles looked around. A person walked into his mind. An old lady, she held some knitting. It was Nora.

"You've been a bad boy, Selig," said Nora from the blackness. "You have to be punished," and she threw a knitting needle towards him.

Giles laughed and the smile disappeared as the needle grew into a javelin. He ducked and it flashed past his ear.

"Plenty more in my bag, dear," and she reached inside, before lobbing a handful at him.

Giles ran into the blackness and turned just in time to weave as five javelins clattered to the floor beside him.

"Say hello to Tyson," Nora said and put the little yappy pooch on the floor. It ran towards him with its legs growing longer and its mouth getting bigger. The eyes became redder, the teeth sharper and it suddenly leapt towards him, with jaws wide enough to take his head off.

"Shit," shouted Giles and grabbed a javelin from the floor, just spinning around fast enough to impale the chest of the beast.

The impact knocked him over and as he landed on the black floor, both Nora and Hell-Tyson vanished.

Giles' heart pounded with fear as he tried to pull his mind out of this nightmare.

Another woman appeared, someone from school, years ago, the Nit Lady. He absolutely hated her, pulling at the knots in his hair with her fine little comb.

"Come on, Selig. I've done the other children. It's time to have your head checked," and she ran towards him with a comb. She grew on approaching and seemed to tower over him, just like at school. She held out the comb which turned into a shiny metal multi-toothed blade and swiped at him with it.

"Shit," he ducked and ran around in circles, trying to escape, just like in junior school. He remembered something and got behind the tall woman, then kicked her hard, in the back of the knee. She crashed down and he desperately tried to think.

Suzie's using bad memories against me, he thought.

He then had to quickly sidestep, as the Nit Lady, still on the floor, rolled over and lunged at his ankles with the overgrown comb blade.

What can I do, he thought, trying to get his breath? An idea seemed to explode into his head…

Maybe if I think of things that I like, he thought, that'll help? He tried to focus on a Sunday morning; lying in bed, with warm sheets and a comfy bedspread wrapped around him…

Suddenly they fell from nowhere out of the black sky. He mentally piled dozens of pillows and duvets on the Nit Lady, more and more Sunday softness, until she stopped slashing.

Another woman appeared, a lady teacher from his school. He couldn't recall her name. She always used squeaky chalk and wore long, red false nails.

"Come here, Selig, you haven't done your homework, you nasty boy," said Miss. She opened her mouth wider and emitted an awesomely loud chalky style screech that lasted a minute. Giles had to put his hand over his ears.

Miss then swiped at him with a long cane that caught him a stinging whack on the bum. "Use a peashooter at me would you?" Giles remembered that bit and wondered what would come next.

A giant peashooter appeared in the hand of Miss. She started pulling off her fingernails and popping them in the end of the weapon.

Giles guessed the next bit and ran.

Several dagger-like nail projectiles flew past his head with a buzzing sound. One just nicked the top of his bald head.

I need some protection, he thought and racked his brain to recall his childhood favourite; bubble gum. A second later, large fully blown bubbles, floated down behind him, popping as the fingernails incised into them. The blowpipe teacher disappeared underneath a bubbly pyramid of gum. The final one went bang and the sticky remains fell on him, covering his head and shoulders.

He had an idea, as he extricated himself from the rubbery pink gel. Why should he get all the hassle? Suzie should share this. He closed his eyes and well… Wished is the only way to describe the feeling.

SuzieEizus appeared, looking around at her new dark surroundings, obviously very shocked at first.

"I underestimated you, Selig. You have the touch of a Mindbender. No matter, I will finish you myself."

Giles watched as the gorgeous Suzie morphed into his most feared child's toy. The Red One-Eyed Teddybear. He hated it when he saw it in his bed, believing that the remaining eye belonged to the devil. He'd hide it under the mattress or in the cupboard but it kept coming back.

This bear appeared even scarier because it stood ten foot tall and this time is built like a brick dolls house toilet.

Its huge leg kicked out, catching his stomach and winding him. A swipe from the left arm knocked him flying onto the hard black floor. Another kick caught him really hard in the legs.

Giles rolled over out of reach and did as before, he ran.

RedTed could run faster. With three huge strides, she caught up and delivered a hammer blow to the back of his head.

Giles went down in a partly conscious stunned heap. He had a feeling about rolling bodily and opened his glazed eyes to realise that the black floor had opened up beside him. He stared into a huge, deep sea of water. He grabbed the cliff edge, just hard enough to avoid being toppled over into the drink.

OneEye shouted down from above "Looks like you're going to get wet soon," and a large furry leg kicked him in the head.

Giles wobbled on the verge of unconsciousness. This felt too hard to bear. The pain from the heavy blows, almost too much. It seemed so easy just to go to sleep, away from all this…

"Ginger, ginger, ginger..."

Someone's voice pulled him back.

"Too hard to bare-bear, how pathetic. It's only a teddy bear, Daehbonk!" shouted the new noise in his head which rose above the pain.

Sandra's voice repeated, "Ginger, ginger, ginger..."

He tried to focus and a TV programme flashed into his head. He listened to his thoughts and spoke out the words.

"Tonight, Giles, I'm going to be a gingerbread man."

Everything went misty. He pulled himself to his feet and felt a bit odd, sort of crunchy.

The mist cleared…

"Déjà vu," he said as he looked down at his orange, rippling six-pack. He was Giles the Gingerboxer. Better than that, he'd become a twelve-foot-tall, mean-fighting, son of a biscuit.

"Fancy a piece of this, squinty?" He shouted to the Red Bear and walloped her in the furry stomach.

Red collapsed and coughed for a few seconds. "Listen," said the bear, "Maybe we should talk?" and slowly struggled up.

Ginger lowered his guard and Red caught him one to the side of the head, followed by one to the ribs. The last one really hurt so he went back at the bear and pounded the living daylights out of her abdomen.

The padding that covered Red cushioned a lot of the blows but she still ended up on the floor, gasping for air.

Sandra's voice started counting. "A-one, A-two, A-three…."

She got to eight and Red started to get up. "I'm afraid that I had to rummage in the toy-box."

Ginger looked down. She had a super-soaker in her hand.

"Bye-Bye, Ginger Selig," and she started squirting his legs.

Ginger's feet went soggy. He couldn't walk. The biscuit legs started bending and he started getting shorter.

"Biscuit into short-damp-bread, Selig, time to be queen. A-one, A-two, A-three…"

Giles tried to think as he collapsed to his knees. There's something else. What is it?

He remembered the silver wand. Did he have it? He reached behind his ear and clumsily grabbed it with his big right-hand ginger boxer mitt.

SuzieRed had closed in now and dribbled the remains of the soaker on his head.

"A-seven, A-eight, A-nine and I'm A-quee..."

GingerGiles struggled to his feet holding the Wand tight in his right mitt and hit her with the biggest left hook that a Gingerbread man has ever thrown.

"A-king" he cried out as he suddenly saw a Neolithic invader superimposed on Eizus.

Everything that is black turned to white... Well, blue sky, concrete and sun actually. Giles slumped to the floor.

The force of the blow lifted RedTed up into air. Only a she-bear, no longer, it had turned into Suzie and he watched her pretty brunette haired face disappear before his very eyes to be replaced by that of a gnarled old woman. A sudden huge gust of wind blew her aged wizened body off her feet, with limbs flailing in all directions. Her body seemed to shudder backwards off the edge of the concrete dam that she had made her throne. Then spinning like a starfish thrown across a beach, it went down and down until it hit the waves with a huge fizzing, bubbling splash.

"Help Giles before she comes back," shouted Rula.

"Eizus went under over a minute ago. There's no sign of her," said Pete, hanging over the dam edge and staring intently into the water.

"She sank like a stone. Keep looking, Pete," replied Pinky, also checking the glistening blue water, lapping quietly at the wall of concrete.

"You took her out, man," shouted Snake "I mean King-Man."

Giles half laid, half sat on the floor. Someone grabbed him in their arms and he felt something hard against his cheek. As he focused he saw Rula cuddling him against her wet T-shirt. Her shoulder strap had fallen down and her nipple pressed hard against his face.

"What the heck were you doing?" asked Pete. "First you were dancing about on your own then you and Eizus were fighting, as though you were on drugs."

"She had you on the edge of the dam. We couldn't touch you. You both had bubbles," said Sandra.

"Sandra read some of your thoughts and shouted at you," added Rula, pulling him tighter.

"Good punch-up though, especially that last left hook, Giles," added Sandra.

Giles had turned partly around to talk to Sandra with Rula's nipple perilously close to his mouth.

"Going to give him a feed for being a good king, Rula?" asked Xena, pointing.

He took the opportunity for a quick nip and made Rula jump.

"You lot are terrible," said Rula, grabbing at the loose strap and dropping Giles in the process.

As he lay there laughing, Sandra asked him what happened at the end. "I can tell that you were fighting in a dream world from your past but all I can dig out from your brain is Mr Crunchy."

Giles started to recover surprising rapidly from his bear beating. It seemed like a hidden repair mechanism had started to work. He pulled himself up to his feet with some help from Pete and checked himself for non-existent ginger crumbs.

He said, "I'm not really sure what happened but at school, I was bullied by some older boys and regularly chased. It ended on one occasion when this kid had knocked me down and as he started to hit me with a lump of wood. I raised my hands over my head to protect myself, wishing really hard that he would go away and when I took my hands down, he lay ten foot away on the floor. His mates picked him up and ran. Another time, the brakes failed on this old car that I drove and it spun off the road down a bank towards a small tree. Again, being terrified I wished so hard that the tree wasn't there. When the car stopped, the tree had been knocked to one side, its roots pulled out of the ground and only a small dent in the front of the car. I heard a load of noise on both occasions. Like a howling wind. I really find it hard to believe that I have any powers, though."

"I'm sure that you have. I think that they are hidden by your dominant Homsap genes but in a life or death situation, the Magi side briefly shows itself," said Sandra.

"The big Ginger and the wishing weren't powerful enough though. I kept trying and Eizus would come back with more. Only when I held the silver wand could I find the strength to finally whack her." He looked around. "Is Suzie really gone?"

"There's not a trace of her and if you mean the stick that you had behind your ear, it flew out of your hand into the reservoir when you fell down. It's with the fishes, like Eizus," replied Xena, looking over the concrete edge into the deep waters below the dam.

"She must have been knocked unconscious. That's why she changed face. That's what the real Eizus looks like," said Sandra. "Ugly bitch."

"What about the Germans?" Snake asked.

"They were typical bullies. If Maria is still at the gate, she'd never have stopped them. I bet they were looking with binoculars from the village. They'll be running now back to Bavaria," replied Sandra.

"Keep watching to see if she resurfaces. We can watch all the banks of the lake from here," said Xena. "She may be dead but even if she regains consciousness, she'll surely drown. That's a deep lake."

"We'll have to wait for several days, I think, to sure. Maybe she will be able to move bubbles of air down under the surface to breathe or something?" asked Pete.

"Indeed. We'll have to set up a watch. I'll stay here with Pete while the rest of you go back to the village. Bring back some women with weapons," ordered Xena.

"Now, now," said Giles beginning to relax a little, because Eizus had not resurfaced and several minutes had passed. "If I make it to be boss, I'll command that male and female are equal… "

Chapter 35

A tired troupe of warriors half walked, half limped most of the half-mile back to the car park, their clothes were ripped, limbs were aching and they were bruised, not just physically but also mentally by the loss of Edgar.

Snake took turns with Pinky to help Rula. She'd broken the heel off one of her shoes and her designer top had snapped a strap. Her left boob hung perilously close to popping out again.

"I'm never going to fight in a battle again. If you and your sister want to take on someone else, just leave me out of it," she said. "This thing about Magi women being the fighting force is a load of balls."

"We're just out of shape, Rula. What we need are a couple of months of intensive training with Xena," said Sandra laughing.

"A couple of months of intensive care, more like." Rula stared at her hands. "Just look at my fingernails."

The remaining heel finally gave way, a few seconds later and Rula tumbled to the ground with everyone laughing. She sat there with one shoe off and examined it.

"I am sick of these shoes. They cost two hundred euros and they're not even lightning proof." She took off the remaining shoe and stood up in bare feet. "You'll have to go on and get me a taxi, Snake. I can't walk any further."

"And Magi women are supposed to be strong," replied Snake, who had walked on twenty yards already.

"You could be eaten by dingoes if we leave you out here too long," added Giles.

"I know there aren't any in Cyprus. I'm an educated Magi woman and I should be treated as such," shouted Rula. She threw a heel-less shoe at each of them.

The final throw at the more distant Snake finished off the stitching on the remaining strap of her top. Her two pert breasts escaped into the sunlight.

"I'm a lady… " she started to shout and her voice tailed off as she wondered why the three men were no longer looking at her face.

"And a fine-looking one at that," said Pinky. "Do you need a hand with those, miss?"

She looked down at her jutting out breasts and clasped a hand over each soft jug, totally speechless.

"Can you pick her up and carry her, Pinky?" asked Sandra.

"No problem," he answered. Before Rula could complain, he bent down, pretending to adjust his shoelace, then in one seamless move, stood up and had her over his shoulder.

He started walking after Snake with his topless burden and after two cries of "Brute" and "Men" Rula looked sideways through her dangling hair and spoke to Sandra who closely followed them.

"Actually, this is quite nice. I used to have this dream about being carried off by a cave-man, you know." Rula then floppily dangled her arms and ended any resistance.

Giles brought up the rear of the victorious column. "We wouldn't be here if it wasn't for Edgar. I feel bad that he's gone. I would have liked to know him better."

"Don't be sad, Giles. That is not the Magi way. He knew his time had come and he aimed to carry out your father's plan. This, he succeeded in doing," replied Sandra. "Edgar felt no pain. He weakened Eizus enough to allow you the final blow. Just remember him as a winner."

"I know, Sandra," he replied "I may be next in line to the throne now that Suzie has gone but tonight we drink in his honour."

"Too right, man," shouted Snake from the front. "Edgar is a legend."

"Who's going to sort out all the stuff with the Elders now?" asked Pinky.

"I'm in charge now," came back a voice, dangling just behind him, through a mass of hair. "By the way, I'm very grateful for this mode of transport, but please don't fart again. I'm in the firing line."

Pinky whacked her on the bum with his spare hand and answered, "Okay, Miss," to everyone's amusement, including Rula's.

Twenty minutes later, they were within sight of the car park. A figure waved at them in the distance and they heard a car start up. Within seconds a black 4x4 belted down the track leaving a plume of dust in its wake. It pulled up just in front of them and a head leaned out of the driver's window.

"Thank the stars that you are alright. We could see the lightning and hear loud noises. Is Eizus defeated? I'm Eric, by the way. Maria's filled me in." The bar owner climbed out to help them in and got a pink and pointy eyeful, as Pinky unceremoniously dumped Rula on the floor.

"I don't care anymore. Everyone else has seen them," as she stood up and pointed her chest in Eric's direction.

"She's not married, you know," said Snake doing an impersonation of her and receiving a whack on the back of his head for his trouble.

Eric passed her a woman's top from inside the car. Rula turned away from the others and took the remains of her designer top off over her head, then dropped it on the floor.

She stood with her long legs akimbo and the sun glistening on her naked back. The eyes of the four men were focused on her sweating pale skin as she ran her fingers back through her blonde hair, several times. Their eyes moved up and down from her torso to shoulder, to the sweep of her hands. When her arms were at their highest point and her elbows horizontal, her pert boobs seemed to point skywards.

"I could do that," said a slightly jealous Sandra, breaking the silence. "You look like a deodorant advert, Rula."

"Were they looking at me? What a surprise," said Rula

giggling and putting on the replacement garment.

The men turned expectantly to Sandra who started to lift her top.

"But I won't," she laughed.

"What about Eizus and what's happened to Edgar?" asked Eric, impatiently.

"Edgar perished in the name of the Magi and we will always remember him," said the fully dressed Rula. "He had prepared him-self. I guess he became his own phrase 'Find The Glory Inside Your-self'."

Eric lowered his head.

"Eizus fell into the lake and did not resurface. My sister and her man are watching for any traces but we are certain that she is dead. You need to send some women… " said Sandra and paused. She looked at Giles' disapproving face, "…or some trust-worthy men, to watch the lake day and night for several weeks."

"You're learning," said Giles.

After a quick argument about where to sit, Rula climbed into the front seat, Pinky climbed into the boot and the other three climbed in the back with Sandra in the middle.

"Can't find the safety belt," said Sandra feeling under Giles' behind, as Eric pulled away.

"You've been fighting thunder and lightning, falling trees, climbing rocky ravines and now you ask for a seat belt," laughed Giles.

"Let's just say I've had enough risk for a few months," replied Sandra wiping the sweat from her forehead with a red cloth that she found on the seat.

"That's a pair of knickers," said Rula, looking back. "There's other clothes in here as well," as she opened the glove-box.

"And some blankets in the back," added Pinky from the boot area. "This must be Eric's passion wagon."

"I cannot deny that I use this vehicle to interview new female staff. I am a lonely man," Eric replied, smiling. "The clothes are just souvenirs."

Rula pulled out a string of bras from the inside of the dash glove-box and looked at the labels. "I have no chance. I guess the bigger the number, the better the CV. I bet some of them can hardly write."

"Knowledge of the language is important to the customers at the bar in particular the alphabet," replied Eric, stopping the car outside his bar and getting out.

Two well-endowed ladies came out to greet him.

"Alphabet…I get it," said Giles "DD and FF."

"Spot on," said Eric. "The blonde is Donna and the brunette is Fiona. The lads love all four of them. Come in and have a drink."

Snake and Giles sat at the bar while the others went to a table.

Snake asked them how they both began working here because they sounded English. They explained how they had Magi parents. Donna being full blood kicked off her sandals to show eight toes. Fiona had a Magi father and a shipped-off mother, when the man started getting too far up in the hierarchy. She showed her feet and produced five toes on the left but only four on the right.

"Apparently, there's not many of us with this combination," she said leaning over and twiddling the fifth toe.

The men could not miss the huge cleavage as she bent down. Giles wondered if she'd be able to straighten back up again with the weight up front. She managed the movement with ease and he noted that although her clothes made her look slim, the well-built lady possessed sturdy legs. Pretty attractive really and he didn't usually go for the larger ones.

"I know my way around a bar," boasted Snake attempting a chat up line.

"Would you like us to show you ours?" said Fiona leaning forward with one hand on a bar pump to counterbalance her top heaviness.

The girl had an awesome pair of knockers and wore a blouse on which most of the top buttons didn't work.

Giles couldn't talk. Snake got straight to the point.

"Are they real?" he asked. "Not that it bothers me."

Giles half expected a real forked snake-like tongue to pop out of Snake's mouth any second.

"Plastic jugs," said Donna coming to the bar. "I'm the real deal and I'm also the senior barmaid. She's under me."

"And you're under Eric," replied Fiona. "Far too often, in my opinion" she added.

"Now, now, girls, fetch everyone a cold beer and look pretty," ordered Eric from over by the others' table.

Giles looked at Donna over the bar. She was another curvy lady. Not as tall and athletically built as her mate but a fine bosom pushing against her top and that certainly scored her points with Giles' imagination.

"We're doing cocktails soon," said Fiona smiling at Giles. "How about Sex on The Beach later?"

"Go girl," said Snake. "You're gonna like being king, Giles."

Giles walked back to the table mentguarding his boob visions.

"Where's Maria?" asked Giles.

"She's borrowed another car and high-tailed it back to Paphos. Rula is getting her to sort out the arrangements there and spread the news amongst the Magi. We'll probably see her tomorrow. I reckon she'll be playing at Eleni Elbon as much as she can, to pick up more info on the Elders for us," replied Sandra.

"Did you just say Pete became your sister's man, a few minutes ago, in the car?" Giles asked Sandra after he had sat down in a rickety chair. "Does Pete know this?" and he laughed.

"He would not dare refuse her. She likes him. He has a sense of humour and is rough in bed. They will bond," Sandra answered.

"How do you know about…?" His voice tailed off. "You have, of course. What about us?" he asked.

"I can no longer share your bed. I am honoured but I was simply carrying out my duties. There is another reason that we must part. I am a believer in the old ways," and she put her hand on her stomach and pressed.

Giles looked at her, not understanding…

"She must be up the duff, man," said Snake sitting down with his pint.

Giles' mouth flopped open.

"You are indeed a father to be, so long as this little escapade hasn't upset anything. It has been a couple of months now and those Magi Homsap unions that abort usually do so in under a month. I will leave you, to bring up the child myself alone, as is the tradition," Sandra replied smiling. "We will annul the Homsap marriage and you are free to take a girlfriend or bride of your choice."

Rula opposite sat up straight and beamed at Giles.

"Fancy yourself as a princess, Rula?" teased Pinky, after downing his pint in one.

"I am available, if necessary, to do my duty," she replied with her nose in the air.

"Can we have some food with this?" Giles called to Donna. "I'm famished and very tired. This beer's gone straight to my head."

"Fiona's warming up her baps for you. Won't be long," DD replied and the three men smiled at one another.

"Why are you men thinking of a sausage between a pair of… Oh I get it…" said Rula. "That's typical men."

"Stop listening to their thoughts, Rula. You know you're not very good at it. Let's just have a bit of food and get some rest. We have to see the Elders soon. We need to decide whether to leave later or wait until the morning," said Sandra.

"Let's wait till morning just to be sure about Suzie. I need some rest to prepare myself for becoming the next Magi ruler, it seems," replied Giles.

They engaged in conversation for the next half hour, the alcohol and food gently relaxing their recently battered minds and bodies.

Xena and Pete arrived after being relieved from sentry duty at the lake.

"We're out there working and you lot are getting pissed," said Pete as he came in the door. They were holding hands or more accurately Xena gripped Pete's hand.

He shook the firm grasp. "She keeps doing that," he explained, looking at Xena.

"Go with the flow, man," said Snake.

They pulled up two more chairs, to the double-table arrangement that had been set up. Pete sat down and Xena sat next to him with her hand on his thigh. Sandra nudged Giles and whispered, "See."

"No sign of Suzie then, Pete?" asked Giles.

"Not a sausage, mate," Pete answered and then he noticed the advancing FF warm baps.

"Not many of those to the pound," he said to no one in particular.

"Ow," he uttered as Xena dug her fingertips into his thigh then rubbed the sore spot.

Donna followed with freshly cut lamb and pork. Eric followed up the rear with beer for Xena and Pete.

"Now we're talking," said Pete, drinking half a pint straight off. "A man's drink," he added, nodding to Xena.

Xena knocked hers back in one and stuck her firm bosom out. She said to Eric, "Bring the Raki. That's a Magi woman's drink," then leaned over and kissed a surprised Pete on the lips.

After a couple of hours they decided to go along with Giles' plan. Eric had a flat above the bar and also owned the villa next door. After taking various verbal measurements from his guests to be, he sent Donna off to town with a fistful of Euros. She came back with several bags of assorted underwear, trousers, shirts and smellies. "All the bedrooms have double beds, one king-sized. I won't ask who's going where, but there are three of them next door and two upstairs here, plus sofa beds in the lounges. The beds are made up so have a good rest. Eric's going over the road to his mates for an all-night poker game so you won't see him," she instructed, after sharing out the haul of shopping.

"There's seven of us so who gets the sofa bed?" asked Giles.

"Doesn't matter, so long as you get the king-size, mate," said Pete. "You're supposed to be their king."

"And as his chief security officer, I get to choose who I guard tonight," said Xena.

"Why are you lot looking at me?" said Pete.

"Argue amongst yourselves," said Giles. "Where's this king's bed then, Donna?"

"Above the bar, Fiona will show you the way." Giles walked after her, as directed.

"I'll take the other room above," said a slightly tiddly Snake looking at Donna's boobs hopefully.

"Follow Fiona then, there's a good boy," and Donna patted him on the bum as he went after Giles.

The other five walked out of the bar door and towards the next Cypriot house.

Xena pulled Pete into the villa front door first.

"Show me the bedroom that you prefer and I will make sure it is secure," she said and they went upstairs giggling.

"I'll take the sofa bed," said Pinky. "You two girls have the beds. I'm used to roughing it in the army."

"You're such a gentleman, Pinky. You could teach the others some manners. Thank you," replied Rula.

"I need to nip back to the bar for something. I won't be long. You lot use the bathroom," said Sandra, putting her fresh clothes at the foot of the stairs.

When she came back, Pinky had made up his sofa bed in the lounge.

"Goodnight," said Sandra, passing the room. She picked up her stuff and went upstairs to the only open door. She looked in the empty room and felt grateful to see an en-suite shower. She closed the bedroom door, looked at the neatly made bed with folded towels on top and breathed out slowly.

Sandra took off her top and placed both hands on her tummy. A tiny movement inside, made her shiver and smile. She carried the new Magi prince, or maybe a princess?

"How good is that?" she said quietly to herself and walked into the shower.

Chapter 36

A gentle shake woke Giles.

"I've come to check if you're all right. Move over," whispered a woman's voice in the dark of the bedroom.

The half-asleep Giles said something unintelligible and wriggled to the centre of the bed. The figure slipped in under the single sheet and soft flesh pressed against his arm.

"I thought you said that you wouldn't be in my bed again," he mumbled.

"I haven't been here before. It's Donna," said the voice.

Giles woke up and turned to the face in the bed. The moonless night and the blackout curtains at the window made it difficult to make her out, but this blonde really wasn't Sandra. He reached over with his right hand to touch the warm skin pressing against his arm, definitely boob and a large one at that.

"Why are you here? I'm alright," he said.

"Sandra said to check on you. She said that you sometimes have odd dreams. The last few days might trigger off strange memories." Donna moved onto her side before putting her left arm across his chest and kissed him on his left cheek.

"Well, I'm flattered and it's nice to have unexpected company. Thank you, Sandra, for thinking about me," and he laughed. He leaned back on the pillow and closed his eyes. "Not that I'm complaining, Donna, but how come you got the job and not Fiona?"

Donna repositioned herself and the bed wobbled a bit. The sheet lifted up a bit again.

"We did discuss it," she whispered and he felt a boob press against his arm. The right one this time and warm lips kissed him on the right cheek. "We're both here now."

Giles turned smartly to his right and could make out a brunette. "Fiona," he stammered.

"In the flesh," she replied leaning over and pressing her right boob against his chest.

"Listen girls, I'm a bit tired now," Giles said, slightly worried, even though he'd day-dreamed about such a scenario.

The girls laughed.

Fiona said "Lean over and sleep on me. It's better than a pillow."

"Well, okay," said Giles. He leant forward as Fiona put her arm under and around his shoulders, cradling him into her soft ample silicone cleavage. "Wow," said Giles.

He lay on her left soft boob and could hear her heart beating in his ear. He reached over and took a handful of her right boob and snuggled up.

Donna spooned up behind him and he dozed off like the meat in a very lucky sandwich.

He awoke several hours later, this time on Donna's chest. Light peeped around the edge of the curtains. She stroked his hair and asked "Okay, King? It's nearly seven."

Giles looked around. Fiona wasn't there but he could hear someone in the en-suite. The single over-sheet had been kicked to the floor and he lay there starkers, on top of an equally naked Donna.

He rolled onto his back to see Fiona approaching him from the en-suite doorway, visible directly between his legs.

"Morning, my Lord," she said and climbed onto the end of the bed, continuing along, with a legs astride him until she sat on his hips.

She leaned over and put a hand either side, her massive orbs dangling down towards his face.

"Anything we can do for you before breakfast, sir?" she asked and deliberately swung her breasts about.

Donna had just got up and opened the curtains. He could now see Fiona in all her naked splendour. She had very large areolar and fat chunky nipples. There were several large veins visible just under the surface of the tanned skin. He could make out the scar on the lower half of each nipple where man had improved on nature.

"Touch them," she encouraged.

Giles couldn't resist any longer. He pulled his arms up from his sides and simultaneously grabbed a handful of both breasts. He had quite big hands but they came nowhere near the diameter of each boob.

He allowed the teats to escape between two of his fingers and gently massaged them. Fiona closed her eyes and softly moaned.

He felt a hand on his leg. He took his eyes away from the soft flesh under his fingers and looked to one side. Donna had come back from the en-suite and began stroking further and further up his thigh. Her hand quickly reached its target and clasped it tightly.

"Definitely waking up," said Donna giving a few encouraging tugs.

Fiona leaned down to kiss him fully on the lips. He could no longer fondle her nipples, as his hands were now trapped between their great bulk and his own chest. The hand on his manhood continued its clever work and he closed his eyes to enjoy the growing sensation.

After a couple of minutes of this, Giles heard a buzzing noise. He opened his eyes to see why Fiona had stopped kissing him and noted that she had moved back into her dangly position. She had her eyes closed and slowly moved her hips in a circular motion, obviously enjoying herself. Giles looked around her, at Donna, who grinned back at him.

"Just winding the lady up," she said, waving a long pink object at him and then reapplying it to Fiona's nether regions.

The buzzing stopped after a couple of minutes and the magic hand began its work again. Fiona leaned a bit further back and he felt his tip nuzzle against something soft. The hand then guided him into a warm, very moist woman.

"Can you feel me hold you, Giles?" asked Fiona, sitting

almost upright, astride him. He looked at her wondering what she meant, then felt her inner walls tightening around him several times.

"Very clever," he said as she started to move up and down slowly on top of him, holding her boobs.

Giles began to notice the bed getting a bit noisy. The thing about women with large boobs is that they frequently come with other large bits. This makes them a bit heavier than the tiny ones like Suzie. Fiona had a bit of a tummy, chubby arms and even a bit of a double chin that he could only see from this impromptu angle. She started to ride him more vigorously and gave up steadying her boobs. As they flopped up and down he put his hands up to catch them and they made a slap noise each time that they landed.

Fiona breathed heavily now and sweated profusely. "Nearly there, King," she said to him and placed a hand between her legs. Giles looked down to watch her fingers dancing across her fun button and then put his hands on Fiona's large thighs. He squeezed and marvelled at their firmness. Obviously, they have to be strong to carry the weight up top, he thought to himself.

He wasn't really able to join in much because of the position and wondered what else to do, when he felt Donna's hand again. She had her hand between his legs again and started caressing his sack. Alternating squeezing the twin contents and when Fiona rose to the tip end of her thrust, being able to pinch that sensitive area at the base of his manhood.

After a minute of her sensual fingers, combined with the vision of the turned on mammary goddess, aboard him, he let go with an "Oh my God."

Twenty seconds later FF stopped rubbing herself and tightened up. "Ooo," and "Ooooo."

"Fuck me," she said.

"He just did," said Donna. "You owe me one now," she added, referring to the hand ball trick.

Fiona remained sitting on top of him, eyes closed, getting her breath back. Donna climbed onto the side of the bed and hovered over Giles' head, to face Fiona, who started laughing. "You wouldn't dare," she challenged her.

Giles looked up between the white thighs of the head barmaid. Her pubic hair had been mostly shaven with the remainder trimmed into a neat little triangle.

"We were joking before about you being the new ruler and doing this to you. I'm going to queen you," and she promptly sat on his face. "Do your stuff, King."

She released the pressure just enough for him to breath and lap at her bits. Giles hadn't done this with a larger-thighed lady before and discovered that he had to time his breaths with her pressing and grinding or he would suffocate. He quickly chose the timing alternative. He also noticed that Fiona moved up and down on his rather sensitive manhood again, making the bed creak even more.

Although he could hardly hear because of the two soft white thighs pressing against his ears, he heard the knock on the door and Fiona shout "Come in" without stopping grinding on his manhood.

"I see you've been looking after him," said Sandra surveying the top heavy girls covering most of the new king.

From the bed's point of view, a bouncing DD and FF were pushing the design to the limit. A leg suddenly decided to let go, catapulting the threesome onto the floor in a heap. Giles looked down at his bits, after his sudden exit from Fiona and happily found himself and his tackle still intact. The two girls were rolling on the floor with laughter. "I'm going to pee myself," said Fiona, bouncing to the bathroom leaving a trail of drips behind her.

"Better wipe yourself," said Sandra, handing a serviette to Giles. "I'll put the tray of coffee over here and breakfast is nearly ready downstairs, so get a move on, King. That is a right royal performance then. I hoped they taped it."

Giles looked around horrified at Donna.

"Just something that Eric does to earn a little money on the side, blackmail and all that. Don't worry. The cameras were off." She wiggled over to a wall mirror, pulled it back to expose a camera. "Oh, that's strange. Someone must have turned it on."

After a quick tousle with the three women, Giles pulled rank and shouted, "I am your ruler, give it to me," and ended up with the memory card.

"I'm going to watch it first before I decide what to do with it. I have to say Fiona that you were fantastic. Still owe you one, Donna," and winked at her as he walked to the shower.

The shower started up and Sandra asked the two girls why they were still giggling. Donna went over to another mirror and showed the second camera and Fiona pointed out the little hole in the ceiling which held the third lens.

Giles became the last one down for breakfast. All eyes were on him as he walked down the stairs into the bar looking as regal as possible. He expected them to be taking the piss and felt surprised to be greeted by a round of applause, from the assembled friends.

"Today we take the fight to the Elders," said Rula.

"Today everything changes," said Snake.

"Are my girls okay?" asked Eric. "Only joking," he added. "They have good heads on their shoulders and work hard. If you get a palace and need staff, look them up."

"Eric won't mind breaking in some new ones," laughed Pete.

"You won't be helping," said Xena, pointing a sausage at Pete, who put his hands up. "Come and eat, Selig."

While he chomped on a bacon-butty, Rula explained their plan for the day and then said, "We've got something for you." She passed him a little box.

He opened it and couldn't believe his eyes.

"It's the Ring, the Magi Ring, the King Ring... What do you

call it?" Giles looked at it closely. "It's not a copy because I recognise that green paint on it."

"When Edgar fought with Eizus, he must have loosened it from her finger. When you finally knocked her over, it must have fell on the concrete. The lake sentry shift found it this morning whilst checking the shoreline," explained Rula.

"I worried that if Suzie had fallen in the lake, then the ring might have protected her but I guess finding it seals her fate," replied Giles.

"Put it on, Giles," urged Pinky.

"And so that's what all the clapping earlier is about? The wearer is the ruler. There's nothing in our way, now," he said.

"Nothing in YOUR way, Selig," and Pete bowed. Pete had hardly used that name but this time it felt right and everyone in the room followed Pete's action.

"The tradition is that the new ruler meets the Council of the Elders with only a trusted adviser. Edgar would have done it so I hope you're happy with me, Giles. Don't worry. I won't get them to make me queen.... " said Rula and paused, "Yet."

"What shall we do?" asked Pinky.

"This shouldn't take more than a day. I have Edgar's paperwork," said Rula.

"We can have a day's holiday?" suggested Sandra.

"Right on, man," said Snake going over to Giles and giving him a high five. "Go kick the Elders' ass."

"I'll do my royal best," laughed Giles and grabbed another piece of toast before Rula hustled him into the waiting 4x4.

Giles looked back at his motley crew as the car drove away and waved at them through the rising dust cloud.

"Someone ought to make a crazy film about my life," he said. Then he remembered the memory card in his pocket and checked he hadn't dropped it. "Hmm. Got one little bit. That should get the viewers."

Rula looked at him wondering just what he meant...

Chapter 37

Giles and Rula stood in front of the red mat.

He toed the material, just as he did with Edgar, the first time that he stood in the building.

"I hate this mat," he said. "Why are they keeping us so long?"

"They'll be talking about you now that's for sure. We will get our turn, shortly," she replied.

Rula wore wearing a smart grey jacket and tight skirt, a little longer than usual. Her tanned long legs finished with shiny medium-heeled shoes. Her blonde hair had been tied in a tight bun with a black clip. A white blouse showing just enough cleavage to be little provocative, completed the ensemble. She looked every inch a young professional lawyer. She had a folder under her arm and when she heard noises from the partly open rear door, behind the line of empty chairs opposite, she put on some spectacles.

"I didn't realise that you wore specs," said Giles looking at the slightly manly rectangular-framed glasses.

"I don't. I have twenty-twenty vision. It just looks more frightening to the other side," she replied. "I have several for different occasions. They're a style accessory."

Giles looked down at his feet and up past his trousers to his shirt. They didn't have time to search out an outfit suitable for a king in the little village shops before they left in the Merc, and although Maria had tried, she'd guessed the wrong measurements.

He stood there in a linen suit and a collarless creamy colour shirt. Maria forgot the shoes so he still wore the same trainers, which clashed severely with the look. At least the trousers were too long and some of the excess material covered the offending footwear.

"I look like a prick," Giles said.

"Kcirp," replied Rula.

Giles laughed. "Kcirp it is then. Do the Magi call it that when you have sex? Or mebbe a Kcoc?"

Rula ignored him.

"Which is best?" he asked deliberately, just as the Elders started to file into the room.

She fell into Giles' trap.

"I like cock."

She blushed. "I didn't say that."

Artis looked at them, "I hope that you are both taking this matter seriously."

"Pompous ass," whispered Giles as Artis turned around to adjust his seat. The others filed in.

"Full complement this time," Giles whispered, as he noticed that it didn't seem there'd be empty seats.

Artis stood up. "Today, we are reviewing the position of Ruler of the Magi. The king or leader as it is commonly known among us. For those of you who were not here last time, there were words spoken against the previous ruler, Selig the Great. For reference, you may break with tradition and call the man in front of us today, by his assumed English name, Giles."

"Cool," Giles whispered.

"The Council decided that, although it disagreed by a majority to allow Seli…Giles to attain the position, due to the length of his absence, a final decision would be made, within an agreed period of a week. This meeting has been reconvened at short notice and I am happy to see a full attendance," announced Artis.

Rula stepped onto the red mat.

"Yes, erm…Rula?" said Artis after being reminded of her name, by a person two seats along.

"We are grateful for your combined attention," she said.

Artis continued, "I am sorry to hear of the death of Edgar, a respected advocate and well-versed in Magi affairs and law. I had known him for years and his presence will be missed. Some of you may not know that he'd been invited several times to join us, which he refused. His opinion of committees is, to quote him, 'I'd rather be outside, pissing in, than the other way about'. He will be missed. I trust that you are familiar with the evidence, Rula."

"Edgar has kept me briefed. Giles has agreed for me to represent him. I believe that he'd been instructed to provide you with certain items that might cause the Elders to rethink their previous decision," she answered.

"Indeed. I have been informed by another member, via his contacts that Eizus has unfortunately perished in the quest for the aforesaid." Artis looked towards Remus who had stood up.

"I request that Selig be put on trial for her death," and he sat down.

"Didn't see that one coming," whispered Giles.

The gathered members looked shocked and spoke to one another.

Rula answered above the noise, "Unlike Remus, I attended the final meeting between Giles and Eizus. She tried to kill him previously by lightning and her companions also attempted to push our vehicle off a cliff."

Volt stood up. "Pure misunderstanding, I'm sure. He should be tried. Selig struck the final blow."

Heads turned and yet again murmurings were heard from amongst the seated Magi.

"And…I hadn't finished. Vipers attacked Giles on a previous occasion and we had rocket launched grenades fired at us. Giles had actually been put in a trance, induced by Eizus, who had attempted to drown him before the final punch."

Another younger man stood up. He didn't attend the last meeting.

"Yes, Nats?" asked Artis.

"I unfortunately missed the last meeting. From what we've been told by Rula, who apparently saw the incident at the dam where Eizus and Edgar perished, it would appear that the deaths were in self-defence. We have been told that Edgar attacked Eizus and in turn Eizus attacked Giles and had done so previously," he said.

Rula butted in.

"Forgive me but Eizus froze Edgar and fragmented him with a bolt of lightning. Edgar did not attack her but merely attempted to negotiate. He kept copious notes and I have his comments and plan from the previous night here in my hand, which shows his intentions." She waved a sheet of paper that she took from her file then took it forward to Artis.

He took his time looking over it before passing it to Remus at his side. After a cursory glance and a sneer, Remus shoved the note over to the man at his other side.

Volt stood up. After being cleared to talk by the Chairman, he said, "No matter if it is self-defence, there remains the fact that has, I think, been hidden for years and that is that Selig is a fraud."

The room went silent and all eyes were on Volt.

"I have been aware of this for only a few days, since a German friend of Eizus spoke to me. It seems that Selig and Eizus physically bonded several times. I surely do not need to remind even the older members sitting here, that during the union, minds may be also joined. This allows the partners to judge one another, for suitable mating. During this act, Giles, as he wishes to be known, the reason which will shortly be apparent, let her know his innermost secret. He is Homsap," and he sat down with a smug grin.

Giles tried to push Rula off the red speaking mat but she stood her ground and shushed him.

Artis stood up. "If this is true, it is of grave concern. There has never been a tainted king."

Rula answered. "Selig the Great knew of this and brought up Giles after his mother died in childbirth. He and others could accept a mixing of bloods and campaigned that the Homsap are not our rivals but our brethren. Although apparently unacceptable years ago, more and more Magi are beginning to believe that union with the Homsap will take us both forward."

Again the seated Council members whispered.

Another man stood up to speak. Longer haired, greying and dressed a little weird, he wasn't at the previous gathering.

"Yes, Yppih, you may speak," said Artis.

"I lost a son. I gave him and my lovely Homsap wife up, to pursue the Magi ways, just so that I could sit on the Council. The fact has haunted me for years. I wonder what he looks like and what he does. It may suit some women to be strong single mothers but deep down many Magi men would like to see their children grow up. I wonder if my son will turn up on their doorstep, one day and I wish for that day. Giles has proven that he is worthy warrior and I see that he wears the Ring of the Ruler," said Yppih.

Artis stood up.

"Show us your hand, Giles," he said.

Giles raised his hand in a fist with the Ring showing.

"We have more," said Rula. "We have the missing part of the scroll. From Edgar's notes, he expects that when joined and translated, you will have the story of the Magi from the very beginning. This part is much larger and the nonsensical part sentences will combine to show that Magi lived side by side with Homsap in Cyprus and islands nearby. Indeed they did interbreed and that means those of us who think that we are pure Magi, myself included, will have some Homsap in our genes."

Giles finally pushed her off the red mat.

"You have been living a lie for centuries. We are all human and we have been denying the benefit of our powers to our friends. I am tired of this crap, Rula. I'm going back to the others. You can all sit here and turn into fossils," he shouted and started walking towards the door.

"Wait, Giles," said Artis. "I apologise for the questions. We will take a vote this instant. Will you please wait just outside the door?"

They did as asked.

"Nice speech, Giles," said Rula as they waited. "You did me out of a job."

Giles and Rula watched through the doorway as the group rose and walked to the back of the hall. After a couple of minutes he could see some arm waving and shouting. It ended with Volt pulling Remus away from Artis. Red-faced Remus pointed angrily towards Giles and Rula.

"He looks pissed off," said Giles, moving to stand behind Rula. "Don't suppose you do that protective bubble thingy?"

Remus started striding towards them with clenched fists.

She reached behind and put her hands on his hips. "Hold my boobs," she said.

Giles quickly did as asked. Remus stopped and stared for a second, dropped his hands and walked silently past, with Volt in tow. If looks could kill, thought Giles, watching the pair pass.

"They might come back, just hold on," warned Rula.

Giles' head swivelled as they walked to the corner of the building and disappeared out of sight.

He turned around to see that Artis had hurried over.

"I see that now you are the ruler, you have utilised the ancient Magi law that the king may have any woman he chooses," he said.

Rula let go of his hips and clasped his hands firmly in position.

"We won, Selig!"

"You can't blow bubbles. You tricked me, Allure," answered Giles. He could feel that her nipples were hard.

"I thought you'd forgotten my Magi name, Selig. Thank you for using it, King Giles, I'm honoured," she said and wriggled out of his grasp.

"May I make commands now and similar stuff?" Giles asked Artis, as the others gathered around.

"I'm sure you'll make some excellent decisions, man," said Yppih. "How about dispensing with this first?" he asked, laughing.

He held up the red mat. Giles noticed that he had several tattoos.

"Put it in the royal bin over there," Giles answered and looked at Yppih's neck as he obeyed.

"The next command, guys. Are you all listening? The Council of Elders is abandoned. I want a CV from each of you on my desk tomorrow, if you want to reapply. Some younger blood is needed and Allure, is the first member on the new Selig Homag Integration Trust," Giles commanded.

"SHIT," replied Rula "Cheers. Nice position, boss of the Shovellers, anything else?"

"And you're also appointed as my new girlfriend," added Giles.

"Cool, that'll be a load of other positions…" laughed Yppih.

Giles joined him in a high five as Rula's unguarded thoughts wandered to royal crowns and marriage…

"Turn around and show me your neck," ordered Giles to Yppih.

He moved closer, looking puzzled and as Giles pulled down the collar and said, "Man, you're one weird ruler."

"I intend to be. Now please tell me this tattoo is in honour of someone very special," replied Giles.

"My son," replied Yppih and removed his shirt to reveal a serpent with the word Ekanz on its back.

"I think we know another Snake who'd like to meet his father…" smiled Giles.

RulaAllure kissed Giles, "Have you got a hungry serpent as well…?"

Roundfire Books put simply, publish great stories. Whether it's literary or popular, a gentle tale or a pulsating thriller, the connecting theme in all Roundfire fiction titles is that once you pick them up you won't want to put them down.